ALABASTER NOON

BOOK TWELVE OF
THE OMEGA WAR

Chris Kennedy &
Mark Wandrey

Seventh Seal Press
Virginia Beach, VA

Chris Kennedy/Seventh Seal Press
2052 Bierce Dr.
Virginia Beach, VA 23454
http://chriskennedypublishing.com/

Publisher's Note: This is a work of fiction. Names, characters, places, and incidents are a product of the author's imagination. Locales and public names are sometimes used for atmospheric purposes. Any resemblance to actual people, living or dead, or to businesses, companies, events, institutions, or locales is completely coincidental.

Ordering Information:
Quantity sales. Special discounts are available on quantity purchases by corporations, associations, and others. For details, contact the "Special Sales Department" at the address above.

Cover Design by Brenda Mihalko
Original Art by Ricky Ryan

Alabaster Noon/Chris Kennedy & Mark Wandrey -- 1st ed.
ISBN 978-1950420339

Dedication

This book is dedicated to the ever-growing number of fans of the 4HU, from the ones who've followed us from Day One to those who've just discovered it. This book pulls together what we've been working toward for the last three years. Don't worry though, we're just getting started.

This book is also in memory of Uncle Timmy Bolgeo, a finer friend to the world of fandom, there never was.

Prologue

São Paulo, Brazil, Earth

The sounds of misery were nonstop as the Besquith specialist team reached their objective: the roof of a five-story building which once housed several hundred Humans. Once in position, they verified none of the occupants remained, alive or otherwise, and began setting up monitoring equipment.

"Filthy Humans," one of the sensor operators said, tossing a severed arm over the side of the building. "It's spoiled. Team Leader Kreth, why didn't they just nuke the entire area—that would have destroyed the Raknar."

"General Peepo wanted the machines intact and their operators alive," his squad leader reminded him for the dozenth time. Grawts wasn't the quickest on the uptake, but he did have a mastery of the finicky elSha-manufactured gear. Several others on the team growled their support of Grawts. "Just shut up and finish deploying the sensors. We have nine more to place before dark."

The five-Besquith team went about their tasks, but Grawts wasn't satisfied. "Okay, I understand preserving the war machines and operators. Peepo has them prisoner now. Why are we looking for the little creatures?"

"Do I look like a general?" Kreth snarled and snapped at the back of Grawts' neck. The hapless sensor tech rolled over and whined, so Kreth didn't rip his rotten throat out. Satisfied, Kreth turned back to look out over the remains of São Paulo.

6 | KENNEDY & WANDREY

The Human city, formerly one of the biggest, if what he'd been told proved true, was largely in ruins. Seven Raknar assaulting the city, along with hundreds of Humans in their entropy-cursed powered armor tended to have that effect. Despite having massive defenses in place to hold the seat of occupation, the Raknar plowed into, and ultimately through, them. The damage was horrendous. Kreth approved.

He shielded his eyes from the setting sun to the west and could see the six surviving Raknar. Dozens of flyers flew around them as heavy equipment prepared to move them. Peepo's prizes; he wondered what she intended for them.

The faked cease fire had worked perfectly, allowing forces to move in close to the Human mercs all over the planet before springing the trap. One Raknar was vaporized by orbital fire. Kreth's unit had been just over a kilometer away, monitoring the mechas' progress, when it happened. They'd been flash-blinded by the orbital particle beam.

The last six went berserk, destroying indiscriminately and totally. They even destroyed the orbiting station *from the ground!* Kreth looked at the building, just one block away—half its height had been severed cleanly by a Raknar particle beam. Then, when heavy Zuul tanks prepared to attack, the Raknar had unleashed what appeared to be nuclear cannon, but much more compact and discrete in its damage.

"Antimatter weapons," an elSha tech with the appropriate knowledge said after the fight. Even Kreth sucked in his breath at the idea. Such unbelievable firepower, and now it was theirs! He desperately wanted to finish this mission so they could move on to the next stage.

"Come on, come on," he growled, "I want to go to the Human's secret base. Oh, to see their end will be a glorious battle." The others grunted in agreement as they worked affixing the sensors. It was no secret the fleet was preparing to go on the final assault. Sure, lots of Humans were still fighting in places, but they wouldn't be fighting for long. What chance did they have? "Aren't you done yet?" he snapped.

"Yes, you're done," a tiny voice said in such perfect Besquith he thought it was a juvenile. Kreth turned, and his jaw fell open in surprise. A tiny furred creature just like he'd been told to look for was framed in the doorway pointing at him.

"Hey—" he said, then something slammed into his throat, and he fell backward, unable to control his body.

"Ambush!" one of his men cried.

Good, Kreth thought, struggling to breath. *My men will deal with them.* Lying on his back on the rubble strewn roof, he heard his men moving, grabbing weapons, and yelling, and then falling bodies. It was all over in two, maybe three, seconds. He exerted all his will and managed to turn his head. Five of the creatures were standing in the center of where his men had been working. None of the Besquith were alive, save himself. He tried to say something, but it came out as a gurgle.

One of the creatures dropped into a partial crouch, its head spinning to face him. One of its eyes was covered in a patch, and it had a cybernetic arm on the same side. The creature grunted and marched over to Kreth.

* * *

"**B**e more thorough, Peanut," Dante snapped as he stabbed the Besquith through the eye, driving hard with his cybernetic arm to be sure the blade penetrated into its brain.

"Sorry, sir," Peanut said.

"Did any of them get a transmission off?" Ryft asked, cleaning her knife.

"No." They all glanced up at their leader. Splunk clung to the half-melted antenna above the roof where she'd been watching the clumsy Besquith set up their instruments. She looked at her frequency scanner one more time to be sure. Nothing within a hundred meters. "They weren't even staying in contact with their command staff."

"Stupid animals," Shadow said, putting away his long blade. "Even the Kahraman would not have wasted their time with this lot."

"They might be pathetic at tactics, but they are strong and numerous," Ryft pointed out.

"Peanut, take their comms gear," Splunk ordered. "Break into their network, and let's get some intel."

Peanut waved, and they piled the Besquith equipment at his feet. Like every Dusman who'd come on the mission, they were all gifted in technology. However, among them, Peanut and Splunk were the most gifted. Since Splunk was in command, she'd delegated the job. The other four moved to the edges of the roof to assume overwatch as soon as the bodies were stripped.

<*The fleet is away,*> Dante sent to her.

<*I felt it,*> Splunk sent back. For 170 hours they would have no contact with their agents within the retreating fleet. She tried to appear confident, despite her inner feelings of failure. Jim was there, only a few kilometers away. She could point to him, if she'd wanted to. They all knew where their operators were, a side effect of the joining. It wasn't like the texts said it would be. She'd tried to explain it to Sly, but he hadn't believed her. Well, now he did.

"Command. Echo-5, report," said a voice from one of the Besquith radios.

Splunk pointed, and Peanut snapped it up. He had a device already set, and he clipped it to the radio. A second later, another Besquith spoke. "Echo-5 to Command, system is almost up."

"What is taking so long, Kreth?"

Peanut cocked his head and tapped a tiny screen with his claws, then the machine said, "My team are idiots."

Laughter replied. "That they are. Hurry up, Command out."

From across the ruined rooftop, Splunk could see Dante nodding without looking over. He approved of efficiency almost as much as he approved of slaughter.

Peanut set the voice duplication device aside. It was the reason Splunk was hanging from the antenna while the Besquith worked; she'd been recording their voices for Peanut. "Here we go," Peanut said, and Splunk jumped down next to him. She moved close, closer than she had to, and surreptitiously set a hand on his shoulder. He glanced at her with a tiny smile nobody else would notice.

You are such a fool, she scolded herself.

Peanut reconfigured the monitor's Tri-V, and a map of the vicinity came up. In a second, a sea of tiny blue pinpoints decorated it. "These are all the units they have searching for us."

"Hmf," she said as she examined the pattern. Efficient, but predictable. All the search teams were using the same type of equipment, too. All the better. "Modify their gear to give a false positive in five minutes," she said and pointed. "Have us going that way, toward where our operators are being held."

"We're not going there?" Peanut asked. He looked surprised and disappointed. "I have listened to Darrel thinking about it. There are almost no guards. We can be in and out—"

"That's what Peepo wants us to think," Dante said from a few meters away. "Use your head for a change, Child. Splunk might be a fool for believing in these Humans, but she's a solid commander."

"So, you agree with Sly putting her in command?" Sandy asked, her voice surprised.

"I didn't say that," he replied, but he didn't add anything.

Splunk knew Dante had it out for her. She'd known it ever since he'd turned up on Karma and tried to make her come back to Kash-Ka. When she'd told him about the Canavar, he'd been as stunned as anyone else. She'd known something was happening when the Human boy showed up suddenly one night. *Known* it in the depths of her being that it was time for them to come out of hiding.

"We're still alive, aren't we?" Peanut snapped at Dante.

"Yeah, we are," Dante replied. "It's the fact she thinks some sort of damned destiny is guiding her that scares the piss out of me."

"Seldia sees it, too," Splunk reminded him.

"Seldia is insane, just like all *K'apo.*"

Splunk couldn't argue. They were a necessary part of Dusman society, though. More so after the Disaster than ever before.

"Speaking of Seldia, when are we going to do it?"

"Better be now," Splunk said, looking at the Tri-V. "We're going to be moving too fast the next couple of days to take the chance. Everyone double check for unwanted visitors."

Nobody saw anything, so they joined her.

Splunk stood in the center. The other five Dusman reached out, touching each other, making a circle, then each put a hand on her head. Splunk sighed, reached within herself, and *stretched.*

<Seldia...Seldia, hear me.>

<*I hear,*> came the reply from light years away. <*What news?*>

<*Defeat,*> she thought, reluctantly. <*Aura is dead. All surviving Raknar and operators captured. We are still free.*> There was a long pause. Splunk knew Seldia was probably contacting Sly, and she feared what he might say. She hoped it didn't take long, the strain was incredible.

Another presence entered on the Far Talker's side.

<What happened?> Sly asked.

<Deception,> Splunk said. <We don't know the full details. Alexis Cromwell is dead. The Humans either fled, were defeated, or have gone underground. Their fleet is en route back now, ETA 169 hours. We expect the Merc Guild to leave in about a day to follow them. They know where New Warsaw is.>

<Can you escape off-world?>

<Not without our operators.> Silence for a moment. <We can avoid capture indefinitely.>

<Do so. I will contact the Humans in command here. We will coordinate their defenses. Contact again in 60 hours.>

The connection cut off, and Splunk gasped from the suddenness of it. She'd been expecting something. What? Anger? Accusations? But there had been nothing.

"He seemed calm," Peanut said.

"A *Koof* always seems calm," Dante said and snorted. "They seldom understand what's really going on."

"Sly will handle his end of it," Splunk said, changing the subject. "Our job is to not get caught and see if we can get our operators out."

"And cause as much carnage as possible in the meantime," Dante suggested.

"Sounds great," Shadow said.

Splunk found herself agreeing. Aura would have approved of some payback as well. Suddenly she felt Jim become highly agitated. Something had happened. Either they were interrogating him, or he'd found some piece of information which made him highly upset. She tried to send a calming thought to him. <*We'll get you out soon, Jim.*>

Splunk knew it was unlikely he would get the thought. Humans were remarkably weak when it came to receiving thoughts. Maybe it was part of what made them so different from the Lumar? The others cleaned up any evidence of their presence, except the five dead Besquith, of course. It was time to go.

* * *

EMS *Pegasus*, Hyperspace, En Route to Prime Base

Sansar Enkh paused to build up her resolve, then knocked on the stateroom door.

"Enter!" Nigel replied.

Sansar smiled. That was a better reaction than the last time she'd been there, two days ago. Nigel's voice sounded neither drunk nor like he was crying. Progress. She opened the door, and he turned from the monitor on his desk. Although he hadn't been crying, there was something different about his eyes, something feral and dangerous, and Sansar had to steel herself to keep from stepping away from the danger she saw there.

"Are…are you okay?"

Nigel smiled, but it never made it to his eyes. "I'm great. For the first time in my life, I have a purpose, something that's bigger than me."

"I'm not sure I want to know what this purpose is."

"Of course, you do, as it's going to be fun for everyone to watch. I'm going to kill all the Veetanho to start, then the MinSha, and probably all the Besquith, too. It's going to be my mission. I like to think I'll be doing the galaxy a service by killing all the ruthless killers."

Sansar's hand went to her mouth, but she couldn't quite stifle the gasp. She'd been wrong to leave Nigel alone for two days. His resolve had stiffened into something entirely unhealthy…not only for him, but for Asbaran, and probably the Human race as well. She thought furiously, using the processing power of all six implants, trying to come up with a way to divert him. Knowing Nigel, though, once he'd set his mind to something, it wasn't going to be easy to change it.

"That's great," she said finally. "If you really want to know the truth, I personally think the galaxy would be better off without the Veetanho. Can I ask you a question, though?"

"Sure."

"Once you cleanse the galaxy of all of these killers, then what?"

"What do you mean?"

"Just what I asked. Once you've killed off three entire races what are you going to do then?"

"Celebrate a job well done?" Nigel shrugged. "Maybe I'll go to fucking Disneyland."

"No. No, you won't. You won't be celebrating anything. You will have just made yourself public enemy number one to the rest of the alien races in the galaxy. You will be seen as such a threat they will *all* unite to destroy *you* in particular, Asbaran Solutions at a minimum, and probably the entire race that spawned you. We're already under attack by the majority of the Mercenary Guild; if you wiped out three races, humanity itself would be under attack…and with the entire galaxy's resources being used against us this time. There's no way we could win. We'd be slaughtered."

"So, what do we do?"

"We take them to court."

"We…what? Take them to court?"

"Yeah, we take them to the Galactic Union court and get a ruling against them. We show them we aren't crazy, and that we have a legitimate gripe. We get the galactic court to go along with it, and then we have a legal mandate to wipe them out."

"Galactic court, huh? What court is that, exactly? And where?"

"Umm…I'm not really sure, but if there are things that are illegal, like nuking planets from orbit or using AIs, there has to be some sort of court to adjudicate it."

"Funny thing, I've never heard of that court. Everything I've ever heard of was done by the Merc Guild…and since the Veetanho seem to be running *that*, I have a hard time believing we'll have a sympathetic ear there."

Sansar ran through the information stored in her pinplants on galactic government and couldn't find a mention of an actual court. "So…uh…you may be right. I can't find any examples of any courts other than those run by the various guilds."

Nigel smiled. "Okay, so your court idea may have merit…but it looks like I'm going to get a chance to kill some of them first. Once we kill off all the Veetanho, MinSha, and Besquith and we replace them with races that aren't completely corrupt, I'll take your court idea under advisement."

Sansar sighed. "Nigel, I'm sorry, but that isn't going to work."

"What do you mean?"

"What I really came here to tell you is I think Peepo knows where New Warsaw is."

Nigel's brows knit. "How can she know where it is? *We* don't even know where it is, and we're on our way there."

"I had a dream—"

"Of course you did," Nigel said. His smile took away some of the sarcasm he couldn't keep out of his voice. Although his mood appeared to have improved, his visage developed a haunted look as his thoughts turned to Alexis.

"—I had a dream you and I were defending a system that was heavily fortified. There were missile stations on asteroids, battle stations with heavy lasers, and a *lot* of ships. It was a battle to decide everything…and at the end of the battle I saw it—Prime Base. That's what we were defending. I had this dream when we were in Golara. Alexis laughed when I told her about it. She said there would never be a battle for Prime Base she wasn't part of...but now she's gone, along with Jim, and it's up to us. *This is exactly what I saw!*"

Nigel thought for a moment and then nodded, his face grim. "With Paka going over to Peepo's side, I guess it's possible she took the coordinates over to Peepo with her." He took a deep breath and let it out, shaking his head. "We're fucked."

"What do you mean?"

"Did you see the fleet Peepo had amassed?" He waved a hand toward his Tri-V display. "I was just going over the battle, looking for things we could have done better, to get an edge for next time. The fleet that was chasing us at the end of that abortion on Earth was huge; how are we going to stop something that size?"

"I don't know," Sansar replied, "but I can tell you we've been working on New Warsaw's defenses for ten years."

"You have?" Nigel asked, a tinge of hope in his voice.

"Yes, the Horde's been working on the system's defenses for ten years."

"Is it going to be enough?"

Sansar shrugged. "I don't know. There was so much more we wanted to do...and that was before Peepo trotted out that dreadnought, or whatever it was." She squared her shoulders, and straightened to her full, almost five feet, height. "Like I said, I don't know, but it's going to have to be, or an awful lot of people are going to die. I doubt Peepo is going to settle for just capturing it; she's going to destroy it. Along with every man, woman, and child."

"A repeat of what happened to my country," Nigel said, with a curt nod. "We cannot allow this to happen. In Alexis' memory, we *will not*." He paused again, then his eyes focused on Sansar. "We won't have much time once we get back; they will surely be hot on our trail. If we have a week to prepare, we will be lucky. What have you done so far, and what do we still need to put into place?"

* * * * *

Chapter One

Major James Good winced as he injected himself with the last dose of nanites from the medkit dispenser. If the alternative—death from radiation poisoning—hadn't been worse than the pain of the dispenser, he doubted he could have pushed the injection button. *I have no idea how those CAS-Per pilots do this all the time,* he thought. He shook his head. He had no idea why he'd thought going to São Paulo was a good idea. *Intel people belong behind the lines, not trying to get first-hand accounts of the battle.*

He looked up once the tears cleared from his eyes. Corporal Bolormaa Enkh was studiously going through imagery on her terminal and had shifted slightly so her back was to him. The small twitches in her shoulders probably weren't from her trying to stifle a laugh because of his scream. Good's shoulders slumped; no, she probably *was* laughing, after all.

Good sighed. "Okay, I'm done. And you don't have to tell me I should have stayed here with you; I am well-aware." She turned around in the chair with a smile on her face, and he could feel his cheeks turn crimson. "I'm also aware that I might have yelled out a little when I dosed myself with the nanites."

Her eyebrows rose. "A little? You squealed like a newborn—"

"Fine," Good interrupted. "I screamed. You dose yourself with one of those things, and we'll see how you like it."

"No thanks, sir. The CASPer drivers have told me how badly it hurts. That's why *I* was quite happy to stay right here."

"Let's just move on, shall we?" Good asked. "Were you able to trace the signal out of São Paulo?"

"Actually, yes, I was. As you directed, I launched all of our new dragonfly drones and had them concentrate on the towers you identified."

"See?" Good asked with a smile. "There *was* a good reason for me to be there."

"Yes, sir. If it makes you feel better to think so; however, these aren't the ones Spartan developed. While you were out playing soldier, we got a shipment of the Mark Two dragonflies, which are bigger and can transmit while they're still in flight. Had you waited we could have searched for the towers from here."

Good frowned.

"But since you *were* there," she said hurriedly, "it allowed me to cut down on the time it would have taken to find and identify the comms sites."

"And?"

Enkh smiled. "And yes, I was able to find the Merc Guild headquarters. It's at a facility just outside Ubatuba, southeast of here."

"How do you know?" Good asked. "I thought we could only get a line of bearing from the dragonfly."

"We could...but they had a primary and a backup laser comm link, and I found both of them. Where those two lines cross...*voila!* There's Peepo's Palace."

"She has a palace set up down here? How did we miss it?"

"We didn't miss anything. It isn't really a palace; from the road, it just looks like a big hacienda outside of town, like many others that exist."

"Then how do you know this is her operations center? Tortantulas at the gates?"

"No, nothing as obvious as that, which is why we haven't found it before now. All the outside security is human, and they aren't in merc uniforms. That said, though, they all *look* like mercs, and I got a facial recognition hit from one of them."

Enkh turned back to her console, tapped a couple of buttons, and the picture of a man in uniform came up. She pointed and said, "Gotcha. This is Major Vels Lucas of the Varangian Guard. He was wandering around, checking out the defenses, and one of the drones got a good picture of him. It's an exact match with his Merc Guild info."

She looked up and smiled. "If that weren't enough, I present to you, Exhibit B." She pressed a button and the Tri-V switched to an overhead view of a cluster of buildings and a small landing pad. "This is on the other side of the hill from the hacienda, out of sight from casual observers. All of these buildings—and especially the landing area—all show signs of having been recently constructed." She zoomed in on an orange blob. "And here are two robotic build-ers, lying on their sides. Looks like they broke, and they were pitched off to the side. Based on the lack of degradation, I would say the landing strip was finished within the past two weeks."

"Well done," Good replied. "It's good to see you weren't just sit-ting around while I was out risking my life to get the intel." He ig-nored her snort. "Did you get anything else?"

"I did, and you're going to like this even better."

"Better than finding the Merc Guild's headquarters?"

"Yes, sir." She tapped a few more buttons. "We've gotten a few reports on what appears to be a group of friendly mercs who are still on the ground in São Paulo."

"Friendly mercs? I thought all of them surrendered."

"I thought so, too, but then I heard about a patrol of Besquith getting slaughtered."

"Maybe it was some sort of rivalry with one of the other races."

Enkh shook her head. "When they reported the patrol missing, I sent a few of our dragonflies to see if I could find them. They were on a rooftop, and they were all dead. There was no evidence of anyone else being there, but they'd all been shot. It looked like whoever'd been there was short, too; the wounds were fired at an upward angle into them."

"So, maybe a squad of mercs firing from prone positions?"

"I thought that, too, so I went looking for them, hoping to make contact. I thought that after killing the Besquith, they'd head toward the Merc Guild—if they could find it—looking for a little payback on Peepo."

"And you found them there?"

"No. Once I found the Merc Guild, I began tracking back from it, looking for them, but never found them. Then I realized that would probably be what Peepo would do, too, when she found out the Besquith were dead, so I landed a spread of dragonflies in the other direction and put them on standby. If there was motion, they would wake up. It was a long shot…"

"But it worked?"

Enkh looked up and smiled. "Here is the current feed from it." The monitor changed to a view of jungle, with the screen panning up and down as if someone were holding it while walking.

"Whoever has it is short," Good said, looking at the perspective.

"Let me back it up a bit." Enkh froze the image and restarted it from when it was activated. There was a flash of brown—the motion that turned it on—then the view shifted as the drone was picked up, and a face filled the camera's view. The creature looked a bit like a monkey, but had huge, intelligent eyes and big ears that sported tufts of fur at the ends. "It's safe to say contact has been made—the Fae have our drone!"

* * *

Merc Guild Detention Facility, Ubatuba, Brazil, Earth

"What do you want?" Jim Cartwright asked the woman at his cell's door.

"I wanted to see if you were okay," she said.

Despite everything, it felt good to hear her voice, and that pissed him off. He stood up, a little too hastily, and the nanite-attached chains around his wrist were jerked hard enough that he felt the skin tear. "Do I look okay, bitch?" he snarled.

"Jim…"

"You don't get to call me that, ever again," he yelled, spittle flying from his lips. She stiffened slightly and took a step back, as if he had the slightest chance of getting free and reaching her. In his mind's eye, he imagined getting his hands around her neck. He shook his head to clear the thought, then took a long, shuddering breath, managing to get a little of his control back. "It's Colonel Cartwright to you."

She took a step forward into the dank cell. The small light showed some detail of her face, so recognizable to him after many hours of time together. He could remember seeing her waking up next to him in the dark—as it was now—the bathroom light of his tower suite casting one perfect breast in profile.

"Colonel Cartwright," she said. "Why did you come back?"

"To kick the stinking aliens off our planet," he said.

"The planet didn't want you to do that. Nobody asked you to return."

"You mean the Republic government didn't want us to return."

She shrugged. "Well, here we are."

She looked him up and down for a second. "You've lost weight."

It was his turn to shrug. "Is Watchmaker okay?"

"Wouldn't you like to know?"

"Can you touch her mind?"

Jim's eyes narrowed. He'd never shared any of that; he'd never told her about Splunk's telepathic ability.

"I can help her," she said. "I like her, and she liked me."

"You had her fooled, too, you know that? Quite the actor, you are."

"Part of my training."

"Captain McKenzie's training?" She just looked at him. "What do you want, Captain?"

"Like I said, to see how you are."

He held out his hands, wincing from the pain. "Well, you saw." Then he thought of something. "Peepo sent you, didn't she?" She didn't respond, and he laughed. "Aliens never understand Humans," he said, laughing more. "Does she know what you did to me?" A slight nod. "But she sent you anyway."

She stood still, less than a meter from him, amidst the dishes from his earlier meal. He couldn't see her eyes, only the slight movements of her shoulders gave any indication she was even breathing. *What does she really want?* "Get out," he said. He backed up to the wall and used it to slide onto the simple bench.

Adayn stood for another moment, then she quietly turned and left. The door closed behind her, leaving him alone in the mostly dark cell.

* * *

Merc Guild Command Center, Ubatuba, Brazil, Earth

"You can go in," the assistant said with a nod.

Paka got up and walked into the office. It was so much more utilitarian than she'd expect her sister to have. Of course, Paka hadn't seen her sister's old office. Her sister stood up to greet her.

"Hail the conquering hero," General Peepo said, bowing her head, whiskers flat against her muzzle in respect. "It's so good to finally see my sister again."

"Just as good to see you, Peepo," Paka said and bowed in return.

"How did you survive so long working for those Humans?"

"It was difficult, sometimes."

"I would think it was difficult *all* the time." Peepo gestured to a chair, and Paka sat down. "I admit, this wasn't what I imagined for the culmination of your mission. I always expected you to somehow slip a data packet to me with the location of New Warsaw."

"As I explained in my debriefing, I couldn't. Nobody knows the stellar location. It's amazingly well hidden for such a distinct system." Paka laughed. "Cromwell is the most suspicious Human I have ever known. Even more so than her mother was. All the program keys written by that AI are carefully accounted for."

"The AI," Peepo said darkly. "I still think you should have blown your cover just to tell us about it."

"Even now? You know if I'd defected at any other point, they would have gone into a lockdown so thorough we'd never have found them."

Peepo looked at her with narrowed eyes, then laughed. "No, I guess you're right." She took a bottle of wine that came from their home world and poured them both a drink. "To the end of humanity's interference in the grand plan, and to bringing them into the fold." Paka raised her glass and Peepo matched it. "The Four Horsemen are gone from Earth."

Paka drank.

"Now, long lost sister, what do you want?"

Paka smiled, showing her tiny sharp teeth. "Command of the fleet attacking New Warsaw."

"I can't give you the dreadnought."

"Why not?"

"It's political. However, I can give you overall fleet command and a battleship of your own." Paka's eyes narrowed. "Who knows, maybe Admiral Galantrooka will err to some degree, and then it will be yours." She finished her drink and handed Paka a data chip. "Courtesy of the Grimm, here's the location to New Warsaw. Go finish what you started."

* * *

After Paka left, Peepo brought her Tri-V to life. She gazed with interest at the numerous reports floating around her office. A hundred scientists were swarming over the Raknar in what remained of São Paulo, though they hadn't made much progress yet because of the radiation levels. The Raknars' power cores continued to be many times hotter than they should be, despite indications of full, unsaturated F11 stores.

"We can only assume the pilots activated a contingency which put the reactors in this mode," her chief researcher, an elSha named Pluis, had reported a few hours ago. Because of the radiation, the researchers could only work an hour at a time, despite the protective gear they wore.

She pressed a virtual button on her desk. This one wasn't the ornate rare wood version she'd had in São Paulo, of course. That one was rubble, along with most of the Cavaliers. She smiled at the thought of how well that plan had come together at the end.

"Yes, General?" her assistant's voice asked.

"Any results on those searches of the Science Guild?"

"Nothing yet," her assistant responded.

"It went out priority?"

"Direct relay," her assistant confirmed.

"Very well." Peepo pressed the virtual button, and the intercom deactivated. One of the Tri-V screens showed a constant montage of the various Human news feeds from around the planet. Of course, all the news was on her stunning victory. A few celebrations had broken out. She slid a personal slate over and made some notes on the cities with celebrations, the cities with protests or riots, and lastly, the ones which were deadly calm.

Prudent action would be required. Between the casualties her forces had taken and the units she'd sent to finish the Winged Hussars, available planetary forces were only around 35%. And, of course, only a few Human units had proven themselves loyal. Those who'd been unreliable were no longer alive.

In the corner of her main Tri-V display, a clock was counting down to zero. It currently sat at 170 hours. Once it started counting down, it would show how long the Winged Hussars and those forces they'd managed to run away with still had to live. She'd rather have gone for the final battle, of course, but it was in good hands with

Paka. She wished she could have seen the look on the Hussars' faces when they saw Paka come for their ending. She smiled and went on to the next item.

* * * * *

Chapter Two

Lieutenant Commander Aleksandra Kowalczy was a legacy. Born from one of the two main families who'd controlled the Winged Hussars from the beginning, she was assured a position within the company. However, she wasn't assured ownership or leadership. The Cromwell line was simple. The Kosmalski family was complicated.

Included in Aleksandra's lineage were the Kosmalski, the Kowalczy, and a few Kowalczyk. Over the last century, her family of Kowalczy had become the most common of those with Polish heritage, and the largest living in New Warsaw. Despite being only a 3rd cousin, twice removed, from the Cromwell family, being a member of the family meant she was still a legacy. A Kowalczy, Lech Kowalczy, was the 2nd in command and captain of *Alicorn*.

Since the Schism, and the brief dark times that followed, the Cromwell family had commanded the Hussars, and the Kowalczy family had handled the financial and logistical affairs. Over the years, some of the Kowalczys had balked at that, and there'd even been whispered rumors of an attempted coup one dark night, decades ago. Despite the rumors, the Winged Hussars' success under the Cromwell family's tactical prowess was undeniable.

Aleksandra was the youngest of four children. Born on Prime Base during a time of growth in the Hussars' history, there were a lot of possibilities for her to rise in rank and responsibility. Despite the

Cromwell family inheriting tactical command, they weren't fruitful, like the Kowalczy family tended to be. Aleksandra was in primary school when the twins were born, and it was big news. Their leader was growing old, and many quietly feared what would happen without a Cromwell to lead them.

Aleksandra was under great pressure from her grandmother to be a ship captain. Unfortunately for grandma, Aleksandra didn't have the aptitude. The Winged Hussars Space Academy was based on Home, the planet Prime Base orbited. Then the curriculum moved into space and the Hussars' kids started training in flight, engineering, and combat tactics.

She did fine in early studies, always managing to maintain acceptable grades. But if you wanted to be a ship captain in the Winged Hussars, especially a combat arms captain, acceptable was as good as failing. By the end of the second year of the academy's four-year program, she started seeing fewer and fewer command-related classes and knew her fate had been sealed.

Ensign Aleksandra Kowalczy entered service as a traffic control officer the year Alexis Cromwell and her sister Katrina joined the academy. Four years later Aleksandra was a lieutenant JG, the same rank the sisters graduated at. Another four years and the twins were full lieutenants and both commanding frigates. Aleksandra was moved to the fleet logistics command at the same rank.

She wasn't the kind of person to be jealous. People like the Cromwell twins, who took to command and combat tactics like a Selroth to water, were a constant source of amazement to her. As the twins began winning battles and proving they were their mother's daughters, the prowess of the Hussars grew, and that meant they all grew with them. The little black unadorned ribbon on her tiny board meant more than any other merc's huge board of ribbons.

Aleksandra did manage to get assigned to a ship for some contracts. She served on *Chimera*, one of the Hussars' drone carriers, as assistant stores purser. *Chimera* completed nine contracts while she was on board as a full lieutenant, falling just short of the ten contracts to earn a better ribbon. She did pick up watch officer and able spacehand ribbons, though.

Thanks largely to the experience she gained while on *Chimera*, Aleksandra was promoted to lieutenant commander and thus entered the Winged Hussars' chain of overall command. It was something to brag about on those rare chances she got to go out on a date or visit a sibling, and not much more. At least, until Alexis Cromwell took every combat ready ship and left to attack Earth, and Lieutenant Commander Aleksandra Kowalczy was left in command of New Warsaw.

The Hussars tradition maintained you didn't move offices when you changed jobs unless the job changed duty stations. Offices and cubicles had electronic signage which could be changed to show a new occupant's position. When her office on C-ring sign changed from "Fleet Supply Logistics" to "New Warsaw Commander," it was a moment of awakening for her.

"I didn't train for this, Colonel Cromwell," she'd said when the commander stopped by before leaving.

"Nobody is able to train for every job they have," she'd said. "Hold the fort; I'll be back in a few weeks' time, and we'll have a drink to celebrate your new rank."

"What?"

"I can't have someone in charge of the system who's only a lieutenant commander. We'll fix that when I get home."

Thus, she found herself handling day-to-day operations of the largest Human merc unit *and* an entire star system.

Aleksandra always kept three timers floating above her desk on a Tri-V. One was the 170 hour clock that started when the fleet departed for Earth; it showed when the assault would be underway. Another was 340 hours, the absolute soonest she could expect word back from Earth. The final was 510 hours, which was the deadline Colonel Cromwell gave her for the drop-dead time she could expect an update. Should nothing arrive by then, she was to open the contingency files.

The first clock had been at 40 hours when Uuth, the commander of New Warsaw's HST—its Home Security Team—came to her office to announce that Dr. Sato had somehow escaped from the system.

"You're kidding, right?" Aleksandra had asked.

"Commander, I wish I was." The Zuparti intelligence officer looked pained. "He had a squad of marines escorting him as he worked on Geek Squad business aboard *Sphinx*."

"The new *Steed*-class battlecruiser," she said, and Uuth nodded. She'd been reading that the ship had moved out of drydock and was undergoing its final fitting. In another few days she'd have exactly one combat-ready capital ship at her disposal, albeit one with only a skeleton crew. "What was he doing there?" she asked.

"I have no idea," he said.

"Do you know how he got out of the system?"

"He had a modified CASPer he used in space. It was programmed to pretend he was still aboard. After finishing his work on

Sphinx, the CASPer accompanied the marines back to Prime Base and to his quarters."

"He never exited the suit? Didn't that attract the marines' curiosity?"

"Dr. Sato is rather...eccentric. Behavior which might be red flags for someone else are probable with the doctor. The suit was programmed to provide basic answers to situations. His absence wasn't noticed until three hours ago when his meal was delivered, and he didn't answer the door. Subsequent investigations found the CASPer unmanned and no log of his departure.

"The only probable way he could have exited the system was on the intel cutter *Virginia Hall*, which passed through the stargate seven hours ago."

"You've conducted a thorough search?"

"Of course," Uuth said, nodding.

Zuparti were most known for their paranoia. In this, they made excellent spies and intelligence staff. She had no doubt he'd been thorough.

"It *is* possible he's down on the planet," Uuth added. "However, you'd have to wonder why he went to such extremes, just to go down to Home."

Aleksandra agreed with that. She'd been born on Home and had spent half her life there. At best, it was beautiful, while still dark and dreary. At worst, it was just wet and dreary. If Dr. Sato had wanted to go down to the planet, he'd merely have had to ask. She accessed his intelligence file and saw he'd visited the planet fourteen times in the past. With the exception of his first visit, shortly after joining the Hussars, every time was on business.

"The timing of *Virginia Hall*'s departure, along with the fact it had a cargo module loaded minutes before departing, and that departure was within hours of his ruse leaves little doubt what happened." Uuth put a chip down, and Aleksandra accessed it. It was a standard cargo module's logistics record. A logistics officer by trade, she knew where to look for irregularities. There were many. Sato was thorough, however, if she'd still been at her job, she might have noticed the hasty order for 122 cases of Japanese rice. Japanese rice wasn't a common commodity on New Warsaw. In fact, she wasn't sure she'd ever seen any come across a cargo log. *Crap.*

"Thank you, Uuth," she said. "File your formal report."

"You'll have it by tonight," the intelligence officer said and left.

Aleksandra sighed and opened a file on her computer to write her own report. Five days and she'd lost the Winged Hussars best scientist. If the file on the enigmatic doctor was half correct, he might well be one of the most brilliant Human scientists in the galaxy.

She pulled *Virginia Hall*'s destination log. Intelligence cutters didn't keep to specific routes. About all she had was its first destination, what area of operation it was headed for, and when it was expected back. The answers were Karma, the Gresht region of the Tolo arm, and three months. During that time it would make contact with far-flung Hussars' interests, drop off some personnel, and gather data. All the while, *Virginia Hall* would be posing as a small independent cargo ship known as a free trader. You'd have to board her to realize the ship had hyperspace shunts—and very little room for cargo because of those shunts.

Forty hours later, she was at her desk reading the final report on Dr. Sato's disappearance when the first clock ground down to zero with a beeping alarm. "The attack has begun," she said to her empty office. It felt disconcerting, knowing her fellow Hussars were fighting and dying thousands of light years away while she was warm, comfortable, and safe in New Warsaw. The second clock was at 169 hours. She heaved a sigh and went back to work.

* * *

Three days later, she was looking at a report from the shipyard staff on misfiled materials when she saw a pattern emerge. All the materials were coming from the same storage facility, which was where the fitting-out materials for *Sphinx* were located. When she examined the materials movement orders, she found Dr. Sato's authorizations all over the place.

"Fleet materials office," she said to her computer, and a connection was made.

"FMO," an elSha answered. "Cafta here."

"Cafta, this is Lieutenant Commander Kowalczy."

"Ma'am!" he exclaimed, obviously realizing he was talking to the current system commander. "What can I do for you?"

"There is a bunch of incorrectly-logged cargo in the construction supply chain."

"Oh? Was there an error?"

"I'm not sure," she said. "Let me email a list for you to review."

"Sure, I'll check them out and get back to you tomorrow?"

"That's fine." She went back to work.

Aleksandra yawned hugely, stretching her back and reaching for the ceiling. It was late, and she was considering calling it quits. Even in the lower gravity of C-Ring, where most of the Hussars' offices were, sitting as much as her current job required was hard on her back. She could walk around and use her pinplants, sure. Somehow, though, she thought the commanding officer of an entire solar system should be at her desk, doing her job.

"Crazy idea," she said. She finished the stretch, opened her eyes, and saw two small creatures standing on her desk looking at her. "Holy shit!" she said and pushed away from the desk hard enough to topple over backward.

She moved the chair, carefully looking around it. The two creatures were now sitting, their short back legs folded under them. One was dark-furred and slightly larger than the other, which was grayish. They both had long, pointed and expressive ears, with little tufts of fur on the ends. They also had tails longer than their bodies, which to her suggested they were arboreal creatures. Only the darker one had a tuft of fur on its tail. The gray one cocked its head at her, and she realized the tufts of fur on its ears were sparkling in the office lights.

"Hello," the dark-furred one said.

Aleksandra sighed as she finally remembered. They were Fae. They were connected with Colonel Cartwright, and they were involved with the Raknars somehow. Alexis had sent out a briefing on them shortly after the other mercs arrived with their asteroid. She'd never seen one in person, though, until now.

"Are you okay?" the same one asked.

"Yes," she said, trying to right her chair with as much dignity as she could muster. "You caught me by surprise."

"This is your day of surprises," the sparkly-eared one said.

The other Fae looked at her with what she swore was a bemused look. "I am Sly," he said, "you can think of me as the leader of our people here. This," he said and gestured to the other, "this is Seldia."

"I am a *K'apo*," said Seldia.

"It means Far Talker," said Sly. "It's a gift that occurs only rarely in our people."

Aleksandra settled back into her chair. She almost caught herself asking the Fae to take a seat. They'd be so far down below her desk she wouldn't be able to see them. Sly was wearing a belt with pouches on it. Seldia only had a simple piece of fabric wrapped almost like a toga. "What can I do for you?" she asked. "For that matter, how did you get in here without someone from security letting me know?"

Sly gave a small smile. "You could say we are experts at getting into places," he said.

"Events are catching up with the galaxy," Seldia said, her eyes closed and ears straight up. "They are closing in like a star circling a black hole. Faster and faster it spins." She opened her eyes and looked at Aleksandra. "There is only one ultimate fate…"

Aleksandra shivered as she looked into the alien's deep blue-on-blue eyes. She felt there was more behind those eyes than she could ever understand. It made the back of her mind itch.

"We don't call them *K'apo* because it sounds nice," Sly said. "Seldia can talk with any of our kind she wishes as long as she's met them in person at some point in her life." Aleksandra opened her mouth to ask why talking to someone was a special ability. "She can do it no matter where they are, whether in the next room or halfway across the galaxy."

"Oh," was all Aleksandra could say. "Oh wow."

Seldia nodded. "Six of our kind went with your fleet to operate the Raknars. One is now dead."

"I'm sorry to hear that."

Sly bowed his head acknowledging her condolences. "It happens in war. Defeat also happens."

"What?"

"Your forces are defeated. Alexis Cromwell was killed."

"No."

"Yes," Sly said. "This is fact. Most of the fleet escaped. There was a superior force in space around Earth. The enemy commander executed a beautiful feint. They waited until your forces were fully committed, then tricked your commander into an ambush. I don't have all the details; however, the Raknar were all captured, and the majority of your ground forces were destroyed or captured. Defeat was total."

"You must be mistaken," Aleksandra said. She straightened in her chair. "Nobody beats Alexis Cromwell."

"She was beaten this time," Seldia said, her tail lazily sweeping from side to side like a serpent. "Beaten and undone."

"What about the fleet?" she asked, ignoring the Far Talker.

"Most of them escaped and are on their way back," Sly said. "They left Sol a little over a day ago."

"Oh, thank God," Aleksandra said.

"Your God can't save you," Seldia said. "There is a huge fleet behind your own fleet. The war is coming to your home."

"How long?" Aleksandra asked. Seldia spread her arms and gave a very Human shrug, as if she didn't know and didn't care.

"We're going to try and find out," Sly explained. "Far Talkers are...different, and their abilities take a heavy toll on them." Seldia snorted, picked up a miniature warship from Aleksandra's desk, and examined it.

Aleksandra opened her computer and found the files labeled "Contingency." Among them was one labeled "Impending Attack." She opened the file and looked at its contents. "Oh, shit," she said, reading the long list of protocols. She looked up at the two Fae, shaking her head. "Some of these are serious," she said. "If I do this, they can't be undone easily. How do I know you're telling me the truth?"

"You don't," Sly said. "You have a choice. You can do nothing until your fleet returns. It will be damaged and war weary. They will be low on supplies and not ready for a protracted battle. When the enemy comes in behind them, since you will probably have little time to make preparations, you will be in a poor position to defend your system. Or, as a better option, you could listen to me and do everything possible to protect yourselves."

"It is a simple choice," Seldia said as she carefully set the miniature ship back down. "Choose wisely, Human." The two Fae jumped off the desk and headed for the door.

"You said the enemy is behind our fleet," Aleksandra called after them. "You are certain?"

They stopped and looked back at her. "Yes," Sly said. "They know where New Warsaw is now."

"How do you know?"

Sly looked at her, his eyes unblinking as he seemed to consider her question. "We have allies throughout the galaxy. Information reaches us through other Far Talkers. All I can say is that your secret has been on the verge of discovery for months, maybe years. It was inevitable."

Aleksandra sighed. The Cromwells had believed that was the case for a long time. Sooner or later, New Warsaw would cease to be a secret. Then she thought of something. "You said our fleet left a day ago. This means we were defeated more than a day ago." Sly nodded. "Why did you wait this long to tell us?"

"A day won't make a difference," Sly said. "You still have almost six days before your fleet returns. Besides, we had some things to set in motion ourselves. Prepare yourselves." The Fae left her alone.

It was as if they had never been there. Her office was unchanged. The same display was frozen over her desk, the art was the same, only the clock showed time had passed. She looked at the "Impending Attack" file again.

Phase 1: Mobilize all reserves.

Phase 2: Initiate economic freeze in preparation for war materials production.

"Entropy," she cursed. "Nothing will ever be the same after I do these things."

The clock clicked forward slowly, every second one less they had to prepare. She clicked the comms control on her desk, and when the screen came up she typed in the code associated with "Impending Attack."

"Enter security access," the computer instructed. She typed in her code, and everything started.

* * *

EMS *Shadowfax*, Hyperspace

Captain Elizabeth Stacy stared dumbly at her Tri-V display and kept shaking her head every few minutes. She'd watched the recording a dozen times, maybe more. The one person she admired more than her own late father, Colonel Alexis Cromwell, had been murdered by her second in command. Shot in the back in cold blood while on a mission to stop a war which now seemed all but lost.

Elizabeth had graduated from the Winged Hussars Space Academy two years behind the Cromwell twins. She'd served with both of them multiple times, including as the XO of *Whirlaway* during the debacle in the Theel system more than 20 years ago. Nobody knew the inner workings of the Cromwell family, only that the two sisters were no longer friends after that.

Twelve years ago, she'd been serving on the intel cutter *John Andre* as navigator when she'd gotten the news that Katrina Cromwell was dead. She'd cried then, just like now. It was all she could do not to cry when Alexis had pinned her commander rank on and assigned her to her first command, the *Legend*-class *Durendal*, just six months later, shortly before Alexis' mother followed her daughter into the void.

She never knew Alexis Cromwell well enough to sit and talk like women do—about her life, her loss, her loves—but everyone in the Hussars knew Alexis was Human and sometimes found companionship. She was unbelievably discreet, but when you run a unit as big as the Hussars, as well as an entire star system, being discreet was easier said than done. She seemed to have no closer companion than Paka.

"Bitch," Elizabeth snarled and closed the Tri-V with a backhanded swipe. She used the same hand to wipe away the tears. "Rotten bitch of a rat," she screamed and pounded her desk. She would have floated away if it weren't for the waist strap around her.

Her ready room was an exact copy of the one on *Pegasus*. When the four new *Egleesius* battlecruisers were brought back from 2nd level hyperspace and went into refit, Sato had matched their design to *Pegasus*. She had to admit it helped. If you'd served on *Pegasus*, you knew your way around *Shadowfax*, *Phaeton*, *Arion*, or *Nuckelavee*. Naturally, though, there were a few design improvements, since they had 90 years' of experience and lessons learned from *Pegasus*. However, none of the new ones would have *Pegasus'* advantage.

There was no official word on what that advantage was, exactly. Consensus among the ranks was that the ghost of Katrina Cromwell haunted her halls and engineering spaces. The command staff believed it was some form of programming wizardry accomplished by Katrina prior to her death. Elizabeth wasn't sure if she bought either of those. Something told her the truth was more complicated and simultaneously simpler than either of those. She believed the ship's edge was a Cromwell, just not Katrina.

"Captain Stacy?"

Her XO, Evie Miller was at her ready room door. "Yes?"

"The damage reports are on your screen, ma'am."

"Thank you," Elizabeth said. "How are the mercs doing?"

"We have them crowded in. Life support is managing."

"No, I mean, *how* are they?"

"Oh," Evie said. "They're quiet. Lieutenant Greeg said that likely means they're more pissed than anything."

If anyone could get the feel of the mercs, it was Greeg. The Aposo was twitchy, like all Aposo, but that didn't detract from him being a good marine, or how well he understood Humans. "Just keep an eye on them, okay? We don't want any trouble. Troopers with anger issues to work off might look for an opportunity to take it out on each other."

"Yes, ma'am," Evie said and departed to see to her captain's orders.

Elizabeth called up the reports on her slate and examined the details. *Shadowfax* didn't fair too badly during the battle for Earth's orbitals. On the retreat things got hectic. After Alexis was killed and another fleet showed up, their situation had been untenable. No one person had assumed fleet command; everything had been too hectic.

The forces that could be evacuated from Earth made a run for transports. Most would never have made it, and, thus, didn't try—they'd gone to ground. She hoped. Jim Cartwright and his fantastic Raknars had surrendered to save themselves. She wasn't sure she would have done that; she'd probably have fought to the last. But he was young and with less experience under his belt.

The Horsemen were what mattered. They were the figureheads that led the resistance. Nigel Shirazi and Sansar Enkh *needed* to be evacuated, but there hadn't been enough transports in place. She'd talked to Lieutenant Commander Akoo—Hoot—the Buma who now commanded *Pegasus*. The only five ships which were in a position to rescue the Horsemen were the *Egleesius*-class ships, as they were the ones with hyperspace shunts.

Elizabeth's idea had been close to insane—dive the five battlecruisers deep into Earth's atmosphere like burning meteors, to intercept as many merc dropships as possible. Her navigator ran it a dozen times as they fell toward the atmosphere. It went from bad to worse. Then, suddenly, navigational data had come from *Pegasus*.

Exact detailed maneuvers, custom made for each of the other four other *Egleesius* ships.

The navigational data was perfect, and it included slight adjustments so they could scoop up every single dropship in their path. Once clear and back out of the atmosphere, they'd used their shunts to escape into hyperspace. Of course, between the high-G maneuver through the atmosphere, friction damage to the hull, and weapons fire from ground units, they'd all been fairly chewed up, although most of the damage wasn't extensive or critical—mostly just a who's who of blown shield capacitors, degraded armor, and hull stresses. The latter was the biggest concern, hull over-stress was the hardest thing to diagnose in hyperspace. The report detailed the progress of the repairs—what would be done before arrival in New Warsaw and what would require assistance after arrival.

Elizabeth acknowledged the report without modification and sent it back to the DCC—damage control coordinator—for her to proceed. A small part of her mind thought of a certain someone back in New Warsaw, then pushed it aside.

"They're coming for us," she said to the empty office. "They kicked our asses at Earth, and now they are coming to New Warsaw." She didn't know how she knew it; she just did. All the years in intelligence had given her some good instincts which were seldom wrong.

The Cromwells had been worried about that, too. Ever since they'd found New Warsaw, they'd spent fortunes developing the system's defenses against that day. Many people considered them paranoid. Now it looked like they weren't all that paranoid after all; the day was coming.

Elizabeth started entering orders for when they arrived in New Warsaw. Normally, when they got back the first thing that happened was injured crew were transferred to Prime Base, damage reports were transmitted to fleet command, and preparations were made to give the ship's personnel a breather. This time things would be different.

If their enemies were behind them, they'd have...what? A day at most? The enemy fleet which had appeared was huge, and it included what must have been a dreadnought. The Winged Hussars had prevailed against catastrophic odds dozens of times, but always with a Cromwell in command. This time they'd have to do it without her.

She shook her head. It didn't matter. The words of her hero came to her lips. "The Winged Hussars are nobody's prey."

We'll be ready for the bastards, Elizabeth thought. We'll be ready.

* * *

Winged Hussars Prime Base, New Warsaw System

Lieutenant Colonel Dan Walker slid into the pilot's seat of the *Avenger*-class space bomber. Although he'd hated being left behind for the assault on Earth, he'd known they would need more combat-ready pilots after the battle, no matter what the outcome, and he was the best person to train them. He was more effective training pilots than being one. The SalSha could pull about fifteen more Gs than he could; he was a liability in battle, and he knew it. Although he knew it in his head, it didn't make waiting for news any easier in his heart. His comrades, including the ones he'd fought with on Paradise—those few who'd survived—had all gone to Earth without him. He shrugged. *Focus on the mission at hand.*

Flying with the SalSha demanded *all* his attention. You never knew when one would get an idea that would have to be squelched. Just because they could do a lot of cool things didn't mean they actually *should*, especially in and around the port facilities.

It tended to make the port officers...cranky.

"I'm ready," his copilot, a young SalSha named Treeg, said.

Walker pulled out his engine start checklist and heard Treeg sigh.

Walker had found the hardest part of training SalSha was getting them to accept that they needed to follow checklists so they didn't forget anything. The entire concept of following set procedures was anathema to them, though, and the youngest ones had to be broken of the mindset of "I have that memorized; I don't need the checklist."

Walker took a breath before reading off the first item, but a call came in on his comm, interrupting him.

"Colonel Walker, Commander Kowalczy."

"Stand by," Walker told his copilot. "I just got a comm from the system commander."

"Doesn't she know we're going flying?" Treeg asked. "Why is she bothering you now?"

"I don't know," Walker replied. When he saw Treeg's mouth open to ask another question—something Treeg did a lot—he added, "And I'll find out what's going on a lot sooner if you stop asking me questions so I can answer her. Why don't you go through the mission in your head while I talk to her? And don't touch *anything!*" Walker added when he saw Treeg reaching for the engine start button.

Treeg pulled his hand back like he'd just touched something hot, and Walker shook his head. *Gotta watch them all the time.*

"Commander Kowalczy, Colonel Walker. Be advised, I am in the cockpit of an *Avenger* and about to go for a flight. Is this important?"

"Colonel Walker, yes, your flight has been aborted. Please come meet me in my office at your earliest opportunity."

"Sure thing. Can you tell me what this is all about?"

"I'm afraid I can't. Suffice it to say that it is extremely important, and I need to talk with you *right now*."

"I'm on my way."

* * *

Walker climbed out of the *Avenger* and—after making sure Treeg got out and went back to the squadron's ready room—hurried to Kowalczy's office. It was located with all the other mid-grade officers' offices in the middle of C-Ring, and far below what a system commander rated anywhere else in the galaxy.

The Hussars had always been a little…different…that way.

The door was open, so he walked in to find the younger officer working at her desk.

"So," he asked. "What's so important you had to pull me from the cockpit to come down here?"

Lieutenant Commander Kowalczy looked up and Walker could see her eyes were red and shiny, as if she'd been crying. "We lost."

"What'd we lose?" Walker asked. "If it's important, I can have a couple *Avengers* out within an hour looking for it."

Kowalczy sniffed. "No. *We* lost—*humanity* lost. We failed to take back Earth."

Walker felt his jaw drop as he struggled for a response. "Shit." It in no way encapsulated the enormity of his feelings, but it was all he was able to come up with. "Wait," he said after a couple of seconds. "How do you know? There's no way word could have gotten back here already. We won't hear anything of at least another...what? Five days?"

"Normally, we wouldn't have, but I just had a visit from two of the Fae. They said one of them was a long-talker or far-talker—something like that. Anyway, they claimed they could talk to the Fae on Earth. They said the battle was over and we'd lost. They also—they also said..." she dropped her head onto her arms and began bawling.

Walker watched for a few moments hoping the officer would get control of herself. When she didn't, he stepped to her side of the desk, put his hands on her shoulders, and gently lifted her. "What?" he asked. "What else did they say?"

"They said Colonel Cromwell was dead!"

Shocked, Walker let go of Kowalczy, and she went back to crying into the crook of her arm. Several thoughts flashed through his head. Cromwell dead—who would lead the Hussars? They were integral to saving Earth...and if they'd just lost the battle for Earth, there was so much they'd have to do. They were on the run again...they were—

"Did you hear me?" she asked, lifting her head again. "I said, *she's dead!*"

"Yes, I heard you," Walker said. "It's bad, and I'm sorry for your loss, but we'll get through this. She's not the first company commander to die in battle. I'm sure there's a plan for succession, and we'll just have to take the time to reconstitute our forces—"

"But there *is* no time!" she exclaimed.

"What do you mean?" Walker asked. "Of course, there's time. As long as the Merc Guild doesn't know where we are, there's plenty of time to fix the things we need to."

"That's just it, though," Kowalczy said. She grabbed one of the three clocks near her and turned it to show to Walker. It was a countdown clock with 142 hours showing on it. "Our forces will be back when that time runs down. Sometime after that, the Merc Guild forces will arrive here. Not only did we lose the battle for Earth and not only was Colonel Cromwell killed, but the Merc Guild knows where this system is, *and they're coming to destroy us!*"

* * * * *

Chapter Three

Winged Hussars Prime Base, New Warsaw System

Walker's jaw dropped for the second time in as many minutes. "They know where we are? How?"

"I don't know, but the Fae said that soon after our forces left Earth, the Merc Guild force followed them, and that they—the Merc Guild forces—were coming here."

"Are they sure? How do they know they're coming here?" He paused and then another question came to him. "Wait. How do you know when our forces will be back? The Fae told you that, too? But our forces have been in hyperspace for over a day now! If the Fae knew about the loss, why didn't they tell us sooner?"

Kowalczy sniffed. "I don't know," she said. "I asked the same thing, and all they would say was they had 'things to set in motion.' They also said the extra day wouldn't have made any difference."

"So, now the Fae are not only able to send messages across the galaxy, but they're fortune tellers as well?" Walker let out a breath explosively. "Fuck."

Kowalczy nodded. "That's about as far as I got, too."

Walker sighed and shook his head, then reached behind him, grabbed a chair, and pulled it over to her desk. He sighed again as he sat. He squared his shoulders and looked up at the system commander as he pulled out his slate. "Okay," he said. "The Fae say the Merc Guild knows where this system is, and we need to begin planning for it. If they don't actually have the coordinates, so much the better...but if they really do, we have to assume we have less than six days to make this system unconquerable. Let's get started."

* * *

São Paulo, Brazil, Earth

"**S**econd squad, move!" First Sergeant Akamai "Buddha" Kalawai barked into his radio, and the squad rose from concealment and moved across the avenue. It had taken over a day to get clear of what was once downtown São Paulo, and what was now a radioactive war-torn ruin.

It took all his years of experience as a CASPer driver and merc to force the feelings of despair from his heart. They'd lost six men from the two surviving companies clearing the conflagration which had enveloped Peepo's headquarters building. His executive officer and longtime friend, Hargrave, was dead. And Alpha Company of Cartwright's Cavaliers had gone with him.

He didn't know what happened in the seconds before the top floors of the building exploded, brought down by controlled demo charges. He'd been too shocked. Luckily for them both, Major Alvarado had assumed command and got them moving out of the armories and barracks which had been their targets. Luckily, because a battalion of Besquith descended on the place like demons. They found nothing, though; the Cavaliers had already pulled back. The battle wasn't over.

Only it was. Colonel Cromwell, commander of the Winged Hussars, had been murdered in a live feed, betrayed by her own XO. The ceasefire violation led to a rout of all their forces. One of the titanic Raknar was obliterated from orbit. Jim Cartwright—in his seemingly invulnerable Raknar—had been forced to surrender or risk losing the other five Raknar. Bravo and Charlie Companies were caught kilometers from any chance of getting off-world. So they stayed and ran.

"Suit check," he called once the entire squad was across the avenue. Each trooper triggered a status report which went to Buddha's suit. The data he constantly received was kept simple to make it harder for the enemy to locate them. A primary status indicator showed the suit was operational, another showed the operator was alive and kicking, and a third showed the suit's position. A suit health squawk gave him more details on their suits' conditions. They weren't great.

Hargrave and Alpha Company were gone, along with all their new advanced Mk 9 CASPers. Bravo and Charlie Companies had older Mk 8s and some ancient Mk 7s, like the one Buddha was driving. The new Mk 9s had fantastic endurance and flight characteristics, but they were gone. The various Mk 8s in his company had 15-22% remaining power. The Mk 7s were worse; all of them were below 10%. They were all out of jump juice and had little ammo.

"Looks grim, Top," Major Alvarado said.

"Yes, sir," Buddha replied.

"Captain Wolf says Charlie Company isn't in much better shape. We need to get off the grid ASAP."

"Yes, sir," Buddha said. "We made it across the avenue without notice; I'm just waiting to get the scouts back."

"Roger."

Buddha released one of the last two drones, its tiny turbines screaming as it took off toward the roof tops. Surrounded by low rent tenements, the entire area was deserted, and it had been so since just after the invasion began. Data flowed from the drone and fed into his battlespace to be reviewed. There were actually a few people around, the drone's multi-spectral scanner showed. Scared, pitiful people hunkering down while their city was torn apart by war. He felt truly sorry for what was happening to them.

He checked his company's troopers in the battlespace, verifying they were all safely concealed in apartments, abandoned shops, or even big rubbish bins. A well-trained unit, despite the horror scenario they were enduring, everyone was doing their jobs. Hargrave would have been proud.

"Scout inbound," reported Sergeant Dixie "General" Lee from Second Platoon, First Squad.

"Upload the report from Private Seeley as soon as you have it," Buddha ordered. A few second later, the data came in, and he examined it. Private Seeley had located a large warehouse just two blocks away. For the moment, nobody was inside. "Major, I think this is our best bet."

The current senior ranking officer of Cartwright's Cavaliers was silent for a moment as he too looked over the results. "If we don't take it, we'll be unassing people in about fifteen minutes," the major finally said.

"That's my assessment as well," agreed Buddha. The endurance report on his suit showed seven minutes of power remaining.

"I concur," said Captain Wolf from Charlie Company. She was young for a company commander. If things had gone better, and the aliens hadn't invaded Earth, she would have had several months of deployment under a more experienced company commander to get her legs. Instead she'd been thrust into command of forty troopers. Now, with Jim captured, the stress in her voice was evident. They needed to get out of the field before things went from bad to worse.

Sure, each CASPer had small arms and survival gear, but the troopers would come out wearing their haptic suits and would only have minimal body armor. Suboptimal, at best.

"Get them moving to that warehouse," Major Alvarado said.

"Roger that." Buddha relayed the orders.

Master Sergeant Scott "Hillbilly" Tackett, command sergeant for Charlie Company, relayed orders to his company and got them moving. The distance was short, and there weren't any intervening large roads. Inside five minutes, the entire command was inside the warehouse. Three CASPers from Charlie Company had to be moved in by other troopers due to power failure.

"Everyone unass if power is under five minutes," Major Alvarado ordered. "Anyone with more, go into standby and hold while we assess the situation."

In minutes, the walls near the main entrance were lined with twenty-nine CASPers, their operators climbing out and accessing emergency equipment. It was a sight no experienced CASPer driver ever wanted to see—powered armor units largely out of power and ammo.

"Private Partlow," Buddha called.

"Top?" the man replied as he safed the weapons systems on his all-but-dead CASPer and put it into shutdown mode.

"Grab a couple others and see what this place has to offer."

"Did you bring your credit card, Top?" Partlow asked.

"Sure did," Buddha said, and removed his personal Ctech CR-26 battle rifle from its storage compartment in his CASPer's thigh compartment. There were appreciative grunts and chuckles from other troopers who were arming up as well.

"Keep your eyes open, Private," Buddha said to Partlow.

"Will do, Top." Partlow and another pair of troopers headed off into the racks full of goods. They returned ten minutes later, and Partlow had a slate he'd found somewhere. "Can't get into it," he said, handing Buddha the computer.

"Corporal Solberg," Buddha called. "Job opportunity."

Solberg was his company's tech specialist. Truth be told, he was a good, old-fashioned hacker. The trooper came over in his haptic suit, his cables held at his waist by a strap. "Let me check it out, Top." Solberg examined the slate. "Hmmm," said the man as he attached a cable from his own slate.

"Simple industrial model," he said after a minute, and the appropriated slate came alive. "Here you go, Top."

"Good job," Buddha said. "Now get your sidearm?"

The man looked down and realized he was unarmed. "Shit. Sorry, Top."

Buddha made a "get out of here" gesture, and Solberg went back to his deactivated CASPer while Buddha began examining the warehouse's inventory. It was a general goods warehouse; however, he immediately noted a large amount of consignments logged as, "Mercenary Guild Property."

"Oh ho," Buddha said, accessing those entries.

"Partlow! See if you can get a lift running." A short time later his worry lines were gone, and he was grinning ear to ear. He made a mental note to thank Peepo later, after he'd shot her between her rat-faced eyes.

* * *

Winged Hussars Prime Base, New Warsaw System

Lieutenant Commander Aleksandra Kowalczy read the report and growled under her breath. Everything was taking three times longer than the tables said it should. Alexis' careful plans for the mobilization and defense of New Warsaw hadn't considered one possibility—that nearly every single hull might be out of the system. She struggled with her emotions for a second, then got them under control, once again replacing mourning with anger.

"Shit," she said quietly.

"Ma'am?"

Aleksandra looked up and blushed. She'd forgotten she had an assistant now. "Sorry Dimitri," she said. "I was just frustrated."

"No problem," he said with a nod of his head. "I have the academy numbers for you." Ensign Dimitri Pavlovich's family was like Aleksandra's—so Winged Hussars they bled black. His family was most known for their tech savvy, though a few had served in the combat arm of the merc company/family. Dimitri was a star in his family for aspiring to command, and he had graduated near the top of his class the previous year. Aleksandra had been a bit of a disappointment. At least, until now.

"Go ahead and give them to me." Dimitri sent them, and Aleksandra saw the files arrive in her pinplants. A total of 192 junior and senior Hussars academy students were being readied for service. Only half even had an able spacehand ribbon on their uniforms. *Entropy,* she thought. *So few, so very few.* "Send out the assignments as we discussed," she said, then remembered something. "They are all volunteers, yes?"

"Yes, ma'am. We had over two hundred volunteers from the underclassmen as well."

Aleksandra felt her heart swell with pride. "Send emails to their parents or guardians. If they approve, the underclassman who are allowed are to be assigned duty on support craft and shuttles aiding in the evacuation of Home."

Dimitri nodded and closed his eyes so he could concentrate to send the messages. The young officer had his first pinplants at age nine, like most Hussars who wanted to serve in the combat or technical arm. Even so, formulating and sending hundreds of emails took a lot of concentration.

Aleksandra input 150 more souls into the support pilots and ratings columns, and shuffled more experienced crews out. She frowned at the results and then shifted more. *Maybe if I only leave one experienced rating on each support ship,* she thought. She made the change, and a hell of a lot of extremely useful crewmembers became available. Also, there were now a great many shuttles and transports being operated by partly trained kids. She gritted her teeth and okayed the redistribution.

Across the star system, she expected her division leaders were looking at her orders and shaking their heads in disbelief. *They're probably thinking I'm insane,* she thought, and they might be right...except, what other choice did she have? Undermanned support ships and unmanned combat vessels? There were still more than 9,000 civilians and dependents to evacuate from Home.

An evacuation drill from the planet hadn't been run in sixty years. When the population had surpassed 5,000, it had become impractical to shut down the planet's economy for a week. Besides, the last time they had conducted one, the operation had taken eleven days to complete. Aleksandra had less than three left. Putting a couple hundred kids on ships before they were old enough to kiss the opposite sex had helped…a little.

"Commander?"

Aleksandra almost didn't look up. She wasn't used to be addressed as a commander. "Dimitri?"

"Kleena is here to see you, ma'am."

Aleksandra blinked as she tried to remember who that was, and why they were coming to her office. She ended up using her pin-plants. He was the head of the Geek Squad. Thinking it might be something in relation to their missing scientist she said, "I'll see him."

The elSha skittered into her office, as was his race's manner. He was old; she could tell by the way his nose scales were flaking off instead of molting regularly. He wore a light jacket, another sign of an aging elSha, and it had the green piping of the Winged Hussars' technical branch.

"Good to see you, Kleena," she said.

"And you, Lieutenant Commander. I don't believe we've ever met." He offered her his tiny clawed hand, which she took. Being from the technical branch and not an armed service member, it was customary, just like how he didn't use her honorific title.

"No, we haven't," she said. "However, Commander Cromwell always spoke well of you."

"A true loss," he said, and shook his long head, casting both independent eyes down at the deck. As one of the top Hussars, Kleena had been made aware of Alexis' death. He was one of a tiny number who knew the truth.

"Do you have news on Dr. Sato?"

"Only that I can now confirm he is not in the star system."

"That is unfortunate." Aleksandra looked down at her drab desk and sighed. The genius doctor could likely have helped pull a XenSha out of a hat. The image always gave her the willies, but it was a popular saying none the less. "Where do you think he's gone?"

"Honestly, I have no idea." Kleena shrugged. "Sato isn't the kind of guy who wants to go places. Ever since he and Nemo came to us, he's been happy to invent, examine, and generally work on any tech we threw his way."

"Except when he unleashed a doomsday weapon on Capital?"

"Yeah, that." Kleena said and gave an all-too-Human sigh. "Even that behavior is in line with him. The only trouble he tended to cause was getting into stuff which would have been better off left alone. Commander Cromwell was always willing to look the other way and considered the small amounts of mayhem Sato created were—what do Humans say—the cost of doing business."

"Yes, we say that. Only we usually aren't saying it in reference to doomsday weapons." She considered for a moment. "Do you believe he's an agent of the Mercenary Guild?"

"Not a chance," Kleena answered without hesitation. "But..."

"But what?"

Kleena scratched his muzzle absentmindedly and his eyes wandered around. "I've always thought his unusual behavior was the result of some past trauma."

"As though he'd been hurt?"

"Maybe, or just mentally effected."

"I don't follow you."

Kleena pointed at her pinplants. "You realize your pinplants are effectively a direct access to most of your brain functions, right?"

Aleksandra nodded in understanding. "It's necessary for you to be able to record vision, control the computer features, etcetera. Well, you can also use those same inputs to mess with your brain."

"Entropy!" she cursed. "Who would do that?"

"I don't know," he said. "However, it could be someone who wanted Sato to either forget something or simply to suppress it. He could have been tortured and escaped. I could also be wrong, and his behavior just a matter of his rearing. I don't completely understand how you Humans raise your broods."

We aren't too sure about that either, some days. "Thank you for your insights. I'll include them in my report for Alexis—" she stopped midsentence and shook her head. "I mean, whoever is eventually given command."

"I understand," Kleena said.

Dimitri got her attention. "Commander, Cafta is here."

"It seems to be my day for elSha visitors," she said and gestured for her assistant to let him in.

Cafta entered, saw Kleena, and the two elSha exchanged a curious, rapid head-bobbing action. Aleksandra guessed it was customary with their race. Her new visitor was carrying a metallic case on a shoulder strap. It reminded her of the standard Hussars' ship damage control case.

Kleena stood to the side and let his fellow approach her desk.

"Why didn't you call?" she asked Cafta.

"I thought you should see this," he said. "If I may?" he said, and held up the case.

"Sure," she said, and gestured to her desk. One of the advantages of the virtual work environment of a pinplanted person was the desk usually remained uncluttered. The person's brain, not so much. Aleksandra moved a couple model ships aside, one of them the one Seldia had examined. She noted it was a *Steed*-class battlecruiser.

Cafta set the case on her desk and unlocked it, but didn't open it. "I know you're busy, and I am sorry to interrupt your meeting. However, I discovered the problem with the inventory mismatch."

He opened the case to reveal a dozen cylindrical devices. Each had a pair of high-power superconducting connectors and a single data connector. "I only checked a dozen—there wasn't time to review all of them. However, the twelve samples I pulled from inventory are all identical to this."

"I've never seen anything like that," Aleksandra said.

"Nor I," Cafta agreed.

"Me, either," Kleena said, leaning in to examine it. "The power cable is a J-class. For a small item like those devices, they must use a horrendous amount of power."

"I agree," Cafta said. "I'm not a tech, but in my duties in the Fleet Materials Office, I see almost every piece of equipment needed to build, repair, and manufacture starships." He pointed at the open case. "I've never seen *anything* like that. Further, I managed to trace them backward and can verify Manufactory #3 produced all of them over the course of a few weeks before Sato disappeared. Within hours of his departure, that manufactory ceased production and purged its memory of all plans."

"I don't understand," Aleksandra said.

"It means Sato wanted us to find them, but not be able to review the plans," Kleena said.

"We would never have found them if I hadn't noticed inconsistent materials IDs and the ship fitters hadn't complained about incorrect shipments."

"Exactly," Kleena said. "Sato is one of the most intelligent beings I have had the pleasure to meet. Do you honestly think he would be able to disappear so thoroughly that nobody notices he's gone for many hours, and at the same time make a sloppy error that allowed these items to be found?" He spread his thin arms apart and shook his head. "No, of course not. He left these devices and guaranteed we'd find them."

"But why?" Aleksandra asked. Kleena shrugged.

She examined the case. It was simple, a utilitarian design of metalized plastics form-fitted for the devices, including insets to hold the cables and wire from being bent or damaged by the lid. She took one out and was surprised how heavy it was. Her eyes moved up to regard Cafta again. "You said there were 105 of these?"

"No, 105 *cases* like that. So, 1,260 modules."

So many, she thought, *it must be important.* "Kleena, can you figure this out?" She handed him one.

"I'll have Patrick Leonard run a diagnostic on it right away," the scientist said. "He's one of my newest Geek Squad members, and he's the best person I've seen with computer systems in many years." He looked at the data connector. "Whatever it is, the computer interface suggests it takes a lot of power and computer processing."

"Notify me as soon as you know anything," she said. "Cafta, be sure they're labeled as experimental ship components, so they don't get shipped to someone under their original label." She glanced at her computer. "Heat deflectors?" She looked at Kleena.

"A component in life support," he said.

Aleksandra rolled her eyes. She examined the case and saw they were labeled "D-Field Generator." "Add this name to it as well. Now, I have to get back to my job. You're both dismissed."

The two elSha left, talking as they departed. Dimitri stood and examined the case with its eleven remaining D-Field Generators. He gazed at the machines for a moment before shaking his head and closing the case. He put the case in a storage area and returned to more urgent work.

* * *

Winged Hussars Prime Base, New Warsaw System

"No, no, no!" Walker exclaimed over his comms. "I don't want the asteroids towed *into* the emergence area; I want them towed to just outside it! Our forces are coming back, and we don't want them to run into them. We're just pre-positioning them so we don't have so far to move them once we are able put them in place."

"But, sir, that's going to take more time because we have to get them moving then stop them. Then we'll have to get them moving again once it's time to position them in the emergence zone."

"I understand that," Walker replied with a growl. He paused a second to take a breath. Yelling at the tug force commander wasn't going to help anyone. "Look," he added, his temper back in check. "Some of the asteroids have to be moved a long way, and we don't know how much time we have. All we know is that we will need them there soon after our forces return. We don't want them there *when* our forces return."

"But, sir, no one has ever emerged into an asteroid or anything like that."

"I am well aware of that," Walker said, just barely holding onto his temper. "Still, Colonel Cromwell and the rest of our folks just lost a battle, and the ships may not be in great shape when they arrive. How about if we make it easier for them by *not* placing obstacles in their path? That will also help them get to Prime Base faster so we can incorporate them in the planning."

"I guess I can see how that makes sense," the tug captain replied. "Still, it's a lot of extra movement, and more wear and tear on my fleet, you know."

"Let me put it to you this way," Walker replied. "I'll send Colonel Cromwell your way, and you can explain to her why you thought it wise to go against the orders of the acting system head of defenses, and why she had to maneuver around the asteroids you allowed to drift into the emergence area, okay?"

"Now, now, you don't have to get your panties in a bunch," the crusty tug captain said. "We'll take care of it as best we can. I'm just letting you know—"

"Look," Walker said, snapping, "*I don't have time for this shit!* Get the asteroids in place, where I told you to, now! You have four days to make that happen, and tow the defender asteroids into place, too. Otherwise, Alexis Cromwell is going to have your ass."

"The defender asteroids, too? There's no way—"

"Yes, them, too! And the sooner you get on it, the more time you'll have. Now do it!"

He terminated the conversation before the tug captain could say another word—Walker really *didn't* have time for it. He also didn't like using the dead as a motivator, but the tug skipper didn't know she was dead, and he doubted Alexis would mind him doing everything possible to protect her system from the enemy.

He looked at the projections for the defender asteroids. Over the years, the Horde had been hollowing out a number of asteroids and mounting huge, ship-sized particle beam weapons on them. After an initial experiment to power them using solar collectors had proven inefficient, they had installed fusion reactors. The cost in F11 alone was staggering, but Alexis had approved it. The asteroids were massive and hard to turn quickly, though, which had required more tunneling, so the individual weapons had more room for independent targeting. The entire project had been one cost overrun after another, to the point that Sansar had almost canceled it, but then Sato made a few changes to the design which made them feasible.

Walker looked at the estimates. Of the twelve *Defender*-class asteroid bases, six would be fully operational when the fleet returned, with four more in various stages of readiness. The last two had been hollowed out and had their fusion plants installed but hadn't gotten any of their weapons yet. His crews were working double shifts trying to get them completed, but they needed more time.

As he thought about the weapons, he brought up the manufactories' schedules. Everyone wanted everything *right now* to get ready for the imminent battle. There had been some jockeying of the schedule that had led to…inefficiencies before Aleksandra had put her foot down. The particle beam weapons he needed were second in line after a massive drone production run that was currently in place. While he didn't know how many drones he'd need to have "enough," he knew the thousands that were being produced would be extremely helpful. As helpful as the twenty particle beam weapons would have been? Walker shrugged.

If they were lucky, the Merc Guild wouldn't show up right on the heels of the Human fleet. He doubted Peepo would give him the extra time he needed to prepare, however, and he had alternate contingencies in place if the weapons weren't available in time. It was all about having good prior planning—luck was never a factor.

* * *

Pesqueiro Arujá, North East of São Paulo, Brazil, Earth

Splunk watched the flyer pass half a kilometer to the south. An unarmored scout; the Besquith crew was visible through the windscreen. It would have been childishly easy to neutralize it. Shadow tracked the craft's passage through the scope on her laser rifle. The weapon had started as a heavy Oogar infantry weapon but had been unwittingly donated by its former owner and repurposed as a sniper weapon. Once you stripped all the extra junk down to the essentials, it was manageable. Only just, though.

"Say the word," Shadow said. Her sharp teeth gleamed as she smiled in anticipation of the kill.

"No," Splunk said. Shadow cast her a baleful stare. "We don't need to alert them to our zone of operation."

Dante nodded his head in agreement from where he was helping prepare the meat for their meal. "She's right," he said. "Give it a rest." Shadow grumbled but lowered her weapon. "Food will be ready in a few minutes."

The house they occupied was empty, and it had been so for a long time. Splunk wasn't used to the kinds of residences Humans preferred, having lived with Jim the whole time she'd known his species. She looked around the dwelling and crinkled her nose in distaste. It was large by her own race's scale; however, it stank and was in terrible condition. Maybe it was abandoned because of that. She didn't know. It was one of hundreds in a neighborhood occupying the side of a hill, which was why they'd chosen it.

"Peanut and Sandy coming in," Ryft called over the tiny radios they all wore in their long sensitive ears. She was two houses further up the hill, carefully hidden in overwatch, observing anyone who approached their hideout on foot.

"Noted," Dante said.

Splunk took her pistol, moved to the door, and waited silently. Despite what anyone on overwatch said, procedure was to observe the facts for yourself before letting anyone in. An overwatch could be eliminated quietly and then impersonated, just like they'd done with the Besquith two days earlier.

Watching through a tiny hole in the door, she saw two small, fast-moving figures loping down the alleyway. Both were heavily burdened with loaded packs and were carrying Dusman-sized rifles at the ready.

"Confirmed," she said and unbolted the door. The defenses they'd set up wouldn't stop anything determined to get in. Stopping an attacker wasn't the intention of the improvised bolts and braces they had emplaced on the entrances, only slow down an intrusion and give the Fae time to respond. She gave a "hurry up" gesture, and the two scouts dashed inside. She secured the door behind them.

"Set a drone and come in," Dante said to Ryft. A single click of the radio came in reply, indicating she was on the way. He turned to the newly returned pair. "Any problems?"

"We saw some Humans," Peanut said.

"They didn't see us," Sandy said and winked.

"Did you have to kill them?" Splunk asked.

"No," Peanut said. "They were fishing at that lake on the other side of the hill. Lots of boats and stuff everywhere, but hardly anyone was around."

Splunk nodded and gestured to the bags they carried. "What did you find?"

They opened their bags to show a vast array of electronics, tools, miscellaneous parts, and spices.

"About time," Dante said, scooping up the spices and heading back to the cooking area.

"Nice," Ryft said and scooped up an electronics repair kit. They all took some of the parts and began working on their equipment while Dante continued meal prep.

Peanut then took a small device out of his pouch. "This is interesting."

Splunk leaned in to look at what he had. It was a small drone. A tiny electronic scrambler had been attached because the drone was still active, though disabled. Unlike their own drones, this one was purposefully designed, obviously one of many similar. It was likely mass produced, or at least a run from a manufactory. She moved closer and examined the construction.

"Human made," she said after a second. "Not terrible—in fact, it's better than most of the Human-made junk."

"It looks like some kind of insect," Sandy said, taking apart a piece of equipment.

"A dragonfly," Splunk explained. "They're native to parts of Earth, including around Houston."

"Why copy an insect?" Peanut asked.

"Camouflage," Dante snapped. "Don't be stupid." Peanut nodded and looked nonplussed.

"Where'd you find this?" Splunk asked. "Did it transmit details before you scrambled it?" she asked after Peanut told her.

"I can't be sure," Peanut replied.

Splunk stared at the immobile machine and scratched her chin. After a minute, she stuffed it into a tiny box, leaving the scrambler in place. She'd have to decide what to do about it later. An hour later, she checked her watch. She'd taken to wearing one some time ago; it helped keep her in sync with the different hours preferred by Humans. It was minutes from the 60-hour mark of their last contact with Seldia.

"Almost time," she told them. Everyone stopped what they were doing and joined her in the center of the filthy home. Dante touched the controls for the various drones the Dusman had out, setting them from observation to sentry, and they all joined hands.

<*Seldia...Seldia, hear me,*> Splunk said across the depths of space.

<*I hear you.*> the K'apo replied. She was waiting this time. <*Update.*>

<We continue to evade. Making progress in locating our operators. Anticipate contact within twenty-four hours.>

<Noted. We are assisting the Humans with preparations for the coming battle. We need exact time of departure for the enemy fleet.>

They were ready to provide the data, and Splunk gave it to her. <The merc guild fleet left twenty-nine hours behind the Hussars. They have a dreadnought.>

This time there was a pause. <*A dreadnought? You are certain?*>

<Completely.>

<Sly asks if you can find out where the dreadnought came from.>

The five Dusman looked at each other. They'd only obtained small amounts of intel via the stolen Besquith comms. Shortly after they'd killed the Besquith and taken their gear, the enemy coordinators had changed the comms encryption. This wasn't a challenge for Splunk, who simply broke the new encryption within minutes of finding it changed. The comms gave them intel on movements of units searching for them, but precious little else.

<We will try.>

<Recontact in another sixty hours.> The connection ended.

"I hate the damned K'apo." Dante spat and went back to the cook fire. The house had a central cooking pit, which served their purpose. Dante had salvaged a power input and put it to work as a heated grill. He put several pounds of meat on the waiting skewers.

The drones showed nothing more than a few, small, local four-legged creatures smaller than the Dusman. Splunk identified them as cats and screened them off the drone's recognition profile. There was no need for overwatch at that time, so everyone grabbed skewers and began roasting meat. The house was quickly filled with the odor and sizzle of cooking flesh.

"Too bad it won't taste as good as it smells," Peanut said, and the others nodded.

"The seasoning will help," Dante said.

It only took a minute before they were taking skewers off the heat and tasting the meat.

"Ugh," Splunk said. The meat was incredibly strong and oily, just like she'd expected. Her stomach roiled in complaint, and she reached for the hot spicy seasoning, adding a large amount. "Disgusting."

"What do you expect from Oogar?" Shadow asked.

Splunk glared at him darkly.

"There are some Humans nearby," Shadow persisted.

"No," she said. "We're here to help these beings, not eat them."

"Only as long as their interests correspond to ours," Dante said.

Splunk looked at the ancient one-eyed warrior then gave a slow nod.

"We can't risk ourselves for the minor races if they don't advance our own interests," Sandy added.

"I don't need to be lectured," Splunk said, and they ate in silence. Splunk detested the meat, but she ate it anyway. It was doubly important just then. Peanut looked up from his meal at her and gave a tiny wink. She smiled and went back to the food. It was what it was. It wasn't like the Oogar needed the meat anymore, anyway. She would worry about the dragonfly drone later.

* * * * *

Chapter Four

*L*ieutenant Commander Aleksandra Kowalczy fumed in her seat aboard Shuttle *322-A* as they entered coast. She had much better things to be doing than flying around inspecting warships. She wouldn't be inspecting warships if they were working properly.

The traffic patterns were chaotic, and she was glad not to be piloting. Her scores at the academy were better than average, but that had been many years ago. New Warsaw's red giant star sported an asteroid belt which was simply massive. Home orbited on the edge of it with thousands of asteroids within easy reach. Many were mineral rich, as well.

Those same asteroids also made navigating around Prime Base an intermittent nightmare.

Aleksandra had seen old 2D movies from Earth—science fiction movies—where asteroids were so close together their distance wasn't measured in kilometers but meters. It was ironic New Warsaw was more like the bad science fiction than most systems in the galaxy.

The academy used the asteroid field as a sort of proving ground—young pilots flew through the chaotic field to hone their navigational skills; the Cromwell twins famously were nearly expelled from the academy a dozen times for it. The most infamous was a typical Cromwell twin dare race through the asteroid field that resulted in a mangled shuttle and a furious academy dean. Had they been anyone other than the Cromwell twins, they would have surely been expelled. All things being equal, Aleksandra would have been thrilled to stay out of the asteroid field entirely.

"Coming clear of the field," her pilot said. She gave a terse nod. She'd passed on the second seat up front despite it being her due. The young woman probably knew how uncomfortable she was, and Aleksandra didn't want to make the pilot nervous as she flew through the asteroids. Aleksandra wasn't trained or qualified for the job foisted upon her. If there was someone—anyone—more qualified to do it, she would have gladly handed off the responsibility.

She watched the display from her seat in the rear of the shuttle as the craft flipped over and began slowing. The camera showed a view of the approaching shipyard complex. One of four, they were placed in an orbital zone within the massive asteroid belt which was relatively clear of rocks. A fleet of tiny robots kept it that way.

This shipyard, like the other three, sported a nearly finished *Steed*-class battlecruiser. The one they were approaching was the most completed of the four, soon to be christened EMS *Sphinx*. The brand-new ship had yet to get her Hussars customary black-and-gold coloring at key points, though her name was stenciled on the bow, printed on either side of the two one-terawatt particle accelerator barbettes.

Moored nearby was *Hippogriff*. She'd been towed back from the battle at Talus in terrible shape. All but one of her reactors were destroyed, and she had severe structural damage. The ship's crew had been devastated. Most of the engineering and damage control crews had been killed. Ship-wide, she'd suffered 45% losses, including half the CIC personnel. Captain Corder was in critical condition and had been evacuated to Prime Base.

The plan had been to refit *Hippogriff* and have her ready for the Earth battle. Unfortunately, after the shipyard personnel evaluated her, it had been decided she was too damaged to have her operational in the time available. Since then, she'd lay at moorage, ignored and all but forgotten. As Aleksandra stared at the wreck, she thought she saw some flashes. *Had someone ordered work to be done on her?* She wondered. She almost picked up her slate to check when the pilot spoke up.

"Braking to dock with *Sphinx*," the pilot said.

Aleksandra looked up in surprise. "Oh, right," she said and cinched her straps. A second later, the image of *Hippogriff* forgotten, the shuttle's engines roared to life, pushing her back into her seat.

A little over fifteen minutes later, Shuttle *322-A* docked to an airlock on *Sphinx*, and her pilot checked the connection manually.

"I appreciate the caution, Ensign," she said, "but I trust the automatic systems."

"With all due respect, Commander, this *is* a brand-new ship…" She left the rest unsaid.

"Oh, I see," Aleksandra said, and she quietly waited while the pilot went through her process. It only took a minute, and then the hatch was opened from the inside.

"Commander Kowalczy," an older man said, floating just inside the hatch. He gave her a formal salute. "Lieutenant Jameson, formerly retired, in temporary command of EMS *Sphinx*."

"Then it is *Captain* Jameson," she replied and saluted. "Permission to come aboard?"

"Granted," he said, smiling.

Aleksandra floated through the open hatch. The shuttle pilot was already closing up; she had a dozen more flights waiting on her roster. The hatch seated with a clank and a hiss of pressurization.

"Well, there goes my ride," Aleksandra said with an uncomfortable laugh. "You might as well show me the problem."

"Sure," Captain Jameson said. She followed him down the shiny new corridor. "I'm sorry my XO wasn't here to meet you, but you see, I don't have an XO right now."

"We're incredibly shorthanded," Aleksandra said.

"I'm sorry we had to ask you to come over, but nobody can decide what to do about it."

"I understand," she said, though she didn't entirely. Had Alexis Cromwell routinely dealt with minor issues like this? Somehow, Aleksandra doubted it.

Though she'd never served on a *Steed*-class, all command-level officers and technical crew in the Winged Hussars were required to have at least a basic familiarity with all the deck plans of the common ship classes. Of course, since she wasn't a serving shipboard officer, she had little experience converting those deck plans into real world experience. She kept the plans constantly running in her pinplants and still couldn't quite get her bearings. Luckily, Captain Jameson seemed to have the knack of it.

They'd nearly reached the CIC when something that had been bothering her finally firmed up in her head: the lack of crew. "She seems so empty," Aleksandra said.

"Normal complement is 225, not counting marines," Jameson said. "I served on *Sleipnir* just before retiring. I have twenty-nine hands on board, including myself, and no marines."

Aleksandra just nodded, because she knew that, she'd signed off on the crew assignments. "You'll have another eleven once the evacuation is complete."

"Kids and old farts like me," Jameson said, shaking his head. "What the hell went wrong back on Earth?" He glanced at her and caught a handhold to bring himself to a stop. Aleksandra did too, though a tad less gracefully. Like so many other shipboard skills, zero-G operations was one in which she was lacking due to insufficient practice. "Ma'am, permission to speak candidly?"

"Granted," she said.

"How the hell do you know what happened?"

Aleksandra sucked on her teeth for a long moment. She'd decided not to make it public that Alexis was dead. Her fear of the company falling into despair was stronger than the need to motivate them. They were executing the needed operations the way they'd been trained and doing it by the numbers. How would introducing the knowledge of Alexis Cromwell's death affect that efficiency? Badly.

The look of profound concern on Jameson's face told her she needed to confide in him. Despite being lower in rank, he was many years her senior, and, as such, deserved to be in her confidence.

"Colonel Cromwell is dead," she said.

The expression on his face went from concern to confusion then to horror in an instant. "No," he said.

"Yes," she stated. "I have high confidence in this fact."

"Why haven't you told the Hussars?"

"Why do you think?" Aleksandra asked. "Can you imagine the reaction? How it would affect morale?"

"Yes...but still..."

Aleksandra shook her head. "It was my decision. The fleet will be back in just a few days. I'll have the full details then." *And someone else from the fleet will take command,* she thought but didn't say.

"And how do you know this?" he asked, some of the concern returning.

"Yeah, that's the tricky part." She took a calming breath. "You've heard about the Fae, the little aliens that came to New Warsaw with Colonel Cartwright?"

"Furry little monkey things?" he asked. She nodded. "I've heard of them but haven't seen one."

Aleksandra described her encounter with Seldia and Sly. The older man listened to every word she said before commenting.

"You believe them."

"What would you do?"

He considered. "I don't know." She cocked her head at him. "I would probably believe them too, I guess. This whole war feels like a reckoning. I met Lawrence Kosmalski once—did you know that?"

"Really?" she asked.

"Sure, it was about fifty years ago. He was old as sin and twice as mean."

Aleksandra laughed and shook her head. It sounded like the founder of the Winged Hussars.

"So much of what the Winged Hussars are today are the result of Amelia Cromwell's guidance that many people have lost sight of Lawrence Kosmalski's contributions. The man was a financial genius who some said could see the future." Jameson made an expansive gesture. "He was responsible for finding New Warsaw and moving us here. Some say he was bitter because his accomplishments were eclipsed; I think he liked the quiet."

"How does that factor into this war?"

"In addition to being mean, he was prophetic. He was the one who was sure war would, one day, come to our home, no matter what we did to prepare for it." He looked her square in the eye. "So, I believe you and the little aliens. War is finally coming here."

"Thank you," she said. "I wish you could take command of the system."

He laughed and smiled. "I wish you could take command of this ship."

She smiled back at him. "We'll see who's left of senior command when the fleet gets back. The Fae didn't have enough details to tell me how badly they were beaten. We might not have much to defend the system, outside of what's here. On that, let's see what it is you brought me here for."

An hour later she was scratching her head in the CIC as a pair of techs ran the fifth diagnostic on *Sphinx*'s tactical systems, with the outcome completely unchanged. The two techs looked at each other in confusion.

"What could it be?" she asked them.

"A fundamental problem with system integration?" one of the techs suggested.

"The shield control system has a deep logic problem," the other said.

"You can't decide which?" Aleksandra asked. They both shook their heads. The pair were young, though not from the academy. Both were qualified to work at the shipyards; however, they were still supposed to be under supervision. Their normal boss was halfway across the system working with the Golden Horde on some of the other defenses. "Okay, how about addressing both?"

"Not practical," Jameson interjected. "You see, the shield control system is dispersed through the hull at several locations." He activated a Tri-V showing a schematic of the *Steed*-class. The named systems were highlighted in blue and showed in a dozen places along the hull. "Trying to see if the shield systems were improperly integrated means a complicated process of running cross-connected diagnostics between each system interacting with the shields."

"Which is half the systems on the ship," Aleksandra said. Jameson gave a sad nod. "How did the ship get moved from the shipyard without testing? I thought it was essentially done before assets were reallocated."

"And there's the problem," one of the techs said. "Those tests *were* completed. We did them ourselves. Full function in standby and under load. No live-fire tests yet, of course; we would have progressed to those as the next step."

"It was working in the shipyard?" she asked. Both men nodded.

Captain Jameson shrugged. "I didn't see her until she was clear of the yard."

Aleksandra acknowledged the fact with a nod; she'd assigned him, after all. "When exactly did you discover the problem?"

"When we were preparing for a simplified live-fire test," Jameson said. "Thirty-six hours ago."

"Thirty-six hours," she thought. Using her pinplants she checked on when the ship was first moved out of the yard. A little over two weeks ago, just before the fleet left for Earth. She continued her research on the process of moving *Sphinx* out of the shipyard and into the final fitting moorage. Everything was routine, as indicated by the work orders, until something changed.

Nine days ago, work began to miss deadlines, which corresponded with the beginning of personnel shortages. It wasn't bad, only notable. Everything which needed to be completed was still being done, it was just taking a little longer than originally planned. Since *Sphinx* wasn't ready for the Earth campaign, and they were short on crew anyway, it hadn't been a priority. She was about to remove the file from her pinplants when a log entry caught her attention.

"Equipment Check—T. Sato."

Instantly, she remembered Uuth in her office reporting Dr. Sato's disappearance. The HST director had told her Sato's last sighting was on *Sphinx*!

"Holy shit," she said, drawing the attention of everyone on the CIC. "I need to check something."

She floated to the side to get out of the way and sent a message to Uuth, as she was too far away from Prime Base to make a live conversation practical. "Please forward the report from the marines who were escorting Dr. Sato on his work aboard EMS *Sphinx*. I need to know precisely where he was working on the ship." She sent the message with top priority, and she got the reply in only a minute.

"The marines weren't familiar enough with the *Steed*-class's exterior to provide those details; however, I have included their suit logs which have camera images. I hope this helps."

"It does indeed," she said as she loaded the enclosed files and ran them forward. She hadn't seen the recording of Dr. Sato's specially modified CASPer going into the ship. She forwarded the recordings before suddenly freezing it. She clipped the image and cleaned it up. "Captain Jameson," she said, "can you show me where access panel 22-A-99 is located?"

"Sure," he said, and the deck plans moved to flash a position. It was next to one of the blue-highlighted shield control systems.

"I knew it," she said. "Please check there, I believe you will find your answers at that section."

"We'll have to go EVA to reach that section," Captain Jameson said. She nodded and waited. The captain looked at the two maintenance techs. "Suit up and have a look."

Despite her meager skills, Aleksandra helped with configuring and checking systems while she waited, and she instructed a young Buma, who was still in the academy, on the ship's damage control station. Those systems were nearly identical across all the Hussars' ships, except the *Egleesius*-class, of course. Eventually the two technicians returned from their EVA carrying a small case.

"Try it now," they said.

"Shields function check," Jameson ordered.

The defensive coordinator activated the system and keyed the shields to life. After a second, full function was confirmed.

"How did you know?" Jameson asked.

"Another event which coincided with your issue," she explained.

"The main shield controller was connected to a slate which was sending an interruption test sequence," one of the techs who'd went EVA said.

"Harmless but intentional," the other tech agreed. He held up the case he was carrying. "This was zip-tied to the sabotage."

Aleksandra took the case. "It's not sabotage," she said.

"Then what is it?" Jameson asked.

"An arrow pointing to this case."

"There's a menu option on the shield control system which isn't normal," the defense coordinator said. He looked at his captain. "Should I activate it?"

"No!" Aleksandra said, louder than she'd intended.

"I thought you said it wasn't sabotage," Jameson said.

"It isn't. Or at least I'm pretty sure it isn't." She looked at the case she was holding for a second, then let it float before her and carefully released the simple locking mechanism. It opened easily to reveal a common slate. "Can I borrow your ready room, Captain?"

"It's not much of an office but be my guest."

Aleksandra forgot to thank him as she pushed off a workstation and floated through the doorway into the captain's ready room, pulling the door closed behind her. Built into the same armored sphere which held the CIC, the ready room was a combination meeting room, office, and temporary quarters for the captain. A fully completed *Steed*-class would have the space appointed with a meeting table, desk, personal effects of the captain, and a tiny toilet. All made to operate in zero gravity or under thrust, of course. This ready room was more an open space with a simple desk.

Aleksandra hooked a foot through one of the fabric loops next to the desk, using it to hold herself steady. The desk had a number of flexible bands built into its surface in order to hold things in place. She secured the case with one and the slate with another, then touched the slate's activation window. She wasn't surprised when it scanned her finger.

"Lieutenant Commander Aleksandra Kowalczy—Identity Confirmed" the screen displayed. The Tri-V came alive, and an image of Dr. Taiki Sato appeared above the desk.

"Hello, Lieutenant Commander, I hope you arc doing well." After the greeting, it went silent. She watched for a while as Sato looked at her without moving.

"Strange recording," she said.

"I am not a recording," the image said.

Aleksandra jumped slightly and would have floated across the room if not for the strap around her foot. "Then what are you?"

"I am a modified ACSP."

Aleksandra used her pinplants for the acronym. Automated Customer Service Program. "You're an AI?"

"That is an over-simplification," Sato's image replied. Then the ACSP gave her a wry look. "Besides, Lieutenant Commander, AI are illegal."

"Okay," she said, giving a little, uncomfortable laugh. "Why did you take the *Sphynx's* shields off-line?"

"Why, to lead you to this slate, of course."

"Sure, but why?"

"I wish to have this conversation with Alexis."

"So do I," she said. "Except Alexis is dead."

The Tri-V image froze for the first time, more closely resembling a static picture. It stayed that way long enough to make her think the program had broken. She was about to see if the slate would reset, when Sato suddenly spoke again.

"I was not programmed with that contingency. Who is in command?"

"I am."

"Processing." The image stilled again for a few seconds. "There are no contingencies stored to match the one you are describing," the program said. "Thus, I am proceeding with the one which most likely matches probable outcomes.

"I have modified *Sphinx* with defensive systems based upon technology acquired from 2nd level hyperspace. I was unable to fully understand the technology involved; however, what I was able to decipher has been produced.

"The plan I assembled was for Alexis Cromwell and her AI to begin evaluations of the new technology and, once complete, to integrate it into the Winged Hussars' vessels in a measured manner to allow tactical doctrine to be adjusted accordingly."

Aleksandra listened and marveled at the program—its intricacies, the level of effort it must have taken to put together, and how well it worked. She'd only met Sato once in passing, although she'd heard all the stories and mentally labeled him an eccentric genius. She now considered her assessment of his genius off by an order of magnitude. This program was only written for one purpose!

"The situation as stated has invalidated all options," the ACSP version of Sato continued. "Information is being copied to a data chip. This information needs to be given to the shipyard personnel. It includes installation procedures for the same modifications I've made to this ship. They need to be given the utmost priority."

The Tri-V began displaying schematics and virtual displays of the new hardware in action. Aleksandra wasn't a front-line combat officer, and she'd never been shot at in the line of duty, but she'd gotten adequate scores on tactical training. What she saw made her gasp and put a hand to her mouth.

"This..." she stammered. "This is a paradigm shift."

The computer-generated Sato gave a slight smile and nodded its head. "You are correct. Please do not try to follow me. I'm going where you cannot follow. I'm sorry for what I've done in the past, even though I had good intentions. Things were done to me by forces I cannot explain for fear of endangering every Human in the galaxy. I hope, one day, to come back and see New Warsaw again. It was the only place where I felt…at home.

"A copy of this conversation has also been saved to the data chip. Please remove it now."

Aleksandra pulled out the chip, and the representation of Dr. Sato nodded. "I wish you luck, Lieutenant Commander Kowalczy, and farewell." With a sudden flash of actinic power, the slate self-destructed.

"Oh!" she squeaked and pushed back from the desk. A tiny puff of smoke came from the slate and was pulled away by the room's air circulating fans. "I didn't know a slate could do that." She examined the data chip. There wasn't anything unusual about it; it was a common data chip. There were probably a million of them in this star system alone. But what this one held might well change the balance of power for an entire galaxy.

She exited the ready room to find everyone in the CIC staring at her.

"The smoke alarm went off," Captain Jameson said. "We were about to call DC."

"It's okay," she said, then gestured back to the ready room. "Though I'd have someone space that smoking slate, just in case Sato was over cautious."

"Ma'am?" Jameson asked.

She shrugged and gave a little chuckle, which she supposed made her sound slightly unhinged. Everyone continued to stare at her. She looked at the data chip again. She now knew what was in the other mislabeled cases in the Hussars' stores. She started making mental notes, including getting hold of the Geek Squad. What was the man's name Kleena assigned? Patrick Leonard? She needed him on this ASAP.

I need to know how long it will take to retrofit the fleet ships when they return, she thought. "Captain, please recall Shuttle 322-A."

"Is it urgent?" Jameson asked.

"Without a doubt," she said.

"Take my personal shuttle. The pilot is standing by."

"Thanks." She started to leave, but she stopped and turned to the defensive coordinator. "Go ahead and access that special menu on the shield systems," she said, then she turned to the captain. "Unless I miss my guess, it's going to be fairly self-explanatory." He nodded his head. "But, Captain, no word about that new system is to leave this ship, is that understood?"

"Of course, Commander. But may I ask why?"

"Once you access the system and see what it does, you'll have your explanation." Aleksandra left, following her pinplant deck plans to *Sphinx's* hangar deck.

* * *

Captain Jameson floated to the defensive station and watched as the tech accessed the menu and read along as instructions appeared. After a minute, he pushed back, his eyes wide.

"My God," he said, turning to look at the hatch Commander Kowalczy had left through. "How is this even possible?"

The defensive coordinator's shocked expression slowly turned to a predatory grin. "Things just got extremely interesting."

* * *

Merc Guild Detention Facility, Ubatuba, Brazil, Earth

"You are weak," the man said and punched Jim again.

He did his best not to cry out, and nearly succeeded. *I'm Colonel Jim Cartwright,* he thought through a red haze of pain, *Commander of Cartwright's Cavaliers.* Another punch. He gasped. *Gah! I am Thaddeus Cartwright's son!*

"Why do you insist on remaining silent?" The man punched Jim in the side of the head and sent him sprawling to the floor for the fourth time. Maybe it was the fifth; Jim couldn't remember.

The cool floor felt good against the side of his face; despite the fact he'd lost some skin with the impact. He didn't try to get up. Even if he hadn't been as fat as he was, there was no way he could have with his arms tied behind his back at the elbows. He felt a heavy boot press against the side of his head and wondered if this was the end.

"No," a new voice said. "That's enough, Corporal."

"As you say, Major."

Jim concentrated on breathing, but broke into a fit of coughing and tasted blood. He hurt; every square inch of his body hurt. He couldn't think well enough to guess how long they'd been beating him. The Eastern European man who had beat him hadn't bothered to ask any questions, either. When the abuse started, Jim had known quite well what they wanted, or rather, what Peepo wanted—the Raknar.

"Can you talk?" the newcomer asked in a thick Slavic accent.

"Piss off," Jim mumbled around bloody, swollen lips.

"You might be fat, but you are your father's son."

"What would you know about that?" Jim asked.

"I knew Thaddeus Cartwright."

Jim tried to turn his head and look at the person who claimed to know his father. He couldn't lift his head off the concrete. More coughing brought up the metallic taste of blood, and, based on the agony the coughing caused, he wondered if some ribs were broken. The corporal had been thorough. He used to watch movies of people being beaten—cops and military movies—and he'd wondered what it was like. His conclusion was that the movies were extremely unrealistic.

"I am afraid Corporal Romanov was overly enthusiastic in the execution of his duties. You likely have internal injuries."

Jim grunted noncommittally. He heard the new man move closer and thought more pain WAS coming. He felt something cold press against his neck, and an instant later his body was flooded with liquid-hot metal.

"Gahh!" Jim screamed and convulsed on the floor. He felt skin tear at the zip-cuffs around his elbows and thought at least that pain was less than what was flowing through his body. *Medical nanites,* he realized as his mind cleared. The bone-deep agony was gone, replaced with a more tolerable body-wide throb.

"You're welcome," the man said.

"Oh, you're generous."

"I know," the man said, missing the sarcasm. "Pick him up."

Jim felt the corporal grab him by the arms and hoist him up. He knew the man was strong, both from the beatings and the way he picked Jim up, as he had many times before. When the man put Jim in a chair, he got his first look at the new man. He wore rather common-appearing fatigues with a logo that said Varangian Guard with two broad-bladed Danish axes on it. The man's name—Major Lucas—was on his other breast.

"Never heard of…the Varangian Guard," Jim said.

Lucas shrugged. "We are not Horsemen, of course. But my company has much history." He reached to his side and picked up a water bottle.

Jim licked his lips, realizing he was both hungry and thirsty. How long had it been since he'd eaten? The answer depended on how long the beatings had gone on. Lucas held the bottle up, a questioning look on his face. "I don't suppose you'd untie me so I can get a drink?" Jim asked.

"You might not be a standard-issue merc," Lucas said. "However, your determination is well known. No, I will not untie you." He stood and came over, holding the bottle up. Jim hesitated a half second then began to drink. "Better?"

Jim nodded, and Lucas did as well. The other man put the bottle down and turned to face the prisoner.

"So, here we are, then, at the point where you provide what I want, and you live. Or you do not, and you die." A half-smile played across Lucas' face as he stared Jim in the eye.

Jim considered his words carefully. The man was hard. As hard as any merc he'd ever seen. He possessed the look Jim had seen on many older mercs. Call it a seriousness beyond any other belief the person held. He was first and foremost a man of business. If he said he would kill you, he would kill you. Jim doubted the man would have a lick of remorse afterward, either.

However, Jim wasn't afraid the man would kill him if he didn't talk. They'd been torturing him for days, and this session alone had lasted a couple of hours. He hadn't talked, and they hadn't killed him, or even increased the torture to the point of endangering his life; in fact, Lucas had just given him nanites when he was afraid Jim might be dying. The conclusion was obvious; none of the other Raknar drivers had talked, either.

"Major," Jim said, "go fuck yourself."

The smile on Major Lucas's face slowly died and became a scowl. "You think you're one tough nut, yes?"

"You just said as much," Jim replied and winked. "Oh, I have something for General Peepo." Lucas raised an eyebrow. Jim turned slightly sideways in his seat, just enough so his jailer could see the upraised finger behind his back.

"Bah!" Lucas spat and got up to leave.

"What I do?" his corporal asked.

"See if you can change his mind," Lucas said. The big Slavic man looked at Jim and smiled.

* * *

EMS *Pegasus*, Hyperspace, Proceeding to Prime Base

The crash, when it came, slammed Nigel into the back of his CASPer. Traveling with his back to the direction of travel, though, the padding absorbed most of the impact as the assault pod slammed into the Merc Guild battleship. His straps kept him from rebounding and absorbed most of the whiplash.

It took him a second to get over something that would have been worse than a car crash back home, but he finally detached from the bulkhead and started moving to the front of the assault pod. The Lumar were already up and heading toward the door. *Tough bastards.*

"Status?" Nigel asked over his comms.

"First Platoon is up and in," Lieutenant Kamali said. "One Lumar injured who will be left behind." Nigel shook his head. The crash must have been bad—as he'd found recently, it took a lot to break a Lumar to the point where they would be left behind. Two broken legs wouldn't do it—they'd just pull themselves along the passageway with two of their arms while the other two fired a rifle.

"Second Platoon, all good, Boss," Lieutenant Davidson said from the CASPer in front of him. He turned to give Nigel a thumbs-up.

"Third Platoon is up, but didn't break in. We're going EVA and will look for a way in."

"Fourth Platoon up and in," Lieutenant Rouhani reported. "Two Lumar dead, one CASPer inop."

There was a pause where fifth platoon should be. None of their icons on Nigel's display were active. He'd hoped that was just a transmission difficulty, but it looked like their shuttle was destroyed.

"Sixth Platoon is up and in," Lieutenant Johnson reported. "One CASPer inop."

"All right," Nigel commed. "Everyone, move in. Third Platoon, catch up with us when you can. Fifth Platoon was supposed to support the assault into engineering; you'll have to do it without them."

"Roger that, Colonel," Lieutenant Rouhani replied. "We're former peasants; we're used to doing without." Nigel smiled wistfully. Fourth Platoon was made up of men from his hometown who'd volunteered for service when he'd gone back to bury his sister. If there was a more bloodthirsty platoon of Human mercs, he wasn't aware of it.

Davidson waved his troops forward, and they entered the battleship, dropping through the hatch in the floor to the passageway beneath them. The squad of CASPers led the way, with the squad of less-armored Lumar in trail. Getting them to understand the concepts of "combined arms" warfare had been…a challenge, and the first simulation hadn't gone very well, but they were doing better with their positioning this time.

Having the Lumar work for him had completely changed his outlook on killing aliens. Unlike a number of other races—and some of the Humans he'd known—the Lumar weren't deceitful. They did what you told them to the best of their abilities. They didn't lie to you or stab you in the back. Oh, he still enjoyed killing aliens and getting paid, but now he looked at it as "just the bad ones." Happily, there were still plenty of those.

He smiled as the platoon worked its way to the CIC, fighting through the obstacles he'd placed in their way. If what Sansar had said was true, he'd get his chance to kill a lot of aliens, very soon. Asbaran Solutions would be ready.

* * *

Winged Hussars Prime Base, New Warsaw System

T he computer simulation finished its run, and Patrick Leonard examined the results displayed on the slate. There was no change from the previous run.

"Holy shit," he said, shaking his head.

"Any deviation?" his assistant, Dana Redcheck, asked.

Patrick looked at her and shook his head. She let out a long, low whistle.

"Yeah," Patrick agreed. Not a lifelong Hussar, Patrick had been born on the Human colony of Talus. Together with his mother, father, and an older sister, his family left—fleeing political persecution—when he was only five years old, and he didn't have any memories of the planet. They ended up being taken in by the Hussars and had eventually relocated to New Warsaw.

His mother and father both held technical jobs with the Hussars while their children grew up. Patrick went into the Hussars as a technician, like his parents, and was eventually recruited by Kleena for the Geek Squad. His sister became a pilot. Both parents had passed away years ago, but his sister was serving on the *Legend*-class frigate *Orcrist* for the assault on Earth.

He'd been given the strange module by Kleena with instructions to figure it out ASAP. The current system commander, Aleksandra Kowalczy, wanted to know what Sato had created. Patrick was still confused why Sato disappeared. He'd met the man a dozen times and had worked directly with him twice. He was a pain in the ass, but the most brilliant mind Patrick had ever met. Sato didn't seem like the kind of person to simply run away. Not even after the incident with the doomsday device.

Regardless, Patrick was given a job, and he immediately turned his small lab in Prime Base to the task. The alarm to begin preparing for invasion didn't affect his work, so he continued with it. Although it was potentially world-ending to all the Winged Hussars, what could he do about it? Nothing, so he carried on with his job.

"I don't see why you're still working with this after *Sphinx* already found out what it did," Dana said.

It was true; word had come from *Sphinx* that the crew now understood the function of the modules since some had been installed on the ship by Sato prior to his disappearance. "Even though we might understand what it does, we don't understand how it does it," Patrick explained.

"Is that important with the invasion coming?"

"It's important despite the invasion," Patrick said. "Besides, we're essential personnel, so we don't evac." Dana nodded and looked away. She was half his age at 22, so he didn't blame her for being scared. He was worried himself, just not *as* worried. His sister was in the fleet, and they were coming back. Alexis Cromwell would deal with the aliens pursing them.

He triggered another test run and watched the miniaturized weapons system fire, with the same results. He'd picked up a side specialization in weapons tech five years ago when Kleena began the project to implement Sato's design for the *Avenger* bomber. The ship had proved impractical, at least until the SalSha had come on the scene. He'd been glad to see the *Avengers* finally in action, even if he was no longer involved. Designed with enough thrust to kill a Human, the crazy space otters seemed to like them.

"Patrick, are you still working on Sato's D-Field modules?" Kleena asked from somewhere else on Prime Base.

He responded through his pinplants. "Yes, Boss. I'm trying to figure out what Sato came up with."

"We know what it does," Kleena replied. "It doesn't really matter how it does it, right now."

Dana gave him a "told ya so" look, and Patrick frowned. "What else is there to do?"

"The fleet is due back in a few hours. I want you to round up as many ship-qualified techs as you can, requisition some shuttles, and head for the emergence point. We can expect the fleet to be damaged, possibly badly damaged."

Patrick and Dana's eyes both went wide in alarm. This wasn't something they'd been told to be ready for. "How many other teams are being sent?"

"General word hasn't gone out," Kleena said. There was a long moment. "The announcement will be coming in a few hours; Alexis Cromwell didn't survive the assault."

"Oh my god," Dana gasped.

Patrick felt his breathing increase, and a sense of panic begin to rise. *Alexis Cromwell, dead? Impossible.* "Are you sure?"

"As sure as we can be."

His mind turned to another, equally horrifying idea. "What about *Shadowfax*?"

"I don't know," Kleena replied. Of course, Patrick's boss knew about his relationship with its captain. Despite the size of the Hussars, it was still more like a small family.

"Wait, there hasn't been time for a courier. How can you know?"

"That's classified. Follow your orders," Kleena said, and cut off the transmission.

"Damn it," Patrick said and began shutting down his lab's testing equipment. Many of the systems, left unattended, could cause considerable carnage. As he worked, his slate chirped with his assignment. "Report to EMS *Shadowfax* and provide all assistance with repairs."

Patrick smiled, silently thanking Kleena for the small consideration. Then he glanced at Dana who was not moving. "Don't just stand there," he said. "Go draw as many shipboard kits as you can find. On the way, shanghai every tech you run into and get them to help you. I'll meet you in the docking bay in thirty minutes." She stared at him. "Dana, damn it, *now isn't the time to freeze up!*" He slapped the test table with the flat of his hand.

She jerked at the sound and looked at him, eyes wide with incipient panic. "She's dead," Dana repeated.

Patrick grabbed the front of her uniform and shook her once, hard.

She blinked and seemed to come out of it. "Did you hear what I said?" he asked.

"No," she admitted. "What do we do?"

Patrick repeated the orders.

"But…"

"No fucking buts," he said and pointed at the door to his lab. "We have to think about those still alive and those that can be saved. Get going, *now!*"

"Okay." She left at a run. Patrick sighed and shook his head. He wasn't an officer; he wasn't even in the combat arm of the merc company. He didn't have rank insignia on his uniform, only a couple of ribbons and the Geek Squad emblem on the arm opposite his Winged Hussars patch. He didn't order people around as part of his job, even though he was a senior member of the Squad. He was surprised it had worked as well as it had.

The lab shutdown complete, he went to the main equipment locker and collected his personal equipment kit and followed her out. A short distance down the hall, he stopped and turned around and went back inside. He removed the connections from the D-Field module he'd been testing and slipped it into his equipment bag before leaving for good. All he could think about was Elizabeth, and he prayed she was alive and well.

* * * * *

Chapter Five

EMS *Shadowfax*, New Warsaw Emergence Point

"Stand by for hyperspace emergence in one minute," the navigator said.

Captain Stacy nodded from her command chair. "Battle stations," she ordered. Her situation controller, or Sit-Con, glanced at her then used his pinplants to follow her order. Throughout *Shadowfax*, the call to stations sounded, and the ancient warship prepared to fight.

Elizabeth didn't think they were going to face battle at New Warsaw. Not yet, anyway. But after what happened at Earth, she simply wasn't taking any chances.

"All stations report manned and ready," the SitCon replied thirty seconds later.

Faster than normal, she thought. Her crew's feelings echoed her own. She waited as the clock counted down to zero. A brief sensation of falling, and the big Tri-V showed the familiar and comforting image of New Warsaw's giant red star. *Home,* she thought.

"Sensors, report," she ordered.

"Multiple emergences from the fleet," the sensor chief reported. "Nine system defense corvettes at emergence point, all with good Hussars' IFF transponders. Also, I show fourteen various shuttles and supply ships en route to the emergence point."

"Very good," she said. "Comms, monitor for traffic with system command."

"Captain Lech Kowalczy on *Alicorn* just reported in to system command," comms reported.

"Let's hear it."

"Welcome back, *Alicorn*," a female voice was saying as the comm switched. Elizabeth was pretty sure the voice belonged to Lieutenant Commander Aleksandra Kowalczy.

"Commander," Lech transmitted, "we have dire news."

"We're aware," Aleksandra said. "You are now in command of the company, sir."

"How did you know?" he asked.

"I'll explain later," she replied. "Repair crews are standing by to assist."

"You knew exactly when we'd arrive as well. It would seem we have a lot to talk about."

"And little time," she added. "Peepo's fleet is right behind you. They know where New Warsaw is."

Silence ruled the net for a long time. "We should talk in person," Lech finally said.

"I agree," Aleksandra replied.

"Please arrange a command staff meeting," Lech ordered, "five hours from now on Prime Base. We are maneuvering immediately."

"Understood," Aleksandra replied.

A moment later, the order was relayed to the fleet, and they got underway.

"Comms, transmit damage assessment reports to the fleet and system command," Elizabeth ordered. "Helm, fall into formation and begin accelerating for Prime Base."

"A lot of ships are moving from Home toward the outer asteroid field," the sensor tech reported.

"Part of the evacuation planning, I suspect," Elizabeth said. All Hussars at the rank of commander or above knew the basics of the plan, if not all the details. What surprised her was that Aleksandra had known to begin the evacuation. They'd left Earth a week ago. Even if a courier had come through immediately after Alexis had been killed, it would have only arrived hours ago. There was no way things could have gotten as far as they had in such a short period of time.

"We have a damage control team matching course and requesting permission to come aboard," comms reported.

"Permission granted," Elizabeth said. "Open the docking bay and prepare to receive the shuttle under thrust."

Landing on an *Egleesius*-class ship while underway wasn't the easiest of operations on the best of days. Elizabeth watched the shuttle approach on the Tri-V with some trepidation. The last thing she needed was a wrecked docking bay with so many other repairs already necessary. The evacuation of Home suggested every certified pilot in the system was flying something at the moment; who was left to handle the shuttle?

"Damage control teams on standby on the landing deck," she ordered.

Her damage control coordinator, or DCC, looked back at her in uncertainty.

"Do it," she said, explaining her concern.

"Good point, sir," the DCC agreed, and transmitted the order.

"We don't need another hole in the ship," her XO, Evie Miller, agreed.

The shuttle matched course and slightly below *Shadowfax's* speed. Slowly it slid even with the warship's nose and then down her length until it came abreast of the docking bay, just behind her midpoint. Whoever the pilot was, they possessed a steady hand. The facing docking bay door slid back, exposing the deck to vacuum. *Shadowfax* didn't yet possess gravity decks, like her sistership *Pegasus*. There'd been no time to add them. In an operation like this, it was an advantage. The four gravity decks would be nestled against the ship's deck just ahead of the docking bay, and thus be a hindrance to close approach.

"Here we go," Evie said as the shuttle began to move toward the bay.

The trick was the moment when the shuttle entered the bay. It would use its ion engines to match *Shadowfax*'s forward thrust as it side-slipped toward the docking bay. However, the moment it entered the bay those engines would have a deck to push against, and the shuttle could crash into the upper deck. The pilot would need to flip the shuttle over and use the belly thrusters to hold approach and, at the last second, cut power on each engine as they passed inside.

If it was performed correctly, the shuttle would settle to the deck, the final velocity scrubbed off as the landing legs absorbed the residual momentum. Every shuttle-qualified pilot needed to complete the docking maneuver under power successfully three times. As a command track officer, Elizabeth did it ten times with only one failure. The shuttle pilot performed the maneuver flawlessly.

"DC stand down," Evie ordered.

"Nice moves," the helm said under his breath.

Elizabeth nodded. She suspected she knew the pilot, and a little grin crossed her face. "Have my assistant bring my kit down to the hangar deck," she ordered, glancing at the Tri-V plot with estimates for their arrival at Prime Base. "I'll shave some time off the trip by taking their shuttle ahead. Evie, you have the conn."

"Yes ma'am, I have the conn."

Elizabeth left the CIC and rode the lift down to Deck 21 where the hangar deck was located. It comprised three decks in total, with 21 being the hangar proper and 22 and 23 holding shuttle stowage and maintenance. Crewmembers nodded to her as they went about their duties. The Hussars didn't go in for lots of saluting, unlike some units. It suited them and created more of a sense of family.

The bay was being pressurized as she reached the hangar. Various engineering and technical crew were entering the bay to properly secure the shuttle, attach power cables, and refuel the craft. Meanwhile the shuttle was unbuttoned, and the passengers were beginning to deboard.

The first one down the ramp was a man roughly her age in Hussars black coveralls with green piping. Like many Hussars techs, there were only a couple of ribbons on his uniform, however, he had the Geek Squad patch as well. His name tape said his name was P. Leonard. He was a pretty good-looking guy and was followed by a much-younger female Geek Squad tech, then three more general technicians, two Human men and an elSha. The older man was obviously in charge, and he came to a stop when he saw Elizabeth.

"Captain," he said.

"Welcome aboard, Mr. Leonard," she said, then they both grinned at each other. Elizabeth could see he was relaxing now, having been worried about her until then. "I need your shuttle."

"It's yours," he said and gestured her through.

"Thank you. My XO, Evie Miller, is in the CIC and can help you coordinate with my DCC." Patrick nodded as his assistant and the other techs floated past. Elizabeth moved her hand over, and he took it. The gesture only lasted a second, and they were sure nobody saw it. "I figured it was you when I saw the way you handled the docking."

"I'm so relieved you made it back," Patrick said.

"Me, too," she said, and they smiled at each other. "I'll be back after the fleet meeting. See if you can put my ship back together; we're going to need her."

"Will do."

"I love you," she whispered.

"Love you, too," he whispered back.

Elizabeth turned and saw her assistant holding out her kit. "Oh, thanks," she said and took the kit before turning back to Patrick. "I need to get going," she explained and climbed into the shuttle.

"You want me to get your flight crew to get you a pilot?"

"Not necessary," Elizabeth said. "I'm a fair stick myself, as you know."

"I believe that," he said, nodding, as she turned to close the door.

Five minutes later she was pushing the shuttle back out into space. *Shadowfax* was in the process of a mid-course flip-over to begin slowing her approach to Prime Base, so her job was considerably easier than Patrick's was. Setting course for Prime Base, she noticed many other ships of the fleet also had shuttles departing.

Autopilot set, she relaxed and waited as the shuttle's engine burned to speed her toward Prime Base. A small shuttle meant a much quicker trip. She'd be at the base while *Shadowfax* was still slowing on approach. Her mind was busy thinking of the upcoming meeting, yet she was also thinking of Patrick and hoping he was still aboard when she got back.

* * *

Winged Hussars Prime Base, New Warsaw System

Nigel Shirazi strode through the corridors of Prime Base as if for the first time. It had a different feel; there were fewer people and those who were still there raced from one place to another as if their lives depended on it. He nodded once—at this stage, perhaps their lives *did* depend on it. He recognized an overwhelming sense of fear and desperation among the personnel he saw and vowed not to give in to it.

His grandfather had taught him that the men under his command would take their cues from him. If he looked desperate, they would be desperate, too, so even though he wanted to race to the conference room for the COs' meeting, he forced himself to maintain nothing more than a purposeful stride. He also tried to engage the few people he passed; if he could spread some hope, it would filter out to others.

That was what they needed. Hope. He didn't need hope; he had something stronger. Revenge. Everything he saw on Prime Base reminded him of Alexis, strengthening his purpose. They would hold New Warsaw and Prime Base. He would make it happen, somehow, for Alexis. It would be his wedding gift for her, even if they were now never destined to marry. Sansar had said Alexis was still alive, and he held onto that hope. He would hold the system, even if it cost him his life.

As he rounded a corner he saw something unusual—someone not racing from place to place. A solitary figure stood unmoving outside an open hatch, and he realized it was Sansar, standing outside the chamber where the Four Horsemen normally met, with her hand over her mouth.

"What are you doing?" he asked as he approached.

Sansar turned to him, tears streaming down her face. "I just...I..." she ran out of words, and he enfolded her in his arms while she sobbed.

After a minute, she tensed and pushed him away. "I'm sorry," she said, wiping away the tears. Some of the steel had returned to her voice, and she had control of herself again.

"You don't need to be sorry," Nigel replied. "Trust me, I understand."

"No, we need to be strong; we need to set the example." She sniffed. "And I was doing that, but I guess I wasn't thinking clearly—I automatically came here for the meeting, like we always have in the past. When I opened the door and saw the table, it suddenly hit me that Alexis and Jim would probably never sit at it again, and it may be the last time we ever do, too. It's just...I was overwhelmed for a moment."

"They *will* sit at this table again."

"How are you able to sound so sure?"

Nigel smiled. "You told me it would happen."

"But that was a dream. They don't always come true."

"This one will, because we will make it."

Her eyes stared up into his, looking for answers. "But how do you *know*?"

"That's easy," Nigel said, his smile fading slightly. "I will accept nothing less. Not from me, not from my men, and not from my allies." He brushed away the last tear on her face, and his smile returned. "Now, if you are ready, let us go put some backbone into the defense of this system."

Sansar nodded and stood straighter, squaring her shoulders. "I'm ready."

"Good," Nigel replied. "Let's go."

* * *

Winged Hussars Prime Base, New Warsaw System

Lieutenant Commander Aleksandra Kowalczy watched the ship captains and commanders filter into the conference room. They'd left the same room a little over two weeks ago, many smiling, all confident of an end to the war and the liberation of Earth from the Mercenary Guild's control. The faces which entered now were, for the lack of a better term, somber.

The gallery of captains was set up to provide each ship's captain a seat with their XO next to them. Three Hussars ships were unrepresented. Two were lost in action. The third missing was the *Crown*-class cruiser *Count Fleet*. The other captains reported she'd jumped to hyperspace with everyone else, but had been severely damaged in the retreat. When she didn't arrive at New Warsaw, she'd been entered into the rolls as missing and presumed lost due to drive failure.

Four merc cruisers were likewise unrepresented, including *Bucephalus*. Many looked at the empty space for Cartwright's Cavaliers as they entered. The storied ship had stayed behind, hoping to collect her surviving mercs. After losing an entire company of troopers to an ambush, including their XO, Hargrave, Captain Su refused to abandon the remaining Cavaliers, and her ship was taken.

They were organized by ship class from small warships in the back to the big hitters up front. Most had arrived late, as they'd facilitated the evac of many mercs.

Fookoolu and Chigaoolu, the Bakulu commanders of their two battleships, sat up front. They might not be Hussars, but after the battle of Sol, they shared the merc's fate.

Aleksandra watched the five commanders of their *Egleesius*-class battlecruisers take their seats. Normally it would be Alexis at the podium, and Paka representing her ship. Instead it was her former 3rd in command, now captain, Lieutenant Commander Akoo. Alexis always called the Buma Hoot.

Next to Akoo sat Captains Stacy, Teenge, and Drizz. Captain Jormungd didn't sit, her long Kaa snake-like frame was curled on the floor so she could observe the proceedings. Aleksandra was suddenly keenly aware Stacy was the only Human among them. It also reminded her how much Alexis depended on and trusted the Hussars' alien members.

Lech Kowalczy entered via a side door and walked to her side. She looked up at him and tried to hold her emotions in check. He put a hand out and rested it on her shoulder. "You've done well," he said.

"I did the best I could," she said. "So much has happened. The Fae showed up and told me of the defeat. They can communicate faster than light, somehow—telepathy I think."

"We can try and understand that later," he said. "Now we have to survive."

She nodded. "I stand relieved of command."

"Not so fast," he said.

Her mouth fell open for a moment. "What? Lech, you're second in command; there can be no question."

"There is no question of my position, but there is one of how much I can do. I'm a ship commander and strategist. You are an excellent organizer, and our people have been following your directions during the mobilization. If what I've read in the last few hours is any indication, you've done a fantastic job."

"I did the best I could," she repeated, unsure how to take the praise.

"No, you did the best anyone could do. I'm giving you a brevet promotion to commander and putting you in charge of Prime Base and all of the logistics support functions of the Winged Hussars, effective the beginning of this emergency."

"Sir, I…" she started to stammer.

"This is the part where you say, 'Yes sir,' and be quiet."

"Yes, sir," she said, feeling the huge weight settle again on her shoulders. "I'll do the best I can," she said, realizing how lame it sounded after saying effectively the same thing three times.

Lech took it well and gave her a tiny smile. "I know," he said. "Just keep doing what you've been doing. We'll talk more after this."

The room fell quiet as Sansar Enkh and Nigel Shirazi entered with their XOs. Aleksandra felt the absence of Alexis Cromwell like she'd never felt any loss before. The two Horsemen took their seats at the front of the audience with an empty seat to the right of each. The last few captains came in, and the doors were closed.

Lech cleared his throat, and all eyes turned to him.

"It comes down to this," he said, looking around the room, then stopped. "There are many empty seats here, and thousands more where brave mercs once lived and fought." He held up a hand. "We mourn for our losses."

"Our fates are shared," echoed through the room.

Aleksandra felt hot tears rolling down her cheeks and tried to swallow her shame. Then she saw dozens of others crying as well. A few lonely sobs echoed in the space. Lech looked down at the deck, and every other head, Human and alien, did as well. In that moment of anguish and loss, they were one.

After a moment, Lech looked back up. "First, I'd like to acknowledge Commander Aleksandra Kowalczy for doing an exceptional job preparing New Warsaw for what is coming." There was a moment while everyone nodded to Aleksandra, who stood quietly, wiping her eyes. "Now we have to discuss what happened and what we are going to do about it. First off, as commander of the Winged Hussars, I have already issued an order that all Veetanho in New Warsaw be immediately detained."

There was a gasp and more than a few shouts. Lech held up his hands for silence. "You must all understand, former Lieutenant Commander Paka had been with the Winged Hussars for decades. She was in the direct chain of command, and Alexis Cromwell's *friend*." He raised his voice several levels when he said the last. "Yet she shot Alexis in the back, betrayed us all, and if what we've heard is correct, she also gave our location away. In every way possible, Paka betrayed us. If we cannot trust her, what Veetanho can we trust?"

Around the conference room there were a few mutters, but no real dissent. Lech's point was accurate and succinct. "They are only being detained. Uuth with HST is trying to ascertain the best way of verifying reliability from those Veetanho personnel. However, for the time being, we simply cannot take the risk."

Aleksandra was shocked by the move. However, if she'd been given the information that Alexis had been assassinated by her own XO, Aleksandra probably would have done the same thing. It just made sense.

"Defense is what's important now," Lech continued. "We know the forces we're facing with a fairly high degree of accuracy. It's unlikely even Peepo could coordinate an attack between two fleets departing from separate systems and have them arrive here at the same time." He gave the room a wan smile. "Now, this isn't to suggest our situation is good."

A Tri-V came alive in the center of the room showing the enemy fleet disposition. "This is built from the data our ships gathered prior to fleeing. The data gathered by our *Egleesius*-class battlecruisers was particularly useful as they were in Earth orbit the longest until they used their hyperspace shunts to escape."

As the enemy fleet disposition built, there were quite a few exclamations and gasps. The ships were shown in order of size, as their order of battle didn't matter for the discussion. A line of frigates was topped by fewer cruisers, then battlecruisers, battleships, and, finally, a truly massive, globe-shaped nightmare.

"Yes, that's a dreadnought," Lech confirmed for them.

Aleksandra shook her head and watched the Hussars' captains gawk at the Tri-V image of a ship class nobody had seen in their lifetimes. She heard someone say "Fleet killer," and the phrase spread around the room like an echo. Lech only let it go for a second before he stepped in again.

"The dreadnought is a serious threat," he admitted. "It's part of why we had no choice but to retreat from Sol. You don't want to fight one of those while giving it home field advantage. With Sol being ceded to the enemy for months, we no longer possessed the home field, which was obvious since we didn't detect the second fleet until it was almost upon us. But now they're coming here." He paused and his gaze swept over the assembled captains. "Coming here to *our home*. What are we going to do?"

Captain Elizabeth Stacy of *Shadowfax* stood and exclaimed, "The Winged Hussars are nobody's prey!"

The room exploded in cheers and people stood to pump their fists in the air. Captain Drizz of *Nuckelavee* and his XO howled in their doglike Zuul manner.

"They're coming here expecting slaughter," Lech said. "And slaughter is what they will find." He blinked, using his pinplants, and the enemy fleet was replaced with a hyper-realistic view of Home, with Prime Base orbiting above. "We've been preparing for this moment for decades." He looked at Sansar Enkh. "Colonel Enkh, are you ready to lead your Horde in the defense of New Warsaw?"

Colonel Enkh looked at her XO, Lieutenant Colonel Walker, who had the look of someone dividing his attention between the ongoing briefing and pinplant work.

After a second, Walker stood. "We've been working on it since Commander Kowalczy informed me…" Walker stopped and looked at the two Hussars standing at the front of the assembly, realizing they were both named Kowalczy. He smiled in acknowledgement. "That would be Commander Aleksandra Kowalczy, of course. When the commander informed me of the situation, the forces I had available at the time were placed on alert, and our contingency plans for the defense of the system were put into effect. I've just reviewed the ongoing process and can tell you we are currently seventy-nine percent complete. I show an estimated completion time of nineteen hours."

"Thank you," Lech said. "I understand the assessment of our remaining ground forces are underway, and we'll be discussing with each unit what their abilities and intentions are." He paused for a second. "I already have requests from a couple of units to be allowed to depart, and I am going to grant them." There was a low rumble from the assembled commanders. "I know what many of you are thinking; how can I let forces leave when we have so few remaining?" Many heads nodded; he could see everyone's eyes on him.

"The answer is simple—what good is it to compel service? We're mercs, and you can't force mercs to fight, especially when there isn't any pay involved. Besides, I understand why they are leaving. These units are based in smaller colonies, and they want to go home to protect their people. Thus, I am sending them on their way, and we should all wish them the best of luck."

Walker nodded. "The members leaving have been withdrawn from our contingency plans, and the defense has been readjusted. Personally, I think they are wrong to leave; we stand a better chance fighting together than we do separately, but I'm not in their place and can't decide for them."

"We *are* stronger together," Sansar Enkh agreed from next to him. "That is the power of the horde. Long ago, we understood the wisdom the American Ben Franklin got credit for—we must all hang together or, most assuredly, we shall all hang separately."

Aleksandra suspected many of the remaining captains wished the deserters anything but luck. She knew which ones were going, including the fact that not all of them were doing it in the interests of others on their worlds. A few had simply had enough. Although Lech hadn't given all the details, their reason for leaving really made no difference. Compelling them to fight wouldn't have resulted in their fighting at their best, and she wouldn't have been surprised if they'd cut and run the first chance they got, leaving a gap in their defenses. Lech had made the correct call, in her opinion. All those leaving had their own ships, and since merc cruisers would be little help in the coming battle, this caused a minimal reduction in force, at best.

"Now, for the forces I have available," Lech continued, "Major Kratlik, our ranking Hussars marine commander, has been tasked to work with the available merc marines, as well as Colonel Shirazi, to prepare for anti-ship actions against the attacking forces."

Kratlik, a MinSha, moved in from the side to stand next to Lech, her blue scales shining and her red, multifaceted eyes gleaming in the conference room light. The Winged Hussars logo was laser-etched on her right shoulder along with her rank insignia and combat ribbons glued to her upper thorax.

Aleksandra caught a glance of Nigel Shirazi's jaw muscles bunching. It was no secret the man didn't like MinSha. Asbaran Solutions had a history with the insect-like aliens—a long history. At the beginning of the war, a MinSha faction had kidnapped Nigel's sister and killed her—along with his father and brother—before he could rescue her. Having Kratlik working with him might be a problem, but nothing could be done at this late hour; Shirazi would have to live with it.

Lech continued his briefing, "The Hussars' combat ships capable of action are undergoing rapid replenishment. We're also going to be moving personnel as time allows."

Aleksandra caught movement and turned to see the Fae had arrived. She touched Lech's arm and pointed. In a matter of seconds, all heads turned. Five Fae entered the conference room, led by the one she recognized as Sly. Seldia was directly behind him.

Lech looked confused at first, then rather surprised; he'd been about to discuss how the various mercs remaining could assist in bolstering some of the shorthanded ships. He turned and looked at Aleksandra, who nodded her head.

"The two in front are the ones who came to warm me about the defeat at Earth," she said.

Lech nodded and addressed the new arrivals. "Welcome. I understand from Commander Kowalczy we have you to thank for having more time to prepare. Sly, is it?"

The dark colored Fae nodded as he approached, and to Aleksandra's surprise, mounted the stage next to her and Lech. "The information was passed to our Far Talker, or K'apo, Seldia." He nodded to the gray Fae with sparkly ear-tufts, but she stayed back with the other three, leaving it to Sly to do the talking this time. Aleksandra gasped as she focused on the other Fae—all of them were armed and armored.

"You brought guards?" Aleksandra asked while looking down at Sly.

"We have been preparing," Sly explained. "There wasn't time to disarm and avoid shocking you. The situation is dire." The tiny alien looked out over the crowd. "Your leader was just explaining some things that could be accomplished, as time allowed. Time won't allow. We heard again from our agents on Earth, through Seldia. The enemy fleet left Earth twenty-nine hours after yours escaped; we have less than twenty-four hours remaining to prepare."

The gasps of the ship captains and merc commanders were nearly universal. Several shouted their doubts, others put hands to their mouths, while still more just stared in shock.

"By now, you must surely know not to doubt us," Sly said. He looked up at Aleksandra, sending shivers down her spine. "You have less than one of your days remaining to complete whatever plans you can." He turned to Lech. "We can help, when the opportunity presents itself. However, if that time comes, you *must* follow our lead, or all will be lost."

Lech was among those who could only stare, nearly poleaxed by the revelation. Sly looked from Aleksandra to him, then nodded and hopped off the stage. His guards and Seldia fell in line with him as he headed toward the door. Nigel and Sansar watched the Fae leave. Neither had expressed much of a reaction to the Fae's pronouncement; Aleksandra guessed that after what they'd been through on Earth, they were inured to further setbacks.

Before the Fae reached the door, Lech finally found his voice. "I have to ask, why should we follow your lead? There are only a few of you here, and without Jim Cartwright and more Raknar drivers, what can you really do?"

"I guarantee you we'll do more than you expect," Sly said, and smiled to show tiny white teeth. They moved to leave again, but Seldia stared at Lech for a long moment, and the others stopped.

"Why should you do what we say?" she asked. She snorted. "Because we're the Dusman, silly Human." Raising her chin, she led the others out of the stunned conference room.

Aleksandra had a great view of Sly, who shook his head and did an almost perfect facepalm before following the Far Talker out the door.

* * *

Winged Hussars Prime Base, New Warsaw System

S ansar waited with Nigel and Walker as the rest of the ships' COs and XOs departed the room, many muttering under their breaths about various aspects of the plan or the fact that some of the other ships were running away. When Lech saw her waiting, he shooed away the remaining captains and came over. "Were you waiting for me?"

"Yes," Sansar replied. She took a moment to look at Lech and had a flash of the dream—the dreadnought going past the shattered hulk of one of the *Egleesius* ships. Lech's ship. "I've seen the battle we're about to fight."

"Seen it?" Lech asked, his eyebrows knitting. "How have you seen something that hasn't happened yet?"

"I don't know, actually," Sansar said. "Some people call it pre-cognition, others some form of psychic ability"—she chuckled—"others just think I'm crazy. Regardless, women in the Horde have long had dreams that foretold the future. While they don't always come true, most times they do."

"And you've had one about this battle?" Lech asked, his voice skeptical.

Nigel held up a hand. "Don't be so quick to disbelieve," he said. "She first had this dream before the loss at Earth. She knew this battle was coming, and that Alexis wouldn't be here to fight it."

"Did she"—he turned back to Sansar—"did you see how it will turn out? Will we win?"

Sansar smiled. Lech sounded like a man grasping at straws, which was probably how she'd have felt in his place. She'd had some time—and plenty of repetitions of the dream—to come to grips with it. It didn't make it any easier. "Honestly, I don't know whether we will win," Sansar said. "I've never seen the ending of the battle. All I've ever seen is that they are unstoppable. Despite everything we throw at them, they break out from the emergence area and make it to Prime Base. We need to make sure all personnel are evacuated."

"All nonessential personnel are already being evacuated," Lech replied. "Aleksandra already had that underway when we got here." He shrugged. "Even so, we still won't get everyone off in time, if the Faes' timeline is to be believed. There are just too many people and not enough transports. We don't really have anywhere to put them, either. There isn't enough shelter on the planet or in the habitations on the asteroids. There are also plenty of people who won't leave..."

"Many, if not all of them, will die if they don't leave," Sansar warned.

"I understand," Lech said. He shrugged again. "There is only so much we can do." He paused a second, then said, "Maybe the Fae— I mean the Dusman—have something planned that will stop them. They said to follow their lead."

Sansar shrugged. "I don't know what they're talking about. In all the times I've seen it, I've never seen them do *anything*. Maybe they're talking about following their lead at some other point? I don't know, but I can't make plans based on a 'Just do what we say when we tell you to;' I need concrete plans that are actionable."

"What if we beef up our defenses in the emergence area?" Lech asked. "Is there a way to stop them if we hammer them with everything we've got right as they show up?"

"I don't know," Sansar replied. "I've seen the battle—Blue Sky Above, I've *lived* the battle—dozens of times. No matter what we do, the dreadnought always makes it through. It's just"—she shuddered—"it's so damned *big* and can take so much abuse. I don't know if *anything* can stop it."

"I have five *Egleesius* ships with 40-terawatt particle accelerators that will carve it up. Now that we know it's coming, we can design a plan to hit it simultaneously. There isn't a ship that's been built that can withstand that kind of firepower." He got a faraway look for a moment. "I'm sorry," he added after a moment, "but there are several issues I need to take care of. If you'll excuse me?"

He turned and left without waiting for an answer, and Nigel turned to look at Sansar. "Will it work?"

Sansar shook her head.

"Any idea why not?"

"I don't know. Maybe it's Paka. If she's truly gone over to the other side, she's as aware of the *Egleesius'* capabilities as well as anyone. She'll have some sort of plan to deal with them." She shook her head again. "Paka's a Veetanho, and she's not stupid. We're going to have to come up with something else to stop it."

"There are several thousand drones that are being built by one of the manufactories," Walker noted, speaking for the first time. "Maybe something small—an asynchronous attack—on something so big is the way to go. Rather than try to meet major force with major force, we go with something they're not prepared for, like a drone swarm."

"Maybe," Sansar said. She didn't sound hopeful, even to her own ears. She shrugged the gloom away; there wasn't time for it. "It's as good an idea as anything else we've got," she added, sounding a little more positive. "You've been working with the Hussars' planners. Go talk with them and pass that along—rather than wasting the drones piecemeal, let's use them all in a mass attack on the dreadnought."

"Yes, ma'am," Walker said. He turned and went out the same door Lech had taken.

Nigel watched him go, then turned back to Sansar with a half-grin. "So, you saw Alexis with my son on the bridge of *Pegasus*, right?"

Sansar nodded slowly. "Yes."

"I never asked. Was I there?"

Sansar was unable to say the word, but she knew Nigel could see the answer in her eyes.

The half-grin turned to a smile, although one that never reached his eyes. "At least that means we win, and that Alexis and my son are safe. I can live with that." Nigel nodded once and then followed Walker out the door, leaving Sansar to her thoughts.

She hadn't had the heart to tell him that she'd only had that dream once, which usually indicated a dream that wouldn't come true.

* * *

Winged Hussars Prime Base, New Warsaw System

Aleksandra reached her office to find Lech and the Buma, Akoo—also known as Hoot—waiting for her.

"You have to be read in on something," Lech said.

"Okay."

"It's some pretty crazy stuff."

"After what I've seen in the last week, I honestly don't see how it can be any crazier."

Lech gave her a strange look she thought was almost sympathetic. Akoo came over and acknowledged her. "Commander," the Buma said.

"Captain," Aleksandra replied. "We're all sorry for what happened."

"I never wanted to command *Pegasus*," Akoo said.

"You're the senior officer remaining," Lech said. "I want you to remain." Akoo nodded his large head. "As Aleksandra is now in the command team, she needs to know about *Pegasus*' secret." Akoo looked at him for a long moment, then nodded. Lech continued, "*Pegasus* has an AI named Ghost which has been one of our most closely guarded secrets, and one of the reasons *Pegasus* has been so undefeatable."

Aleksandra gawked. There were many theories as to why *Pegasus* was so successful in combat, but this wasn't one of them. Lech addressed Akoo directly.

"Has Ghost spoken to you since this happened?"

"No," Akoo admitted. "I've tried several times. Ghost sent the flight profiles which allowed us to dive through the atmosphere and rescue the mercs, and that was the last time we are certain anything came from it."

Lech looked at Akoo and rubbed his upper lip. "Have you gone down to try and talk to it directly?"

"How do you do that?" Aleksandra asked. Akoo and Lech looked at each other uncomfortably.

"I'm sorry," Lech said, "this revelation has always been handled by Alexis. Let me start a little further back." He paused as he gathered his thoughts. "Shortly after the original commander, Lawrence Kowalczy, found *Pegasus*, the legend of the Ghost began. It wasn't until Alexis and her twin sister Katrina took over the Hussars that the legend was proven. You've heard the story about Katrina Cromwell dying in an incident on *Pegasus*?"

"Everyone has," Aleksandra confirmed.

"Of course. Well, Katrina didn't truly die. In that incident, the AI which had been aboard *Pegasus* for thousands of years overwrote itself on Katrina's brain. In essence, it took human form. It's been there, in the body of Katrina Cromwell, ever since."

Shocked, Aleksandra put her hand to her mouth. What must it have been like for Alexis to have the *dead* body of her sister inhabited by an alien AI program? The AI gave the Hussars considerable power, but she somehow doubted it made up for the horror of an undead, AI-infested sister to forever remind you.

"So, you see it *is* possible to have a face-to-face with Ghost," Lech finished.

"It won't let anyone in," Akoo said. "Food continues to be delivered, but the AI won't talk to anyone, not even to the crewmember who brings the food."

Lech nodded and sighed. "I was really hoping for help from Ghost. Counting on it, actually. Please keep trying," Lech said, and Akoo nodded. "But don't harass it. Maybe it's working some angle."

"Would you like my opinion, sir?" Akoo asked.

"Of course."

"If Ghost were a Buma, or even a Human, I'd think it was sulking."

The three regarded each other in silence.

* * *

Winged Hussars Prime Base, New Warsaw System

"There you are," Lieutenant Colonel Walker said as he came upon the solitary SalSha staring out the viewing window of the observation deck. "Your squadron is looking for you."

"Squadron?" Thorb asked without turning around. "I don't have a squadron anymore. They're all dead. Eleven bombers and twenty-two SalSha. *All dead!*"

Walker nodded. *So that's what this is all about.* He'd gotten a call thirty minutes earlier that Thorb couldn't be found and had turned off all methods of communication. Walker knew the observation deck was his favorite place to come and had come up looking for him. *Because I don't have anything better to do with my fucking time at the moment than look for a sentimental alien. Less than a day until the Merc Guild arrives, and I'm now the head psychologist for an otter with PTSD.*

"I don't know if I can do this anymore," Thorb added. He continued to look into space. "Is it always like this?" he asked after another moment.

"What do you mean?" asked.

"Does losing people under your command always hurt so much?" Thorb asked. "That I can't stop seeing their faces or hearing their voices?"

"Losing your troops is like the pain from a wound," Walker replied. "It hurts a lot while it's fresh, but the pain becomes more tolerable after it heals." He shrugged. "Some wounds are worse than others, though, and they stay with you longer...sometimes the rest of your life. Like losses where you could have done...where you *should* have done something else, something better. Those can really haunt you. When you didn't do the things ahead of time to prepare—when you should have done something else but didn't—those hurt the worst and the longest."

"*But I did everything I could!*" Thorb exclaimed, the anguish in his voice plain. "We trained as hard as we could!"

Walker raised an eyebrow but didn't say anything.

"Yes, we played, too..." Thorb replied to the look. "That's just how we are. We may even have practiced the Kloop, some—so we could welcome everyone home appropriately—but that type of flying was practice, too. It helped us practice flying in close formation!"

"I could tell you'd been practicing," Walker acknowledged. "And the people who saw the Kloop were all very impressed. Even Alexis Cromwell told me she was impressed."

"But it didn't matter that we practiced! I still lost my entire squadron!"

"I heard," Walker said. He could see Thorb shaking and stepped forward to put a hand on the SalSha's shoulder. "I also heard that you took out your target, and that the attack was only able to proceed because you did."

"Well, yes, but the attack was a failure. All those lives, lost for no reason!"

"But you didn't know it at the time," Walker replied. "That attack was necessary to help the overall battle plan succeed. The fact that it didn't isn't your fault. From what I've heard, we were out-played by that rat-bitch Peepo and her minion Paka. Sometimes that happens in war, and sometimes you lose people. I survived a total wipeout of my company; I know how badly it hurts to be one of only two survivors. I also know that it gets easier."

"How does it get easier? What do you do?"

"You go on. You keep putting one foot in front of the other. You make your unit better, so the next time you *don't* get wiped out—you wipe out the enemy, instead."

"I don't know if I can," Thorb said, his eyes on the deck.

"I know you can't do anything else," Walker said.

"Oh?" Thorb asked, looking up. "Why is that?"

"You haven't heard? The Merc Guild is coming. They are coming *here*—to New Warsaw—and what do you think they're going to do when they get here? Offer us tea and cookies? No! They are going to kill every single one of us. Men, women, and pups. And then they're going to enslave both of our races—those they don't kill—and use them as fodder for the Merc Guild's plans. Is that what you want?"

"Well, no…"

"You once told me that when the grahp comes, everyone fights—everyone does their part. Well, the grahp is truly coming this time—for both our races. What are you going to do? Are you going to continue to sit here and feel sorry for yourself, or are you going to organize what remains of the SalSha squadrons so we can beat the ever-living shit out of the Merc Guild forces when they get here? You're the senior ranking SalSha officer—they need you to lead them. You may see something with your experience that everyone else misses—something that could be the difference between victory and defeat, yet *you don't know if you can*? Don't whine to me—I don't have time for it! Just tell me one thing—*what are you going to do?*"

Thorb took a deep breath and let it out slowly, then Walker saw him stand a little straighter and square his shoulders. His eyes gleamed as he said, "When the grahp comes, everyone fights. I will grieve for them when this is over, but for now, I will organize our squadrons, *and we will fight!*"

* * * * *

Chapter Six

EMS *Shadowfax*, New Warsaw

"And frames 19 and 44 have been over-stressed...."

Patrick Leonard rubbed the bridge of his nose and tried to will away the growing headache. The report from the structural specialist wasn't helping. The five *Egleesius*-class battle-cruisers had been through hell on their dive though Earth's atmosphere to rescue a group of mercs trying to escape. The ship's condition was a testimony to that hell.

For the last seven hours, since he'd arrived aboard *Shadowfax*, he and his team had worked non-stop trying to deal with the damage her crew had been unable to fix in hyperspace. Patrick had expected to spend a few hours getting started, then rotate back to Prime Base for more assignments. Only it didn't work out the way he'd planned. Shortly after arriving on board, he'd gotten word the alien fleet was due to arrive in less than twenty-four hours.

So they'd stayed on board, prioritizing vital combat and flight systems first, popping the stimulants known as CASPer Candy, and working nonstop. The problem was that his people kept locating problems faster than they could be fixed. *Shadowfax* might be just as old as *Pegasus,* but she'd been sitting for eons without any maintenance, and it showed. He suspected a lot of the issues they were struggling with might not have been a problem if the ship had been better maintained.

"Can the frames be reinforced?" he asked over his pinplants.

"Sure," the engineer replied. "But it won't be as strong as a drydock repair."

"Doesn't matter," Patrick stressed. "Get it done, ASAP." He waited for a second, half expecting another of his team to call with a problem. Nothing happened, and he sighed in relief; He could go back to the diagnostics he'd been trying to finish for more than two hours. The secondary charging coils on the ship's ancient particle accelerator spinal mount weren't cycling properly.

<Patrick Leonard.>

He looked up and checked his pinplant comms. No channels were open. *What the heck,* he thought.

<Patrick Leonard, Winged Hussars Geek Squad technician, I must speak with you.>

More curious than freaked out, Patrick didn't know how to respond. It sounded like an artificially modulated voice. Was someone playing a trick on him. Of course, the question was how he heard it at all. How could he be hearing a comms signal without receiving one? He decided to just think a reply, and see what happened.

"Who is this, and how are you talking to me?"

<Who I am is unimportant.>

"Then why should I talk to you?" he asked. "You've hacked the comms system or broken into my privileged channel."

<You need to talk to me, because the survival of everyone in this star system is at stake.>

"I doubt there's anyone in New Warsaw who doesn't know that by now," Patrick replied.

<You could well be correct, but this does not change the importance of what I have to say.>

"I'm listening."

<I analyzed the dreadnought and its escorting ships in the Sol system and have completed a series of probable attack profiles.>

"Pass them along to Commander Lech Kowalczy," Patrick said. "Why tell me?"

<Speaking with Commander Kowalczy would not prove productive. I calculate only a 9% probability of him following the advice.>

"Then I shouldn't follow it either," Patrick said.

<You should if you want to continue surviving.>

The last statement made Patrick pause. Was this person expecting him to take some sort of tactical data from a mystery comms hacker?

"Even if this data is somehow useful, why are you giving it to me?"

<I have reviewed the files of everyone in the star system, and you are the only one who will be able to correlate the data. You also have the background knowledge to put it to use, and you are here, now.>

Patrick floated in the auxiliary power room and considered. It sounded like whoever he was talking with was delusional. He ran his comms log back and found nothing since speaking with the engineer. *Nothing.* Even if the mysterious voice was crazy, it had ability. "*Okay, give it to me.*"

<It cannot be imparted from a distance.>

"*I have to meet you in person? Fine, where are you?*" Patrick thought it was a perfect opportunity. He'd write a report to HST, Home Security Team, once he had a name to go with the voice. The whole affair was highly irregular. Elizabeth would want to know what was going on aboard her ship as well.

<Come to the auxiliary computer core.>

"I'll be right there." Patrick left his analysis tools floating where they were and fished a micro-recorder from his tool kit. His pin-plants could record anything he saw, but the recorder could see in low light and infrared. Besides, if the mystery talker turned hostile, a recording would remain. Once he'd clipped it to his uniform in a way unlikely to be noticed, he consulted the ship's deck plans in his pin-plants and headed for the auxiliary computer room.

Just before he arrived, Patrick took one more precaution. He wrote an email on the encounter, complete with a recording of the conversation from his point of view and left it in his outbox. Now confident it would be extremely difficult to make him disappear without at least some clues remaining, he opened the airtight door and looked inside.

The space was the size of a tiny apartment on Prime Base. Every wall was lined with the high-density computer cores used for storing data needed to bring the starship back online should the main computer be destroyed. While there were countless glowing and flashing indicators, the room itself was in darkness.

Patrick ran his hand along the inside door frame and found the light control. Flicking it caused no change. The lights were either broken or disabled. His every instinct told him to flee. "A-are you here?" he stammered.

<Yes.>

"Come out so we can talk," he said.

<Come inside, I cannot exit.>

Patrick ground his teeth, stuck between wanting to get answers and wanting to run for his life. He hadn't thought to bring a weapon; however, he had a small tool kit and several screwdrivers rested inside. He popped open the kit and took the longest, sharpest-looking one. If the mystery talker was armed, the screwdriver would be less than useless. Patrick's hand-to-hand training went no further than the mandatory four-hour familiarization course.

<You have nothing to fear.>

Easy for you to say, Patrick thought. He chastised himself for being a coward. The space was small, and the ship's security was tight. Whoever it was couldn't be an alien spy or an assassin. Even if it were one of the legendary Depik, why would it go through all the effort to get him alone? He was just a Geek Squad tech, not a Winged Hussars command-level officer.

He took a deep breath and floated into the space.

The door closed behind him with a sickening *Clang,* followed immediately by the locking mechanism engaging. "Shit!" he squeaked in a most undignified manner. It took a long moment to get a hand-hold and spin around, and even longer to find the locking mechanism in the near-total darkness. He jerked on the lock with no result. He jerked harder and harder, and still nothing. A sound behind him made Patrick spin around, holding onto the lock with his hands behind his back.

"Don't come any closer!" He yelled. "I have a gun!" In addition to not getting a weapon, he'd left the portable light in his tool kit. *Shit, shit, shit,* he mentally moaned, feeling his panic growing by the second.

"I mUst sHoW yoU," a voice spoke aloud, a voice like fingernails screaming across a chalkboard. Then out of the gloom floated a skeletal woman with wispy hair as white as hyperspace.

By the time he could bring his hands around to defend himself, the woman's equally skeletal hands had reached out and grabbed his head. Patrick screamed as the fingers searched along his temples.

Patrick's own hands closed on the tiny wrists just as her fingers touched his pinplants, and liquid fire poured into his brain, burning away everything.

Somebody screamed.

* * *

Shadowfax's medical alert blared, and a team was dispatched. They reached their destination in moments, having trained for weeks and become battle-hardened after Earth. They found the door open to the auxiliary computer core and a member of Geek Squad floating there, her face ashen. Her name tape said D. Redcheck.

"What's the situation, ma'am?" the medical team head asked.

"He's in there," she said and pointed into the room. "I-I think he's dead."

One of the techs floated in while the leader questioned Redcheck. "What happened, exactly?"

"No clue," Redcheck replied. "I couldn't find Patrick and used his pinplants and the ship's locator to find him. When I got here, he was dead."

"He's alive," the other med tech called out. "Unconscious— maybe in a coma—but alive."

The team leader floated in and checked the patient. Another Geek Squad member, a male in his forties. Her assistant had him hooked up to a medical monitor and was running tests.

"Severe shock, it looks like. I'm getting strange signals from his pinplants." He reached into his kit for an instrument then fumbled it, the device spinning away into the dark room. "Can you hit the lights?"

"Sure," the team leader said and floated back to the doorway where Redcheck was watching. He flipped the switch. Nothing. "It's broken." He looked around. Spaces like the one they were in were seldom visited by medical personnel. He grabbed a light from his toolbelt and flicked it on. "Holy shit!" he yelled and pointed. The body of an old woman slowly spun further back in the center of the bay, toward the rear.

After the shock wore off, the med tech anchored on a handhold and caught the woman. He felt for a pulse. "She's dead," he said.

"Sure," the team leader said. "But who the fuck is it? Nobody on this ship is that old."

"I'm not sure she's really that old," the med tech said, examining the body. He took out a sequencer and pushed the needle into the corpse's skin. "If she was in New Warsaw, she has to have a record." The machine only took a second to respond. "That's not possible."

"What does it say?" the team leader asked.

"Lieutenant Commander Katrina Cromwell," he replied. "But she's been dead for more than a decade."

* * *

Merc Guild Detention Facility, Ubatuba, Brazil, Earth

Jim Cartwright had no idea how long he'd been in his prison cell; he only knew pain and despair. He'd tried counting meals for a time, then they stopped feeding him regularly. Then he counted what Major Vels Lucas euphemistically referred to as questioning sessions, until he lost track of those as well. He'd nev-

132 | KENNEDY & WANDREY

er considered that nanites could be used to help torture; now he wished he still didn't know.

He was pretty sure it had been a couple of days since he'd last seen anyone, when the door creaked open. He didn't bother getting up off the floor; what good would it do?

"Oh God, Jim," a feminine voice said.

"I said you don't get to call me that," Jim said with a growl. "What the fuck do you want, Captain McKenzie?

"I'm here to check your medical condition," the woman he'd known as Adayn said.

"Don't want your prisoner dying before he spills his secrets?" he asked. "Right."

"Something like that," she said and came closer.

Jim briefly considered grabbing her and choking the traitor to death. They hadn't replaced his nanite-bonded shackles after the first torture session. Unfortunately, he doubted that he could choke out a kitten just then. He elected to glare at her as she held a medical scanner next to him and ran it through a diagnostic.

"You've lost ten kilos," she noted.

"The quisling torture diet. I'll write a book and make a fortune."

"You're showing evidence of malnutrition and massive deficiencies in multiple dietary categories."

"They stopped feeding me," he noted.

"Damn it," she said and looked back at the door.

Jim followed her gaze and saw Major Lucas standing in the doorway, silently watching. Somewhere in the back of his mind his curiosity sat up and took notice.

"He has plenty of fat to live off of," Lucas said.

"He'll still die if he doesn't get enough vital nutrients," McKenzie said.

"Fine," Lucas said and made a dismissive gesture.

She took out an injector from the medkit, inserted a vial into it, and pressed it against Jim's forearm. He felt the slight sting of an air-injector as it worked, then she took it away. "You'll feel a little better in a few minutes," she said, then she left without another word. As Jim watched her leave, he felt a couple strange twinges in his back and base of his head, then it was gone.

"Food will come," Lucas said. "I suggest you eat it. We'll talk in a day."

"I can hardly wait," Jim said.

The Varangian commander sneered and slammed the door.

Jim sat up slowly and stared at the closed door. There was more going on than he'd originally thought. Although he was sure of it, he had no clue what it might be.

Just as Lucas had said, a meal arrived within minutes. It was soup with two slices of bread and a pitcher of iced tea. The soup was full of bits of fish and vegetables. Jim ate every single bite but did it with measured patience as his mind tried to understand what was happening.

As he finished the soup, he felt something he hadn't felt in a long time: a ready indicator from his pinplants. *What the fuck?* They'd disabled his pinplants immediately after taking him into custody. He'd tried to access them a few ways without success, but then he'd stopped trying.

He reached for them in his mind, though tentatively, like a man dying of thirst tries to reach out to a mirage for water, and found a single function control—music. Jim activated it and the sounds of

Crowded House's song "Don't Dream It's Over" began to play. Tears rolled down his filthy cheeks.

* * *

EMS *Shadowfax*, New Warsaw

Captain Elizabeth Stacy found out about her boyfriend's medical status as her shuttle was docking. She was forced to wait as the reaction mass tanker cleared its umbilicals and an ordnance shuttle flew clear before she could land her own craft in the bay. Even if the entire crew knew of the relationship, she wouldn't let herself show her fear. She'd already instructed her XO, Evie Miller, to get *Shadowfax* under power the instant her shuttle touched down. Elizabeth engaged the magnetic grapples on the shuttle's landing legs and almost immediately felt thrust begin to build as the ancient warship accelerated.

It took another minute before the bay was pressurized, then Elizabeth undogged the shuttle door, set her course, and jumped. It would only have taken another few seconds for the guy ropes to emerge from the deck, but she leaped anyway. It was just under ten meters to the bay exit, and she nailed it perfectly. The deck officer nodded as she shot by without acknowledging he existed. Despite her personal promise not to show her feelings, she caught herself heading for the medical deck. It was easy with her ship under increasing acceleration.

The ship's chief surgeon looked up from his slate as Elizabeth entered. "I've been expecting you."

"I just wanted to check on your patient," she said, and looked away. "He was injured on my ship, after all."

"Sure, Captain." The surgeon gestured for her to follow him. Patrick was in a medical hammock which would keep the patient contained regardless of whether there was thrust or zero gravity. Even though it was obviously Patrick, she couldn't quite believe what she was seeing.

"What's his condition?" she asked in a hushed voice.

"Physically fine; there's no sign of trauma." The surgeon used his slate to display a Tri-V image of a brain scan. "His brain is showing highly unusual signs of activity."

"Do you know what he was doing in the auxiliary computer core?"

"I don't, sorry." He pointed at a doorway. "The body I mentioned is in there."

She nodded and moved into the adjacent room. This one wasn't full of stowed hammocks; it was lined with slide-out lockers, all with dim status indicators, save one. The surgeon went to that one and pressed a control. It slid out like a filing cabinet drawer. In the morgue drawer was what she could only describe as a specter, or a ghost.

Her recollection of that fateful day on *Whirlaway* when the Cromwell sisters had their falling out was as clear as the day it happened. She'd been siting watch and saw the aftermath. The body lying before her was unmistakably Katrina Cromwell, who'd died twelve years ago. Her looks matched her sister in every way possible, with the exception of her general appearance. This woman looked like she was the survivor of a concentration camp, gaunt and undernourished. Her hair was ratty and unkempt, and her fingers bent like a raptor's talons.

"What the fuck happened?" she wondered aloud. She turned to the physician. "You've compared the DNA?"

"A one hundred percent match," he confirmed. "That is Katrina Cromwell. However, I need your authorization to conduct an autopsy."

"Do it," Elizabeth ordered. He nodded his head.

Her XO's voice came over her pinplants. "Captain?"

"Go ahead, Evie," she replied.

"We are ready to begin high-G maneuvering on your orders."

Elizabeth walked out of the morgue into the sickbay, stopping to look at Patrick one more time. He lay in the hammock, eyes open and staring. Other than the regular rise and fall of his chest, there was no sign he was alive. *What did you stumble upon?* She thought. When her love didn't respond, as she knew he wouldn't, she hurried toward her CIC, and her duty.

* * *

EMS *Alicorn*, Winged Hussars Flagship, New Warsaw

"Commander Kowalczy, we are getting indications of ships entering the system."

Lech looked up from his personal Tri-V on the CIC and to his sensor tech. He pointed at the central Tri-V and an image of New Warsaw appeared on the screen. In the center was the system's emergence point. The stargate was on one extreme side, Prime Base and Home on the other. His fleet assets were highlighted as green points, each with their own indicator for class, name, and status.

"It's hours early," he said and searched the emergence point in vain. "Where are they?" A section of the map flashed deep in the asteroid field, almost a light minute from the emergence point. "Confidence?"

"Neutrino sensors in that region received between five and twenty pulses. Confidence is high."

Lech chewed his lower lip and considered the development before speaking. "Any of our assets in the area?"

"One non-Hussars asset," his SitCon said. "Upsilon."

"Cartwright's pet asteroid," Lech said and shook his head.

"Should I order a fleet element to investigate?" TacCom asked. On the Tri-V, sensors in the region of the new target began to build on the readings, but only slightly. Hazy, indistinct traces showed the vessels' general delta-V and course. No estimates were available on their type or tonnage.

"No," Lech replied. "They're not enemy."

"Are you sure, sir?" his XO, Lieutenant Commander Akers asked, casting a worried look at the new arrivals.

"Yes," he said. "Those aren't enemy ships."

"With all due respect, sir," Akers said. "How can you be sure?"

"Because they can arrive anywhere they want, just like *Pegasus*. If those were enemy units, they would have appeared next to Prime Base, where we have exactly dick." He looked at her. "If you could appear anywhere in a star system, would you show up in an asteroid field, or right next to your objective?" She pointed at Prime Base. "Right, exactly. Also, they have almost no delta-V." He shook his head again. "No, those are our friends, the Dusman."

All around the CIC, *Alicorn*'s command staff exchanged looks. Lech saw everything from concern to hopelessness.

138 | KENNEDY & WANDREY

"They made the *Egleesius*," his TacCom said. "I mean, didn't the Dusman build those ships?"

"Maybe," Lech said, then shrugged. "I know we're hoping for a big fleet to come and rescue us—I certainly am. But we have to be realistic and hope our little allies have some sort of ace up their sleeves." He didn't say it, but he didn't think it was the case. The Dusman had been hiding for 20,000 years and had done it so thoroughly everyone thought they were extinct. The idea they'd also have some super-secret fleet of badass warships didn't strike him as all that probable. For that matter, why had they decided to come out of hiding now?

Maybe they aren't really the Dusman, he thought. Before the thought was even fully formed, he *knew* they were. Who would claim to be what they weren't? After all, they'd apparently come to New Warsaw in a number of different ways, both on Cartwright's Upsilon asteroid and various merc ships. They could just as easily have run after the battle on Earth was lost. Instead, it appeared they were bringing reinforcements of some kind.

"We have no choice but to trust them," Lech said. He remembered the leader of the Dusman saying to "Follow our lead, or all will be lost." They'd sounded so arrogant. He sighed. "Continue acceleration and give me an update on the status of indicators."

As Lech listened to his TacCom recite data, he watched the vicinity of Upsilon. The sensor data on the new arrivals slowly fell off the scale of improbability until there was nothing left to report. Either the Dusman ships had stealth—something which was all but impossible in space—or they'd concealed themselves in the thousands of asteroids in the vicinity of Upsilon. Whatever the case, he didn't have more time to waste on the mystery.

* * *

EMS *Pegasus*, New Warsaw System

Captain Akoo, currently in command of *Pegasus*, sat in his position uncomfortably. He'd had more than a week to get used to it, but it wasn't nearly enough. *Pegasus* had been under command of a Cromwell from the early days of the Winged Hussars. Alexis Cromwell's presence was profoundly missed by *Pegasus'* new master.

After this battle I'm going home, Akoo thought. He'd been with the Hussars for a decade and had loved every minute of it, until now. He was coming to realize he didn't like being in command. At all. He fully intended to see this battle through to a win, at which point he would probably be offered command of another ship. He didn't want it.

Akoo liked comms and had maintained his old post in addition to being in command without an XO. It was a nest full of dung, but he felt he deserved it after watching his beloved commander be murdered.

"Squadron is in formation," Abby Smith, the SitCon, reported. As situational controller, she monitored the ship's position and those of the ships around them to coordinate their actions. It took an open mind with an eye toward details many would miss.

"Enemy emergence expected in twenty minutes," Xander, the ship's TacCom, said. The tactical commander handled the ship's offensive and defensive systems. "Commander Kowalczy says to prepare to launch drones in five minutes."

"Understood," said Akoo. He looked down at the seat he sat in—the commander's seat—and ground his beak. He wished with all his being to not be in the hot seat. He used his pinplants and sent a message to the dedicated channel he'd always known existed, but never used.

"*Drone control, are you there?*" Silence answered. "*Ghost?*" More silence. He sighed and spoke aloud. "Xander, order drone operations to prepare for launch."

"Standing by," she replied. Xander looked at the closed door to the captain's ready room then back at her controls. How drones were controlled, or even who did it was one of the mysteries of *Pegasus*. Now, without much explanation, crew were assigned to the task in the same manner as the other *Egleesius* ships. The entire command crew felt a profound difference in how the ship was about to fight. Even more than the absence of Alexis, it felt like a bit of their soul was now gone as well.

As the minutes ticked down, dread hovered over the crew of the *Pegasus* like the Grim Reaper. With fifteen minutes remaining, the five *Egleesius* ships released their complement of drones into the black, and they raced ahead on tiny tongues of fusion fire.

* * *

CIC, New Warsaw Defense Command, New Warsaw

"The *Egleesius* ships are launching their drones," one of the comms techs said as Sansar sat in the command chair. It seemed like everyone needed her for something—a last-minute decision, a question on positioning, or a missing detail about the plan—and she had been delayed to the point that she almost hadn't made it back to the command asteroid in time.

One of a plethora of asteroids near the emergence zone, the command asteroid was a little further back and didn't have any offensive weapons. It did, however, have an excellent communications suite and a bevy of defensive measures so it could stay alive while it coordinated the defense of the system.

Although the Golden Horde had been working to upgrade and integrate the system's defenses for years, the asteroid hadn't been completed when Walker had been given the word that the Merc Guild was coming, but he'd at least been able to get it up to initial operating capability in the time he'd had. Many of the redundant backups weren't in place yet, but she had full control of the operational defenses.

The command center sported one of the biggest Tri-Vs she'd ever seen in the center of the space, with three levels of technicians ringing it. One group controlled the fixed defensive positions, the second operated the mobile defenses, and the third group was responsible for the command and control of any ships in the system. Not all of the stations were manned, though, as many hadn't been brought online yet. They would make do with what they had, and a number of extra technicians stood nearby to fill in or assist where necessary. One display screen was blank at the moment—the one directly in front of her that showed unidentified and enemy ships.

"Very well," Sansar replied. "Give the order to launch all available drones and asteroids into the emergence area. Tell the tugs to cut and run."

"Yes, ma'am," the comms tech replied.

Sansar watched the massive Tri-V in the center of the CIC as little points of light—the drones—streamed from the ships surrounding the emergence area as well as the defensive asteroids. Larger points of light joined them—asteroids that had been towed to the edge of the emergence zone. Some were armed; others were no more than giant rocks designed to make targeting and maneuvering difficult for the Merc Guild ships upon emergence. Some tugs were still bringing some in; those were released and allowed to fly through the emergence zone on their own. Others had motors, limited sensors, and comms suites; those could be guided to make them deadly instead of merely annoying. Unfortunately, there hadn't been time to bring the overwhelming majority of them close enough—nearly all of them waited in the asteroid belt due to a lack of towing capacity. Only nine of them were in place, but their motors fired, and the massive hunks of rock began moving into the target area.

"Arm all weapons; fusion plants to full power."

Sansar glanced at the status boards and watched as the lights on the various defensive platforms turned from yellow to green. Her mind raced with the power of six pinplants—what was she forgetting? What else could they do? She couldn't come up with a thing.

The emergence area was a spherical area with defenses everywhere along the periphery. While there were no gaps she could see, there were some concentrations that were stronger than others due to the way the ships had set up and the directions that the asteroids had been towed in from. If she'd had more time, she would have worked that out better. But she didn't have time, so she took a deep breath and released it. It was as good as she could get it; it would have to do.

"Ready?" Nigel asked from behind her. He'd brought her back to the asteroid on *Revenge*, which was now tied up on the backside of the asteroid, hopefully out of harm's way, but near enough to use, if necessary.

"As much as we can be," Sansar said as the last light on the status board changed to green. She looked over her shoulder. Nigel was staring intently at the Tri-V display with the look of a predator.

He nodded once. "Now all we need is the enemy."

Sansar turned to check the countdown timer on the wall. Less than a minute remained until when the Fae—the Dusman—said the Merc Guild would arrive. She hoped they were right—having to recover and rearm all the asteroids if the enemy didn't show up would be a bitch.

* * *

CIC, BMS *Trushista*, Hyperspace, Approaching the New Warsaw System

Admiral Paka's eyes surveyed the CIC of the Bakulu battleship she'd been given. While it still rankled, a little, to have not been given command of *New Era*, she was sure that she would have it after this battle. Galantrooka would either be too aggressive or not aggressive enough; it was inevitable he'd do something stupid, and she'd be able to blame the loss of *something* on him. After all the time she had lived with the Humans to bring about this end, she deserved it. Besides, as Peepo's sister…rank did have its privileges, after all.

Although she wouldn't have expected to be commanding the fleet from a Bakulu ship, she had asked for the best and received it. *Trushista* was supposed to be the best-crewed ship in the fleet, and she had seen nothing so far to prove otherwise.

With fifteen minutes to go until emergence, the ship's captain had called the crew to battle stations, and every station was manned

144 | KENNEDY & WANDREY

and ready as the timer counted down through the final minute before emergence, and her chance to make a name of her own. Although it had been Peepo's plan, Paka had been the one who'd gone under cover *for decades* to make it all possible.

All she needed to do was win this battle, and her name would be as acclaimed as her sister's; maybe even more. She doubted the Humans would appreciate the grand strategy she had been a part of—it was more likely they would consider her a traitor—but she was first and foremost a Veetanho, and the Veetanho ruled the galaxy because they were the best and the brightest. The sooner the Humans came to terms with this, the fewer she would have to kill. There was no doubt in her mind, though, after all her time with the Humans, she knew they wouldn't go down without a fight.

Which was just fine with her.

* * *

CIC, MGS *New Era*, Hyperspace, Approaching the New Warsaw System

"Twenty minutes until emergence," the Bakulu navigator said, looking at his console.

"Set Battle Stations," Admiral Galantrooka ordered. "This unprofitable war has gone on long enough; it is time to finish it. The Humans have nowhere left to run and nowhere left to hide."

Lights and sirens flashed, though there was very little movement throughout the massive dreadnought. Nearly the entire crew—including its admiral—had kept at least one eyestalk trained on the emergence timer for the last day and had begun massing around their battle stations some time earlier. All were excited to finally bring Peepo's plan to its successful conclusion, and the admiral was proud to be the one chosen to command the Merc Guild's new flagship.

Galantrooka bobbed an eyestalk—although not the one watching the timer as it relentlessly counted down. "I just hope they don't surrender *too* quickly."

* * * * *

Chapter Seven

"Well, that's strange," Corporal Bolormaa Enkh muttered as she reviewed "the take" from their remaining dragonfly drones. They would need a new shipment—and soon—or she would soon be without them. Built to look like one of South America's dragonflies, apparently they were "too real," and one of the local predators was picking them off, hoping to get a meal, and a large percentage of the drones they launched never came back. It didn't help that the nimble craft usually flew straight and level, where the natural ones zipped and flitted everywhere, making them tough targets to catch. Her drones were almost too easy for the predators.

She turned around from her terminal. "Hey, Major, I've got something."

"What is it?" asked Major James Good.

"Do you know of any high value targets that escaped the massacre in São Paulo?"

"Do you mean the Fae that got away?"

"No, sir," Enkh replied, turning back to her terminal. "I have a dragonfly sitting on the comms antenna at the Merc Guild's headquarters, and I just got two hits of traffic on high value items. Based on the intercepts, though, I don't think either of them are our wayward Fae."

Good's eyebrows rose. "What have you got?"

"Well, the first one originated *from* the headquarters. They contacted some of the local quislings and asked what the best trauma center was in the country."

"So? Maybe one of their troops got plugged on a patrol."

"No sir; that's not it. The quisling asked if the injured was an alien or a Human, and he was told that the injured party was a high-value Human. I just wondered if we knew who that was."

"Not that I'm aware. Maybe we can send a drone or two to the hospital they sent the patient to? Where is it?"

"I think it was the Hospital Samaritano in Rio de Janeiro. There were two others the quisling recommended, but they were both in São Paulo and got destroyed in the Raknar attack. The problem isn't with 'where' they're taking the victim, though; the problem is we don't have enough of the drones left to spare one without pulling it from the search grid, and I got another hit on *that*, too."

"You found the CASPers that were reported missing?"

"Well, no, sir, I haven't yet, but one of the Merc Guild's informants reported a group of giant metal men just south of Taubaté."

"And where the Blue Sky is that?"

"It's a small town about thirty-five kilometers northeast of here."

"So, you think whoever stole the CASPers is headed toward the Merc Guild headquarters?"

"Might be, sir. That position's up the road from São Paulo and near the HQ. All they'd have to do is take the 383 highway and they'd be there. If someone escaped the devastation in São Paulo, stole the suits, and figured out where the guild's headquarters was, that's probably about where they'd be."

"That's a lot of ifs."

"Yes, sir, it is. But nothing else makes sense. We know the CAS-Pers were reported stolen. We also know it would take a group of mercs to operate them, and the only mercs who would have been in that area were ones assaulting the city."

"So that would have been the Cavaliers, then. I thought they were all wiped out assaulting the fake Merc Guild headquarters in São Paulo, though."

Enkh shrugged. "I don't know; I thought so, too. At least some of them were in there—we saw the video Peepo broadcast of when she blew up the tower with the Cavaliers' XO inside it. We thought all of the Cavaliers were with him…but what if some *weren't* in the building at the time and escaped?"

Good nodded. "Their suits would have been about out of power and ammo by now. They would have needed replenishment…or new suits."

"And if they happened to find the ones Peepo had…"

"They would have taken them and gone after Peepo to get some payback for the people who died."

"That's what I think, sir."

"I think you're right," Good replied. He thought for a moment and then said, "We need to get in contact with them."

"How are we going to do that, sir?" Enkh asked. "Tie a little note to a dragonfly and send it out? What happens if it falls into the Merc Guild's hands?"

"I might be able to help you with that," a new voice said from behind them.

* * *

Somewhere near Taubaté, Brazil, Earth

"Where are we, Sergeant?" Major Alvarado asked over the comms.

"Lost, sir," Buddha replied sullenly.

Their convoy of thirteen trucks was not distinctive in and of itself, despite being composed entirely of stolen trucks. What was unusual was the distinct lack of darker-skinned teamsters to operate them. Buddha and the other surviving senior NCOs had scoured the Cavaliers for everyone who bore even a remote resemblance to a native of the region. Two men were of Indian descent, another was from Jamaica, and another woman was Native American. That left nine trucks driven by light-skinned people, a job seldom done by such people in Brazil.

"We can't risk uplinking with the planetary navigation network," Private Aidan Lynch said over the squadnet. A young member and a recent addition to the Cavaliers, his only real faults were over-eagerness and an unwillingness to follow the chain of command.

"The first sergeant is well aware of that, Private," Corporal Solberg replied.

"Sorry, Corporal," Lynch said.

Buddha knew they were somewhere between São Paulo and the northern coastal region. Their theft of Peepo's brand new Mk 8 CASPers and tons of supplies had also yielded intel that Peepo had another base on the coast north of São Paulo. The same intel confirmed the Raknar pilots weren't in São Paulo. After Buddha consulted with Major Alvarado, Captain Wolf, and the other senior NCOs, they'd agreed their objective was probably there.

"If the Raknar drivers aren't there?" Wolf asked.

"Then we still get another swing at Peepo," Alvarado said.

Everyone liked the sound of that. Since they'd already stolen everything not nailed down in the São Paulo warehouse, it wasn't much of a leap to help themselves to a small fleet of heavy transports next door. As an added bonus, that facility was a food distributor. They had brand new CASPers, ammo, batteries to bring the Mk 7s back online (for those who couldn't fit into the Mk 8s, like Buddha), and plenty of grub. What they didn't have was a map.

"You'd think someone would have thought to steal a map," Solberg mumbled to Buddha off the radio.

The big Polynesian first sergeant just shook his head in frustration. CASPer drivers were used to having all kinds of intel and orbital data feeds, or, worst case, their suits had built-in navigational aids to get them to their target. They didn't have *any* of those things this time.

The thirteen-vehicle convoy had pulled over along the SP-070 to try and get their bearings, and instantly began drawing attention. So, Alvarado ordered them onto the side streets. Nobody in the unit spoke Portuguese, which all the street signs were printed in. The trucks were also big and couldn't fit down many of the small side streets. They'd been forced to make several turns, and the result was their current predicament.

"We're going to have to send out scouts," Buddha finally said to his commander.

"I think that's too risky," Alvarado replied immediately.

"Getting caught here is more risky," Buddha countered. "Send out Private Seeley with three others in the new Mk 8s. They aren't painted, so there's nothing to identify them. Even if they're spotted…"

"Which they most certainly will be," Captain Wolf interjected.

"But nobody will know it's us," Alvarado finished. He sighed. "Peepo and her people are bound to figure out we were the ones who stole those CASPers sooner or later, anyway. Very well, First Sergeant, do it."

The thirteen trucks were more or less hidden on a rundown road near some abandoned apartment buildings. Buddha watched via a pair of newly "acquired" drones as the four CASPers slipped out of the trucks and quickly moved into the shadows around the surrounding structures. The new CASPers had all been given quick and dirty paint jobs of black and brown primer; the new suits had come out of their boxes as shiny as rolls of aluminum foil. Buddha and the rest of his squad were geared up as well, just in case.

In moments, the four scouts were gone, and Buddha watched their progress over his battlespace Tri-V projected inside the CASPer Mk7 cockpit. The four scouts moved out quickly, their sensors extending the battlespace in leaps and bounds. He quickly saw their problem. The vicinity they'd found themselves in was made up of many circular roads, each tending to branch in and around to others. It was like a damned maze.

"Find a thoroughfare," he ordered.

"We're not looking for a pizza," Seeley responded.

"Don't be a smart ass," Buddha replied. He could almost see Seeley mouthing a less than appropriate reply. Then he watched as one of the scouts sailed over an alley on his jumpjets, with a civilian watching in surprise below. *Damn it,* he thought, *so much for stealth.*

"Got the main road," Seeley said a second later.

Buddha watched the map fill in, and the computer automatically drew a path for the convoy to reach it.

"I've got recon flyers in the area," another scout reported in.

"Road is out of the question," Alvarado said.

"Concur," Wolf agreed.

"Find us some cover, First Sergeant," Alvarado ordered.

"Roger that," Buddha said, and analyzed what the scouts had found so far. It only took him a minute to locate something. "I have a commercial vehicle maintenance facility, less than a kilometer to the north east. Bonus, it's in our direction of travel."

"Facilities for the troopers?" Alvarado asked.

"Only just," Buddha said. "But the trucks won't stand out."

"Another recon flyer transiting our AO," Seeley, reported.

"Buddha, transmit the location and get them moving."

Buddha fed the coordinates to the squadnet. In a moment, the trucks' hydrogen engines came alive and the convoy moved out. The four scouts also zeroed in on their destination. Maybe when night came, they could send out more scouts. He was keenly aware they still lacked even the most basic plan. All he knew was they needed to find their commander and the other Raknar drivers.

"Hang on Jimbo," he said inside his CASPer as the truck rumbled along. "We'll find you."

* * * * *

Chapter Eight

CIC, New Warsaw Defense Command, New Warsaw

A new point of light appeared, slightly left of center in the emergence area.

"Emergence!" several voices cried simultaneously.

"Steady!" Sansar ordered as she waited to see if this was indeed the main assault, and where the bulk of the enemy's fleet would show up. "Hold your fire. Get me an ID."

There was a pause, and a second light appeared close to the first, then a third. "Maki battleship!" the sensor tech called. "Maki light cruiser! Another light cruiser" Lights began separating from the first ship that had emerged. "Riders detaching from the battleship!"

Sansar nodded. The Merc Guild had arrived. "All weapons, target the battleship and fire!" Hopefully, they could pick off some of the riders, too, before they all detached, giving them two kills for the price of one. "Drone and asteroid controllers, move forward and attack!"

"I had expected better of them," Nigel said from behind her. "They were five seconds late."

* * *

155

CIC, MMS *Morning Dew*, New Warsaw System

"Emergence!" the battleship's sensor tech noted. Captain Sartyl nodded as the Tri-V began filling in. "Cast off all riders!" he ordered. "Fire on targets as they are identified." The one good thing about being the first ship in an assault was that you didn't have to identify any contacts as friend or foe—if you were the lead ship, everyone else was the enemy.

"Damage control reports several large explosions on decks 11, 44, and 9. Unknown origin."

"Dispatch control teams," the captain ordered.

"Targets everywhere!" the sensor tech exclaimed. "I have multiple targets...no, hundreds of targets inbound."

"They're everywhere," someone said.

"Target the riders on the biggest concentrations of inbound targets and fire! Individual weapons, fire as targets bear."

The motors on several of the riders ignited, and they roared off to intercept the incoming streams of what were probably drones, based on their numbers and flight patterns. Then it seemed like every system defender in range fired at him. His shields fell in under two seconds, and the ship was destroyed half a second later.

He had just long enough to note that the *bad* thing about being the lead ship into a system was also that everyone else was the enemy, and they could concentrate an awful lot of firepower on you if they were all waiting to do so, as it appeared the Humans had been.

* * *

CIC, New Warsaw Defense Command, New Warsaw

"Target One destroyed," one of the ship controllers noted, and a small cheer went up.

"Focus!" Sansar ordered. Enemy ships were now showing up faster than they could be targeted. Twenty-seven ships had emerged so far, although the dreadnought had yet to make its appearance. The four riders that had detached from Target One before it was destroyed raced forward faster than she would have believed a ship could go. "What did Target One launch?"

"I don't know, ma'am," the closest sensor tech replied. "They were too big to be missiles, but they are accelerating on a near-missile profile."

Sansar watched the ship riders continue toward the drones that were inbound to where the Merc Guild ships continued to emerge. *What was big enough to be seen detaching like a rider, but could accelerate like a missile?* Sansar didn't know, but it had to be something defensive in nature. "Scatter the drones!" she ordered.

The drone formation had just begun to open up when the first not-missile arrived and detonated in a massive explosion, wiping out dozens—if not hundreds—of the agile drones. "What the hell was that?" she asked as the second, third, and fourth not-missiles exploded, destroying huge chunks of their drone formation.

"Captain Teenge of the *Arion* on comms."

Sansar gave a "go ahead" motion, and the Aposo captain's voice came over the radio.

"That was an antimatter blast," he said.

"Are you sure?" Sansar asked.

"Trust me, Colonel, I was pretty damned close to one a few months ago—a lot closer than I would have liked. We're feeding the data to Commander Kowalczy on *Alicorn* now so we can factor it into the main attack, but I am sure that was an antimatter blast."

"Thank you, Captain. Good luck." Sansar said, and the direct channel closed.

"I guess the gloves are off," Nigel noted.

Sansar nodded. "This is bad."

"What do you mean?"

"They're prepared to use antimatter weapons, and they aren't worried that we know about it."

It took Nigel a little longer to figure out what Sansar had already realized. "This is winner take all, then, isn't it?"

"Yes," Sansar replied. "Peepo knows word of this can't get out. They intend to kill all of us—every man, woman, and child in the system is going to have to die."

"We can't allow that to happen," he said.

"No," Sansar said, her voice grim, "we can't."

Nigel nodded toward the Tri-V. "It looks like the battle is going well, though."

"Yeah, so far." Sansar studied the battlespace. Merc Guild ships continued to materialize—*How many of them did they have?*—but the defenses were holding. Many of the ships had the antimatter-warhead riders, though, and a number of them had been used on the drones and asteroid bases. "Target any of those riders you see!" she ordered. "They can't be allowed to take out any of our bases or, even worse, our ships!"

Sansar shook her head as the battle continued to develop. *What was she missing?* It was a slugfest, and her forces were starting to take losses, but it didn't look like a "maximum effort" attack—*Blue Sky Above, they weren't even clustered that tightly!*—and Peepo was throwing away an awful lot of ships for little actual effect. A mobile asteroid intercepted a Maki cruiser and its light winked out. *This is too easy; this isn't what I saw!*

A new light illuminated on the far side of the Tri-V display from where the battle was being held. Then a second. Then a third, a fourth, and a fifth, all at random spots in the battlespace. The ships immediately began maneuvering toward each other.

"This was all a ploy," Sansar said as the realization hit her. The initial ships had gone through the stargate and all arrived in one place. Their mission had only been to draw in the static defenses and destroy some of her forces with their antimatter missiles. They weren't the main assault, though; those ships had jumped with internal shunts so they would arrive somewhere else in the emergence area, away from the other ships where they could hopefully catch the defenders out of position and stage a breakout from the emergence area. Her inexperience in space combat had led her astray. She'd never even considered that Peepo would split her forces and make multiple simultaneous emergences.

Sansar had reserve forces, but nothing that could contain the forces which had just appeared in the system, all of which were close to joining up. Most of her forces were engaged in stopping the initial assault, and they were now out of position to stop the invaders.

The Merc Guild's plan was beautifully executed, and she'd fallen for it. She began giving orders to reorient her forces and call in the reserves, while a lead ball formed in her stomach as the ships turned toward Prime Base.

"Defense Command, *Alicorn* Actual," Lech Kowalczy called. "Don't reorient on the newcomers. You finish with the first group; we've got these."

Sansar breathed a sigh of relief. More experienced at space combat, Lech had seen the need, and the Winged Hussars forces had peeled off to take them under fire. She hoped he knew what he was doing—five battlecruisers and their escorts seemed vastly underarmed versus the battleships. Regardless, she'd let the mobile forces deal with them while she concentrated on the first wave.

"New emergence!" a sensor tech cried.

Sansar's eyes whipped to the display, where a new dot was displayed. Its representation in the battlespace was so large that it gave no doubt as to what it was.

"*Dreadnought!*" the sensor tech yelled in fear as the light cruisers it carried began to detach.

This was what she had seen. More ships than she had defenses for. The battle was now truly joined, and she was an hour late and a whole pile of credits short. Then she saw the direction the dreadnought was heading.

"They're going for Prime Base, too," Nigel muttered, "aren't they?"

Sansar nodded as she continued to send out orders via her pinplants.

"Are we going to be able to stop them?"

Sansar stopped for a second to answer. "No," she said with a shake of her head. "We aren't." On the wider fleet action feed into her pinplants, she saw the Hussars' main fleet element approaching the engagement zone. While they could hit the battleships, they were out of position to turn on the dreadnought. Despite all their planning to stop it, the dreadnought was going to get away.

* * *

CIC, EMS *Shadowfax*, New Warsaw System

"They got one!" Evie Miller, XO of *Shadowfax*, called out. The entire CIC erupted in a cheer. Elizabeth was somewhat skeptical of Sansar Enkh's ability to run the defenses of New Warsaw. After all, ships weren't her thing. The plan had always been for Alexis Cromwell to handle space defenses, and, should anything get through, Sansar would then deal with it. This wasn't the plan—not at all—and the Winged Hussars lived or died by planning. *Plan, prepare, strike.* This fight was shaping up to only be prepare and strike.

The hapless Maki battleship which arrived first—and was promptly destroyed—was more a victim of poor fleet logistics than a successful layered defense. The Hussars training emphasized tight formations through stargates to make what just happened extremely difficult. First-year students knew the first ship out was the unluckiest ship.

"We're just getting started," Elizabeth reminded her command crew.

"Multiple emergences at a second emergence point," SitCon reported. "Various hull sizes from battleships to cruisers. They are one point nine-two light seconds off from the first emergence."

"Very good," Elizabeth said. "Prepare for an attack run on them. Helm, alter course to intercept. Comms, signal *Alicorn* we're ready."

"Target assignments received," TacCom responded.

"Explosions in the enemy fleet's midst. Two cruisers have exploded from internal damage, one battleship similarly damaged."

"The interdiction drones are working," Evie said, and Elizabeth nodded. The Tri-V showed a second group of ships struggling to launch their parasite craft while simultaneously fighting off a swarm of drones.

The emergence area was millions of square kilometers flooded with specialized drones. Once activated, the drones—nothing more complicated than fusion bombs with tracking systems and a drive—would attack anything without a clear IFF transponder. They were lethal in great numbers. The ships which exploded no doubt emerged into normal space with a drone next to their hull. The energy release from such an event was spectacular.

"We only get one clean pass," Elizabeth reminded them. "Forward shields to maximum, charge the spinal mount, prepare for combat."

The enemy fleet was emerging en masse now. Only a few seconds after they started to emerge into normal space, the big Tri-V in *Shadowfax*'s CIC revealed the enemy hadn't sent the earlier fleet assets by mistake. It was an expensive feint which had gotten Sansar to commit a large percentage of her defensive assets toward that zone, expecting the remainder of the fleet to arrive there as well. Tactical assessments continued to arrive from the flagship, *Alicorn*. Based on the data they'd gotten on the way out of Sol, there had to be at least a third element coming as well; no one had seen the dreadnought yet.

"Weapons range in twenty seconds," SitCon reported.

Too late to worry about a third element, Elizabeth thought. "Assigned targets in alignment?"

"Almost there," helm reported.

Elizabeth watched the closing tracks. It would be close, but then again when wasn't it? She missed Alexis running the show. This attack wasn't as creative as what she would have set up. This was more blunt force than surgical.

"On target," helm confirmed.

"Weapons range in ten seconds."

"More emergences," a sensor tech reported. "Different area of emergence."

"Acknowledged," Elizabeth said. "Data recording on automatic, concentrate on this engagement."

"Weapons range in three, two, one…"

"Fire," Elizabeth ordered.

* * *

The squadron of five Maki and Bakulu battleships and their escorts immediately began forming up upon their emergence into the New Warsaw system. For decades, the Winged Hussars' hidden base had haunted many space navy merc companies' dreams. The ability to destroy the Hussars and remove some of their best competition was a desirable goal. So, when General Peepo handed out the assault assignments, the Maki and Bakulu were only too happy to take a vanguard position in the second element.

"The Hussars are surely going to position their best ships to defend the emergence point," the Bukulu commander had said.

"And they'll be no match for five battleships and our squadron of escort ships," the Maki commander had completed the thought. The two races were not really enemies, but they weren't really allies, either. In situations where they were both under Mercenary Guild command, though, they worked together, if reluctantly.

The squadron was not in full formation yet when a dozen ships reported damage, including two Maki cruisers that were destroyed outright from internal explosions.

"Drones!" the TacComs of both races' ships called out. "Thousands—no tens of thousands of drones!"

"Sensors to close range, maximum sweep! Order the battleships to bring weapons online. Escorts, set CID weapons on automatic!"

The close-in defensive lasers were designed to intercept missiles or drones. Many of the Maki and Bakulu ships could also re-task their main laser batteries for defensive fire, as well. In an instant, thousands of lasers crisscrossed space, slicing drones apart and causing many to prematurely detonate. Tactical screens were awash with interference due to the radiation waves from nuclear detonations.

Despite the unrelenting torrent of fire, ships were still hit. Several were cruisers and frigates struggling to undock and get clear of the battleships they'd rode into New Warsaw. They were caught with their shields down and torn apart.

The losses were inconsequential. The squadron had more than 100 ships, and, although one was damaged, the five battleships were intact. Within a minute, the battleships' powerful defensive lasers were employed, and the anti-drone weapons-fire doubled. They'd destroyed about half when the squadron's sensors detected the enemy ships.

"Attacking squadron, inbound!"

"Five battlecruisers, unknown configuration. Two battlecruisers, *Steed*-class. Eight cruisers, *Crown*-class. Passing average 4,000 kilometers astern, direction 1-0-4 mark 3-5."

The Maki and Bakulu commanders both regarded the data and the speed of the approaching ships. It took a second to process what they were seeing and realize the drones weren't the main attack. They'd expected a static defense waiting for them, like what had met the first wave. The Hussars were going to pass at speed and rake them with fire. Instead, the entropy-cursed Humans had known when they would be arriving. They had to; it would have taken hours to push up to such a speed.

The commanders were stuck in a quandary. Change defenses to face the hurtling Hussars' ships and open themselves to the still significant swarm of drones? Or weather the coming attack to keep the drones off them?

The Maki, favoring a strong offense, elected to have their three battleships reorient on the attacking forces, counting on their escort frigates to protect them.

The Bakulu, being more defensive, had their two hold their ground.

* * * * *

Chapter Nine

"What are we going to do about the dreadnought?" Nigel asked.

"I'm still working on that," Sansar said. "I'm hoping the Hussars have something they can use to stop it, or at least slow it down a little."

"If we finish off the first wave quickly, can we reorient what we have to take on the dreadnought?" Nigel asked.

Sansar shook her head slowly. "A little, but most of what we have are the static defenses—the asteroids and mines. The ships we have are mostly mercenary cruisers and lighter-armed ships. If they go up against the dreadnought…"

"It would be a slaughter," Nigel finished.

Sansar winced as one of the asteroid bases was taken out by an antimatter "missile." Although the weapon functioned like a missile, they were ships in their own right; each was almost the size of a corvette, and it took a lot to stop one. The defensive lasers weren't enough to take one out with a single shot; the ships' defenders had to hit them multiple times with the defensive lasers—no easy task when they were going so fast—or use the offensive lasers to burn them down.

And each offensive laser was one that couldn't be used on the enemy forces.

Losing an asteroid base was a considerable blow, and that was the third one the Merc Guild forces had destroyed. In addition to the weapons on the station, they had also drilled out hangars in them. The last one to be destroyed had taken a squadron of the *Avenger* bombers—along with their SalSha crews and maintenance folks—"into the light."

Although Sansar wasn't as experienced as the Hussars at space combat, even she could see that the Merc Guild forces were starting to make gains as the defenders ran out of mines, drones, and asteroid bases. She had hoped to save the *Avengers* to go after the dreadnought, but hope wasn't an actual strategy, and she needed the extra throw weight.

"Launch the bombers," she ordered. "We need to finish this group off."

* * *

Ferret One, Asteroid Defense Base Kilo, New Warsaw

"Ferrets, check in," Thorb's bombardier, Second Lieutenant Skald, called.

"Two, up and ready." Thorb nodded as the rest of the bombers checked in. He could see some of the twelve bombers in his squadron on his right wing—they were far too close to each other, but it was necessary so they could stay hidden in the asteroid's shadow.

"They are ready," Skald said. "At least, they think they are."

Thorb winced but didn't say anything. He'd had the same thought. While there was almost nothing he wanted less than having to take an entire squadron of newbies into combat, one of those few things was to give the Merc Guild uncontested access to Prime Base and all of the women and children—both Human and SalSha—who hadn't had a chance to evacuate yet. Having lost eleven crews from his squadron in the assault on Earth—most of whom had been well trained—he knew it was statistically unlikely that he would return with all of his crews—most just out of training—this time. Still, the grahp had come to the system, and it was time for everyone to go out and face it. And, the truth of the matter was, sometimes when the grahp ate one of the inexperienced warriors, that gave the seasoned ones a chance to sneak in and kill it…not that anyone would ever say that, of course.

And, if worst came to worst, they were all in two-person bombers. No one would go into the light alone.

"The Badgers, Minks, and Wolverines all report ready, too," Skald said. "The asteroid the Weasels were based on got hit. They've gone into the light."

Thorb sighed. They'd already taken 20% casualties, and they hadn't even gone into battle yet. If he had to lose a squadron, though, Space Attack Squadron Five was the least experienced—they had just finished training and none of them had seen combat. The Badgers, Minks, and Wolverines had all participated in the assault on Earth and had come away with minor losses, so most of their crews were combat veterans.

He dialed up the airwing net. "All SalSha, this is Thorb. On my command, we will accelerate into a skew turn up and over our asteroids, spreading out as we go. Hit your targets then regroup back here for rearming in case we're needed for additional attacks. We cannot let the Merc Guild make it to Prime Base. It's either kill or be killed, and I'd rather do it to them than have them do it to our pups."

Several excited calls came back. He could tell they were mostly from the new crews in his command, who didn't know what they were getting into yet. The other squadrons' crews knew very well what war looked like and focused on getting themselves and their ships ready for combat, double- and even triple-checking checklists and settings.

"Here we go," Thorb transmitted. "Three, two, one, mark!" He smoothly pushed the throttle forward. "Tighten it up, Four," he added as that ship started to drop behind. "Everyone, fly off me, not your wingman." With twelve bombers in a row, if everyone tried to stay in position on the craft to their left, the last craft would be playing crack-the-whip the whole time.

"Defense Command, Ferret One," Skald called as Thorb began the pull up and over to head toward the battle. "We are up with twelve Avengers, looking for a target."

"Good to have you, Ferrets," the controller said. "Sending targeting data now."

Thorb glanced down at the display and tweaked his steering marginally as the new heading came in. "What are we going for?"

"We drew the short end of the seaweed," Skald replied. "The Badgers are with us, but we got the last Maki battleship. Defense command thinks they can contain the rest of the Merc Guild fleet, but they can't do anything with the battleship as it is now. We either have to destroy it, or at least wear down its defenses so someone else can."

Thorb shook his head. While they were wearing down the battleship's defenses, it would be wearing down his squadron…and there weren't any more SalSha available to fill the empty seats this battle was going to cause. But it had to be done, for the good of all.

He advanced his throttles. "Follow me," he commed to the squadron. "We have a battleship to kill."

* * *

CIC, EMS *Shadowfax*, New Warsaw System

"Just as we expected," Elizabeth said as the five *Egleesius* class battlecruisers opened their bow doors and unleashed hell.

At 40-terawatts each, the five battlecruisers volley fired on the three Maki battleships advancing toward them. The two *Steed*-class, *Sleipnir* and *Alicorn*, added their own twin one-terawatt particle cannons to the attack. The eight *Crown*-class cruisers; *Sir Barton*, *Gallant Fox*, *War Admiral*, *Whirlaway*, *Secretariat*, *Affirmed*, *Seattle Slew*, and *American Pharoah* added their own single one-terawatt particle cannons. The smaller ships' weapons weren't as powerful as the ancient *Egleesius*-class battlecruisers, but they had a higher rate of fire. All told, the fifteen Winged Hussars' warships pumped 350 terawatts of concentrated particle beam energy into the five battleships in less than one minute.

Two of the three battleships were torn to pieces, either destroyed outright or crippled so badly as to be rendered combat ineffective. The third was badly damaged but managed to return fire. She lashed out with particle cannons, heavy lasers, and missiles.

The missiles were easy to counter. Each of the *Egleesius*-class battlecruisers had two frigates docked, and they provided substantial anti-missile fire. The enemy lasers and particle beams were not as easy to counter. *Sleipnir* was hit twice by 5-terrawatt particle beams, causing heavy damage to her engines, while *Alicorn* took a beam through her bow, which took out one of her two particle beam barbettes and heavily damaged her shields. The cruiser *War Admiral* was wrecked, hulled bow to stern. Her sister ship, *American Pharoah*, was grazed by a particle beam, disabling her shields while a trio of 50-gigawatt laser batteries chopped her into pieces of spinning, exploding debris. The gigawatt lasers were only nuisances to the five *Egleesius*.

"Commander Kowalczy, what is your condition?" Elizabeth asked.

"*Alicorn* has seen better days," he replied. "Ship's still functional. I'm ordering the fleet to perform a skew turn and come back around for another pass. The third fleet element is the dreadnought and a bunch of escorts. We can't help with that; not yet anyway. If these ships join up, we're screwed."

"What about the reserves in the asteroid belt?" Captain Jormungd asked.

"Yes, it's time," Lech said. "Let's see if we can winnow them down a little more."

Elizabeth looked at the Tri-V in her CIC. Despite knocking out two battleships, the ruined behemoths were still managing to launch their escorts. The *Egleesius'* escorts were undocking, while the additional escorts and formerly Maki cruisers began emerging from the asteroid field, burning their fusion torches to link up with the rest of the fleet. Only the carriers stayed hidden; they were more of a liability in a moving engagement.

She snarled as *Shadowfax* burned her powerful engines, converting forward momentum into a turn, and tried to will her ship to come around faster.

Elsewhere the enemy dreadnought and its escorts maneuvered toward Prime Base.

* * *

Ferret One, Asteroid Defense Base Kilo, New Warsaw

"Well, it could be worse," Skald said as the *Avenger* rolled out on a heading toward their target.

Thorb looked at the flashing lasers and the sporadic blossoms of explosions in front of him. They were still a way off from the battle, but with the magnification dialed up, it looked like they were flying into a near-solid wall of death. While he knew in his head there was a *lot* of space between the tangled lines of lasers questing for his ship— and if he were lucky, he could fly between them when he got closer—his heart sank at his current view. He'd never seen that many ships all firing at each other before.

He sighed. "Okay, I'll bite. How could it be worse?"

"We could be going up against the dreadnought and its pile of escorts," Skald replied.

"Be careful what you ask for…" Thorb said. "This is bad enough."

"Truth."

Thorb looked closer at the Tri-V display. "Hey," he said as he pointed at a spot in the battlespace. "What's this?"

"That's what used to be Asteroid Defense Base Foxtrot," Skald said after a moment. "That's where the Weasels were. It got hit by a couple of antimatter missiles."

"So now it's a big expanding pile of rocks and metal?"

"Yes. And the bodies of Space Attack Squadron Five," Skald added wryly.

"Good."

"Good?" Skald asked, looking across the cockpit. He cocked his head. "How are their deaths good, oh glorious leader?"

"They aren't, of course," Thorb said, "and I wish it were otherwise. Still, that is a big debris field." He pointed to the navigation monitor. "Look. If we divert a little to the left and down, we can get behind it and use it for cover as we run in on the battleship. Then we pop out, launch our missiles, and return to base."

"The battleship will still have a chance to hit us once we clear the debris field, but you're right, that should give us some cover." He punched the buttons on his system, updating their navigation, and then pushed the button that sent steering commands to Thorb with a flourish. "Follow that."

Thorb nodded as the system showed he needed to fly down and left. "All Ferrets, all Badgers, this is Ferret One," he transmitted as he turned to follow the system's navigation. "Follow me and close up."

The ship raced forward as the rest of the squadron closed in on him. The destroyed asteroid wasn't perfect cover—the battleship's crew would still be able to see them both through the other networked sensors of the fleet and through the gaps in the debris field, but hopefully it would give them a little more protection and make it harder for the Merc Guild to hit them. It was a calculated risk flying in close formation—you couldn't maneuver as much or as violently, and it would be easier to target the relatively non-maneuvering group than a single maneuvering ship—but he thought it a worthwhile strategy.

It didn't take long for it to become readily apparent, though, that the strategy wouldn't last as the battleship's weapons began annihilating the largest remaining pieces of the asteroid, and stray laser beams began getting through. Thorb winced as the light for *Ferret Eleven* went out. Through some vagary of combat, the Badgers had already lost two ships, even though they were in trail of the Ferrets. *You never know when the laser beam is going to come for you.*

Thorb wished he could go faster—every fiber of his being wanted to push the throttles to the firewall—but that would have caused the squadron to spread out, weakening their combined attack. The Human attack training was good for maximizing efficiency, if nothing else.

Ferret Two winked out, followed shortly by *Ferret Six*, but then they were almost to the destroyed asteroid and in danger of running into the expanding debris themselves.

"Here we go," said Thorb as he pulled up, cleared the debris, then rolled until the craft was inverted and pulled back to their attack vector. The nice thing about space combat—even more so than combat in the water—was there was no "up" or "down;" you just reset your horizon accordingly.

Ferret Four winked out, but then they were within range, and the Rapiers began launching from both the Ferrets and the Badgers.

Although the Rapier missiles were smaller than the missiles the warships carried, proportionally, they carried a much greater payload. Since the missiles were already boosted to great speeds by the bombers that carried them, they required less fuel to get them to their extremely fast attack speeds, which were hard for even the modern computer systems to defend against. Armed with one of the Winged

Hussars' modified "squash-bomb" warheads, the slender missiles were not only tough to defend against, they also carried a big punch.

The battleship exploded as several detonations went off across the center of the ship, breaching its hull. Additional missiles made last minute corrections to target the initial detonations, and they flew deeper into the ship before exploding. Several of these set off the battleship's ammunition stores, and the ship cracked in half. The front half continued to burn, and the fires illuminated it as that section lost power.

"Hah!" Skald yelled as Thorb pulled the bomber up and away from the hulk. "Gotcha bitch!"

Thorb looked over to say something to his bombardier, which gave him a great view of the first Izlian battleship as it materialized.

* * * * *

Chapter Ten

CIC, New Warsaw Defense Command, New Warsaw

*B*lue Sky Above! *Would it never end?* Sansar asked silently as the rest of the Izlian fleet emerged from hyperspace. The dreadnought was going to get away, and she couldn't help it. She'd been drawn in by the first group and had already committed her forces to defeating them when the second group arrived. Thankfully, the Hussars had taken them on, but then the *third* force—with the dreadnought—arrived. She'd hoped to finish off the group that had arrived via the stargate, so she could turn her attention to the dreadnought, but it wasn't to be as the massive Izlian fleet maneuvered into formation.

Even worse, the ships had appeared right as the SalSha had finished their runs, and, not only were they out of ordnance, but the Izlian fleet was now between them and the bases where they could rearm. Looking at the status board, she saw she was out of forces to commit. There was only one weapon system remaining, but it was out of position to do anything about the Izlians.

It was enough to stop them, but she had to get the Izlians closer...*but how?* Then she saw the stream of lights, and she smiled. While she felt badly for the SalSha, they would make the perfect bait. As Sun Tzu had said, you just had to know yourself and your enemy...

* * *

Ferret One, Asteroid Defense Base Kilo, New Warsaw

"*Ferret Three*, break right!"

"Badger Seven—" Static.

"Break! Break! Attention on the net! This is New Warsaw Defense Command on guard. All *Avenger* bombers come to a heading of 2-7-8 mark 2-3. I say again, all *Avenger* bombers, come to a heading of 2-7-8 mark 2-3. New Warsaw Defense Command on guard, out."

"Shit!" Thorb said as he snap-rolled the bomber to the new heading and pushed the throttles to the firewall. That heading would take them within weapons range of one of the strange new light cruisers that had just emerged.

"What do you suppose that's all about?" Skald asked as he fired the *Avenger*'s gun, more in frustration than anything else. It wouldn't penetrate a ship's shields, but there was always a chance they might be down, or that the little bit of energy the *Avenger* spit out would be that one last thing that made the ship's shields drop for someone else.

"No idea," Thorb replied as he jinked the ship around. They were far enough away from the ship—and headed outbound—that the ship probably wouldn't decide they were a threat and shoot at them...but Thorb didn't want to give the Izlians any more opportunity to hit his ship than he had to. "But this is all sorts of fucked up."

He glanced at the battlespace. *Avengers* were fleeing from all over on the new heading. For some of them, it was easy; for others, who had turned the opposite direction when the new ships started arriving, it was a little more...problematic as they had to fly back past them, and some of the younger crews just blindly turned to the heading without looking to see where it took them.

The icon for one of them went out as he watched.

"All *Avengers*, this is *Ferret One*," he transmitted. "Join on me as soon as you're able. Do not fly within range of the ships if you are able and maintain defensive maneuvers while you are. *Ferret One* out." He shook his head as another icon was extinguished and a crew went into the light. Each one was a gut punch—what could he have done to train them better?

He shook off the thought as he realized where they were heading. "There's nothing on this heading but the asteroid field," Thorb said. "Call up Defense Command and ask them what we're supposed to be doing here, would you?"

"Sure," Skald said, safing the *Avenger*'s gun. After a few seconds, he said, "Well, you're not going to believe this, but they want us to lead the Izlians into the asteroid field."

"Oh?" Thorb asked. "Are there forces I am unaware of hiding out there?"

"No idea. I don't think so."

"Then what am I supposed to do to get them to follow us?"

"I don't know…look like a good target?"

Thorb shook his head. "This is the dumbest plan I've ever been part of. All I can hope is that we are just delaying them so Defense Command can come up with a better plan or send additional forces. The Izlians aren't stupid enough to run into the asteroids on their own, and we're going to be out of fuel before too long. Did they say how long we were supposed to do this?"

"Nope. Just that we'd know when it was time to return."

"Well, I hope Sansar—Colonel Enkh—has a plan, because this is stupid." He shook his head again as he pulled back the throttles and slowed the *Avenger* bomber. The Izlians—four battleships, fifteen cruisers, and ten frigates—continued to accelerate toward them. "I don't understand Humans, sometimes."

* * *

IMS *Fresha Two Seven*, New Warsaw System

"Admiral Epsilon!" the sensor tech exclaimed. A squid-like being, it floated next to its station and spoke through a combination of radiations. "All of the little ships are slowing and gathering together at the edge of the asteroid field."

"Aha!" the admiral replied, watching the Tri-V intently. "It is as I thought. Their carriers are nearby! We can follow those bombers back to their mother ship, and they will lead us to the remainder of the fleet. Once they have been eliminated, we will be able to finish the attack on the base without having to worry about any additional space-based attacks.

"Turn to a heading of 2-8-1 mark 1-7," he added. "We will follow them home to victory!"

* * * * *

Chapter Eleven

Prime Base, New Warsaw System

"Dreadnought and escorts inbound." Sansar's voice came into Aleksandra's mind via her pinplants. "I repeat, the dreadnought is inbound. They slipped our cordon... <*crackle*>...jamming...<*crackle*> ...ETA two hour.... [signal lost]"

Aleksandra looked up at her assistant in slowly dawning horror. Dimitri looked back in surprise. She'd been working on trying to complete the last of the evac while simultaneously hoping Sansar and the Hussars' fleet would hold the merc guild fleet at the emergence point. Now she realized she'd been wishing for the impossible. The improbable at best.

"Entropy," she cursed.

"What do we do?" Dimitri asked. "They'll blow us up in a second!"

"That's not the goal," she said, and called up the system status on her Tri-V. A map of New Warsaw appeared, which included the battle around the emergence point and the inbound dreadnought. No missiles had been launched at Prime Base, even though they were well within range. "They're going to take Prime Base."

"*Bozhe moi,*" Dimitri said.

Aleksandra only knew a little Polish, even though she'd gotten plenty from her grandmother growing up on Home, but some phases in Russian were nearly identical to Polish.

"Again, Commander, what do we do?"

"We fight," Aleksandra said, and triggered the General Quarters alarm for Prime Base.

The few thousand people left onboard looked at the strips of lights flashing red throughout the vast multi-ringed space station. Every Winged Hussar spent time on Prime Base, and many had spent all their time on the hub of Hussars' operation, but none had ever seen the General Quarters lighting. The ones in combat arms immediately sprang into motion. The rest simply stared in confusion or horror.

"Commander!" Three marines in CASPers stood in her office doorway. She glanced at the one who'd spoken.

"Sergeant Hedrick?"

"Yes, ma'am. Privates Hamill and Barnes and I have been assigned by Major Kratlik as your personal detachment." The two CASPers behind him stood waiting.

"I don't need a detachment," she complained.

"Not up to you, ma'am." Hendrick put a case on the floor next to her and opened it. Inside was a suit of light combat armor and a sidearm with extra magazines and a belt. "Please put this on. Quickly."

"What about my assistant, Ensign Pavlovich?"

"I have no orders concerning the ensign, Commander."

Aleksandra stared at the gear for a second, then grabbed the armor. "Well, you do now. Get him some armor and a weapon."

"Ma'am, we don't have time—"

"Make time," she said. "That's an order, Sergeant."

His CASPer didn't move for a second, then one of the other two left. She nodded and began slipping the armor on. She'd put it on more than once, in training, years ago. Those skills were as rusty as her Polish. She managed to avoid embarrassing herself, though only just.

When she was done, Hedrick's CASPer stepped closer and took the gun belt out of the storage case and handed it to her. She put the belt on, feeling the weapon's weight as she fastened the strap around her thigh. With the CASPer looming over her, she had a flashback of being a little girl with her mom helping her get dressed.

Aleksandra glanced at the gun and shook her head. Sergeant Hedrick's suit could bend steel bars with ease. *How many thousands of hours do you have to spend in one of those in order to have such control?* She silently wondered.

"You ready, ma'am?" the sergeant asked.

"Just a second," she said, and grabbed her command tablet. It would boost her pinplants and allow her to control almost anything on the station remotely. "What about the ensign's armor?"

"Private Barnes will meet us on the way to the CIC."

"Okay," she said, and took one last look around her office. "Let's go."

* * *

CIC, EMS *Shadowfax*, New Warsaw System

Elizabeth concentrated on breathing and watching the Tri-V update the order of battle. A new swarm of green indicators raced in from the asteroid belt. They weren't as fast as drones but were a lot faster than normal manned ships. *SalSha,* she thought. *Tough little fuckers.* They were arrowing toward the original battleship squadron.

The two remaining Bakulu battleships were acting in an extremely coordinated manner. In Elizabeth's experience, battleships didn't play well together. If you used them right, they could be utterly devastating, what with their overlapping fields of fire and massive shields. However, it seemed, more often than not, that battleship commanders were individualistic and protective of their own little space-fortresses. It was one of the many reasons Alexis had never brought them into the Hussars. That and they were slugs, which didn't fit the Hussars' nimble strike-and-run tactics.

"Someone is pulling the strings," Evie wheezed, also suffering under 5Gs of thrust. She could barely hold up her arm to point at the Tri-V.

"You saw that, too," Elizabeth said. Yes, the SalSha were definitely going for the remaining Maki battleship. She nodded. A tough nut to crack and the best choice. "Time to maneuver completion?"

"Two minutes," helm replied.

"Spread attack," Lech called over comms to the fleet.

Elizabeth pursed her lips. It would make their ships more challenging targets, but it would also reduce the effectiveness of their fire. She examined the Tri-V again. They had one big tactical advantage: the enemy didn't have carriers. The Hussars had wrecked every carrier in the system during the battle at Sol. The status indicators for the Hussars' four carriers showed only 25% for available drones, but the carriers were tucked away in the asteroid field making new ones. Most of the initial wave of automated killers were dead, though, and it appeared it would be an hour before more would be ready. *This is liable to all be over in an hour,* she thought.

"Enemy fleet is repositioning," Evie said.

Elizabeth's eyes darted over the display, then looked at it with her pinplants for the "bigger picture." *What the fuck?* she wondered. The enemy ships were repositioning, transitioning from the defensive sphere around the damaged Maki battleship to a vanguard aimed at the approaching Hussars attack.

The formation was right out of the Winged Hussars tactical training—layered offensive nose-on formation of escort frigates, cruisers, battlecruisers. Even the battleships were integrated!

"Commander Kowalczy!" Elizabeth snapped. "It's our own tactics. Paka is in command of that squadron!"

"I know," he replied, his tone fatal.

* * *

CIC, BMS *Trushista*, New Warsaw System

The Bakulu captain of *Trushista*, Glashpooka, focused all three eyes on the Tri-V in surprise. "Just like you said," he spoke.

"Just like I said," Paka replied. She sent a file to the *Trushista* TacCom. "There is the location of the *Egleesius*- and *Steed*-class CICs; target those shield grids with the battleships' main weapons. Have your cruisers concentrate on the *Steed*-class escort frigates, their anti-missile laser screens are the most effective. Beyond that, pick your targets at will."

Glashpooka regarded her for a moment, then nodded his eyestalks before passing on the orders. Paka figured he didn't like having orders given to him. Battleship commanders liked their autonomy. The Maki commander didn't much care for her ordering him to become a static defense, either. Too bad; the little idiot shouldn't have gotten shot to shit in the first place.

Finding herself on the other side of a Winged Hussars assault wasn't something she'd ever looked forward to. But without Alexis Cromwell in command, Paka wasn't afraid. She knew their tactics, and they didn't know she was commanding their adversaries.

As the engagement began to develop, she wondered how they'd known when the fleet was arriving. Sure, the ships which escaped Sol might well have realized the Mercenary Guild forces were coming for them and that they would know where New Warsaw was. But when the invasion forces began arriving, the Hussars were ready with their planned defenses, timed almost to the minute. *How had they known?*

"Enemy entering our threat box," the *Trushista* TacCom announced.

"You may begin firing," Paka said.

In the seconds before her ships began firing, the Hussars started maneuvering again. Too little and too late, but at least they started to *evade. Someone figured out I'm here,* Paka thought. *Probably Captain Stacy or Jormungd, though Kowalczy could have put the pieces together.* Paka decided to let the engagement play out the way she'd planned. Altering the order of battle wouldn't alter the outcome much.

Missiles launched from both sides in waves as dense as the stars. The Hussars were broken into groups, like petals on a flower, surrounding Paka's ships. The ships were facing outward. and oriented to not provide a side to any of the attackers, something they could only have done in time if they'd known what was coming. A dispersed attack made the most sense, by Hussars doctrine, so Paka was ready for it. Of course, if Alexis had been there, things might have played out quite differently.

The guild Maki cruisers concentrated fire on the former Maki *Seed*-class escort frigates fighting for the Hussars. Designed as anti-missile screening ships, the escort frigates lacked the shields to resist concentrated laser fire. The cruisers overwhelmed them, and all four escort frigates fell. All five of the Maki-standard *Bloom*-class frigates also fell, along with two of the Hussars' *Sword*-class, *Osman* and *Honjo Masamune*. In seconds, the Hussars lost more ships than in any engagement ever before.

Missiles tore into the Hussars' cruisers and battlecruisers. Bereft of screening ships, they were forced to use all their lasers, both offensive and defensive, for anti-missile fire. It wasn't as effective, and their offensive fire was seriously reduced. The cruiser *Omaha* was peppered with missiles. Her shields went down, and she was cut in half by a two-terawatt particle beam from a battleship.

The five *Egleesius*-class battlecruisers lashed out with their 40-terawatt particle beam spinal mounts. The guild ships used overlapping screens to protect the larger, more vulnerable battleships. When screens failed, they used their hulls. Seven enemy frigates, three cruisers, and a battlecruiser were disabled or destroyed.

Missile and laser fire also reached the *Egleesius* ships. Unable to maneuver as effectively, they suffered multiple hits but maintained their shields and kept the battleship's particle beams away from their hulls.

The more lightly shielded *Steed*-class battlecruisers didn't do as well. *Sleipnir* took a beam through her engine room and lost all power. It spun out of control, unable to fight. *Alicorn*, the flagship of the Winged Hussars, was shot through with a pair of two-terawatt particle beams. The last went through her CIC—based on the data provided by Paka—killing everyone inside.

Paka scowled as the Hussars swung away, regrouping and using their own overlapping shields. A pair of Bakulu battlecruisers managed to take out the two remaining *Sword*-class frigates, *Mercy* and *Bishop*, screening for the fleet. She'd wanted the *Eglessius* taken out and was worried where the newly acquired Hussars battleships might be. Still, the Hussars lost fourteen ships, and she'd only lost eleven. With forty-one ships still functional to her adversary's twenty-eight currently in the field, it looked bad for her former allies, and good for her.

"Initiate pursuit," she ordered.

"What about the damaged Maki battleship?" Glashpooka asked.

"It can fend for itself."

* * *

CIC, EMS *Shadowfax,* New Warsaw System

"Captain Jormungd on comms."

"Go ahead," Captain Stacy said, looking up from her small Tri-V status display built into the command chair.

"Captain, *Alicorn* took one through the CIC. They're under control and withdrawing to the asteroid field. But all command staff are dead, including Commander Kowalczy."

"Oh no," Evie said from across the bridge.

"You're the next most senior, Captain Stacy," Jormungd said. "You are in command of the Winged Hussars."

Elizabeth watched the fleet's movements for a moment; the enemy was forming up to pursue. Their attack on Paka's fleet had used a lot of fuel and didn't leave them with much surplus velocity. It had also consumed a lot of ships and lives, and none of the enemy battleships were gone.

"I'd like to offer my congratulations," Captain Teenge said from *Arion.* "But that doesn't seem right. What are your orders, Commander?"

She rubbed her face and examined the tactical map again. Sansar was sending what ships she had after the dreadnought, but it was precious little. Besides the dreadnought, there were dozens of cruisers and battlecruisers as screening vessels. The friendly forces only had a couple of cruisers. They didn't have a chance.

"Send a lasercom to Captain Fookoolu and Captain Chigasoolu," Elizabeth said. "Order them to do what they can to assist the assault on the dreadnought and its squadron. Maybe they can pull off a miracle." She turned to Evie. "Order the fleet to come around. Prepare for attack." *I'm coming for you, Paka.*

* * * * *

Chapter Twelve

Prime Base, New Warsaw System

Commander Aleksandra Kowalczy reached Prime Base's CIC. It wasn't where she'd expected it to be.

"Shouldn't this be in the center of the hub?" she asked Sergeant Hedrick.

"Of the station?" he asked, his voice coming over the CASPer's external speaker. She nodded. "You mean right where the enemy would expect to find it? Ma'am, this isn't some bad sci-fi thriller where the command center is on top of the ship with windows out to space."

Aleksandra felt her cheeks getting hot and she looked away. The CIC was not large; it was smaller than any she'd seen in the Winged Hussars warships. As she'd found out, it was off center from the stationary core of Prime Base, but it was still in zero gravity. Although it was nothing more than a ring of six seats with a central command and control position, it was still like a starship, despite its small size.

"This was set up in the old days." Aleksandra turned and saw Kleena of the Hussars' Geek Squad working on an open system panel. "It hasn't been used in decades."

"Why put it here, then?" Aleksandra asked.

"Back in the day they considered defending the system from here. When the Golden Horde was contracted to build defenses, they created a defensive command center in a large asteroid." He

189

shrugged as he took out a chip and inserted it into his slate. "Makes sense, not having it here." He removed the chip, then inserted it back from where he'd taken it. With a flicker, all the CIC's Tri-Vs came alive.

"Why are you here?" she asked him.

"Where am I supposed to go? Besides, Nemo wouldn't leave; I couldn't abandon him. I figured I could at least help here."

Aleksandra nodded, not understanding why Nemo wouldn't leave, but knew Kleena had nowhere else to go. Over the next few minutes, a tactical staff assembled in the tiny CIC. Aleksandra Kowalczy, who'd never commanded a ship, was suddenly in command of a massive space station with more than a thousand of her fellow Hussars and dependents.

"Full battlespace coming online," her TacCom announced.

"Prime Base sensors are tied into the system's sensor net," Kleena said, who'd elected to be her chief sensor operator.

"We stand ready to defend Prime Base," Major Kratlik said. Her multifaceted eyes reflected the lights from the various Tri-Vs. The MinSha marine commander had 96 troopers at her disposal, most either young or old. The majority of the most able marines were on the ships. Of the ones remaining, only 42 were in CASPers.

Aleksandra's other controllers verified their functions. Her assistant, Ensign Pavlovich, manned a computer station, ready to fill in however he could. As promised, he was now wearing light combat armor and a sidearm, the same as everyone else in the space. Only one thing was left. "I have command," she said, and Prime Base was placed on the battlespace as a combat unit.

"We have an update on the inbound forces," Kleena said.

The central Tri-V of the CIC wasn't as impressive as what a regular combat information center normally had. The original had been removed years ago, so Kleena had appropriated a trio of mid-level Tri-Vs and pressed them into service. An armada was centered on the display, composed of dozens of warships, everything from frigates to battlecruisers, with the simply titanic dreadnought at its center. It wasn't moving fast, because dreadnoughts *couldn't* move fast, but it was obviously heading toward Prime Base.

As Kleena mentioned, the armada had changed formation. A wedge of eleven ships had broken formation and were accelerating quickly toward Prime Base.

"Those three are troop transports," Kratlik said, pointing a jagged-edged arm at the Tri-V.

"The other eight are assault cruisers," her TacCom said. "It's a boarding party."

"How long to engagement range?" Aleksandra asked.

"One minute," TacCom replied.

"Fire on closing," she ordered. "Target the troop transports."

The seconds ticked by until the enemy was in range, then the TacCom launched his long-range weapons. Hundreds of missiles streaked toward the advancing enemy units. As soon as the missiles left the launchers, the enemy assault cruisers maneuvered in front of the troop transports to perform anti-missile laser screening.

"I don't think we can get through those screens," TacCom said. "I have a total of 20 gigawatts of laser fire at my—" He cut off as missiles began launching from the assault cruisers. "Make that 10 gigawatts of offensive laser weapons. I'm going to need the rest to hold off those inbound missiles."

"They were counting on that," Kratlik said.

Aleksandra could see the Hussars' naval asset board. There were almost no reserves left. The two battleships were being held back to preserve their effectiveness. Against a dreadnought and its dozens of escorts, the battleships would be nearly useless. "Commander, I have more than one hundred assault shuttles at my disposal. With your permission, I'd like to take this fight to them."

"Major, you only have forty-two CASPer equipped troopers, which isn't even one per shuttle."

"The CASPer drivers are staying behind, I intend to take the fifty-four light armored troopers on just five of the assault shuttles. The rest of the shuttles will be empty."

"Still not good odds," TacCom pointed out.

"If we can get to that dreadnought, it might work."

On the Tri-V, a force left the protection of the asteroid field. The datalink indicated it was heading for the dreadnought as well. Kratlik clicked quickly, a noise translated as laughter.

"You see, Commander, I am not the only one with this idea."

Aleksandra looked at the board and considered for a moment. "You have my permission," she said. "Give 'em hell, Major."

The MinSha nodded, then turned to Sergeant Hedrick. "Sergeant, protect the commander at all costs. Is that understood?"

"Nothing will touch her. You have my word, Major." The MinSha marine commander left, moving quickly on four chitinous legs.

"You think she has a chance of taking the dreadnought?" she asked Sergeant Hedrick.

"She has no intention of taking it," Hedrick said. "She'll ram her shuttle at maximum thrust against the troop transports. It's why she didn't take the CASPers. If they can't stop the transports, our tiny force won't be able to hold anyway."

Aleksandra watched the Tri-V until she saw the wave of assault shuttles race away from the docking bay, accelerating at over five Gs. The CIC was silent as the marines shot toward their fate.

* * *

CIC, BMS *Trushista*, New Warsaw System

"Admiral Paka, the Izlians are turning away," the SitCon reported.

"Turning away? What do you mean?" Paka said, hoping this wasn't another one of their foibles. The problem with exotics was that they were…exotic, which for them usually meant, "eccentric" or "idiosyncratic." Unfortunately, they didn't think like normal races—she wasn't sure if they really, actively thought much at all, sometimes—and they weren't the best race to have as allies, as they had shown by leaving the field for months after their worthless Admiral Omega had eaten an asteroid. How stupid did you have to be to sit there and watch a group of asteroids wreck your fleet? You could ask the Izlians—except all the ones who'd done it, including Admiral Omega, were dead now.

"They appear to be following the Humans' smaller craft out toward the asteroid field."

"Are they brain dead or just exceedingly stupid?" Paka asked, shaking her head.

"I'm not sure, Admiral," the SitCon replied, turning two eyestalks toward Paka questioningly.

"That was rhetorical," Paka replied with a scowl as she watched the Tri-V. She shook her head. The Izlians were definitely headed off after the *Avengers*…right into the asteroid field. "Get me a channel to Admiral Epsilon, please."

"You have it, Admiral."

"Admiral Epsilon, Admiral Paka. I notice your trajectory is no longer toward our intended target. Can you explain, please?"

"Yes, Admiral Paka. We will be back with you soon enough. Our doctrine indicates that we need to destroy all mobile forces prior to attacking stationary targets, so we are not attacked by the mobile forces while already in the midst of another engagement. We are following the Humans' bombers back to their carrier, so we can destroy that and any other forces accompanying it. Once this is completed, we will rejoin you for the assault on Prime Base."

"Admiral Epsilon, I must insist that you turn away from the asteroid field. It is a known Hussars trick to use asteroids as weapons. We've already lost several ships to them in this engagement. Turn away from the asteroid field and rejoin us *now* for the assault on Prime Base. After it has been captured, you can go hunt any additional ships down."

"I'm sorry, Admiral Paka, but you are making no sense. The bombers are out of weapons and I'm sure they're nearly out of fuel. Following them back to their ship, or ships, is the tactically sound thing to do. We can hit their ships while the bombers are rearming so we don't have to face them. If we let them go now, the next time we see them they will be refueled and rearmed and a much bigger threat to the fleet. Now is the time to attack their mother ships, and fleet tactical doctrine supports this strategy."

Paka took a deep breath, trying to control herself. She let it out slowly then transmitted, "Admiral Epsilon, I am well aware of your fleet doctrine, as are the rest—as are the Winged Hussars." She hoped no one caught her slip. After decades of being one, it was hard not to identify as a Hussar. "I can almost guarantee you that the Hussars are baiting you to go into the asteroid field, because they've set up an ambush there. Turn around, *now*, and rejoin the fleet!"

"I'm sorry," Epsilon replied, "but who are you to tell me what to do or not do? I have thousands of years of experience and a fleet tactical manual that has withstood the test of time. Do you? I do not believe so. Besides, I seriously doubt Prime Base is where you say it is. It does not make tactical sense; it is too out in the open. The object you are proceeding to is nothing more than a decoy, a distraction. It is probably loaded with defenses, and when we get there it will blow up in our faces. No, I am going to follow the bombers back to their real base—or their carriers, wherever they are headed— and destroy what we find there so we do not have to worry about them attacking us again. That is the real target, not some bait that you dangle in front of us."

"You fool!" Paka exclaimed, losing her patience. "You arrogant windbag! What do you think happened to your precious Admiral Omega? It was something similar that Cromwell used to kill him. I should know—I was there!"

"I see," Epsilon replied. "So you were part of the sneak attack to kill our beloved admiral, and you are now probably trying to use us as cannon fodder for your precious Mercenary Guild! Just because we aren't part of the guild doesn't mean we don't understand military tactics! We understand them very well—even better than you, as has been laid plain for all to see here today. And to besmirch the honor of Admiral Omega? Once we are done dealing with the Humans, we will be back to deal with you."

"Stupid fucking Izlians," Paka said with a growl as she disconnected the channel. "They build decent ships, but the Merc Guild would be better off without them."

"New forces entering the battle zone."

Paka turned at the SitCon's announcement and examined the CIC's huge Tri-V. A force of between twenty and thirty ships were accelerating toward the emergence point. For some reason the sensor ops couldn't lock down the exact number of ships, or their types. *More asteroids?*

"Why can't you firm up that data?" she demanded, and used her pinplants to highlight the inbound ships.

"I don't know," the Bakulu sensor ops burbled. Paka knew from extensive time dealing with the two long-standing Bakulu command officers on *Pegasus,* Glick and Chug, this particular Bakulu was disconcerted at the least. "I thought it was active jamming, but there is no indication of EM bleed, which would be indicative of it."

Like the indistinct number and class, the tracking information, displayed as lines leading out from the ships, kept swinging back and forth. The targets were going hundreds of kilometers per second. In order to deviate their courses that much, they would have to be pulling hundreds of gravities. Impossible for a manned craft.

"Launching sensor drones," the Captain Glashpooka announced, acting on his own initiative.

Paka nodded in agreement with the move. The sensor drones were capable of incredible speed and would provide steadily increasing data starting in only seconds. It was eleven seconds before the plots of the new ships cleared up even a small amount. *Entropy, what are those?* Paka wondered. She'd served with the Hussars for most of her adult life after Peepo helped get her inserted as a sleeper agent, and she'd never seen anything remotely like this.

"I have high confidence on their target," the sensor ops said. "It is the disabled Maki battleship." The Bakulu worked his sensors for several seconds. "Entropy, they are fast!"

"Can you get a visual from the drones?" Paka asked.

"Coming up now."

On the main Tri-V, images formed. At first Paka thought it was a distorted image, then she realized it was the ship which looked distorted. No ship she'd ever seen looked like them, more akin to a fish than a starship, though a fish with radial symmetry. She thought there were aspects which reminded her of the *Egleesius*. Their hulls seemed to scintillate in the starlight, and she decided it was a form of ECM built into the ship's very structure.

"Targets are no larger than corvettes, or light frigates," was the final report.

Paka shrugged. Combat ships as small as those were no real threat to a battleship, not even one that couldn't maneuver. Besides, with the amount of Gs those craft were pulling, they were certainly unmanned. *They're coming into the battleship's weapons range,* she noted.

Thanks to the sensor drones, she knew there were twenty-eight of the craft and in three sizes, though precise displacements were not forthcoming. Shortly before the battleship would have been able to begin firing, the twenty-eight tiny ships exploded into motion, splitting into seven groups of four, spinning around each other and the central point of their flightpath. Then the flightpath altered, and they came together, dancing like a kaleidoscope before again breaking into four groups of seven but spinning but in a different pattern.

The movement patterns seemed to have infinite variety and were almost hypnotic to watch. It took a full minute for Paka to realize she'd been staring, and the battleship hadn't fired. "Why haven't they engaged?" she asked.

"I don't know," Glashpooka replied. Then the dancing ships fired their own weapons.

Paka had been expecting missiles, or lasers. The crackling actinic light left no doubt in her mind—they were particle accelerator weapons.

"Estimated yield 40-100 gigawatts per beam," the TacCom said upon reviewing the data.

"So, between one and three terawatts total?" Paka asked. She watched as the ships fired over and over, timing the shots at three second intervals between pulses.

"That is accurate," the TacCom said. "They are firing using the same rotating patterns as their evasion. The effect on the battleship's shields is...energetic."

The Tri-V centered on the battleship as the smaller ships assailed its shields. Not having to use power to maneuver, because its engines were wrecked, the battleship could apply most of its energy to tactical systems. Particle accelerators were the most effective weapon against a ship's shields, able to impart vast amounts of energy into them until their capacitors overloaded. A ship compensated by either being multiphasic and able to move them as they were depleted or roll the ship to bring new shields to bear. The new ships' attack made both tactics useless by chewing at the shields like a chainsaw.

The battleship unloaded with everything it had at the dancing and spinning little ships. It was like hitting a ghost. Missiles flashed away in waves, then the battleship's shields failed, and the particle beams tore into it, carving through armor and exploding magazines. It was over in less than a few heartbeats.

"Entropy," one of the Bakulu CIC officers cursed. Tactical showed one of the enemy ships was destroyed, though Paka thought it might have been more of an accident than a successful shot.

"They're changing course," TacCom said. "The ships are coming for us."

Paka examined the Tri-V and scowled. At the other end of their engagement zone, the surviving Winged Hussars ships were lining up for what would be their final attack. The new ships might be a threat to a single disabled battleship, but Paka had two perfectly operational battleships and thirty-nine screening ships; she wasn't nearly as vulnerable as the stupid Maki had been.

"Allocate a squadron of escort ships to intercept the small, unusual ships," she ordered. "Prepare to destroy the inbound Hussars."

* * *

Ferret One, Asteroid Defense Base Kilo, New Warsaw

"*Power spike!*" Skald exclaimed as a warning illuminated on his system. "More! Multiple power spikes all around us!"

"Power spikes as in not the remaining *Avengers*?" They were down to a total of sixteen, Thorb knew. He'd tried to stay out of range, yet close enough to the Izlian ships that they continued to follow, but two more of the bombers had been picked off by the chase armament on the Izlian ships. "Where are they coming from?"

"They're coming from all over!"

"What do you mean?" Thorb asked, his head snapping back and forth. He had so few bombers left, and each was precious. He didn't want to lose any more to a sneak attack, or...whatever this was. Then he saw the flare—no, multiple flares—from an asteroid as they raced past it in close proximity.

"It looks like there's something on the asteroids," Skald said. "There are at least twenty separate power sources!"

"It *is* the asteroids," Thorb agreed. He watched on the battlespace Tri-V as the gap he had just flown through closed behind him. It had been big enough for a battleship to fly through; now, a frigate wouldn't have been able to squeeze through.

"The asteroids—they're moving!" Skald said, as the giant hunks of rock began accelerating back toward the ships following them.

Thorb gave a sad smile. As he watched, the asteroids picked up speed. "I think that's our sign," he said as the adrenaline of being chased drained from his body. "Let's go home."

* * *

IMS *Fresha Two Seven*, New Warsaw System

"Admiral, I have ship engines lighting off in the asteroid field in front of us!"

Admiral Epsilon pulsed in self-satisfaction. "I told the stupid Veetanho the fleet was out here," he said. "What is it? What do we get to destroy?"

"I am not sure," the sensor operator replied. "There was nothing, and now there are twenty-one ships heading toward us. They appear to be cruiser class, but I am having a hard time identifying them. I don't know what kinds of shields or screens they have, but it is like nothing I have seen before."

"The screening frigates are coming within range," Epsilon said, looking at the Tri-V. "Tell them to fire!"

The SitCon gave the order, then turned to face Epsilon. "They are firing, sir, but they say their weapons are having no effect. They are missing more often than they're hitting, and even when they hit, nothing happens. They can visually see flashes of light on the targets, so they know they are hitting something, but it's not having any effect."

"The incoming ships are continuing to accelerate toward us," the sensor operator reported. "They are now accelerating at just over twenty gravities…now thirty gravities, and still accelerating. They will be within range of the main body shortly."

"Admiral," the SitCon said, "the frigates are concerned that their weapons aren't having any effect, and that the Humans appear to be on a collision course with them."

Epsilon waved a tentacle at the SitCon in derision. "Tell them to keep firing. Their weapons will burn through the shields eventually. Besides, it is important to know your enemies. The Humans value their lives, no matter how unworthy they are, and they would not ram our ships. They are obviously planning close aboard passes to limit the amount of damage they take getting past our screen. They want to get to our battleships with their ships as intact as possible."

The icons for several of the frigates winked out, and Epsilon floated away from the Tri-V in concern. The data didn't make sense. The Humans didn't use ramming attacks, but that was the only possibility, based on the evidence. Something had smashed through the

three frigates, destroying them utterly. *What was it that Paka had said?*
The Hussars used asteroids to attack?

"Skew turn!" Epsilon ordered. "Reverse course! Get us out of
the asteroid field immediately!"

* * * * *

Chapter Thirteen

CIC, New Warsaw Defense Command, New Warsaw

"That's going to leave a mark," Nigel said as the first three asteroids collided with the screening frigates of the Izlian fleet. "Lasers just don't work very well on nickel-iron asteroids, now do they?" The frigates had been primarily armed with lasers and must not have had many missile launchers. They had only fired a few missiles; not enough to make a difference.

"Yeah," Sansar said with her first smile of the day. "That kind of damage won't buff out."

"Ma'am!" the SitCon called. "It looks like the Izlians are waving off the chase. They have all gone into skew turns."

"Very well," Sansar said with a nod. "This is our only chance. Continue the attack. Target two asteroids on each of the battleships and one for as many of the cruisers as we have asteroids." One of the more recently added system defenses, Alexis Cromwell had modified their contract to add a series of asteroid kinetic impact devices to the area around the emergence area, based on the results of a battle she'd had. Although the Horde had started on them, and had gotten the motors and shield generators rigged to twenty-six of the asteroids, only five had actually been emplaced. The other twenty-one hadn't been towed to their intended positions; they were still in the asteroid field and hadn't been close enough to use during the battle...until the Izlians had gotten too close.

Now, however, there was no escape. Powered by micro-drone fusion engines, the asteroids were able to accelerate at over 90 gravities for several minutes—far faster than what the manned ships could. Once a ship wandered too close—like the Izlian fleet had—there was almost no escape.

"Two minutes to impact on the first battleship," the sensor operator noted.

"Ah, Colonel Enkh?" one of the comms techs asked. "I think the Izlians are trying to contact us?"

"They are?" Sansar asked with another smile. "I wonder what that could be about?"

"They don't want you to break their shiny toys?" Nigel asked in return.

"Open a channel to them," Sansar said. After a second, the comms tech nodded; Sansar was online.

"Admiral commanding the Izlian fleet, this is New Warsaw Defense Command, Colonel Sansar Enkh commanding. What can I do for you?"

"We surrender!" a strange, obviously synthetic voice said. "This is Admiral Epsilon. We surrender! Do not hit us with your asteroids! We surrender!"

"Want me to call them off?" the SitCon asked.

Sansar sighed. She'd really been looking forward to destroying the battleships, but at this point, it would have been wasteful, especially with the dreadnought still heading to Prime Base. She needed to focus on that.

"Yes," Sansar said. "Divert the asteroids." Sansar examined the system with its myriad engagement zones and found a spot deep in the asteroid field. She switched back to the comm. "Admiral Epsilon, we will accept your surrender. I am transmitting coordinates to you. Divert to those coordinates and power down all defenses. We will send someone over to formally take your surrender when we are able." She closed the connection.

"When do you suppose that will be?"

"No idea," Sansar replied, "and not my focus anymore." She looked at the Tri-V, which showed the dreadnought getting ever closer to the largest icon on the display. "How much time until the dreadnought reaches Prime Base?

"The dreadnought will arrive in the area of Prime Base in two hours," a sensor tech noted.

"Two hours?" Nigel asked. "We still have two hours to catch them?" Sansar turned as he nodded, obviously making up his mind. "That's still time to run them down. Okay…I've got this." He turned to leave.

"Where are you going?" Sansar asked. "You can't take on that dreadnought with your merc cruiser. *You'll be slaughtered!* You have absolutely zero chance! Don't throw your life away! If nothing else, think about your son!"

"I'm not going to duel with the dreadnought, I'm going to board it and take it over from the inside. It's our only chance at this point. We just don't have anything that can take that beast on."

"You've got to be kidding!" Sansar exclaimed. "A ship that big has to be *filled* with marines. Even if you *could* get inside its defenses, you'd still be vastly outnumbered."

"Be that as it may, my honor will not allow me to stand by while the Merc Guild savages Prime Base. It. Will. Not. I don't know whether or not I will be successful; all I know is I have to try."

Sansar nodded once, slowly. She understood. It was all she could do to remain at the command center while the battle raged all around her. She had been raised as a fighter, born and trained to lead troops in battle, and she wanted nothing more than to fight. Still, someone had to coordinate the defenses, and there was no one better left to run them than the person who had designed them, especially since Alexis—who had co-designed them, and who she'd always expected to be in command—was no longer with them.

"I know you do," she finally said in a small voice, fighting back the tears. She knew, with all her heart, that she would never see him again. "Blue Sky watch over you."

"You're not going alone," Walker said, vacating the SitCon position. He turned to Sansar. "Ma'am, the fight is almost done here, and you don't need me, but it looks like Colonel Shirazi surely does. I owe him, ma'am, and he's going to need the assistance. Let me take the *War Pony*, since it's got our boarding pods, and go with him. I heard what you said—he's going to need every bit of help he can get. Even just getting aboard will be difficult, but maybe we can overload their defenses if we send enough assault pods. Thorb's squadron is landing here. Maybe I can get them to support the attack. Regardless, we can't let the dreadnought get to Prime Base. We've got to do everything we can to stop it. *Ma'am, we've got to try!*"

The loss hit Sansar like a blow to the gut. Her XO and one of her closest friends were both going off to die together, in some insane effort to stop something that couldn't be stopped. She didn't trust herself to talk; she merely nodded her head. "Go," she finally said as she fought back the tears welling in her eyes.

Walker saluted and Nigel gave her a sad smile. "Tell my boy I loved him, even if I didn't know him. I do this for him." He spun and strode off toward the docking bay, his magnetic boots clicking purposefully, and Walker had to hurry to catch up.

* * *

CIC, New Warsaw Defense Command, New Warsaw

"Son?" Walker asked, coming alongside him. "I didn't know you had a son."

"I didn't either."

The silence went on for a few seconds, and then Nigel said, "Sansar had a dream that Alexis wasn't dead. She said she saw Alexis on the bridge of the *Pegasus,* bouncing our son on her knee."

"But you weren't there?"

Nigel's voice, when he finally spoke, was flat. "No."

Not sure how to answer that, Walker filled his time calling in all the members of the Horde who were available for the assault. Several platoons' worth of troops met him at the entrance to the docking bay. "What's up?" Walker asked. "I said to meet me at the shuttle."

"Can't go in yet, sir," Corporal Nicholas Melton replied. "Some of the *Avenger* squadrons are landing. Apparently, they got hit pretty hard."

"Do you know which ones?"

"I think they said the Ferrets and Badgers," Corporal Jerome Everett said. "May have been more."

"Damn," Walker muttered.

"What's wrong, sir?" Melton asked.

"I know the CO of the Ferrets," Walker replied. "Hard luck squadron. They lost all but one in the battle for Earth."

"Damn, that sucks," Staff Sergeant Yvonne Jacobs said. Everyone else nodded in sympathy; they'd been around long enough to see it happen before. That still didn't make it any better.

"Okay, so here's the deal," Walker said, mentally shaking it off. "The Merc Guild has a dreadnought, and, so far, nothing we've thrown at it has been able to stop it. Despite our best efforts, it's going to reach Prime Base if we don't stop it. What it will do there...I don't know, but they've given every indication so far that they don't intend to spare anyone in this system."

"That's fucked up, sir," Corporal Matt Horan said. "There are still women and children aboard it."

"Yes, Corporal, there are," Walker said with a nod. "Colonel Shirazi here is going to take his cruiser and attempt to board the dreadnought, but he's going to need help, both getting onto the ship and then capturing it from the Merc Guild. I told him I would help, as he's saved the Horde on a number of occasions; it's time for us to pay him back. We—Colonel Shirazi and I—expect the dreadnought to be heavily defended, but we cannot—we *will* not—allow it to get to Prime Base. We will *not* allow them to kill our women and children. Now, this isn't something that the Horde normally does—we hold what you've got, we don't normally take it away from someone else—however, we've all trained to this mission before, even if it was all the way back in cadre. Due to the nature of the mission, though, I won't take anyone who's not a volunteer. If you don't want in on this, you are clear to go back to whatever you were doing with no stigma of not being part of it.

"Anyone want out?"

The men and women looked at each other with fear in their eyes, and Walker knew it could go either way. The first person to talk—for good or ill—would probably sway everyone. The Horde members *wanted* to help…but the odds were long that any of them would even survive to make it *to* the dreadnought, much less successfully complete their mission.

"Hell, sir," Corporal Melton said, "my wife's on the station. I don't want those rat bastards getting her. I'm in."

"Can't let you do it by yourself," Corporal Everett said. "If you got killed, I'd have to spend the rest of eternity with you never letting me live it down. I'm in."

"Me, too," Corporal Eric Chase added from the back of the group. "It's time to show them who's boss." Everyone else began nodding. "What's the plan, sir?"

"We hit them with everything we've got and kill anything that isn't Human. We don't stop until the CIC and engineering are in our hands."

"I would ask you to not kill the Lumar I am bringing along," Nigel said with a smile. "They are good troops and have proven to be allies in our fight against the Merc Guild. They may not be the smartest troops, but they are some of the most loyal, which is something you can't say for most of the aliens." The smile fled from his face as he added, "Speaking of which, if you see any Veetanho and can kneecap them, I'd love to get my hands on Paka, who used to be the second in command of the Winged Hussars. In case you haven't heard, she shot Colonel Cromwell in the back. I know she has to be part of this force, somewhere, and I'm betting she's on the dreadnought. If you can take her alive, I'd like to have…a talk…with her."

Walker suppressed a shudder; that "talk" would be far from pleasant. Or survivable, if he had to guess. Still, it was nothing more than Paka deserved when it came right down to it.

The light to the bay went green, and the door unlocked. "All right, let's go," Walker said and led them into the shuttle bay. He started toward the shuttle, but then saw several figures walking toward the door he'd just come through. "Mount up," he said, pointing to their shuttle. "I'll be right there."

He scanned the bay and counted; only six of the squadron's twelve bombers were present. The Ferrets had gotten hammered...again. Of the 60 bombers the SalSha had started with, he could only see sixteen.

Thorb saw him waiting and came over to him. "We won," he said, his voice lifeless, and his fur matted. His bombardier trudged alongside him, head down. "We lost almost three quarters of the SalSha crews, including six more of my own crews who went into the light, but the Merc Guild assault has been repulsed." He didn't stop to talk, but shambled past, his head down.

Walker opened his mouth, but then closed it again as he watched the small alien, who'd become his friend. Thorb's shoulders were slumped, and Walker could tell he was spent, physically and emotionally. It didn't take a psychologist to tell him that all the SalSha were heavily in the throes of PTSD—all he needed to do was look at them as they shuffled out of the landing bay, heads bowed. He had intended to ask for Thorb's help reaching the dreadnought's defenses, but found he didn't have the heart. The creatures—always full of life and having fun—looked like they'd reach the end. They'd given all they could.

Fine. Between the Asbaran Solutions forces and the Horde forces under his command, they'd make do.

Walker turned and hurried to the shuttle.

* * *

CIC, New Warsaw Defense Command, New Warsaw

Thorb entered the command center but was too tired—too emotionally spent—to be impressed with all of the displays. Sansar turned toward him as the door opened, and one of her hands went to her mouth in dismay. He was too tired to care about that. All he could feel was the soul-crushing loss of the 90 SalSha who'd gone into the light. Another battle like the one they'd just fought, and there wouldn't be any more SalSha outside their home planet—they'd all be dead.

He sighed and then shuffled over to Sansar to make his report. Drawing up stiffly, he saluted. "Major Thorb, reporting as ordered."

"Thank you for coming," Sansar said. She started to say something, then thought better of it and said instead, "Thank you also for all of your races' contributions today. I am greatly sorry for your losses."

"Some days, the grahp fights back," Thorb said with a shrug. "At least we won."

"Well, not yet, we haven't," Sansar said.

"What?" Thorb asked, looking up in surprise. "We destroyed the last battleship in the emergence area. Didn't the other supporting ships there surrender?"

"They did...but there was one that got away. The Merc Guild's dreadnought broke free from the emergence zone and is headed toward Prime Base. Didn't you pass Walker on the way here? He is assisting Colonel Shirazi. They are going to try to board the dreadnought. It is a huge gamble, but we've got nothing left which can stop it. He was going to ask you to help."

"He didn't...he didn't say anything to me..." Thorb said, not understanding why his friend hadn't mentioned it. "I don't know why."

A small sad smile crossed Sansar's face. "I'm going to go out on a limb and say it's because you don't look like you have anything left to give. I suspect he took one look at you—and the losses you took today—and decided the SalSha race had done its part. That he couldn't ask for anything else from you."

"But...but...he can't attack a dreadnought by himself. That's..." Thorb searched for the right word, but only one came to mind. "That's stupid."

"Well, it's been attacked a couple of times, and I guess he's hoping that its defenses have been beaten down some so they can find a way through them, or at least give the defenders so many targets to shoot at that at least some of them get through. He didn't confide his plan to me—probably because he knew I would order him to stand down."

"Why did he go then, if he knew there was so little chance of success?"

The sad smile returned to Sansar's face. "Humans are funny that way, sometimes. We don't want to give up when there's a chance we can still pull victory from the jaws of defeat. It doesn't even have to be a *big* chance...sometimes it's just the slimmest glimmer of hope. I think the worst part—for both Colonel Shirazi and Lieutenant Colonel Walker—was that they couldn't stand around and watch the destruction of Prime Base—with all of its women and children onboard—and not do anything to try to stop it. I don't think they would have been able to look themselves in the mirror tomorrow morning if they had. They'd rather go down fighting, knowing they'd done their best, rather than give in."

"But I could have helped them. I could have given them a better chance of success!" Thorb looked around the command center for the first time and saw all the Humans who were still fighting, still doing their best, to bring the battle to a successful conclusion. The grahp was still outside their caves, it had not been destroyed as he'd initially thought, and he had taken himself out of the fight; he wasn't doing his part.

"You still can, you know," Sansar said.

"What?" Thorb asked, spinning back toward her. "What can I do?"

"You can still help them. They are only now getting underway. You can pull a whole lot more Gs than they can. There's still time to get back to your bombers, get them armed, and get to the dreadnought ahead of them."

Thorb nodded. "I will not allow my friend to go into the light; not without me at his side." He took two steps toward the door, then turned and saluted. "Sorry, Colonel, I have to go." He dropped the salute and raced through the door.

"Hey, Skald," he commed as he ran toward the hangar. "Looks like you're going to get your chance to see the dreadnought after all."

* * * * *

Chapter Fourteen

"Concentrate main guns on the lead battleship," Elizabeth yelled. The CIC was chaos as everyone tried to deal with more events than they had attention to give to them. A hundred damage reports blared for attention—missile magazine #2 had feed problems, the forward ventral shield generator was fluctuating dangerously, and a main power relay was out, among others. Among the many messages on Elizabeth's console was a low priority status report from the sickbay. She hadn't noticed it.

"Comms are spotty with the other *Egleesius*," said Evie. She was sitting in for comms and SitCon, both of whom had been injured during the last attack only five minutes ago. They hadn't lost any more ships, but only because they were sparring from a longer range. Minus screening vessels, the enemy battleships and missile cruisers were scoring hits. "It's making it hard to coordinate!"

"The Lightships are harassing the enemy fleet, but are unable to get through their screen," TacCom said. "They've lost three total."

When the new ships appeared and destroyed the damaged Maki battleship, they'd looked like dancing light on water the way they maneuvered. "Lightships" had stuck. Remembering the briefing back on Prime Base, Elizabeth was sure they were Dusman ships. Impressive, sure. Sort of. She'd rather they had battleships or their own dreadnought.

"We're going to have to get in closer," Elizabeth said. Her surviving command crew looked at her with somber expressions. "If we can punch through the screens…"

"Maneuvering closer," helm said.

The *Egleesius'* particle accelerator spinal mounts possessed slightly better range, firepower, and flexibility than the ones on the battleships. Even though the battleships had more of them, they were located in bays scattered all around the ships' spherical superstructure. Both of them also rotated steadily, allowing their shields to regenerate between attacks.

A wave of missiles lashed out at them. Their four surviving former Maki light cruisers and one heavy cruiser, *Stonewall Jackson*, all screened for the jockeying *Egleesius*. Dozens of missiles made it through the cruisers' laser defenses. The light cruiser *Langur* disappeared in the nuclear fire, and *Tamarin* was battered and fell out of formation, unresponsive. *Stonewall Jackson* soaked up unbelievable amounts of fire and kept going.

"There!" Evie yelled as the CIC's Tri-V showed a window.

"I see it," Elizabeth said. "All *Egleesius*, on my mark…*FIRE!*"

The ancient battlecruisers lashed out with their 40-terawatt spinal mounts. An enemy battlecruiser side-slipped directly into the line of fire and was obliterated. Two of the five powerful beams found their mark. The battleship they'd targeted lost a shield and took damage, though not much.

"Son of a bitch!" Evie yelled. Elizabeth nodded.

Return fire flashed back as a dozen five-terawatt particle beams fired from the battleships' bays. Captain Dan Corder of *Stonewall Jackson* took a page out of the enemy battlecruiser's book and moved his ship directly into the line of fire. He suffered a similar fate.

With most of their remaining screen gone, the *Egleesius* tried to maneuver for another attack. Particle beams ripped through *Arion*, *Phaeton*, and *Pegasus*. *Pegasus* and *Phaeton* both had their CICs destroyed; *Arion*'s computer deck was ripped apart.

"No," Elizabeth gasped. *This can't be how it ends.* Another particle beam hit *Shadowfax*. The energized particles sliced one deck above her CIC, cutting away controls and overloading system. Half the panels went dead in the CIC, and the armored door slid open for no obvious reason.

Shadowfax listed badly from uncontrolled attitude jet inputs. Elizabeth was thrown sideways in her chair; her head hit a support, and she saw stars.

"*Shadowfax*, what's your status?"

Elizabeth recognized the voice of Captain Drizz of *Nuckelavee*. She tried to respond, but her mouth was full of cotton. She managed to focus on the Tri-V, which, somehow, was still functioning. The enemy battleships were rotating to bring more particle beams to bear. She was about to die.

Another ship slid into screening position. It was the newest *Steed*-class, *Sphinx*, which had been completed while they were fighting at Earth. It only had a skeleton crew and had been kept in the middle of the formation to provide fire support.

"*You fool,*" she thought, as a half dozen five-terawatt particle beams lanced out at *Sphinx*. All six ricocheted off.

* * *

CIC, EMS *Sphinx*, New Warsaw System

"It fucking worked!" the TacCom yelled, pumping his fist. Overload alarms blared as two more particle beams rebounded from her shields.

"Good job," Captain Jameson said to his shield tech. The man had been working nonstop since the fleet first engaged in combat to get the new systems working with the rest of the ship's shields. When Jameson ordered her into the line of fire, nobody knew if it would work.

"Nothing like a good old-fashioned live-fire test," the tech laughed. "Deflectors. Who'd have thunk it?"

"Dr. Sato, apparently," Jameson said.

"Power drain is critical," the engineer yelled.

"Bring #3 to emergency power," Jameson ordered. "Everything to deflectors and maneuvering." He looked up at the two massive battleships which seemed confused by their inability to destroy the relatively tiny battlecruiser. "Let's see what these things can do."

* * *

CIC, BMS *Trushista*, New Warsaw System

Paka felt a tiny twinge when her battleship burned a meter-wide hole through the CIC on *Pegasus*. Only a tiny one. Her future was almost assured; only a few more distasteful acts were needed. She tried not to remember how she'd been welcomed as a Hussar and treated like family. The trust Alexis had bestowed upon her. She washed it away remembering her race's ways; trust was for the weak. You watched your back, because nobody else would.

"Clear our screening ships," Paka ordered. "Let's finish this."

The battlecruisers who'd been screening moved aside, and the battleships fired again. The Hussars' lone ancient heavy cruiser they'd salvaged from 2nd level hyperspace moved into the way of the withering fire and died. There was nothing left to protect the surviving *Egleesius*. One more volley.

Then a *Steed*-class battlecruiser moved into the line of fire, blocking their shot at *Shadowfax*, which Paka had believed to be commanding the fleet after *Alicorn* was destroyed. It took her a second to recognize the ship. *Sphinx*, the newest *Steed*, which Paka hadn't known was operational. When she used her pinplants to review the battle at high speed, she saw *Sphinx* had stayed back and avoided the worst of the fight.

"A skeleton crew then," she said, shrugging. "Destroy it."

Six 5-terawatt particle beams might have been overkill, sure. But they were lined up on *Shadowfax*, so one or two would destroy the new *Steed*, and the rest would pass on to *Shadowfax*. The weapons fired…and bounced off.

"What did I just see?" she demanded.

"I don't know," the TacCom admitted, looking back at her with a single eyestalk.

"Some strange fluke?" Captain Glashpooka asked.

"Hit it again!" Paka yelled.

This time ten particle beams lashed out…*and they all bounced off!*

"Coordinate *all ships' weapons* on that battlecruiser," Paka ordered. Fear made the hair on her muzzle stand up and her whiskers flick. First the strange ships, now this? "Destroy it!"

The captain made the order, and the fleet fired.

CIC, EMS *Shadowfax*, New Warsaw System

Elizabeth felt an injector jammed into her arm and cried out as medical nanites flooded her body with fire. Clarity returned a few seconds later. Not even bothering to thank whoever did it, she pushed the arm aside and leaned forward in her command chair, her brain racing to clear her tactical view of the battle. She saw *Sphinx* with dozens of high energy weapons beams bouncing off her shields like an old sci-fi movie, and she wondered if she had brain damage.

"*Sphinx* says it's a system Dr. Sato installed before he disappeared," Evie told her.

Elizabeth noted dimly that her XO had been the one to give her a nanite jolt. She struggled to understand how a ship could just deflect weapons' fire with some sort of gimmick the loony scientist installed. Then she saw her XO look up, eyes wide in surprise. Elizabeth turned and saw Patrick floating in the open CIC hatchway.

She was excited to see him up, then she saw his body language and black expression. "Patrick? You okay?"

He didn't look at her, instead he reached out with both hands and touched the CIC bulkhead. "*I mUst acT!*" he said in an ethereal voice that she felt in the core of her being. His eyes began to glow, and sparks jumped from his fingertips.

The Tri-V drew her attention away from him as she felt the ship maneuver. Suddenly the five *Egleesius*, even the ones critically damaged, were all moving in perfect coordination. The CIC bridge lights dimmed.

"I've lost helm!"

"Weapons are off-line."

"The spinal mount is overloading!" Evie said.

Elizabeth looked from Patrick to the Tri-V, her mouth beginning to form a question. All five *Egleesius* fired as one.

* * *

CIC, BMS *Trushista,* New Warsaw System

"All beam weapons are ineffective," TacCom announced.

"Then use missiles, you idiot!" Paka all but screamed.

"Ready a missile barrage," Captain Glashpooka ordered, rasping his radula in distaste at his commander's public show of emotion.

"Standby," the TacCom said.

"The enemy battlecruisers," SitCon said, and the five *Egleesius* were immediately the center of the Tri-V focus.

Paka gawked as the five ships changed bearing in perfectly synchronized motion. They reminded her of the Kalta birds native to the Veetanho home world. Only the Kalta birds didn't fire 40-terawatt particle accelerator spinal mounts in equally perfect precision. She just had time to open her mouth to speak a warning when the beams struck.

The other battleship was hit precisely in its main engineering section. The *Egleesius* ships not only fired in precision, their angles adjusted while firing, delivering all 200-terawatts of energy to the same point. Shields failed in a split second, and the beams cut through the battleship's armor and into its engineering section. As the beams penetrated, the *Egleesius* ships performed a tiny spin, widening the damage to ravage the battleship's engineering section.

Eight of the battleship's twelve fusion reactors were breached, filling the engine rooms with star-hot plasma, setting off scores of rampaging secondary explosions. The battleship ruptured like an overripe melon.

"Defensive screen!" Paka ordered, and the screening cruisers and battlecruisers moved to intercept positions, changing focus from the untouchable battlecruiser to the strangely acting *Egleesius*, all of which accelerated and began maneuvering in excess of 10 Gs, making them much more difficult targets.

The swarms of missiles intended for *Sphinx* were instead launched against the *Egleesius* ships, which swept them from space with unbelievable accuracy. Nearly every laser fired by the *Egleesius* ships hit a missile, and all were destroyed before they could get to the ships. Paka had never seen such a display of accuracy.

"Ghost!" she hissed. The damned AI was controlling all five *Egleesius* at once! *I should have thought of that,* she realized in horror, but the damned AI hadn't done it in the previous battles. With Alexis out of the game, she'd been counting on the AI's inability to affect the battle. She'd never completely understood how it worked, anyway. When it hadn't produced any magic as dozens of the Hussars' ships died, she'd ceased worrying about it. It was a mistake.

"Withdraw behind the screen," she ordered.

"Our screen will have to stand in the face of their fire," Glashpooka said.

"Do it," Paka said.

Glashpooka stared at her with all three eyes.

"Do it, or I will relieve you on the spot!"

ALABASTER NOON | 223

Many eyes in the CIC turned to regard their captain, and the Veetanho placed in charge of their ship. A moment passed before Glashpooka passed along the order.

"Prepare for high-G maneuvers," the battleship's automated system announced as the ship's engines poured power into the void. The escort ships moved to screen the battleship, and the five *Egleesius* killed them in ones and twos.

"We'll join up with the dreadnought's squadron," Paka said to herself, not aware the Bakulu were listening. "The entropy-cursed AI can't defeat the dreadnought, even *with* five *Egleesius*."

* * *

CIC, EMS *Shadowfax*, New Warsaw System

"We have injuries all over the ship!" Evie said with a groan as she fought the effects of the intermittently horrendous gravity. Every tactically important system on *Shadowfax* was no longer under their control; the announcement to warn the crew about coming maneuvers had to be passed via the damage control teams. Some sections hadn't gotten it in time; others were simply unable to resist 10 Gs of force.

"Have medical do what they can," Elizabeth said helplessly. Her seat was one of the most padded in the CIC, and she was still in hell. She carefully turned her head and saw her boyfriend, only she was sure it wasn't him anymore. Shortly after he'd shown up and started talking like a horror film—glowing eyes and all—robots had appeared out of the walls and created a support framework for him that responded to each maneuver to minimize the effects on him.

All the captains in the Winged Hussars had heard of the Ghost which haunted *Pegasus*. Some even spread rumors of how Alexis was friends with it. Elizabeth never believed in her wildest dreams that Ghost was real, though, or that some kind of poltergeist could possess people. *Patrick, why you?* she wondered.

"Status on *Sphinx*?" she asked her XO.

"Captain Jameson reports no damage from enemy fire, only overloaded power systems. He's still fully operational."

Shadowfax maneuvered so hard to the side Elizabeth felt ribs pop. She cried out and held onto her couch arms so tight she felt her fingernails crack. *He's going to kill us trying to save us,* she thought.

"The enemy battleship is disengaging," TacCom said. "The *Egleesius* are destroying the screening ships wholesale."

Elizabeth could see her TacCom coughing up blood. The med tech who had reached the CIC was lying on the floor, possibly dead herself. She saw another wave of missiles from the enemy escorts. Her ship and the other *Egleesius* swatted them from the black with ease. One laser, one missile destroyed. *What was a space battle like in these ships' heyday?* she wondered.

She watched her command station's little Tri-V; her head was G-locked in place, and she couldn't see the main one. On the display, the twenty-odd Dusman ships darted around the battleship, joining in the slaughter of the enemy's screening ships.

Elizabeth might have blacked out for a minute because she realized she was floating in zero G, and a med tech was attaching a medical scanner to her arm. "What happened?" she asked, gasping. Every breath felt like there was a knife sliding between her ribs.

"We're adrift," the med tech said. "The DC teams are working on it, but nothing is working right now."

"Did we get hit?" Elizabeth asked.

"No," Evie said, floating into view. The right side of her XO's face was a nasty, bloody bruise, and blood matted her hair. "The enemy screen is destroyed, and the battleship is running to join the dreadnought's squadron. As soon as it moved away, *he* relinquished control of the ship's main system." Evie nodded to where Patrick still floated, but the bots were gone.

His eyes glowed dimly, and static discharges leaped from his fingertips where they floated near the CIC wall.

"Why don't we have control?" she asked.

"The computer's OS has been completely overwritten. We're trying to rig a workaround, but we have nearly fifty percent casualties."

Elizabeth noted the majority of her command crew was incapacitated. Her DCC officer, Ensign Todd Stone, who'd only come aboard during the attack on Earth, was dead. A med tech had wrapped a blanket over his head and torso, and it was stained crimson.

"Do you know what Patr…do you know what *he's* still controlling?" Elizabeth asked, looking at what had once been her boyfriend.

"We have no control over the high-gain comms. All five *Egleesius* are transiting toward Prime Base."

"But not *to* Prime Base?"

"No," Tesk'l, her comms officer said. The Aposo had a med tech working on her. Both arms were obviously broken, with one an ugly compound break. She winced continuously as she continued to do her duty using her pinplants. "It looks to me like the target is either the shipyard, or the parking zone."

"But no warships or combat assets are there," Evie said.

Elizabeth's eyes got wide. "No conventional assets." She gestured to Tesk'l. "I know you're hurt, but can you focus a telescope there? If they're working."

"Sure," Tesk'l said, her fur glistening from sweat. She closed her eyes, and the big Tri-V changed to show a swinging view. It stabilized and began to zoom in quickly, making Elizabeth dizzy. "Coming up in a second."

The shipyards with their manufactories came into view, as did a series of astcroids the Hussars used as moorings for ships under construction or needing repairs. Several also served as temporary warehouses for construction stores. Elizabeth knew what had been there. Seven incomplete warships in various stages of construction, the *Hippogriff*—which was being repaired after an earlier action—and one more ship.

"*Hippogriff* is missing," Evie noted.

Elizabeth nodded, then pointed. "Tesk'l, can you focus on grid 5-A?" The view moved and zoomed a little more. A ship which looked a lot like an *Egleesius* was under power, its fusion torches burning as it moved away from the mooring area.

"Is that what I think it is?" Evie asked.

"Yes," Elizabeth said. "It's the *Keesius*. The other one almost destroyed Capital Planet."

On the Tri-V, the doomsday ship continued to accelerate.

* * * * *

Chapter Fifteen

CIC, EMS *Revenge*, New Warsaw System

"They didn't destroy the dreadnought," Captain Gallagher noted, "but at least they damaged it some."

Nigel raised an eyebrow at the ship's captain. "Will it be enough?"

Gallagher started to shake his head but stopped. "I don't know," he said after a second. "The ship's damaged, but it looks like the crew—and the ship—has still got plenty of fight in them. I'll get you as close as I can...but it's got a lot of active defenses on it you're going to have to get through."

"Do what you can," Nigel said with a shrug. "That's all I can ask of you." He looked at the Tri-V a moment. "Looks like the *War Pony*'s at least holding up with us."

"Aye, the *War Pony*'s hanging in there like a champ," Gallagher said.

The Horde's transport was an older model and had seen plenty of use, Nigel knew. Walker had told him before they'd left that it might be a struggle for them to keep up. It was only lightly armed and shielded, and it had never been meant to be taken into combat like this. Walker and the Horde troopers with him had all of Nigel's respect for being willing to ride it into battle.

Nigel nodded. "Well, with both the Horde and us launching pods, hopefully at least some of us will make it through."

228 | KENNEDY & WANDREY

"What the hell's *that*?" the sensor tech exclaimed.

"What is it, O'Neill?" the CO asked.

"Sir, we just got overflown by what looks like almost twenty little ships!"

"Ours or theirs?" the CO asked, tension in his voice.

"Ours...I think," O'Neill replied. "Looks like they're setting up for a run on the dreadnought, but they weren't part of the plan."

"See if you can get hold of them."

"Got 'em," said the comms tech after a moment.

"This is *Ferret One*," a voice Nigel recognized as Thorb's said. "We will make a hole for you. Tell Walker no one goes to the light alone."

The CO nodded. "You better get to your pod, Colonel," he said. "We're almost there, and even if they're able to knock down some of the defenses, things may get...rough."

* * *

Zhest Squadron, New Warsaw System

Peskall smiled, his tiny sharp teeth glinting in the cockpit fluid. "Come around, bearing 1-7 mark 1-1-4," he said.

"The dreadnought?" Bruxo asked.

"Yes," Peskall answered.

"Oh, this is awesome," Buzz cackled.

"Nobody lives forever," Dapple said.

"Only fourteen of us left," Wisp reminded them.

"Plenty more *Zhest*," Peskall said.

"Just nobody to fly them," Neagle noted.

Peskall grunted and watched the squadron, in *Akee*, come about at 85 Gs, then push their drives to their top speed of 200 Gs.

"Yesssss!" Lyra screamed in exultation.

"After so long, we get to fight!" Zeeta agreed.

"Too bad it isn't the adversary," Jocko lamented.

"Bite your tongue," Burro said.

"He's right," Shiroi said. "The last thing we want is that."

"Is it?" Wisp asked. "We've all heard what Seldia and Splunk have said."

"*K'apo* are crazy," Sadoo said.

"And Splunk?" Peskall asked. Silence greeted them all.

"I'm down to forty-four percent fuel," Stryker noted. "A few of us have more, but I think I'm the lowest."

"I'd like to know where the dreadnought came from," Skye said.

"They're trying to find that out on Earth," Peskall told them. "Sly told me just before we launched."

"There were twenty-eight of us then," Shiroi said. "Only fourteen now."

"Enough," Peskall said, and worked his comms. It wasn't easy to interface with the Humans' pathetic system. They used so many frequencies and systems, it was amazing they could manage to coordinate any kind of fleet action. He chose a series of frequencies the Humans were using to coordinate their command. Their squadron of *Zhest* would be in range within a few minutes.

* * *

CIC, Prime Base, New Warsaw System

"Commander?" Comms called. "I have…"

"What is it?" Aleksandra asked. She hadn't taken her eyes away from the Tri-V showing Major Kratlik's force of 100 assault shuttles accelerating toward the dreadnought and its escorts. In minutes they'd be within enemy range.

"They say they're a squadron of *Zhest*, whatever that is."

Aleksandra scowled at the comms tech. The last thing she needed right then was craziness.

"The pilot identifies as Peskal and says Sly told you to expect him? He also provided their coordinates."

The Tri-V flashed a sector of the battlefield showing a series of unspecific targets. The computer was struggling to identify how many or even their precise course. The comms tech lifted a hand. "Hold a second, I have Captain Wolfsong of *Sir Barton*."

"Go ahead, Captain Wolfsong," Aleksandra said. "Situation update?"

"We've defeated the enemy fleet out here," Wolfsong said. "But we've suffered more than fifty percent losses, including the *Alicorn*." There were gasps from around the CIC and Aleksandra sighed. "Two of the *Egleesius* are also out of action, and all are experiencing system failures. Something happened; I can't explain it."

"Do you know anything about these ships called *Zhest*?" she asked.

"We called them Lightships. They headed in your direction."

"Thanks, we needed confirmation." She turned to the comms officer. "Put them through."

"Human commander? We were expecting the one named Kowalczy."

"He's gone," Aleksandra said.

"I see. Well, we are going to attack the dreadnought. There are other ships heading toward it as well. As we said, follow our lead."

"The signal has cut off," comms said.

"What do we do?" her TacCom asked.

"Fleet wide, inform Major Kratlik so he can coordinate, also tell Sansar what's happening. This needs to work, or we might lose it all."

"Did someone authorize moving a ship from the yard?"

Aleksandra turned her head to look at the SitCon. He pointed at the flickering Tri-V which was showing the Hussars' shipyard. As before, it only held a few incomplete or non-functional ships. Only, one of the non-functional was gone. *Hippogriff* was not ready for the battle, but now it was gone. They'd been too busy to notice. However, in addition, another ship was moving.

"What is that ship?" she asked. "It looks like one of the *Egleesius*…"

"It's the other *Keesius*," TacCom said. Aleksandra cocked her head. "The doomsday ship."

"Oh, my God," she said. "Where's it going? Stop it!"

"It's accelerating toward the enemy fleet," TacCom said. "I can't stop it, ma'am—we've never had control of those ships. They were inactive, at least until that scientist Sato activated one. I don't know who's controlling it, and there's no way—short of destroying it, and we don't have anyone in position to do so—that I can stop it."

Unable to do anything except watch, that is what Aleksandra did.

* * *

Ferret One, **Approaching Prime Base, New Warsaw System**

"Hang on everyone," Thorb transmitted. "Here we go!" He advanced the throttles almost to their stops, and the formation of bombers leaped forward. He looked over to his bombardier. "You've got the target."

"You mean that small moon in front of us?" Skald asked. He paused and then added in an ominous tone, "That's no moon…"

"Yeah, and that's not funny right now," Thorb said. "You need to focus."

Skald looked over to his pilot and smiled. "Can I at least say 'I've got a bad feeling about this'?"

Thorb sighed. The crews had been watching old space fighter movies again. "Okay," Thorb said. "Me, too. Are you happy now? Can we focus on blowing this up without losing any more of our squadron?"

"Just trying to have a little fun," Skald muttered, turning to look at his displays again. "You know, embrace the suck? That kind of thing."

"Yes, I know, but Walker thinks we need to be more serious."

Skald shrugged. "That's not us, though. You're taking all this too seriously. We can't train like the Humans; we *need* to have fun, too. That's just who we are. You seem to have forgotten that recently."

"Well, the number of crews we lost—"

"Yes, we've lost crews," Skald interrupted. "Yes, many of our people have gone into the light, including many of our friends. But that's part of life; it's part of making the world better for our families and our people. People used to die on our home world fighting the grahp, but did that make us train any differently on how we fought it? No. We mourned them, then we carried on with our lives. We celebrated them by having fun in their honor. *That's* who we are.

"The Humans' training—in all its seriousness and lack of fun—works for the Humans. That's who they are. It doesn't work for us. We have to have fun. As a matter of fact, if we're *not* going to have fun doing this, I'd rather go back to our home world and fight a grahp by myself. I'm going to die either way, but at least I'll have fun doing it."

Thorb thought back to his first mission. He'd ended up wrecking his fighter, but he'd accomplished the mission, and he'd done it with swagger. Somewhere along the way, he'd lost that swagger in trying to become more like the Humans they served. But Skald was right; that wasn't who the SalSha were—that wasn't who he was, either.

He nodded to himself. They would do this, but they needed to do it as Salusians would; they needed to be true to themselves first. That way, if it was their day to go into the light, they could do it with smiles on their faces.

An idea came to him immediately, and he smiled. "You're right. We can't win like this." His voice took on a mysterious tone. "But there are alternatives to fighting…"

* * * * *

Chapter Sixteen

CIC, EMS *Revenge*, New Warsaw System

"What the hell is that?" the sensor tech asked.

"What?" Captain Gallagher asked. There hadn't been any alarm in the tech's voice, so he wasn't sure if he should be worried. Well, more worried than he already was as his ship streaked at full power toward the massive ship that had been built for the sole purpose of killing him. "What's what thing?"

"The SalSha bombers. They're almost in range of the dreadnought, and they just went into some sort of…I guess it's a defensive formation? I don't know. It's the damnedest thing I've ever seen."

"What do you mean?" Gallagher asked.

"I don't know. It looks like some sort of spiral pattern with a really complicated reverse-helix thrown in. Like I said, sir, I have no idea what they're doing."

"Entropy," Gallagher muttered, shaking his head as he watched the formation maneuver. Every couple of seconds a pair of *Avengers* would pass within what seemed like meters of each other as they raced around in their pattern. "It almost looks like some sort of ballet, but I wouldn't want to be doing something like that, that close to other ships. That's just a recipe for disaster."

"Have you ever seen anything like that, sir?"

"Me? Never." The captain said as a smile crossed his face. "And I'm betting the Merc Guild forces never have, either."

* * *

MGS *New Era*, Approaching Prime Base, New Warsaw

"Fast movers, inbound," the SitCon reported. "Looks like the bombers we saw earlier."

"How many of them?" Admiral Galantrooka asked.

"I show sixteen," the sensor operator said. "They are approaching in a line abreast formation."

"Why are you even asking," Galantrooka inquired. "Kill them."

"Locking lasers…" The defensive weapons operator's voice trailed off.

"What?" Galantrooka asked.

"Well, sir, they just went into some sort of formation maneuver that the computer is having a problem with. They are going really fast past each other in what appears to be a random maneuver, and the system is having a hard time keeping a target locked as they pass. The system keeps jumping from ship to ship. They have to be unmanned; they're pulling nearly 25 Gs!"

Galantrooka focused all three eyes on the Tri-V. The bombers approached at an incredible velocity as they swung through a pattern that made no tactical sense. As the computer struggled to keep a target locked long enough to fire on it, he realized it made *perfect* tactical sense—*the* New Era*'s weapons couldn't shoot the bombers because of it!* Sweat started to pool inside his shell as the small craft got closer and closer, and nothing was done to them.

"Put the weapons in manual control!" he shouted finally. *"Shoot them!"*

* * *

Ferret One, **Approaching Prime Base, New Warsaw System**

"I wonder why they haven't fired on us yet?" Skald asked via his pinplants. At the speed they were going, the Kloop—an underwater ballet normally used to welcome an honored warrior home after a successful battle—required 20- to 25-G maneuvers.

"They are in *awe* of our Kloop," Thorb announce proudly. "They are so distracted by the grace and beauty of it that they can't take their eyes away long enough to press their firing buttons."

"If they would hold off a little longer, we'll be in firing range."

The first laser stabbed out at them from the dreadnought, followed quickly thereafter by a number of others.

"Just had to say something, didn't you?" Thorb asked.

"Oops," Skald replied. In addition to training methodology, the SalSha had also picked up a good amount of superstitions from their Human pilot counterparts. "At least it's only random and light."

The intensity of the defensive fire picked up noticeably, and one beam flashed close by them, enough to illuminate the cockpit like a stroke of lightning.

"Oops," Skald repeated.

"How about you just shut up now and let me concentrate," Thorb said, "before you make it any worse?"

In addition to the lasers, which admittedly were not well aimed, despite the level of fire being fairly heavy, missiles began leaping from the dreadnought. "It's going to be close," Thorb noted as he watched the icons closing on the bombers while the distance to firing range counted down.

"Now!" Thorb transmitted. "Roll out! Fire!"

The pilots used the G-forces of the reverse helix pattern to throw them out into a large circular pattern, and Skald armed and fired the six Rapier missiles under their wings. As the last one launched,

Thorb initiated a skew turn away from the dreadnought. He wasn't able to stifle the sigh that bubbled from his lips—they'd been in straight and level flight for less than five seconds, but six of the sixteen bombers had been destroyed, and twelve more SaSha had gone into the light.

* * *

Zhest Squadron, New Warsaw System

"Crazy, stupid Humans," Shiroi said as the last of the bombers finished its attack and tried to flee. He shook his head at their losses. Many of the bombers had been destroyed once they finished their interesting maneuvers and had initiated their attack runs.

"Not Humans," Peskall said. "Didn't you see how many Gs they pulled?"

"More than fifty at one point," Zeeta said.

"Exactly," Peskal agreed.

"Then what race?" Sadoo asked.

"Probably the one they uplifted, the SalSha." Peskall said.

"The Humans are a little too like them," Shiroi said.

"Perhaps," Peskall said. "But we need to aid them in this war. Seldia says the Humans are important. Besides, it's obvious what the SalSha and the Humans are trying to do, they just need help. *Zhest*, let's open the door for our clumsy allies."

"Akee!"

The fourteen ships exploded toward the dreadnought at 150 Gs. Their combined firepower was insufficient to knock it out, or even do substantial damage. However, they *were* able to disable a sector of its defenses—the sector facing the incoming assault ships.

Fourteen particle beams pulsed and struck with pinpoint accuracy. Already weakened shields failed, and command pathways were cleanly severed. In just a few seconds, they were done and dancing away. Unlike the SalSha, they were easily able to make it out of range safely; the dreadnought never got a clean shot at them.

"Okay," Peskall said. "Return to base. We opened the door, let's see if the Humans can walk through it."

* * *

CIC, EMS *Revenge*, New Warsaw System

"Whatever the hell it was, it worked," Gallagher said as the *Avengers* launched their missiles. If even half of them hit, and it looked like more than that would, a large portion of the defenses on this side of the dreadnought were going to be destroyed.

"If you thought that was interesting," the sensor tech said, "you're going to love this."

Gallagher looked at where the tech was pointing on the Tri-V display. A group of dots accelerated toward the dreadnought from a different angle, faster than any manned ships he'd ever seen. "Are those missiles?" he asked. "Where did they come from?"

"I don't know," the sensor tech replied. "As strange as it seems, though, I think they're manned. They've flown further under power than any missiles I've ever seen."

The tiny ships raced past them, destroyed more of the dreadnought's defenses, then darted back out again, like a little school of minnows, all turning together as if they had some sort of ESP that allowed the individual ships to function as a group.

As the tiny ships turned away from the massive dreadnought, though, its defensive focus turned to the next wave, and the dreadnought's defenders targeted *Revenge* with their remaining lasers and missiles. There were a lot fewer defenses in the wake of the combined strikes...but "a lot fewer" wasn't the same as "none." A far bigger target than either of the preceding waves—and less maneuverable, as well—it wasn't long before the first laser strikes hit *Revenge*'s shields.

"We're in range for the pods!" the SitCon exclaimed.

"Good," Gallagher replied. "Launch all pods, and let's get the hell out of here!"

* * * * *

Chapter Seventeen

Boarding Pod, New Warsaw System

Nigel forced himself to breathe as the breaching pod went into coast mode. Although they'd practiced with them in the simulators a number of times, he'd never done a real breach before—Asbaran assaulted ground forces; they weren't marines and—normally—not dumb enough to do something like this.

He was pretty certain *Revenge* had taken at least one hit during the ingress, if not several, and now comms with the cruiser were out. The last call he'd heard was Gallagher telling the CO of the *War Pony* to tuck in behind him. That would have made *Revenge* an even bigger target but might have given the Horde CO time to get his pods launched, too.

Nigel's ship was aptly named—he intended to take his revenge on the dreadnought for everything they'd had to go through, then he *would* find Peepo. Regardless of whether or not Alexis still lived, only one person was going to exit that conversation alive. It drove him and kept him focused as the attitude jets came alive, and the pod began maneuvering.

"One minute," the pilot said from the controls. "Everyone, make sure you're locked in," she added.

Nigel watched as First Sergeant Thomas Mason, his senior enlisted, made sure everyone's restraints were in place. Each of the pods held a mixed squad of five CASPers and five Lumar to ensure that, even if only one pod made it, they would have CASPers to fight with.

The clock in his head ticked down to zero. There was a momentary queasy sensation as they passed through their target's shields, then the craft's motors went to full power, pushing them away from their rear-facing seats as ten gravities of thrust threw them into their harnesses.

"Brace for impact!" the pilot yelled.

Mercifully, the boost was short, and the harness retracted as it cut out, pulling Nigel back into his seat. Involuntarily, he tensed, even though he knew he wasn't supposed to. *How could you not?*

SLAM!

The boarding pod crashed into the dreadnought at over 300 miles per hour, and the long nose on the pod pierced its outer skin. The armor-piercing shaped charge fired on impact, blasting a hole into the ship that the pod followed, forcing the gap wider as it shouldered its way through the hull with a rending and tearing of metal.

The nose of the pod, having survived the initial breach, began collapsing back onto itself, cushioning the impact—marginally—and slowing the pod like crumple zones absorbed some of the impact from a car crash. Automobiles were never meant to go 300 miles an hour, though, and the crash was substantially more violent. In less than half a second, though, it was over, and the pod had come to a blessed stop.

"All ashore who's going ashore," the pilot called. Cushioned in her crash cocoon, she'd come through the impact better than the people in the tube, and Nigel wished he'd had something similar as he tried to shake off the effects of the crash. The suit, recognizing his mental incapacity, administered a low dose of nanites and a stimulant, and his head cleared quickly. The Lumar—hardier than Humans and better able to shake off the blow—were already getting out of their seats.

Nigel tried to call the other squads of the Golden Horde force but didn't get any response. He unbuckled and went to the front of the craft, using his magnetic boots in the lack of gravity. "Thanks for the ride," he said to the pilot, who was putting on her combat armor. "Although I hated the sudden stop at the end."

"Just be glad we didn't hit one of the main structural members," she replied.

"How do you know we didn't?" Nigel asked. "That was a pretty violent crash."

"Easy—we survived it. If we'd hit one of the main structural members, we'd all be paste right now."

Nigel could feel his face turning red. Happily, the woman couldn't see it through the suit. "Well…uh…thanks for missing them, then."

"My pleasure. Now, if you'd move to the back, sir?"

"What?" Nigel asked.

"I need to blow the nose of the pod, but I'd like to not be next to it when I do."

"Oh, yeah." Unaccustomed to using the breaching pods, Nigel had forgotten that part. He was happy the woman couldn't see him blushing more as he moved to the back.

The pilot entered the bay, locked the door, and then a jarring *Boom!* rocked the pod as 100 pounds of C8 blew the nose off it.

The pilot opened the door, took a look through it, then stood to the side. "There you go, sir. I'll let the guys with the metal suits lead."

"The Merc Guild's the problem!" Nigel roared.

"And we're the Solution!" the combined squad yelled back.

"For Alexis!" Nigel yelled, then charged though the door...and into some sort of duct. It was big enough for a Tortantula, but it was obviously an air duct—or something—and not a living space. It flexed as the combat suit ran across it but held. After several steps, Nigel pulled up short.

"Well, shit, sir; that was anticlimactic," Mason said, stopping behind him. "Now what?"

"We can either try to move through this ducting or we can cut our way through and go through the normal spaces. What do you think, Top?"

"There's no telling what they can flush through this ducting," Mason replied. "We'd probably survive it in the suits, no matter what it was, but it might suck to be the Lumar."

"Good point. Cut us a way through."

While the troops cut out a section of the floor, Nigel tried to reach the other groups, but was still unable to get hold of the others. He had Mason try, as well, to no avail.

"Suppose we're the only ones who made it?" Mason asked over a private circuit.

"I don't know," Nigel replied. "It seems odd that only one ship would make it. Perhaps there is something interfering with our comms." He paused, then added, "Well, they all know where we need to go. We'll count on them to do their part, and we'll do ours." He pointed to where the Lumar were pulling up a large square they had cut out of the ducting and the floor below it. "Looks like it's time to go."

One of the Lumar was about to dive through the opening, but Nigel held out a hand. "Before you go diving into who-knows-what, let's announce out presence with authority." He pulled two K-bombs off his suit and pointed across the gap to Sergeant Rahimi. "If you'd grab a couple, too?" He asked, holding up a K-bomb.

"Sure you want to do that, sir?" Mason asked. "They're going to know where we are if we do."

"I have a feeling that crashing a breaching pod into their starship at 300 miles an hour probably alerted them to that fact. If they know we're here, I'd like to soften them up a little." He paused, then asked, "Ready, Rahimi?"

"Yes, sir!"

Nigel counted to three, then hurled his oversized grenades into the passage below them, with Rahimi throwing his in the opposite direction. "Follow me!" Nigel yelled as the detonations erupted below them. He dove through the gap and found himself in a side corridor. The K-bombs had done a good job shredding the bulkhead in one direction and the group of Oogars in the other.

Blood and purple fur floated in the air as two of the four struggled to bring their lasers up. Nigel shot them both as the members of his squad poured through the hole in the ceiling. As Mason got the troops organized, Nigel found a diagram of the ship on a bulkhead. As expected, the CIC was in the center of the giant vessel, 103 decks down from where they were.

"Let's go, Asbaran," he said. "We've got a long way to go, and a short time to get there."

"You've got the lead, Taheri," Mason said. "Move out."

* * *

CIC, Prime Base, New Warsaw System

"They did it," the TacCom announced. "It looks like the boarding is successful."

"How many got through?" Aleksandra asked.

"Looks like just over half. Less, if any of the boarding pods didn't function as advertised or they went splat into a main structural member, or something like that."

Aleksandra sighed and shook her head.

"They might have fared better than we will," the TacCom said. On the Tri-V, dozens of enemy boarding pods were racing toward Prime Base. "Initiating close-in defense systems."

Prime Base opened up with all the point defense lasers it had in a blinding crisscross pattern of lethal energy. Dozens—hundreds—of the alien boarding pods were destroyed. More passed through. Then the enemy screening vessels opened up at extreme range.

Aleksandra yelped in surprise as Prime Base shuddered from weapon impacts against her shields. The intensity of fire ramped up by an order of magnitude. Shields failed, and the station took damage.

"Damage control teams!" the SitCon called and began listing areas with damage. In seconds, Prime Base lost most of her close-defense lasers.

On the Tri-V, twenty-two alien boarding pods fired their braking thrusters. Close-defense lasers managed to pick off a few more before the remaining nineteen slammed into the station, breaching its hull. All had targeted the central hub.

"They knew right where to board," the TacCom spat.

"Paka," Aleksandra said.

"Section Seven!" A voice screamed over the internal comms. "Tortantula have boarded the station—" the speaker cut off with an explosion, then silence.

"Evacuate all non-essential personnel from the hub," Aleksandra ordered.

"Commander," Sergeant Hedrick said. "I need to defend the station." She looked at him in alarm. "I'll be back. You'll be safe until then. I promise."

She nodded, and he left with the two privates, their CASPers hurrying through the CIC doorway despite the tight fit.

Aleksandra tried to concentrate on the fight out in space. The remains of the main Hussars fleet were still out near the emergence point, with many of its ships wrecked or disabled. The surviving enemy ships were racing to join up with the dreadnought and its task force. The dreadnought itself was slowing as it approached the base, and the dozens of screening vessels were pulling ahead to engage what remained of Prime Base's offensive firepower.

She didn't know what to think or do, and she shuddered as despair wormed its way up her spine. Their forces had boarded the dreadnought, but even if they succeeded and captured the ship, what good would it do? Despite the losses they'd inflicted, there were still scores of screening vessels and several battleships left. *Maybe if the Egleesius ships could get back into the fight?* She shook her head. The TacCom's data on the five heavy hitters showed them either disabled or non-responsive. She didn't want to be known as the person who lost Prime Base. *There had to be another option!*

"What's the status of *Lubieszów* and *Byczyna*," she asked. The TacCom looked back at her, his mouth pressed into a line. The bat-

248 | KENNEDY & WANDREY

tleships were the last of their reserve forces. "Send a message and see if they can expedite."

The two captured battleships had been waiting on the far side of Home, and were now swinging around to join the fight. Her comms officer nodded, and the order was transmitted. Seconds later the Tri-V showed the battleships firing their engines harder to speed their orbits.

Prime Base resounded with the sounds of weapons fire.

Everyone in the CIC stared at the door where the sounds of fighting echoed. Aleksandra drew her sidearm and checked the load. She hadn't handled a pistol for years, not since initially qualifying on the weapon. She remembered enough to do a simple function check on the autoloading firearm and loaded the chamber.

Dimitri watched her check the weapon, his eyes wide in fear, then quickly did the same with his own. He was a little more comfortable handling his firearm, having qualified more recently. All around the CIC, the rest of her staff did the same.

"Sergeant Hedrick, update please?" she commed through her pinplants.

"We're falling back to the center zone," he replied immediately. His words were punctuated by intermittent heavy weapons fire. "Private Barnes took two men and tried to lead the spiders toward the hangars. It didn't work; they obviously have deck plans."

"What happened to the private?"

"He didn't make it," Hedrick said. A thunderous explosion shook the CIC, making the main Tri-V flicker.

Kleena snapped something in his native language her translator didn't catch and started working on his computer. "I'm going to throw a curve at them, but I need your authorization," he said to Aleksandra.

"Show me," she said. The little Tri-V built into her command chair came alive with deck plans and flashing red pinpoints where the invaders were, then highlighted the corridors and what was next to the corridors. "That's going to make a mess of those power systems," she said.

"The enemy ships already blew out the lasers they were feeding," Kleena said.

Aleksandra nodded and transmitted her authorization via her pinplants. Kleena re-routed the main power through the sub-system relays.

"Heads up, Sergeant," she commed, and send a schematic of what was about to happen.

"Roger. Go!"

Aleksandra nodded to Kleena who triggered the overload. Power in a plasma state was interrupted. The safeties had been removed, and the result was to turn the conduits into bombs. A 20-meter long section of hull was blown out, causing an explosive decompression.

Kleena brought up an exterior camera which gave them a beautiful view of a dozen Tortantula blown out into the black, their ten legs spinning as they flew away. Everyone in the CIC cheered. A series of staccato explosions echoed through the CIC door, killing the celebration.

"Thanks for the help," Sergeant Hedrick said.

"Can we do that again?" she asked Kleena.

"No," the elSha said. "They're only a few sections away now." An alarm sounded and Kleena moved to another system. "They're breaching the exterior hull in multiple places," he warned.

"Helmets," Aleksandra said, and grabbed her own. The flexible helmets were clipped to the armor opposite their weapons. It wasn't designed for space so much as to keep the wearer from being exposed to vacuum during combat. It locked into place, the gloves were sealed, and with the touch of a control on the armor's arm, the suit pressurized. Seconds later, the station core depressurized with a bang and a hurricane of escaping wind. "I guess they didn't like our little trick."

"No, they didn't," Sergeant Hedrick said. "We'll be there in less than a minute."

Aleksandra knew what that meant—the marines hadn't been able to hold the enemy. She examined the CIC, taking a moment to see how it was put together. Warships had CICs with meter-thick armor, which was all but impenetrable by the small arms carried by boarding teams. You could use explosives, but that would pretty much destroy the CIC. If you wanted the vessel as a prize, wrecking the CIC was contraindicated.

She examined the Tri-V for another moment. The battleships would be in combat range in five minutes. There was no sign of the *Keesius*. Maybe the enemy stole it? If they did, there was nothing she could do about it. CASPer-equipped marines sailed through the door, and she knew time was up.

When a dozen had entered the CIC, it began to feel crowded, and Aleksandra didn't see Sergeant Hedrick. She commed him though her pinplants. "Sergeant, are you okay?"

"Fine as frog hair," he replied, and she laughed despite herself. "You miss me?"

"Just worried about my guardian angel," she said, a little embarrassed.

"I'm covering the retreat. Private Hamill should be there any second with some equipment."

As if on cue, the private floated in along with another CASPer, the two maneuvering a trio of heavy plates. "Commander," he said. "Please move all your staff to the rear of the CIC."

"What are you doing?" she asked. "It will be hard to manage the battle without workstations."

"I can teach, or I can do, sir," Hamill said.

"We'll use pinplants," Kleena said.

Aleksandra, not being a combat arms officer, wasn't used to exclusively using pinplants. She also wasn't used to being shot at. She gave the order, and all her people left their terminals and moved to the far side of the CIC.

As soon as the middle was empty, the troopers took the steel plates and assembled a barricade in only a minute. They used their lasers on lower power to weld the plates in place, including jamming them into wall-mounted workstations with tiny explosions of ruined technology. Watching them work, she realized this was a last stand, and she was in it.

The entry to the CIC was at an angle on a corridor going from left to right. A laser beam flashed past the entrance, making her jump slightly. Sergeant Hedrick swung into the CIC with another trooper behind him. Before the trooper could make it in, though, a laser transfixed his CASPer from behind. Sparks and molten metal flew from the top of the cockpit. The armor jerked and floated past the entrance.

Sergeant Hedrick turned, saw the dead trooper, and gave the armor a shove to clear the entrance. Aleksandra swallowed. *That armor once contained a living, breathing human being.* Death had arrived.

All the surviving marines were now in the CIC. Aleksandra counted twelve, including Sergeant Hedrick. Thirty had died trying to stop the boarders. Aleksandra's eyes swept the space, unconsciously looking for a way out. Her back was against the rear wall of the CIC, the metal cold and unforgiving, just like the attacking alien troopers. Her pulse raced, and her breath came in quick gasps. *I'm going to die here.*

"I'm tying you into the squadnet," the sergeant said. "You need to know what's happening."

"Okay," she said, her voice sounding tiny.

"Just lost the drones," one of the marines said.

"Confirmed, we have no visibility," another added.

Hedrick tensed. "Here they come."

A trio of massive Tortantula shot into midst of the CASPers. The two troopers closest to the entrance produced meter-long switch-blades from their right arms and chopped at the ten-legged nightmares. These spiders weren't armed beyond their natural weaponry. Despite that, Aleksandra saw sparks fly from armor as the aliens used their powerful claws and fangs to tear at their armored foes. Blue Tortantula blood sprayed in globs as the aliens were dispatched.

"Scouts," one of the marines said. Others grunted in agreement as they finished the final touches on getting the armored plates into place. As the last weld was completed, the Tortantula entered in force.

Aleksandra couldn't control her shaking and realized she was hyperventilating. To try to combat the feeling, she closed her eyes and went into the virtual command space. She was in a white featureless room with three Tri-Vs arrayed before her. She didn't have a body so much as a presence. A lot of pinplanted people liked to use this place, but it disconcerted her, and always had.

Through the Tri-Vs, she could see the other members of her command staff and was surprised to see them all using virtual space, too. She took a deep breath and went to work.

"Update on offensive situation," she asked.

"We're down to five of the larger laser batteries, but they're all on angled bearings to the enemy," TacCom said.

"Our fleet?"

"No change," he said.

"SitCon, how about the Horde's command?"

"They baited the Izlians into the asteroid field and were going to swat them when the gas bags surrendered."

"Surrendered?" she asked in surprise.

"Yes, they've been moved to a staging area and have shut down their tactical systems. They're out of the fight."

"Score one for us," Aleksandra said. Something exploded in the CIC, and she cried out but didn't open her eyes. She couldn't. The sounds of men screaming in rage and pain over the squadnet echoed in the back of her mind.

She checked the hub evacuation progress; it had been completed. She ordered other station personnel to prepare to defend each section of the rings from assault by the hub. The glideways would provide natural choke points, although they wouldn't stop the enemy from simply landing more boarding pods. The room shuddered, and someone's gurgling scream was cut short. Her SitCon's screen disappeared.

Something smacked against her. The man formerly her SitCon had been cut completely in half, and horrendous amounts of blood were floating everywhere. The blood boiled, drying in vacuum. Some hit her helmet and left little red-black marks. Two burned and ruined CASPers floated next to her. They bumped into each other and drifted in opposite directions. One left a stream of bright red globules in its wake.

Pieces of metal bounced off her armor. The metal shield by her head deformed several centimeters inward. She yelped and pushed as far away from it as she could. Everywhere around her was complete chaos. She rose a few centimeters to see the door. CASPers were using the metal barriers for concealment as they fired their arm lasers, autocannons, and MACs at a swarming mass of Tortantula.

The multi-legged aliens were struggling to get through the relatively narrow door, due to their size. They fought the fusillade of fire from the CASPers, the tight entrance, and dead or dying Tortantulas. She had read a story called *Dante's Inferno* in school many years ago. Here it was, alive and in killing color.

There was an explosion in the midst of the struggling mass, sending bodies and parts out in a shockwave of horror. Through the newly created opening came three more Tortantula, with tiny furred and heavily armed riders on their backs.

Flatar, Aleksandra thought. There wasn't a Human merc in the galaxy who didn't know what a Flatar was.

The earlier Tortantula fought differently. They didn't carry weapons, and they threw themselves at the CASPers with zero regard for their own lives. These three were different. They dodged and raced sideways in the body- and debris-clogged CIC, away from the doorway and the chokepoint it represented.

The surviving marines rose again from cover and fired on the doorway, only to find riderless Tortantula there. They fired several rounds before any of them realized it.

"Flanking!" Sergeant Hendrick yelled. He rotated his shoulder-mounted MAC, and a meter-long tongue of soundless flame spat from it. It would have been quite loud, if there had been any atmosphere. The shot missed, and one of the Flatar spun its improbably huge handgun to loose an equally impressive gout of fire. The hyper-velocity round tore through a CASPer at short range, killing the trooper inside instantly.

"Something is happening in the fight against the dreadnought," her TacCom said.

"What is it," Aleksandra asked, shaking uncontrollably.

"The shi—" A laser fired from one of the Tortantula carrying a Flatar bisected the TacCom's neck and head, ending his life.

"Dimitri?" Aleksandra asked. "What did he see?"

"I-I'm checking," the young ensign answered, his voice stammering badly.

A Flatar rained fire on the surviving CASPers, dropping three before it and its Tortantula were torn apart by a MAC round from Private Hamill.

"Yeah, eat that!" the private yelled, then was felled by a hypervelocity round through his cockpit.

"Got it," Dimitri said. "The *Kleesius* is closing with the dreadnought. They're firing on it, but the thing has unbelievably powerful shields. It's taking damage but not stopping. It looks like the hull is splitting. Maybe they finally hit it badly? *Ghagh!*"

Aleksandra turned and saw a Tortantula had impaled young Dimitri from behind. Long, deadly fang tips protruded through the front of his combat armor; air hissed out and blood pumped forth in gouts.

"No!" Aleksandra cried. Just like that, her fear and shaking were gone, and her pistol appeared in her hand as if it had a will of its own. Dimitri's eyes glazed over as she leveled the pistol at the ring of black beady eyes of the Tortantula and pulled the trigger over and over. The gun wasn't very powerful, but at only a meter away, the Tortantula's head exploded. She shifted her aim, looking for the Flatar. There wasn't one, nor a saddle; the Tortantula who'd killed Dimitri was riderless.

She pushed off the wall and turned, looking for one of the little chipmunk bastards. She fired the rest of the magazine at another Tortantula forcing its way through the door. The rounds mostly bounced off, and she marveled how the aliens didn't need space suits. The little Flatar did, though.

Something hit her in the back, forcing her forward against the now badly perforated and bent metal shield. She craned her neck and saw a spacesuited Flatar on her back, its gun pointing at her head. The barrel's muzzle looked big enough to dock a battlecruiser. The Flatar was smiling, and then it wasn't. It was difficult to smile without a head.

The metal-alloy blade glistened in blue and red blood from its passage through various species as Sergeant Hedrick swiped the dead Flatar's body from her back. "Get behind me," he said over her pin-plants. She moved. As she did, she saw his suit was pierced in many places. Some were stained red; all had a black goo in them she guessed was a sealant.

"You're hurt," she said.

"I don't have time to die," Hedrick said, raising his arm and unleashing a burst from his chain gun. A Tortantula slammed into his armor, bearing him backward.

Aleksandra only just managed to move aside and not get pinned between his armor and the wall. The huge alien reared back and rammed its fangs into the CASPer's bulbous forward cockpit armor. One fang broke off in a shower of splinters, the other penetrated.

"Eat this, you bastard!" Hedrick screamed, pushing the barrel of the chain gun against the Tortantula's underside he fired a long burst. The alien was blown apart in a fountain of blue gore, sending all ten legs spinning in different directions.

A Tortantula/Flatar team came at Hedrick from behind and Kleena came out of nowhere, leaping in zero gravity to hit the Flatar in a football tackle. The little alien was locked into the saddle, and not thrown clear. Kleena took out an electronics tool of some kind, jammed it against the Flatar's armored torso, and triggered it. An intense burst of lightning enveloped the two, then the Tortantula. When it stopped, none of them moved again.

Hedrick moved and shot, then moved and shot again. Aleksandra let her gaze move around the CIC, now a slaughterhouse of Human and alien bodies. She was the only one of the CIC staff still alive, and it looked like Hedrick was the only marine. She remembered earlier thinking it was a last stand. An accurate assessment, she realized; Hedrick was barely moving.

"You okay?" she asked.

"Not really," he said. "Fang got me, and the cockpit is leaking."

"I think we won," she said. "There aren't any more spiders."

"Great job," he said, then coughed. "I knew you had it in you."

A cylindrical object floated in through the door, spinning lazily and bouncing off the various dead spiders and inactive CASPers, toward her.

"Sorry we couldn't make it to the end," Hedrick said.

It's a grenade, she realized, far too late to do anything about it. There was a strange sensation and a wave of static passed through the CIC, sending spitting arcs off every metallic surface.

What was that? she wondered, then the grenade detonated.

* * *

MGS *New Era*, Approaching Prime Base, New Warsaw

"Well, this sucks," Corporal Melton said, surveying the corridor. "No one else made it?"

"I don't know," Walker replied. "I can't raise anyone. Doesn't matter, though. They're paying us by the job, not by the hour, so let's get this done. The number one priority is the CIC, so that's where we'll go first. Move out."

Melton led the way forward, and Walker shook his head, finding it hard to believe they were the only group alive. They'd all survived the breaching operation with minimal damage to their suits and had fought their way through the first group of mercs—a patrol of Zuuls—they'd run across.

"I've...explosions...me," Melton commed a minute later as they advanced toward the ramp that would lead them "down" to the CIC.

"What?" Walker asked. "Say again, over."

"...got sounds...in front..." Melton commed.

"Anyone catch what he just said?" Walker asked.

"He's got sounds of explosions coming from in front of him," Corporal Horan replied. "He's breaking up a lot, though."

"Tell him to hold up," Walker commed, nodding. So, it was the ship, he thought. It either prevents comms...or they're actively jamming us. Good to know—there may be more of us.

He jetted forward to where Melton was waiting at an intersection. "There's a barricade around the corner and down the passageway," he said. "Looks like more Zuul, and they're shooting at someone coming from the other way."

"If they're enemies of the Zuul, they must be part of our group. We'll charge the barricade on three," Walker said as he came alongside the trooper. "Hopefully, they'll all be looking the other way and won't see us coming."

"Sure thing, sir, but you need to stay back. Me and Horan have got this." Melton patted the top of the mech behind him. "Ready, Matt?"

"Ready as I'm going to be."

Melton counted down from three, then the two soldiers raced around the corner, with the rest of the squad following. As Walker cleared the corner, he could see a barricade set up about twenty meters away at the cross-passage. It was manned by at least half a squad of Zuul, firing off to the right. The Horde troopers made it halfway to the barricade before one of the Zuul noticed them and turned in their direction. He got a single shot off, before a deluge of laser and MAC fire caught him.

The other Zuul started to turn, but the CASPers were already on them, and all were killed in the brief firefight.

"Thanks to whoever just hit the Zuul checkpoint," an Italian-accented voice commed. "This is Lieutenant Colonel Valenti. We're coming up the passageway and would appreciate it if you didn't shoot us, too."

Walker went to meet him, then noticed Horan's icon had gone red in his display. The one shot the Zuul had gotten off had gone through his chest, killing him instantly.

Damn it.

* * *

CIC, MGS *New Era*, Approaching Prime Base, New Warsaw System

"We've lost the Zuul checkpoint, Admiral," the TacCon reported. "They got hit by a second group before they could deal with the first."

"What are your intentions for dealing with the boarders?" Admiral Galantrooka asked.

"Until we get our boarders back from Prime Base, I don't have a lot of forces to use against them," the TacCon replied. "I'm going to pull back most of the remaining forces to defend engineering and the CIC so I can hit their groups one at time."

"Will that be enough?"

"Absolutely. There are several barricades set up to stop them or at least delay them until our forces get back. And besides, we haven't used the Goka yet."

* * * * *

Chapter Eighteen

MGS *New Era*, Approaching Prime Base, New Warsaw

Nigel's force covered about half the distance they needed to go before they ran into their first barricade.

"Looks like I've got a Zuul position on the ramp below us," Corporal Taheri said as rifle fire and a couple of explosions could be heard from down-ramp.

"Stand by," Nigel said. "I'm coming."

He worked his way to where he could see the Zuul further down the circular ramp. They had a pretty good position where anyone coming down the ramp at them would be exposed, and what looked like several heavy lasers positioned to cover the approach. *They'd be hell on the CASPers.*

Fortunately, the Zuul had either neglected to protect themselves from fire from above or hadn't had time yet to get the defenses in place to do so. Nigel's forces could trade fire with them from above and get the better of them. It would take a while to whittle them down, of course, but it would be a lot safer than charging the heavy lasers. While he felt the press of time and wanted to hurry, getting to the CIC without enough forces to do the job wouldn't work.

He moved back from the edge to find Major Sulda, the leader of one of his Lumar companies, waiting for him.

"Dogs dumb," the Lumar said, pointing with the hands on his right side toward the Zuul below. "No have roof."

Nigel nodded. Although they may not be mental giants, the Bold Warriors' leader had seen plenty of action and knew how to fight. "No, they don't. We can shoot at them and kill them without needing to charge those guns."

The Lumar shook his head. "Lumar pet good dogs; Lumar break dumb dogs. You shoot here," he said, indicating where they stood, "and we go break."

"Okay…" Nigel said, not entirely sure what the Lumar planned, but trusting him to know his job. He shrugged as Sulda turned away and began giving orders to his troops. "Asbaran CASPers, move to the side of the ramp and take the Zuul below us under fire."

After a couple of minutes of trading somewhat ineffective fire with the Zuul—they had better cover than Nigel had first realized— Major Sulda tapped Nigel's CASPer on the shoulder. "We ready," the Lumar said.

Nigel turned to find two of the largest members of the Bold Warriors behind him. They had removed four of the ship's watertight doors and spot-welded them together with their lasers into a large shield.

"Bold Warriors go spank bad puppies," Sulda said. "You shoot from here and keep Zuul heads down."

The other three Lumar, including Sulda, got behind the Lumar carrying the improvised shield and began marching down the ramp.

"Cover them," Nigel ordered, moving to the side of the ramp so he could fire down at the Zuul.

While the Zuul were able to return fire or operate the heavy lasers, it quickly became apparent they couldn't do both at the same time, especially since the heavy lasers weren't as well protected. Although the Zuul got off a few shots, including one that put a wicked line across the Lumar shield, the Asbaran forces quickly killed any of them that went to operate the lasers, and the Lumar reached the impromptu barricade without loss.

The two Lumar carrying the shield raised it and threw it into the remaining Zuul, then hopped over it and engaged the Zuul hand to hand.

"Let's go!" Nigel yelled, going over the railing so he could fly down to the barricade.

By the time he got there, though, it was over. The thrown shield had killed several of the Zuul, nearly cutting them in half as it squashed them into the bulkhead, which had deformed with the force of the impact. It appeared the ones that remained had had their necks wrung.

Nigel shook his head. Say what you want about the Lumar, they're certainly strong.

* * *

CIC, BMS *Trushista*, New Warsaw System

Paka clicked her tiny claws rhythmically on the arm of her chair on *Trushista*'s CIC. A short distance away, Captain Glashpooka had all his eyes retracted, a sure sign he was using his pinplants heavily. The entire CIC staff were occupied similarly. The battleship and a mere nine of its formerly large squadron of support ships was closing in on the dreadnought, which had a fraction of the battleship's meager acceleration. The dreadnought was also slowing as it approached Prime Base.

I will be the first to walk into Prime Base, she said. I will claim it for my sister and the Mercenary Guild. That will end it. Nobody will care about a few wrecked Bakulu and Maki ships.

The ship's battlespace contained data on all the different battles underway, including the traitorous Izlians who'd surrendered and the battle for Prime Base. The strange ships which had showed up to harass her squadron had then gone on to help a force board the dreadnought. The boarders appeared to be causing all kinds of hell on *New Era.*

Admiral Galantrooka wasn't having an easy time of it. Paka's muzzle curled into a tiny smile at the idea. She decided after they took control of New Warsaw, there would be plenty of time to find out what was behind the little Lightships.

"There is another *Egleesius* approaching the fleet from the vicinity of Prime Base," the TacCom announced.

"That's impossible," Paka said. "All five *Egleesius* were at the emergence point battle."

"Then you are wrong," Glashpooka said, indicating the Tri-V. "That is another."

"You don't understand," Paka insisted. "I was there when the other four were found..." She trailed off as she remembered. "Show the scan of the new ship." He regarded her with a single eye. "Now, entropy take you!"

Glashpooka looked at the sensor tech, and the data was relayed to Paka. She took one look at it and felt ice tripping off her tail. *It's not an* Egleesius, *it's a* Keesius*!* The captain stared at her with a pair of eyestalks. On the verge of telling the Bakulu captain, Paka paused to consider for a moment. If the *Keesius* took out the dreadnought, it would be a loss, certainly. But there were more than enough ships left—even in the meager squadron she still commanded—to finish the job.

"What is it?" Glashpooka.

"Nothing," Paka said. "You were right; it is just an *Egleesius*, and one is no danger to the dreadnought. Still, we had best keep back while Admiral Galantrooka deals with it, just to be safe."

All three of Captain Glashpooka's eyes regarded her for a long moment, then one looked at the SitCon and another at the TacCom. The battlespace showed the screening ships beginning to fire on the *Keesius* with lasers and missiles. All were dealt with by the ship's shields. Over the next several minutes, the weapons fire intensified quickly. The *Keesius* burned all four of its fusion torches—one more than the *Egleesius* possessed—at maximum output, driving the ship at greater than 20 Gs of thrust. Then, the entire forward section opened up like the petals of a flower.

"What is happening?" Glashpooka asked as the *Keesius* ran through the enemy screen. Cruisers, frigates, and battlecruisers desperately tried to get out of its way while still maintaining fire on the insanely acting ship. Glashpooka turned all three eyes on Paka.

Paka saw the open petals of the *Keesius*' superstructure sparkling like slag dropping from a welder's torch. She calmly disconnected her pinplants from the ship's direct data relay and waited. A second later, in the midst of the dreadnought's screen of dozens of ships, the *Keesius* detonated.

The antimatter explosion was several orders of magnitude larger than the missiles the merc guild fleet had employed. The blast was a light second across while the radiation and EMP shockwave ripped out over three light seconds. In a fraction of a second, all the dreadnought's screening vessels were destroyed or disabled.

* * *

MGS *New Era*, Approaching Prime Base, New Warsaw

After a quick meeting between Walker and Valenti, the Asbaran Solutions' forces had continued to the engineering section, while the Horde forces had continued on toward the CIC. They needed control of both spaces in order to fully capture the ship, and they were playing for the win. Joining forces would have increased their odds of taking one or the other, but they needed both.

Walker wasn't sure who'd gotten the better of that deal; the Asbaran troopers had to walk about 1/3 of the way along the outer deck to get to engineering, while his troops had to get to a ramp and go about half a mile into the core of the ship to reach the CIC.

No matter which way they went, he expected that the command element in the CIC was watching their movements and setting up blocking positions in front of them. A loudspeaker announcement had played several times warning of their arrival and had instructed the ship's crew to stay out of the corridors. It only made sense—it kept the Horde forces from killing any of their technicians they'd need later. Even though the technicians might be able to get in a lucky shot that killed or disabled a CASPer, the odds were that the unarmored Bakulu would die in prodigious heaps compared to any real damage they'd do to the invaders.

That part was helpful to Walker, as it kept the noncombatants out of the way. As the ship was already at battle stations when they'd boarded, he was sure the ship's marine forces were already wherever they needed to be, and he doubted those forces were Bakulu; those positions would either be subcontracted out to more warlike races, or other races like the Zuul that had been hired by the Bakulu company that had the contract.

Walker noted after a few minutes that, in fact, they hadn't seen *anyone* besides the mercs at the barricade. Whoever was handling the damage control must also be routing their forces around his, because they hadn't seen any of them, either. It was obvious they were being watched and it made his skin crawl…it was just a matter of *when* they would be hit. And the longer they went without being hit, the more time the defenders had to make the traps they were setting nasty.

They'd also lost comms with the Asbaran Solutions force once they'd gone a little farther down the passageway, confirming his feelings that their comms were being jammed. There might be additional Horde or Asbaran forces that had made it…but they wouldn't be able to coordinate with them. He was sure the defenders were working to pick them off piecemeal, and he shivered involuntarily as he wondered when it would be their turn.

Two minutes later, they made it to one of the ramps and started down. Staff Sergeant Jacobs indicated the empty ramp in front of them. "Where the hell are they, sir? I would have thought they'd put up a bigger defense than this?"

"I don't know," Walker replied. "Maybe they're waiting until we're more concentrated—" Then realization hit him. "Damn it; I know where all their damn troops are—they must have attacked Prime Base. If they sent boarding parties over, they would have a lot fewer marines left here to defend the ship. And, if that were the case, they'd be waiting closer to the CIC if multiple groups made it aboard here, so they could shift from one group to the next without having to cover a lot of ground."

Walker nodded to himself. "We aren't alone here; other forces are advancing with us, and we probably have less time than we originally thought. Prime Base was basically undefended, and if they sent forces over, it won't be long before they capture it. The only way we can save them is to end this *now!*"

"You heard the man," Jacobs roared. "What are you waiting for? *We've got civvies to save!* At the double time, march!"

The Horde forces raced down the ramp, going around and around as they descended into the ship. "Oh, screw this," Jacobs said after about ten circuits around the ship. "I ain't doing this ninety more times." She flipped over the railing and into the center of the shaft, using her maneuvering jets to fly down it.

"Should we follow her?" Sergeant Wyatt, the squad's medic, asked.

"Damn right!" Walker replied. "Everyone into the shaft!"

The squad followed Jacobs down toward the center of the massive ship. Five decks down, the lighting went out, and they were forced to turn on their exterior lights. Although the shaft was fairly well illuminated by the ten suits, the changing direction of the lights as they moved toward the center of the ship caused shadows to jump out at them from everywhere and frayed everyone's nerves.

Although traveling down the shaft was inherently more dangerous, it also was faster, and they made it to Deck Two faster than they would have if they had taken the ramp all the way down.

"Careful," Walker said as they proceeded down the passageway. "I've got a bad feeling about this."

"I don't see anything in front of us," Corporal Melton, who was on point, replied. "It looks like it's clear all the way to the CIC."

"I know," Walker said. "That's what's bothering me." On a ship as big as the dreadnought, there had to be a lot of marines. Even if they'd sent the bulk of them to attack Prime Base, certainly they would have kept some in reserve to defend the dreadnought, wouldn't they? He would have, if he'd been in their place.

The squad continued down the hall, slowing as they neared the hatch to the CIC.

Melton was just reaching for the hatch when shaped charges blew along the length of the passageway.

Corporal Eric Chase's suit went red—he'd been in front of one of the charges and something large had gone all the way through his suit at chest height. Nearly everyone in the squad took at least some damage, and all their cameras were degraded by the smoke and dust in the air.

Then the Goka dropped on them from above.

* * * * *

Chapter Nineteen

MGS *New Era,* Approaching Prime Base, New Warsaw

Nigel inspected the remains of the barricade with disdain. That was the best they had? On a ship this size? Then he realized what was wrong—there should have been more forces. Up to that point, he'd thought the Merc Guild troops had been just biding their time, but as he looked at the defensive position, he realized their objective at Prime Base wasn't its obliteration, but its capture, and most of the marines on board must have gone to participate in the assault. That meant there probably weren't as many currently aboard the dreadnought, and if the Humans hit them hard and fast, they might be able to push through any defenses and maybe catch the CIC unaware.

Even if they didn't, they needed to hurry and get to the CIC before the marines returned. He looked over the railing and into the darkness of the shaft. *It* would *be a lot faster that way.* "Anyone tired of going down the ramp and want to go down the shaft to speed things up?"

"I thought you'd never ask," Sergeant Rahimi said. He flipped over the railing, oriented his CASPer, and maneuvered down the shaft.

"What are you waiting on?" Mason asked when no additional forces attacked. "Everyone in a CASPer, grab a Lumar and let's go!" He swung the closest Lumar onto his back, pushed off, and joined

Rahimi in the shaft. The rest of the Asbaran CASPers grabbed a Lumar and followed.

Nigel smiled as Major Sulda grabbed hold of his suit. *Now this is more like it.*

* * *

MGS *New Era*, Approaching Prime Base, New Warsaw

*F*ighting Goka sucks, Walker decided. *But fighting them in zero gravity sucks even worse.* It was a lot harder to stomp on them or pin them to a floor or wall, and they could use their wings to fly. The suits could maneuver, too, but the Goka had a marked advantage.

"Back to back!" Walker yelled, positioning himself with his back to Jacobs' suit. The Goka were everywhere, and one sword blade was not enough. He felt like he needed three or four, as they came at him from all sides. In the time it took to rip one from his leg and stab it, two more had attached themselves to his other side, and he spent more time knocking them off than he did actually killing them. One by one, additional caution lights illuminated for the members of his squad.

Somehow, one got behind him, and he felt a blade pierce his left shoulder. He swung hard into Jacobs and was rewarded with a *crack!* as the Goka's carapace shattered. The knife dropped away. He stabbed a Goka coming in high, then fired a MAC round through one crawling along the deck. Thrust. Shoot. Slash.

A red light illuminated as one of the Goka pulled out a laser and shot Corporal Melton through the chest in front of Walker. Corporal Everett killed the Goka with the laser, but as he moved three Goka landed on his back and went to work. Before Walker could come to his aid, Everett's icon went red as well.

Jacobs slammed into Walker as he was moving, trying to dislodge a Goka from her back, and hit Walker so hard it dislodged his magnetic boots, and he was propelled to the side. Before he could maneuver back, two Goka landed on her. One stuck a knife through the joint in the back of her knee, cutting her hamstring, and the other got a blade through the back. Walker cut both away with a single stroke of his blade, but he was too late. With a muttered, "Fucking bugs," Jacobs' icon went red.

Now lacking a partner, Walker backed up against the wall to protect his back and killed two more. Another suit went red, and then another, and it was all Walker could do to keep them off him—he was no longer fighting to win, just to survive another few seconds.

A Goka landed on his non-sword arm, but before he could cut it off, it was ripped away, and he had to twist at the last second to make the sword blade miss the Lumar in black armor that was now happily pulling the Goka apart. He turned the other way to see CASPers and additional Lumar marching up the passageway in an alternating line abreast, driving the Goka in front of them. If one of the aliens tried to attack, it was shot, stabbed, or grabbed and then torn apart. Many of the giant cockroaches were too busy attacking Walker's group and didn't see the new arrivals in time. Within a few seconds, it was all over, and the Goka were dead or dying. The Lumar moved down the passageway with glee, finishing off the ones that were still kicking.

"You seem to attract them," Nigel noted as he came over to Walker. "Maybe you should shower more."

"You should talk, Camel Boy," Walker replied as he injected himself with his nanobot injector at the worst of his wounds. It burned like the surface of an O-class star, but the wounds began to close. "Thanks, though. That's the second time you've arrived without a moment to spare."

Sergeant Wyatt went past, going from CASPer to CASPer, but Walker could tell there was nothing he could do; all of them were dead.

Walker shook his head. He was down to three troopers plus himself; however, he'd made it to the objective. "Let's end this," he said as he walked over to the hatch into the CIC.

The hatch was locked, of course.

"Now what are you going to do?" Nigel asked over a private channel.

"I'm going to ask them to open up." Walker replied.

"And you think that is going to work?"

"Yes, I do."

"And why is that? What reason do they have to let us in?"

"I'm going to ask nicely."

Walker disconnected a package from the back of Jacobs' CASPer and held it up in front of the camera over the hatch. "In the CIC!" Walker said over his external speakers. "I know you can hear me! Here's the deal. Your part of this war is over, and one of two things is going to happen. Either, one, you let me into the CIC, and we take you prisoner, to be repatriated at a time of our choosing, or two, I blow this up and kill you all. Which is it going to be?"

"There isn't enough explosive in that pack to breach the CIC's armor," a voice said through the speaker next to the camera. "I doubt that is enough to even dent it."

"You'd be right," Walker agreed, "if this were conventional explosives." He pulled a deadman's switch from the pack and pushed the button. "This, however, is a nuclear bomb, and I just activated it. It definitely *is* big enough to blast through the hatch, and it *will* kill you. So, what's it going to be? Death or repatriation?"

"How do I know you're not bluffing?"

"You don't. But you can watch the way my people run and guess that it's real. Of course, if you do that, I'm going to make sure you die, just out of spite, and we won't be returning you, safe and sound, to your home world. I'm willing to do what it takes to save Prime Base, so it's your choice. Do you surrender, or do I blow us all up?"

Walker counted to twenty in his head and was just about to issue his final ultimatum when the lock clicked on the hatch. Nigel moved forward and undogged the hatch. It opened easily. Walker followed Nigel into the CIC, before safing the weapon.

"Was that a real nuclear weapon?" a Bakulu sitting in the command chair asked.

"Yes, it was," Walker replied. "You chose wisely."

"There was little reason to continue," the Bakulu said. "The attack on Prime Base has failed, and one of your other groups has captured our engineering section. Hopefully, you will honor your promise to repatriate us."

"What the hell is this?" a voice yelled from behind them. "What are you doing, Admiral?"

Walker turned to find a large Goka standing at the hatch. *Oh fuck. More Goka? How many of them are there on board?* A mass of the giant cockroaches could be seen behind him in the passageway, and Walker stifled an involuntary shudder. All were armed with laser rifles, although he knew they also had knives hidden on them somewhere—all of the insectoids seemed to have knives, as well as the training to use them effectively on the CASPer suits. Perhaps something about their eyes allowed them to see the joints and gaps of the suits easier—Walker had no idea—but they always seemed to find them easily enough while in combat.

All of the CASPers turned and leveled their weapons at the Goka, who aimed their rifles back at them.

"I have surrendered the ship," Galantrooka replied. "Lay down your rifles." When none of the Goka moved to do so, he yelled, "Lay down your rifles, now!"

The Goka leader slowly placed his weapon on the deck, although without gravity, it rebounded slowly upward. The other Goka behind him did the same.

"Why are we surrendering?" the lead Goka asked. "There aren't many more of them than us." He looked up and down the closest CASPer to him. "I think we can take them."

"We have lost all our screening ships," Galantrooka replied, "and the assault on Prime Base has failed."

"Should have sent us," the Goka leader replied. "We could have chewed them up. Of course, we still can…"

"That is enough!" Galantrooka roared. "I have surrendered the ship; you will follow my wishes!"

"The Black Death doesn't surrender, Galantrooka. Perhaps you've forgotten that? Maybe we need to kill all of you useless Bakulu and take over the ship ourselves."

"Look," Nigel said, stepping in front of the command chair where the smaller Bakulu had adhered his viscous foot. "It's over. The assault on Prime Base is over. We hold engineering and the CIC.

Stand down. Hasn't there been enough lives lost in this war? Stand down, and let's end it."

"No surrender!" the Goka yelled as Walker moved to stand beside Nigel. "Not to the likes of you!" It reached up under the shell protecting its wings and whipped out a laser pistol.

"Move!" Walker said. He'd seen plenty of Goka treachery before and was prepared for it—he tackled Nigel out of the way of the laser blast as the Goka fired.

* * *

CIC, MGS *New Era*, Approaching Prime Base, New Warsaw System

The rest of the Goka troopers exploded into action, pouring into the CIC. They came in high and low, spreading out like a plague.

Several of the Human troopers got off MAC rounds, but then it was hand-to-hand combat in the enclosed area, and the Humans' sword blades snapped down. Nigel pushed Walker off him and climbed to his feet. At least ten of the Goka had made it into the CIC, and they worked to get behind the CASPers, where they could stick their long knives into the suits' joints.

The battle didn't last long. Although there were an equal number of Humans and Goka, the additional five Lumar made the difference, as they were able to grab a Goka with two hands, hold the Goka's knife arm with a third, and disarm the giant cockroaches with their fourth. The Lumar then pulled them apart, ripping off legs until they had an opening where they could stab them. Some just turned toward the closest CASPer, which would stab it while the Lumar held it incapacitated. A blue mist filled the air, joined with plenty of red globules, as knives and sword blades flashed.

Within seconds, all the Goka were dead, as was one of Nigel's troopers. One of the Goka had charged the ship's crew, and several of the Bakulu appeared to have been killed as well. As Nigel surveyed the room, he realized Walker had never gotten up. His CASPer floated near one of the terminals with the nuclear weapon close by. Nigel raced over and found a laser hole through the center of his chest.

"No!" Nigel yelled. He toggled the canopy release and pulled it open, and a huge spray of red was sucked out to float nearby. Walker's eyes were half open, and his hands covered a leaking wound over the center of his chest.

"Oops," Walker said, gasping. "Fucking hate...Goka."

Nigel opened his own canopy and grabbed his first aid kit. He pulled out the auto-injector, set it to max, and tried to move Walker's hand so he could use it.

"Too late," Walker whispered. "Don't want...that pain...too."

"*Why?*" Nigel asked. "Why did you do it?"

"You have..." Walker's voice trailed off, but then he added, "...Son."

"No!" Nigel yelled. "No! I won't let you die. Thorb said to tell you no one goes to the light alone."

Walker reached up, his hand twitching, and grasped Nigel's hand. "I'm not...alone." He gasped once more, then his whole body relaxed.

"He's gone," Sergeant Wyatt said, confirming what Nigel already knew.

Nigel looked away from his friend, trying to control his breathing and his emotions. He could barely see through the tears welling in his eyes. He wanted to kill something—anything—as long as it was associated with the Merc Guild, who'd already been responsible for killing his family, possibly his girlfriend, and now the man he considered his best friend. His eyes filled with murderous intent, looked across the CIC to where most of the Bakulu huddled, but then he looked back down at Walker. Killing the entire bridge crew, even the entire crew of the dreadnought, while satisfying, wouldn't bring Walker back or get him any closer to his number one goal, and that was the one thing he *would* do, even if it ultimately cost him his life. He would kill the rat-faced bitch, even if it was the last thing he did.

"What is the status of this ship?" he asked the Bakulu sitting in the command chair.

All three eyestalks turned to look at him. "We are damaged, but still operational."

"Good," Nigel replied. "Turn this thing around. There's a Veetanho on Earth I want to talk to."

* * * * *

Chapter Twenty

CIC, BMS *Trushista*, New Warsaw System

"It is confirmed; the Humans have taken the dreadnought," comms reported. "The Hussars' battleships and remaining screening vessels are changing course for our vector."

"Get us out of here," Paka ordered the captain.

"We need time to recover our screening ships," Captain Glashpooka said, looking at Paka with a single eyestalk as he issued orders to the squadron.

"No!" Paka barked. "Set course for Sol. Use your shunts and get me out of here."

"You knew that ship was a bomb, didn't you?" the captain demanded, now looking at her with all three eyes. "You knew and didn't warn Admiral Galantrooka."

"I suspected," she said and shrugged. "It doesn't matter; get us out of here."

"You mean get *you* out of here. That's what you said a second ago."

"You know what I meant. We have to escape."

"Why did you not tell me about that ship? Tactical analysis suggests it was a doomsday weapon. At its full potential, it could destroy an entire planet!"

"The merc guild planned to capture it," Paka said, making a dismissive gesture. "We didn't expect the rotten Humans to use it against us. Antimatter weapons are illegal."

"Just like the ones we used against them earlier? Why else did you want to secure it?"

"By order of the Mercenary Guild Council, you are to get me out of here. I cannot be allowed to be killed or captured."

"By order of the Mercenary Guild Council," Glashpooka repeated.

Paka was surprised her translator could convey such a level of disgust from the speech of a mollusk. "Yes, by the guild's orders."

"The guild is why this all happened in the first place. How many millions have died? How many ships have been lost? How many of my people, the Maki, the Izlians, were sacrificed at the guild's orders? And why? Just to stop the dangerous Humans? They didn't start this war. They are a merc race, doing what merc races do."

"They broke every law they could," Paka snapped. "The trial of Sansar Enkh proved that."

"Yet the Besquith have perpetrated all manner of atrocities over the centuries and have never been subjected to this sort of vendetta. This sort of slaughter. Why?"

"General Peepo has her reasons."

"Oh, General Peepo. I thought it was the will of the Mercenary Guild Council."

"Same thing," Paka said, filling with rage. "The Veetanho *run* the entropy-cursed council! We have since shortly after the Great War. We move events in their correct direction. We keep the peace. We decide who lives and who dies." She gestured at the captain. "What are you, in the grand scheme of things?"

Glashpooka stared at her for a second, one eye turning to look elsewhere before returning to Paka.

"Now execute my orders."

"Execute," the captain agreed, and Paka looked in surprise as a laser burned through her chest from behind.

She gurgled as blood filled her lungs. Reaching down she disconnected her safety harness and floated free, struggling to breathe. Glashpooka's XO held a laser pistol in a pseudopod behind her, its emitter glowing slightly. "You…you…" Paka stammered, trying to concentrate with a mind filled with pain and outrage. "You will pay for this."

"No," Glashpooka said, and his XO fired again, this time hitting Paka in the center of her chest.

She screamed as blood pumped from her chest while she tried to stem the flow with a paw.

"You asked what I am in the grand scheme of things? Why, I'm the captain of this ship, and my word is law."

Paka struggled to breathe, each breath becoming harder and harder. She tried to catch hold of her chair—there was an emergency medkit inside. If she could just reach it…but she couldn't. It seemed a light year away. "Pay…" she whispered. *They will all pay.*

"Comms, signal the Winged Hussars that we surrender."

Paka wondered how it all went so desperately wrong as she quietly died.

* * *

Conference Room, EMS *Shadowfax,* New Warsaw System

Captain Elizabeth Stacy floated into the conference room, a med tech close behind her. The surgeon hadn't wanted to let her out of sickbay, but Elizabeth had ordered her to do so. The surgeon assigned a young female medic to follow Elizabeth and constantly monitor her condition. Elizabeth had also had the level of pain killers reduced so her mind was clear. But damn, she hurt.

In the conference room waited the remnants of the Winged Hussars' captains. Only twenty-eight captains of the sixty-three who'd left for Earth a few weeks earlier watched her enter. *So few.* Along with them were Sansar Enkh and Nigel Shirazi. Every one of them looked tired, beaten, bruised, and bloody.

"Captain Stacy," Evie, her XO announced. "Commander, Winged Hussars." Everyone saluted, and Elizabeth struggled to keep the tears at bay.

"I am in command," she said. "For now. Let's get through the rest of this war before we get ahead of ourselves." She looked at the faces, Human and alien, all of which didn't want to hear what she was about to say. "Make no mistake, this war isn't over. We know from information surrendered by the Izlians and Bakulu ship commanders, Peepo intends to bring more forces here to take control of New Warsaw. If any of us escape, we will be hunted down. The same goes for all Human mercs."

"We already know they tried to enslave our colonies, from the biggest to the smallest," Sansar said. Heads turned to look at her. "I know you've all lost friends and loved ones; so did we."

"Some of us lost our closest friends," Nigel said, his expression dark.

"We can't let our sacrifices be in vain," Elizabeth said. "Lieutenant Commander Kowalczy fought to the last to hold Prime Base, and in the end gave her life." She wanted to mention Patrick, yet she dared not. He was somewhere in *Shadowfax*; she didn't know where. What she *did* know was he wasn't who he had been.

"What are we going to do?" Captain Drizz of *Nuckelavee* asked. Others nodded.

"We need to go back to Earth," Sansar said. She nodded as the assembled captains gasped.

"How?" Captain Eshek of *Franklin Buchanan* asked, his elongated Sidar face unreadable. "Half of our ships are damaged."

"Doesn't seem possible," Captain Sarauw of *Seattle Slew* added.

"And yet we *must*," Nigel said with complete conviction. "The only way we can end this is to go after that bitch Peepo in her own lair. Look around you. She sent such an unbelievable and overwhelming force, and we kicked her ass."

A few chuckles.

"A lot of it was luck," Elizabeth said. *Luck and magic?* "Yet as Colonel Shirazi said, we *did* win."

Nigel nodded. "Plus, there are hundreds of mercs prisoner on Earth, including Colonel Cartwright. He doesn't deserve to be left behind any more than the others." Nigel seemed about to say something more, then pursed his lips and shook his head. "I am going back, with or without the rest of you."

"What kind of forces can we muster?" Captain Corder asked. Just out of medical after weeks in recovery from a previous battle, he already looked resigned to the task.

"First and foremost, we have the Merc Guild's dreadnought that our forces captured. Although it was roughed up in the capture, even at fifty percent it's much more powerful than anything the guild forces have."

Many of the commanders nodded, having fought—and lost—to it.

"We also have the surviving Izlians and Bakulu. I've spoken to both their commanders. The Izlians seem to think we're some sort of legend come true." She shrugged. "Who knows what a freezing bag of gas thinks?" A few people laughed. "The Bakulu realize they've been used by Peepo, and they would like to get a little payback. Either way, they didn't have to surrender.

"The captain of Paka's battleship, the one who had her killed, spoke with the dreadnought commander, Admiral Galantrooka. There is an understanding between them. Galantrooka isn't happy about the situation or about being used by Peepo. The Bakulu don't throw away their lives like some merc races. They want to go back and settle up with Peepo. I trust them, which is good, as we don't have the personnel or the know-how to man that monster."

She used her pinplants to examine the information. "The fleet resource officers are evaluating the rest of our ships now," Elizabeth continued. "I've already gotten commitments from two Maki battleships. It seems that, like Colonel Shirazi's Lumar troops, they were quite tired of being on the losing side and have switched their allegiance to us." Many shocked faces were evident with the revelation as she continued: "Everyone here is best able to evaluate his or her own ship's capabilities, though. Given three days to repair and rearm, please indicate by a show of hands how many would be prepared to deploy." Elizabeth raised her own hand. "To go kick Peepo's scrawny ass off Earth? I know I will."

It took a few, long seconds, but Captain Drizz put his furred hand in the air. "*Nuckelavee* will answer the call."

"Count *Seattle Slew* in," Captain Sarauw said. "It seems like suicide, but I'll be damned if we don't take the fight back to them. That's *my* planet that bitch is squatting on."

Within seconds, every captain's hand was in the air. Elizabeth gave a little sigh and nodded. "Okay, three days. Everybody get to it."

Nigel immediately caught her after the meeting broke up. "Commander," he said. "Can I ask a favor?"

"If I can accommodate you, I will," she assured him.

"*Revenge* was badly damaged in the assault on the dreadnought. Is there any chance it can be repaired in time to participate?"

Elizabeth reached for her slate and hissed in pain. Her arm was far from healed, so instead she used her pinplants. "There isn't a detailed assessment of your ship on file," she said. "I'll see if I can get a team there. That said, I can only allocate staff as available. I need to prioritize forces. There are other merc units who weathered the battle in the asteroid field; perhaps you can use one of their ships?"

"I will see," he said. "Although I admit, I'd rather have *Revenge*." He got the same look on his face he'd had earlier in the meeting.

"Is there something more?" she asked.

"Yes," he said. "We haven't talked about it with your people for many reasons, but you should know." Nigel gestured to Sansar who was waiting by the conference room door. The other Horseman floated over. "Tell her about the dream."

A minute later Elizabeth was reeling yet again. Her med tech turned to look at her from across the room, obviously in response to her suddenly elevated bio-signs. "A dream?" she asked Sansar.

"You do not have to tell me how it sounds," Sansar said. "Believe me, I know. But the fact cannot be denied that our family has the gift—or curse—of visions of the future. I saw the attack on New Warsaw months before it happened, and in great detail."

"So, you think Alexis Cromwell is alive?" Sansar nodded. "I don't know how to process this," Elizabeth admitted.

"She's also pregnant," Sansar added. Elizabeth's eyes went wide, and she turned to look at Nigel. "And yes, he's the father."

"Entropy." Both Nigel and Sansar nodded this time. "So, you want *Revenge* because you're going to get her back."

"The very hounds of hell could not stop me. I will wade through a sea of blood to save Alexis."

Sansar chuckled. "That means yes. If given the opportunity, he intends to rescue her."

Elizabeth used her pinplants to alter orders. "A team is heading for *Revenge* as we speak. As long as its damage isn't critical enough to require drydock, I'll have it ready."

"You have my thanks," Nigel said and bowed his head.

"If she's indeed alive, bringing back Alexis Cromwell is all the thanks I need." She looked at the two. "I cannot tell the Hussars about this, although this added hope would be a powerful tool, if they believed it. Morale is already holding on by a slender thread, and if it were to turn out you were wrong—"

"Which is possible," Sansar interjected.

"—it would be devastating," Elizabeth finished. "For now, this is not public knowledge."

"I agree," Sansar said. "It's also why we haven't shared this information previously. We wanted you to know, however, because if the opportunity exists to rescue her, we intend to do so."

"Good. Well, I've got a lot to do." The others nodded and left the conference room. A thousand messages clogged her pinplants, much of it fleet logistics. *I wish you'd made it, Aleksandra.* Her expertise in logistics would have been incredibly useful. *I'm sorry I left you there to get killed.*

"Commander?"

She glanced over to see Captain Corder waiting nearby. "Captain?"

"Forgive me. I didn't want to interrupt your conversation with the Horsemen."

"It's fine. What can I do?"

"I don't have a ship," he admitted, and gave a nervous chuckle.

"Oh, hell, I forgot." During the height of the battle, *Hippogriff* had disappeared from the shipyard. None of the Hussars' monitoring assets had been focused on that area of New Warsaw; the shipyard and parking orbits hadn't been a priority. It was pure luck anyone noticed the *Keesius* being activated, although no one still knew how it had happened. Its use saved the day…but its activation was a mystery.

In addition to the missing *Hippogriff*, four incomplete *Crown*-class hulls were also missing. Sato had moved them out of the shipyard before he'd left to allocate construction to the *Avenger* bombers for the SalSha. The hulls weren't much more than superstructure, powerplants, and engineering spaces. Still, they were missing. Elizabeth wondered if the Dusman were responsible. Back when they'd been known simply as the Fae, helping themselves to various assets had been their hallmark.

"Well, the problem of crew shortages is gone," Elizabeth said. "We lost a lot of ships, yes. However, many of the crew survived either by ejecting, or by holding out in wrecked hulls prior to being rescued. In fact, I have several ships with no command crew assigned." Corder nodded as she looked at the list.

"You're familiar with battlecruisers, so I'm going to give you *Pegasus*."

"Commander!" Corder exclaimed. "You can't be serious. You should take it."

"That isn't how this works," she said. "I'm familiar with *Shadowfax* and my crew is used to her. I'm not uprooting my crew. In addition, *Pegasus* has most of her crew intact, she just lost her command crew. Captain Akoo managed her fine until the traitor took her out."

They only referred to Paka as, "The Traitor." Many felt calling her by her name was simply wrong; she didn't deserve the honor. When it was revealed the Bakulu captain of *Trushista* had her shot, it had been considered poetic justice. Especially since Paka had been using the Bakulu and Maki as pawns in the Veetanho schemes. Now, with their schemes laid bare, the Bakulu had become allies as well.

"Fleet repair is already on board *Pegasus* and *Phaeton*. They're sure they can get *Pegasus'* CIC back into shape, although probably not *Phaeton's*, which has a newer design. Teenge has *Arion* underway, although her computers will need more repairs. She'll be ready. I'd rather have all five *Egleesius*, but I'll settle for four." She looked at Corder. "Your assignment is *Pegasus*, Captain."

He blinked, then saluted. "Yes, Commander. I won't let you down."

I just hope I don't let you *down,* she thought as he left. One item off her checklist, 999 more to go. Nearly at the top of the queue was a message from Laras, now in charge of the Geek Squad after Kleena gave his life in Prime Base. He said the modifications on the *Egleesius* were possible and would be given priority. Elizabeth grinned, caught Evie's attention, and they headed for the CIC. Her med tech followed closely behind.

* * *

Upsilon Asteroid, New Warsaw System

"I didn't tell you to go out there and get half your forces shot to entropy," Sly said.

"You said to help them the best I could," Peskall countered.

"And *that* is the best you could do?" Sly jabbed a claw at the stringer dock which extended from Upsilon's main maintenance bay. There were twenty-eight moorings, but fourteen had cables floating where the ships should have been. "We have so few of the *Zhest*-equipped ships left, and you use them like markers in a *L'oopo* game?"

Peskall floated without comment. Neagle, his second in command, stayed back. His black-brown ears were folded back.

"The other factions won't commit," Sly said. "I'm only a *Kroof.* I have no power to sway this decision. Reporting we've lost fourteen *Zhest* won't help our position, or Splunk's."

"How will her position be helped if she's dead?" Peskall asked, uncowed.

Sly ground his rear teeth together. The pilot had a point. "That female has been a thorn in my side from the day she left the creche."

"Yet you cannot deny she has influence," Neagle said, breaking his silence. Sly was about to tell him to stick to flying when Seldia floated in. The other three lowered their eyes in reverence.

"Splunk is key," she said. Even though she hadn't been there for the discussion, she always knew what had been discussed. "Her and those who follow her."

"Fine, whatever," Sly said, then gestured for Akl'a to come over. She floated over, bowing her head to Seldia, who merely stared past the new arrival. "How comes the work?"

"We'll have it ready in six days," Akl'a said. "After the Humans have left."

"As fast as possible," Sly said. "But do the job right."

"Of course," Akl'a said and gestured to the bay. *Hippogriff* was in several parts as hundreds of Dusman in powered suits moved among the parts, cutting and welding. "Their ships are unimaginative, to say the least. Still, we'll make it work."

"We must be there," Seldia said, gazing at the ship. Everyone near her listened. "We must be there when they join the fight, at the end."

* * *

CIC, EMS *Shadowfax*, New Warsaw System

The Tri-V showed the fleet forming up.

Elizabeth flexed her arm. It was healed, though still stiff. She was better off than more than 5,000 Winged Hussars. Luckily, very few of their dependents had died. Another debt they owed to Aleksandra Kowalczy.

The fleet formation was a total of thirty-nine ships, including transports, carriers, and merc cruisers. They were desperately low on escorts and frigates, and the SalSha were spent with only ten combat crews remaining. The survivors would remain on New Warsaw. Their carrier, *Dragon*, would stay back, as well; there weren't enough bombers to make it worthwhile, and there wasn't enough time to equip it with a useful drone payload.

The good news was that all five *Egleesius* were operational, crewed, and armed. Dan Corder was in command of *Pegasus*, and Elizabeth assigned Lieutenant Richard Wilde as captain of *Phaeton*. Fleet crew cohesion was a mess, with hundreds in positions they were either unfamiliar with or weren't entirely qualified to operate, but at least they were fully manned.

The Izlians and Bakulu squadrons were at the forefront of the fleet. Just behind them, the bulk of the dreadnought, *New Era*, eclipsed the starscape. Elizabeth shuddered at the sight of it. Hundreds of damaged points were visible, even from hundreds of kilometers away, and still it was strong enough to fight.

She examined the merc cruiser formation and nodded to herself. Only twelve merc units remained or were going with them to Earth. They were crowded onto the six Hussars transports and three of their own cruisers. *Revenge* was in the formation, repaired and ready for action. She caught her gaze straying to the ship several times and tried not to think about their mission. It was too crazy to consider real.

"Everything looks good on the modifications," Evie told her, floating nearby. "We'll just have to see how they work when the time comes."

Elizabeth glanced at her and nodded, then looked down and caught sight of her own rank insignia. The eagle made her scowl. *Find her,* she sent to Nigel Shirazi. *I don't like the weight of these fucking things.* Fifteen minutes later, the fleet began passing through the stargate. Just before *Shadowfax* touched the event horizon, she again thought about Patrick, or whatever he was now. She didn't know what to think about him, and, right then, she didn't have time.

* * * * *

Chapter Twenty-One

São José dos Campos, Brazil, Earth

Good and Enkh spun around. Neither had heard anyone enter the building, and none of their sensors had indicated anyone was even nearby. Good's hand instinctively went for his pistol, before his rational mind kicked in. If the Depik sitting on his desk had wanted him dead, his body would already be cooling. He carefully removed his hand from the pistol and the alien slow-blinked at him.

"I greet you, Hunter," he choked out, although every fiber of his body yelled, *Flee!*

"I am Tsan, Dama of Whispering Fear Clan," the Depik replied, slow-blinking again. "Welcome to our negotiation."

"What...who is that?" Enkh asked. Her hand still rested on the handle of her pistol.

"That is a Depik," Good said, "and if she wanted us dead, we would already be dead. You can take your hand away from your weapon. I do not believe she is here for us." He turned back to the alien. "At least it would not appear that way."

"You are safe, at least for the moment," Tsan said, flicking her tail. "Although you may not know it, your contract was bought out."

"That is good news, certainly," Good said, although he was far from relaxed in the company of an assassin, whose race had tried to kill him once before. "Can I ask how this happened?"

"Our last Governor, Cahli, chose to allow your Sansar Enkh to buy it out, and she did. As such, you are safe. As I said, I am not here

for you; I am here for the murderer of my race, Peepo. Cahli swore Peepo would bleed, and I am here to see that she does."

Good nodded. "In that case, our goals are allied. I would like nothing more than to kill her. We thought we had her, but she proved more elusive than we thought and killed many of my people. My corporal and I are now looking for other options to fulfill that task." He paused as what Tsan had said finally dawned on him. "Wait. The murderer of your race?"

The Depik's furred fluffed out, and Good could see her tense. He carefully kept his hand away from his weapon, praying he hadn't brought about his own doom by asking the question. After a couple of seconds, though, her fur flattened, and she preened herself for a moment in an obvious attempt to regain control of herself. He remained silent, willing to give her all the time she needed if it allowed him to continue breathing a little longer.

"Hunters don't have enemies," Tsan finally said. "We have prey, and one does not hate prey; we just kill them and move on. But for that Veetanho—and Veetanho in general—I am willing to make an exception. Peepo tried to enslave our race; the Depik chose mass suicide instead."

"I don't understand," Good said. "How did Peepo think she could compel your obedience?"

"She had some kind of ray that froze us." She shuddered. "When it was turned on us, our muscles locked up, and we were unable to move or act. We were powerless." She shuddered again. "It is an awful thing, to be held against your will."

"Kind of like what Earth is going through now," Enkh noted.

Tsan nodded. "Peepo and her race have enslaved many other races, but we refused to allow her to enslave us. It is my goal to make sure she is unable to enslave anyone else."

"How do you intend to do that?" Good asked.

Tsan slow-blinked. "It will be difficult for her to enslave anyone if she is dead." She preened her tail for a moment, then added, "It may be possible for my race to still survive; there are efforts proceeding to ensure our survival. I am here to ensure those efforts have the opportunity to be successful."

"But if the Veetanho have the ability to freeze you, how are you going to get into the Merc Guild's headquarters?" Enkh asked.

"You said it earlier," Tsan replied, her gaze going to Good, "our goals are allied, and I would propose an alliance of our efforts, as well."

"You need help," Good said with a nod.

"I do *not* need help," Tsan said. She paused and then added, "It is just, for once in my life, I find myself needing...support."

* * *

Merc Guild Detention Facility, Ubatuba, Brazil, Earth

Jim was waiting as his evening meal arrived. The man wore the Varangian Guard uniform and gave Jim a distasteful look as he handed the prisoner a plate.

"Thanks," Jim said. The man snorted something Slavic, likely a curse, and left. Jim gave a little laugh and took the meal inside. He'd gone through his memory upon waking up and, to his best guess, it was more than a week since the disastrous battle for Earth. The survivors were probably back on New Warsaw, waiting for the coming invasion, or worse.

He sat and listened to Metallica as he ate. The music was a big part of why he was feeling better. Jim was positive whoever monitored the cameras in his room would be confused as to why the prisoner in his disgusting dank cell was in the best mood he'd been in for some time.

In the quiet dark stretches of time, Jim spent a great deal of time trying to get into the other functions of his pinplants. He had yet to have any success but refused to stop trying. The effort kept him from obsessing on the why of it. His former girlfriend, who'd been spying on the Cavaliers for the world government, had given him a targeted nanite treatment which removed part of the lock on his pinplants. It made zero sense.

As he chewed the tasteless bread, taking a bite of the bland fish with each bite, he probed every area of the pinplant's mental access menus. His plants were advanced compared to most. Well, not compared to Sansar Enkh who had three sets; Jim's two sets were way beyond what most other people got, though. He didn't think the Human brain could handle four. He'd used his for everything from storing data and analyzing company reports to helping interface with his Raknar.

Jim jerked in surprise. At the thought of his Raknar a new menu had appeared in his pinplant access area. He dropped one of the pieces of bread and didn't even notice as he looked around, stupidly afraid someone was watching. *Who could be watching my thoughts,* he chided himself, and hit the menu selection.

"Option Currently Unavailable"

Damn it, he thought. There was a help feature to the menu, so he selected it.

"I open at the close."

Jim sat back and ran a hand across his mouth, scattering crumbs as he thought. The line was unmistakable, as was the fact that Adayn knew the line. They'd sat together and watched that old 2D movie at least twice, maybe three times. The menu help message could have several meanings, most of them ominous.

Why, he kept asking himself? Why would she help me?

He was surprised when the door opened again to reveal General Peepo. He hadn't seen her since shortly after his capture. She was smiling until she saw him, then her grin turned to a bit of a scowl. Jim guessed she'd expected to find him upset by her arrival, which begged the question if they'd been spying on him or not.

"Colonel Cartwright," Peepo said, quickly recovering.

"General Peepo," he replied. "To what do I owe the pleasure of this visit?" He set his mostly finished meal on the filthy floor.

Peepo again looked slightly confused. Only somebody who had familiarity with the Veetanho would notice, and it was gone in a split second. "I wanted to commend you on your ability to withstand questioning."

"Is that what your pet monsters have been doing, questioning? The Varangian Guard are everything you'd value in humanity—no self-respect and a complete lack of compassion for their fellow man."

"Compassion for their fellow man," she repeated and walked into the room, moving closer to him.

He wasn't restrained anymore. She weighed maybe 40 kilograms to his 150. If he could get his hands on her for just a few seconds… Jim saw movement on the other side of the door. It was too dark to see who or what was there. He relaxed as she spoke again.

"If your race could learn what it means to serve a greater good, you might understand the irony of your statement."

"We believe our freedom *is* part of the greater good."

"You have no idea what's out there," she said.

"Why don't you tell me?"

Peepo stared into his eyes, searching, thinking. She seemed to be considering. Jim had no choice but to acknowledge she was one of the smartest beings he'd ever met, if not *the* smartest. For the first time he wondered at her motivations in the war, *really wondered*. Were his fellow Humans really such a huge problem that she'd mount a war costing millions, or even billions, of credits to enslave them?

"No," she said. "What I came here to tell you was that despite your stubbornness, my techs have managed to secure the Raknar for transport."

It was Jim's turn to pause slightly. "Makes no difference, you'll never understand how to operate them."

"After wringing your fellow Raknar operators dry, I agree. Only you seem to have that information."

"And I'll die before I give it to you," Jim said.

"Willingly, this is true." Peepo smiled. "Regretfully, I don't have the means to get it from you here. However, in the Betall system, I have a Wrogul standing by. It will gladly wring the information from your brain, whether you want me to or not."

"Wrogul," Jim repeated, his confidence gone in an instant.

"Yes, Colonel Cartwright. The Raknar are difficult to handle in the damnable condition you left them, so it will take some time. But in a week at the most, we'll be bundling you and your fellows off to Betall where I'll get my answers."

* * *

São José dos Campos, Brazil, Earth

Good smiled. "Support then," he said with a nod. "I would be happy to give you our support in your mission, if you could give us your support as well. There are a number of things which we need to do, many of which would be far easier—and safer—if you were to do them than if either the corporal or I were to do so. Peepo has shown herself to be quite...inhospitable... to the mercs remaining on Earth. She captured our last operative in Europe, a man working with Taranto S.L.R., and he wasn't seen again.

"We have great capabilities—like the Raknar the Cavaliers use, but we need to get hold of the Fae and break out the Raknar operators from where they're being held."

Tsan drew up and cocked her head. "I'm afraid you will have to start at the beginning, Human, as I am unaware of what either Fae or Raknar are."

Good explained the situation to the Depik, who appeared to listen intently.

"I do not understand how these Fae—or even the Raknar will help us," Tsan said once he finished. "They seem to be blunt instruments—giant hammers, perhaps—that inflict great amounts of damage indiscriminately. They are not instruments of stealth. They would be good for destroying the Merc Guild headquarters, but I don't see how they would be of any use getting us into it. *I* will be the one to bleed Peepo, not some giant mecha which will kill her by knocking down the roof on her."

"I understand," Good said, realizing his error. "While they might not be helpful to you in your immediate mission, recovering the Raknar operators will help us afterward."

"I am not sure what use that is, either." Tsan jumped down to the floor and stalked the room, looking annoyed. "Even if you had the Raknar, complete with their Human and Fae crews, what good would that do you? You would be no better off than the first time they surrendered. They could be surrounded again, or even destroyed, and to what end? They may devastate more of this country, but in the end, *what good does that do?*"

"Well, uh—" Good realized the Depik had a point. He'd been more focused on recovering the men than doing his job and thinking about a long-term plan. He finally shrugged. "I guess I thought that once I recovered our personnel, Colonel Cartwright would know what we needed to do next. At a very minimum, we need to get the captured mercs away from the 'tender mercies' of the Merc Guild. I've heard about what being locked up in a Merc Guild prison is like."

"Yes, I heard about what they wanted to do with your Sansar," Tsan said, flicking her tail. "I suppose they will have their show trials for Colonel Cartwright and his troops soon, too."

"Show trials?" Good asked. He raised an eyebrow at Enkh, who shook her head.

"I haven't heard anything about a trial for Colonel Cartwright," she said. "In fact, they never even issued a statement that they had captured him."

"And now that I think of it," Good said, "that worries me a lot. If they aren't planning a trial, that means that they're probably planning on getting rid of them once they've extracted whatever info they're trying to get out of them. That could be any day now. We need to get them out of there, ASAP."

"What we *need* to do is kill Peepo," Tsan said. Good noticed her tail had fluffed out, and she was pacing faster again, which was decidedly *not* a good thing. "Anything that doesn't help us accomplish this is irrelevant. If rescuing your people ties into killing Peepo, then I will support it. Otherwise, it isn't worthy of discussion."

"Rescuing our mercs isn't entirely irrelevant," Corporal Enkh said. "The Raknar pilots are being held at the Merc Guild Headquarters, and we believe Peepo is in the headquarters as well. Perhaps if we were to contact the Cavaliers soldiers and use them to break the Raknar pilots out of jail, this would give you the diversion you needed to slip in and kill Peepo."

Tsan stopped pacing, sat, and slow-blinked at Enkh. "This plan has more promise." She slow-blinked again. "I only need a few minutes with her. I would like a few hours…days even…to truly show her my displeasure, but five minutes will be enough."

Good smiled at Enkh, happy she had calmed the Depik somewhat. No one wanted to be in close proximity to an unhappy killer. "I agree," he said. "In addition, the Fae have shown themselves to be very handy as far as technology goes. It would be good if we could bring them in and incorporate their skills as well. I'm sure they would be very interested in breaking the Raknar pilots out of jail."

Tsan flicked her tail. "If they can be of use, then that would be acceptable. I also have someone else who may be of assistance."

"Who is that?" Good asked.

Tsan walked to the back door and opened it, and a young black girl walked in. Good blinked in surprise. The girl looked like she was in her mid-teens but was on the thin side and appeared shy. Her eyes never left the floor. If there was a "look" that Good had been expecting, the girl's appearance was about as far from it as was possible.

"This is Sunshine," Tsan said.

"You're kidding, right?" Good said. "How is a little girl going to help us? Perhaps you don't know very much about our race, Tsan, but she is nothing more than one of your cubs."

Tsan slow-blinked. "I know enough to know that, in general, Humans are often more than they seem. I think you will find the same to be true with Sunshine." She waved a claw at the girl. "Please introduce yourselves."

"Hi, Sunshine," Enkh said. "I'm Corporal Bolormaa Enkh."

"And I'm Major Good," the officer said, still sounding put-out.

The girl chuckled.

"What?" Good asked with an exasperated tone.

The girl looked up with fire in her eyes. "I think it is funny that you dismiss me so easily, while calling yourself, 'very good.' You don't look much like a typical warrior, either—and I have known all sorts of soldiers and warlords, and yes, even some of the best warriors my continent ever produced. I fought alongside them in battle. Have *you* shot down a MinSha fighter? No? I have. Have you operated a CASPer in the defense of your country against a horde of alien mercenaries? No? I have. I've fought Tortantulas and Besquith, and I lived to talk about it. I'd like to see you do any of that, Mr. Very Good."

"Is this true?" Good asked.

"I can't confirm it's true," Tsan said, "as I wasn't there for the fall of Monrovia, but she has told me about it, and I believe her. What I can confirm is that she walked nearly all the way across the Sahara Desert, by herself, in a CASPer that had been modified for her to operate. She understands very well how to operate a CASPer, and I am sure she would best you in hand-to-hand combat using them quite easily."

"You were at the fall of Monrovia?" Good asked. "That was…it was awful what the Merc Guild did there."

"Yes, I am a member of the Kakata Korps," Sunshine said proudly. "We defended Monrovia, by ourselves, to the last person. Me."

"If everyone else was killed, I am not sure the Korps still exists. How is it that you made it out?"

"I did not want to leave, but my *bass* made me leave. He programmed information into my CASPer that will make the Peacemakers intervene and stop this war. My mission is to get that CASPer off-planet and to the Peacemakers so we can stop this war."

"What information do you have?" Good asked. "We have countless examples of the Merc Guild breaking the rules of combat—nearly every single one of them—yet the Peacemakers haven't intervened so far."

"I don't know what it is," she said looking down in embarrassment. After a second, she looked up again. "But I do know that it is there, though, or Colonel Mulbah Luo would not have sent me on this mission. It is too late to save him and the rest of the Korps, but it is not too late to save Earth."

"Well…that certainly is interesting, if nothing else." Good turned to Tsan. "Any other surprises?"

Tsan looked up from where she was preening her tail. "I think that is all," she said. She slow-blinked. "For now, at least."

"Okay," Good said. "In that case, let's reach out to the Cavaliers and the Fae, and bring them here so we can coordinate our efforts. The Cavaliers will be helpful in the attack on the headquarters, as will the Fae. They may be able to figure out the message, too, which will be a lot easier to get off planet if it isn't stuck in a CASPer. Tsan, it would be easiest if you could go and get them—" He stopped as Enkh sat up straighter and turned to her system. "What is it?" he asked.

"I just intercepted a transmission from the guild headquarters. They've found the Cavaliers and are sending out a force to trap them."

Good turned to Tsan. "Can I convince you to do it now, actually?"

* * * * *

Chapter Twenty-Two

Southwest of Taubaté, Brazil, Earth

"I told you they wouldn't believe me," Sunshine said as she raced along the Via Dutra—Brazilian Highway 116—toward Taubaté.

"The size of a warrior doesn't matter as much as their spirit," Tsan said. "Compared to some of your Human CASPer drivers, I am tiny, yet would you want to face me?"

"No," Sunshine said, trying to hide a small shiver that went down her back. She'd seen the assassin in action and knew that fight could only have one outcome—Sunshine's death. Worse, when time wasn't of the essence, Tsan tended to like to play with her victims rather than give them a quick, clean kill, which remind her far too much of when she had been in the service of one of Monrovia's warlords. He, too, liked to play with his victims as they died, and Sunshine had always found that disturbing. If someone needed to be killed, kill them and move on. Causing them more pain than was needed indicated a darker, more sadistic, side. Having seen it too many times in the streets of Monrovia, it wasn't a place she wanted to go.

Like many other vehicles they'd used in their travel from Africa to Brazil, Tsan had "acquired" the automobile. Sunshine was less worried about something so transient as theft; it was just part of life where she'd grown up. Besides, she wasn't going to actually *keep* the vehicle when they were done, so it wasn't really stealing; Tsan would clean it of their presence and they would leave it somewhere for the local authorities to return to its owners. It did, however, cause small flashes of guilt, as it was something Colonel Luo probably wouldn't have approved of, stealing being bad for the image of the Korps, after all, but she thought he would have allowed it, maybe, as it helped ensure the successful completion of her mission.

"Easy," Tsan said, looking at the map on her slate. "We will take the next off-ramp."

Sunshine forced herself to slow down. The fact that the Merc Guild was coming was in the back of her mind, and every time she looked down, she found her speed was much higher than the last time she'd looked. Driving was a skill she'd never expected to have, or to need, for that matter, but she'd had to learn along the way. While Tsan *could* have driven, it would have attracted too much attention.

Sunshine followed Tsan's directions and drove past the address they'd been given. A man stood outside a large warehouse smoking.

Tsan made a coughing noise. "Like *that* isn't obvious," she said.

"What?"

Tsan made the coughing noise again, and then said, "Look at that man. He looks different from everyone else here in town. His skin is too lightly colored. He's obviously bigger and better fed, while the locals look malnourished. He's smoking a cigarette like he does it daily, but the locals here treasure their cigarettes like there's a shortage; they smoke a little then stub it out to save it for later. That's the wrong place for him to stand, too, if he didn't want to draw attention. There are deeper shadows over to the side of the building. Besides, there are lights on in the building. How many other buildings are so well-lit?"

"So that's one of the Cavaliers?" Sunshine asked as she pulled over. He *did* look much larger than anyone she'd seen in the area and was larger—bulkier and more muscular—than probably anyone on the continent of Africa.

"I think it's obvious," Tsan said, "even without needing to see the drone flying overhead." She slow-blinked, which Sunshine had come to realize was Tsan's way of smiling.

"Stay here," Tsan said as she got out of the car.

"Why? Don't you trust me to come along? I can hold my own!"

"I know that, young one," Tsan said with a slow-blink, "but I can convince them faster than you can, and I don't want to come back and find out our car has been stolen by someone who recognizes it's from out of town. We may need to leave in a hurry. I don't know if you've heard, but the Merc Guild is coming." She went invisible and shut the door before Sunshine could reply.

* * *

Taubaté, Brazil, Earth

Tsan made a quick lap around the warehouse, then jumped up onto the ledge of one of the open windows. They needed to have the windows open, she saw. With all the big humans inside, working to fix their metal suits and the vehicles they had acquired to transport them, it was warmer than she would have liked. She would have had them open, too.

After surveying the scene for a few moments, she jumped to the floor and bounded over to where a knot of men stood talking.

"—it triangulates somewhere near Ubatuba," a large man was saying as she approached. He pointed to something on the slate he was holding. The man was enormous—probably one of the biggest Humans she had ever seen—and she had no idea how he wedged himself into one of their metal suits.

"Where the hell is Ubatuba?" asked another male with a gold oak leaf on his hat. As Major Good wore the same device, she decided he was probably a major, too.

"It's about seventy kilometers from here," Tsan said, dropping her quintessence field. "If you want to meet the Merc Guild, though, you don't have to go there; their forces will be here within the next thirty of your minutes."

"*Who the hell are you?*" the major exclaimed. All of their hands went to their pistols, but no one drew. The interior of the building went quiet, too, as everyone stopped what they were doing to see what had caused the major's reaction.

"I am Dama Tsan of the Whispering Fear Clan. Major Good of the Golden Horde sent me. You need to leave, right now."

"Wait. How did he know where we were?"

"They are monitoring the Merc Guild's comms. That's also how he knows they are sending a force to trap you here."

"Wait. How did *they* know we were here?"

"It wasn't hard. This is the only building in town with a white man smoking a cigarette in front of it, with lights on inside it and a drone flying overhead. You're lucky; I would have just called in an airstrike. You're obviously not very smart or good at stealth." She yawned as all of the men started talking at once.

"Humans!" she exclaimed, and they all stopped to look at her. "We don't have time for this." She took the slate from the large man and typed an address. "Here is where you will find us—Major Good and me, as well as a few others. It is in the town of São José dos

Campos, southwest down Highway 116 from here. You need to leave, now. There will be time to discuss our options once we are there. I will see you there." She turned to leave.

"Wait!" the major called.

It seemed to be his favorite word. That, or he used it to cover the pauses he needed to think. *Humans, sometimes, did not adapt to new information well.* "What?" she asked, turning, as her tail flicked impatiently.

"Where are you going? Why don't you come with us?"

She cocked her head, as she'd seen Humans do. "Who is going to kill the MinSha spying on you if I do that?"

"There's a MinSha spying on us?"

How Humans had become a threat to the Merc Guild was beyond her sometimes. "Yes, there is a MinSha. Yes, she is watching you and reporting your movements. If I don't kill her, she will likely follow you and report where you go, giving away our location as well. As I am more concerned with killing Peepo than I am every single one of her minions, I would rather this not happen. It is inefficient. Now, do you have any more wasteful questions, or can we leave before they get here?"

The major looked at her with his mouth open as he processed the information. Before she could say something else—or stab him, something to get him going—the large man began giving orders for everyone to pack up in preparation for moving out. She took that as a good sign and drew her quintessence field around her.

The Humans' trucks were just rolling out of the warehouse when she returned to the car ten minutes later. She opened the door and got in before becoming visible again.

"It's about time," she said shaking her head at the Humans. "Let's go; the guild forces will be here any minute."

Sunshine started the car. "Sure thing, *bass.*" She drove off down the street and looped back on the next street over. She could see the lights of the Humans' vehicles a couple of blocks down. Shadows flitted from building to building as they passed the street with the warehouse on it. More MinSha; they had cut it almost *too* close.

"Did everything not go well?" Sunshine asked.

"It all worked out," Tsan replied. "Why?"

"You've got a little blue on your tail."

* * *

Taubaté, Brazil, Earth

"It's a MinSha scout, no doubt about it," Ryft said as she observed through the drone.

"Let us see," Dante said. Ryft sent the feed through the others comms, and they all looked. The insect form was cloaked with a highly advanced image-blurring cloak. It would have been hard to both notice and pick up on most scanning devices. The Dusman had been using the tech for thousands of years, though, and weren't impressed.

"Let me kill it," Shadow said. He had the MinSha firmly in the crosshairs of the former Oogar laser rifle, his finger just outside the trigger guard.

"No," Splunk said, shaking her head. She was a hundred meters away on another rooftop. The Dusman were in their element in the city full of two- and three-story buildings—many of which had balconies or even flat roofs. Humans so seldom looked up, she doubted anyone had seen them. If they had, the Humans probably thought the Dusman were cats, or other small creatures. "We need to get the scout's comms before killing it."

"She's right," Dante agreed. "Sandy, Peanut, go get the bug's communication gear then kill it."

"Done," Peanut replied.

"Whoa, what was that?" Ryft asked.

They brought up Ryft's view and found a completely different scene. The MinSha was spinning around, flashing its razor-sharp midarms at something they couldn't see. Blue blood splashed, and one of the arms fell off. A split second later, the MinSha collapsed to the ground in a heap, blood pumping from the center of its torso.

"Peanut, Sandy, move!" Splunk ordered.

A kilometer away the two Dusman flew across the intervening territory, jumping from rooftop to rooftop.

"Shadow, be ready in case whatever it was is still there," Dante said.

"On it," Shadow said.

"Wait," Rfyt said. "I have vehicles entering the area." He paused and then added, "Two...no three truckloads of Oogar just arrived. Gah. I can smell their oily taste from here." They could hear him spit, then he picked up his commentary. "They are forming up to assault the building where the Cavaliers were...and there they go. Not a bad job, assuming everyone within a mile is deaf and didn't hear them coming. Oops, sorry stupid Oogar, you're too late."

Ryft chuckled. "They're standing around looking confused...still confused...ooh, we have a newcomer; a Veetanho just entered. It's not Peepo. Request permission to kill her."

"Denied," Dante said. "Hold your fire, and let's see what they do. We don't want them to know we were here, too."

"I can kill them all before anyone notices," Ryft noted.

"No," Dante said. "Do not give away our presence. What is happening now?"

"She's yelling at the Oogar...Still yelling...Now they're going back to their vehicles. Yeah, they're leaving."

"Okay," Dante said. "Shadow and Peanut, go see what you can find out."

The two appeared on the monitor, coming in from both directions with blades drawn and at the ready. Splunk watched them sweep the area and eventually give the all-clear signal.

"No sign of an attacker," Peanut said.

"Be thorough," Splunk implored him. "If we have a new player, we need to know."

The two spent several more minutes using their gear and going over the scene millimeter by millimeter. Eventually, they shook their heads and came back to rejoin the others. Together they moved into one of the plentiful abandoned apartments.

"Report," Splunk ordered them.

"The MinSha was taken out by a pro," Sandy said.

"No doubt," Peanut agreed. "They knew the perfect kill-spot. You'd have to know their physiology to stab one in the brain. Not many know their brain isn't in the head."

"Not that they have much of a brain," Ryft said.

Dante nodded, then spoke. "Clues?"

"Not a one," Peanut said. "The weapon was a blade, though not a special one. No residue. No footprints."

"No such thing as invisibility," Splunk said. Ryft had the recording of the attack running, going through it over and over.

"The SooSha are close," Shadow said.

"They have to know you're there to blank your memory," Dante said.

"Look," Ryft said. She had the recording frozen at the second of the MinSha's death. The blade, coated with blood, was visible as it punched into the insect's torso along with a crackle of discharge from the cloak. She zoomed and enhanced the knife until a tiny hand was partly visible. It was distorted to the point it was more spectral than real.

"Depik," Dante said.

"What are *they* doing here?" Splunk wondered. "Not only that, why are they taking out a scout watching the Cavaliers?"

"Safe to say the Depik isn't working for the Merc Guild," Dante said.

"Can't we find the Depik and ask it why?" Shadow asked.

Dante laughed and shook his head. "Little one, you don't find a Depik; it finds you. They go back to the great war. Haven't been many of them around since, though. They keep a low profile. They've got skills, and you don't want to mess with them."

"How do you take them out?" Shadow asked.

"Preferably from orbit," the old, one-eyed warrior answered.

Splunk nodded and considered. They still had the drone from earlier, the one belonging to the other group of Humans in the area. Maybe it was time to link up, and possibly combine their resources. Besides, if they turned out to be on the wrong side, it would be easy to have her team liquidate them. "We'll do our best to give the Depik a wide berth," Splunk said, before mentioning her plan.

* * * * *

Chapter Twenty-Three

Merc Guild Command Center, Ubatuba, Brazil, Earth

"General, we have a message from the emergence point. *New Era* and a fleet have returned to Sol."

"The whole fleet?" Peepo asked, looking up from a slate of reports.

"A partial fleet," the comms tech replied. "Report says twenty-two ships, light on escorts. Mixed Bakulu and Izlian, including *Trushista*, the ship Paka was commanding. It appears most have suffered damage."

"I expected losses, but why so few, and why *Trushista* and *New Era*?" It wasn't actually a question and she didn't expect an answer; what would the stupid elSha know of the tactical situation? "Send messages to Admiral Galantrooka and Paka. Give them my regards and tell them to report the status of the New Warsaw conquest immediately; signed, my office."

The comms tech saluted and left her office. Peepo scratched her chin and considered. The fleet had orders to send a courier reporting success as soon as the battle was won. A fleet wasn't a courier. *New Era* and *Trushista* had returned, which meant they hadn't lost. She couldn't conceive of a scenario where the dreadnought would survive the attack to withdraw and return; Admiral Galantrooka wasn't the type to give up. Besides, dreadnoughts had only slightly more acceleration than a behemoth; they weren't made to run. If it was

317

back—and they had an overwhelming force compared to the fleet they were facing—they had won and were back to report that something unexpected had happened. Perhaps the remainder of the Golden Horde had blown themselves up and there was now nothing left in New Warsaw and no reason to stay.

Her mind tried to come up with another possible outcome as the minutes ticked by from the lag time of message transmission to reply, but there wasn't one. Using her pinplants, she called up the data for the newly arrived fleet, including velocities and disposition. Initial scans showed *New Era* had taken a beating but wasn't severely damaged. This was to be expected, but the fleet's composition was strange—like the sensor ops at the emergence point said, the ships had almost no escorts. The fleet was comprised solely of battleships, battlecruisers, and cruisers. And the dreadnought. Where were the escorts? Surely Admiral Galantrooka hadn't left them to guard New Warsaw; that made *no* sense. Their entire presence and their disposition made no sense, their comms procedures were abnormal…nothing about their appearance made sense, and that made her fur stand on end.

"Operations," she called. "Order the fleet to a defensive posture."

"Against our own ships?" the operations officer asked.

"Do it." Peepo cut the line and waited. Less than five seconds later, the system's operational status switched from alert to defensive. Starships began breaking orbit to maneuver toward the emergence point.

Something went desperately wrong at New Warsaw.

A number of seconds after the reply should have come back from *New Era*, two dozen more ships emerged from hyperspace. The group was led by the two Bakulu battleships the Humans had captured and flanked by five ancient cigar-shaped battlecruisers that made her whiskers twitch in pent-up rage.

"No reply from the *New Era*," the comms tech reported.

"You don't say," Peepo snarled, and threw a slate at the stunned elSha. She called operations again. "Delay the inbound attack fleet as long as possible," she said. "And get me the file on *New Era*."

Peepo grabbed a slate and quickly composed a message to Pluis instructing him to get the Raknar and their operators off planet immediately. She'd dearly wanted to have the Fae as well, but that wasn't to be. For now, anyway. But they wouldn't escape.

As soon as she finished the order and saw its receipt confirmed, another message came in. The Oogar strike team sent to take out the probable Cavaliers unit hiding to the south had arrived and found no trace of the mercs. There were remnants of a bivouac inside the warehouse and evidence the Humans left only minutes before. She ordered a sweep of the area and leaned back in her chair.

* * *

CIC, EMS *Shadowfax*, Sol Emergence Point

"The fleet is out of hyperspace and forming up," Evie reported.

"Roger that," Elizabeth replied and watched for herself on the Tri-V. No losses in hyperspace. So far so good. A light second closer to Earth, *New Era* and the other new allies of humanity were falling toward the blue planet. A fleet was climbing to meet them. "It seems our surprise was not total." She shook her head. *Where did they come up with so many ships?*

"Tactical, give me a breakdown on enemy fleet composition, ASAP."

"Working on it."

The Tri-V battlespace evolved quickly, painting and identifying targets. There were four battleships, 11 battlecruisers, 15 cruisers, and 31 frigates of various sizes. Captain Glashpooka commanding the Bakulu battleship and screening vessels for Admiral Galantrooka was maneuvering to flank Peepo's forces. The dreadnought was moving toward Earth at a painfully slow rate.

She'd expected the forces Peepo was mustering to engage hard and fast. They didn't. Instead the enemy ships were engaging at extreme range with immense amounts of missiles. It forced the screening ships to move at the pace of the dreadnought, *New Era*, or risk having it overwhelmed.

"Whose ships are those?" Elizabeth asked her TacCom.

"Jeha," he answered. "Mostly Jeha ships, though some Bakulu, Izlian, Maki, and even a few Buma."

"It's a motley crew she's assembled," Evie pointed out.

"Still formidable," Elizabeth said.

<Formidable and desperate, it seems.>

Elizabeth jumped. *Shadowfax* was coasting, and she almost launched herself out of her chair. "Patrick?" she said aloud, but didn't receive any response. The voice had appeared in her mind, so she replied in kind.

"Is that you, Patrick? Where are you?"

<I am near. Not Patrick, as you knew him.>

Elizabeth was aware Evie was looking at her, so she tried to appear to be studying the Tri-V tactical board. *"Then what are you?"*

<Alexis Cromwell knew me as Ghost, just as her mother before her.>

"Entropy," Elizabeth hissed. "Why did you…why did you take Patrick?"

<There are many reasons, but chief among them is compatibility.>

"Is he dead? Patrick?"

<Not dead in the sense you know that state exists.>

"That isn't much of an answer."

<It is the best I can offer.>

"You can read my mind?"

<The connection to this body is part of the reason I chose the Human known as Patrick. Observe sector 11-A.>

Elizabeth checked the battlespace. The sector Ghost noted was on the enemy upper left flank, where they were not keeping proper pace. "Assign Captain Sarauw in *Seattle Slew* to take *Howler, Marmoset,* and *Tamarin.* Include *Damocles* and *Excalibur* for escort. Have them break off and intercept sector 11-A to exploit the flank. Have *Chimera* initiate drone launch to cover the move."

Evie checked the board and nodded at the move. The TacCom stared, abashed that he'd missed the weakness.

"Is this what you did for Alexis?"

<Among other things.>

"You know Alexis might be alive?"

<I do.>

"Then why did you move to Shadowfax and take my Patrick?"

<It was the only way to save her.>

She was about to ask how that would matter when the enemy fleet responded to the movement of ships she'd assigned. The move opened up a fissure. "Drone strike, there!"

"Got it!" Evie said.

"All *Egleesius*, advance at best acceleration."

* * *

São José dos Campos, Brazil, Earth

Major Good looked up from his slate as Sunshine and Tsan walked into the command post, followed by a huge Samoan and a Hispanic man wearing a gold oak leaf.

"Welcome," Good said. "I'm glad Tsan and Sunshine made it in time to get you."

"It was a close thing," Tsan noted, preening her tail. "They need to move faster when told to move. The Merc Guild almost caught them."

"I'm Major Alvarado," the Hispanic man said, "and this is First Sergeant Akamai 'Buddha' Kalawai." He waved toward where Corporal Bolormaa Enkh was processing video imagery on a Tri-V. "As you may have figured, we're from Cartwright's Cavaliers." He paused a second then added, "Can I ask just what the hell is going on here?"

Good smiled. "Absolutely. Welcome to the headquarters of the resistance. I'm Major James Good of the Golden Horde. Like you, we escaped the failed assault on São Paulo, and we've been working on our options for what to do next." He indicated the other two members of the conference. "Along the way, we picked up Tsan and Sunshine, who's the last member of the Kakata Korps. They tried to keep the Merc Guild out of Monrovia. Like São Paulo, though, they weren't able to."

"I see," Alvarado said with a nod to Sunshine. "I'm sorry for your loss." He turned back to Good. "So, you have been working on options? What have you come up with?"

"Until your arrival—"

"I'm going to kill Peepo," Tsan cut in, "while you provide a distraction as you rescue the rest of the mercs." She turned to Good and slow-blinked. "Sorry, but you have a habit of talking around a subject." She turned back to Alvarado. "That is what we are going to do."

"I don't remember agreeing to participate in this plan," Alvarado replied.

"That's because you didn't know about it until now." Tsan paused as she licked an errant hair on her paw back into place. "Now that you know, though, you will do it."

Alvarado gave her a small smile. "And why's that?"

Tsan gave him a drawn out sigh. "Because Peepo is holding your leader. You don't want her to have him in her claws any longer than you have to. She may extract information from him, or she may kill him in the attempt. Either way, you need to rescue him as soon as you can. I need to kill Peepo before she moves somewhere else. It is all very simple; I don't understand why you Humans have to talk everything to death before taking action. Can we all agree to that, and move forward with the planning?"

"I agree that needs to be our plan," Good replied. "But there's one more player we haven't taken into account. They could be very helpful."

"Who's that?" Alvarado asked.

"I'll show you," Enkh said, indicating the Tri-V. On the display, a MinSha lay in a puddle of blue. "Here's the sentry Tsan killed." She fast-forwarded the image, and a Veetanho and an Oogar appeared. They looked at the MinSha for a few moments, the Veetanho yelled at the Oogar's incompetence, then they left. Enkh fast-forwarded the image again. This time when she stopped, two small aliens were searching the room.

"Who...or what are those things?" Sunshine asked.

"Those look like Fae," Alvarado said thoughtfully, looking at Buddha. "I don't think either of them are Splunk, though, do you?"

"No, sir," Buddha replied. "I can confirm; neither of them is Splunk."

"What are they doing?" Sunshine asked as the Fae stopped to look at the MinSha.

"Looks like they're admiring Tsan's handiwork," Enkh said. Tsan slow-blinked back at her. "The question is whether they will find your camera," Enkh added.

"They will not," Tsan said. "Similar to how I can go invisible to your eyes, I can make other things invisible to your eyes and technology, at least for a time."

"The Fae are reputed to be very good with technology," Good said.

Tsan slow-blinked. "It won't make any difference."

Good nodded as the Fae walked off, apparently without noticing the camera.

"If there are two of them here, Splunk is probably close by, too," Buddha said. "I guarantee you that if we can get in touch with her, whatever Fae are in the area will help us get Colonel Cartwright back."

Good stared at the image of the Fae. Enkh had frozen it just before they disappeared. "That is…weird," he said finally.

"What do you mean?" Alvarado asked.

"Tsan kills the MinSha spying on you folks, and then immediately after, the Fae drop by for a peek at the assassin?" Good shook his head. "Too coincidental. How would they have found the MinSha? They just happened to be in the neighborhood? I don't buy it."

"What are you thinking?" Alvarado asked.

"I don't know," Good said. "Maybe they were about to make contact with you, but the Merc Guild attack spooked them? Maybe they were positioning themselves to hit the Oogar, but Tsan came in and swept you all away?" He shrugged. "The only way we'll know for sure is to ask them, and I don't know how we're going to be able to do that."

"*Shit!*" Enkh exclaimed. "Time's up."

"What do you mean?" Good asked.

"The Merc Guild just got a message from the picket at the emergence point. *New Era* and the Merc Guild fleet have returned to Sol."

"Damn," Good said. "That means…they were only there, what? Three days? They must have wiped out everything there if they are already back."

"Wiped out?" Sunshine asked.

"Nuked it all," Good replied. "Like what they did to Monrovia."

"Are they going to do that here, next?" Sunshine asked.

"What they decide to do next doesn't change anything," Tsan said. "Whether they decide to destroy the other pockets of humanity doesn't matter, nor does it matter if they decide to nuke Earth. All that matters is that Peepo will die, and I will be the one to kill her."

Her tail flicked once. "You can either help me or get out of my way. Which is it going to be?"

"With all due respect," Buddha said, "I care an awful lot about what happens to Earth. I'm kind of attached to it." He turned to Alvarado. "With that said, sir, I say we help her. You've seen what Colonel Cartwright's Raknar can do. They're all we have left to defend Earth. If we can rescue the colonel and find out where the Raknar are being held—"

"We know where they're being held," Good interrupted.

"Even better," Buddha replied. "If we can break out the colonel, find the Fae, and get them both to the Raknar, maybe we can hold them off Earth."

"Weird…" Enkh interjected. "Peepo just moved the fleet to a defensive status."

"What?" Alvarado asked. "Why would she do that?"

"She wouldn't," Good replied. "Unless…"

"Unless what?"

"Unless she thought the fleet was being chased. The only reason she would do that was if the Merc Guild fleet failed to capture New Warsaw, and Peepo thinks she may have to defend this system." He turned to Enkh. "What else do you have? Has the fleet given any sort of update on the battle in New Warsaw?"

"No sir, and that's another thing that's weird. The guild keeps calling the fleet, but it hasn't replied, not once. It's almost like it's a ghost—*More ships at the emergence area!* It's the Hussars! The Hussars are chasing them! We must have won!"

"Wait," Good said. "Let's not jump to conclusions. There's no way the Hussars could have beaten that dreadnought. Are you sure it's the Hussars?"

Enkh pressed several virtual buttons, and her Tri-V display changed to show two battleships, flanked by the distinctive cigar-shaped *Egleesius* ships. A number of smaller ships were moving into screening positions. "I present to you, the Hussars," Enkh said, pointing to the *Egleesius* ships.

"Well, there's no doubt that the Hussars' *ships* have returned. But have the Hussars, themselves? Maybe they surrendered, and the Merc Guild forces captured them?"

"Not the way they're forming up," Enkh replied. "They're organizing for an attack, not to move into some parking orbit...and the earlier Merc Guild forces are aligning to meet the ships coming up from Earth orbit, not to stop the Hussars! What the hell happened in New Warsaw?"

"And what does it mean?" Alvarado asked.

"It means we have a chance," Buddha replied. "If we can get the colonel to the Raknars, they can get back into the fight, like at Karma. They might be able to help."

"What it really means," Tsan said, "is that everything we thought we knew just became as useful as GenSha shit. Whatever Peepo *was* going to do, now she is going to do something else. Her prisoners? She may decide to kill them rather than let them be recaptured. Same thing with the Raknar; she's probably going to move them. *Deep night!* She's going to move herself, too. If it looks bad, she's going to try to flee. We don't have time! We have to attack now, or we're going to miss her."

"There is no need for you all to get so excited," a new voice said from behind them. "The Dusman are here now, and we will tell you what to do."

328 | KENNEDY & WANDREY

Good did his best to commit the moment to memory. He didn't think he'd ever again have a chance to see a Depik look surprised.

* * *

Tsan was only able to avoid pulling quintessence through force of will. She hadn't heard them coming. She turned to regard the newcomers, forcing her fur to lay flat. The newcomers looked somewhat like monkeys, but with large blue eyes and big ears sporting tufts of fur at their ends. The one who'd spoken was the only one who looked different—he had a cybernetic arm, a patch over his left eye, and his tail looked like it had been partly amputated at some point.

"I don't care who you are," Tsan said after a moment's inspection had determined the newcomers were unlikely to be of much assistance, despite the big rifle one of them carried, "and I'm not taking orders from you. I already know what to do—I am going to kill Peepo. Do not get in my way; I will kill you."

The one-eyed Dusman straightened like he intended to respond; however, Major Good stepped between them.

"Let's try to remember we're all on the same team," the Human said, making patting motions with his hands. "We have a number of targets that need to be attacked simultaneously. If you will all work together, I'm sure there is a way to accomplish everything that needs to be done."

"We need to recover Jim and the other Raknar drivers!" one of the Fae—a female by the sound of her voice—exclaimed.

"I agree," Good replied, "and I think that if we get the Cavalier forces in place, stealthily, while the other groups infiltrate, we can use them as a distraction to free the Raknar drivers and kill Peepo."

"You're not listening!" Tsan's tail lashed, her patience growing thin. "We have to get in there now, or we're going to miss Peepo!"

"I agree, sir," Buddha said, looking to Alvarado. "We can hit them hard and give the other groups time to accomplish their missions." He pointed to a dirt road that ran along the other side of the hills from the complex. "If we unload here, we can jump into the complex."

"That's thick jungle in between," Alvarado warned. "If we have to set down, its likely to result in the loss of the CASPer. They also won't be able to jump again—any further progress will have to be overland."

"So, we don't land," Buddha said with a shrug. "We have enough jump juice to make it in one jump. We won't have a whole lot left over when we get there, but it shouldn't be a problem. Then we hit them from the side, and the other groups advance while we're stomping spiders and such."

"We need an hour to prepare," the Dusman with the eye patch said. "We will need access to parts and materials during this time."

"What for?" Good asked.

"We need to assemble *Konar* so we can participate in the attack. With these suits, we will be able to provide key assistance when and where it's needed, which will allow us to help turn the battle."

Tsan swished her tail angrily. "More delay."

"Can you do whatever it is that you need to do en route?" Good asked. "Like in the back of a truck?"

The Dusman with the eyepatch turned to another, who nodded slowly. "It will take us a little longer," Eyepatch said, "but it can be done."

"I'm good with this plan," Alvarado said. "I'm sure Captain Wolf will be as well. Hitting hard and fast is what the Cavaliers do best." Buddha nodded.

"Okay, then," Good said. "As far as timing goes, here's what we'll do…"

* * *

Merc Guild Detention Facility, Ubatuba, Brazil, Earth

"Get up, scum!"

Jim jerked awake at the sharp kick to his side. He rolled away from the kick, hissing in pain and trying to wake up. "What the fuck do you want?" It was one of the loathsome Varangian Guard. Not the sadistic Corporal Romanov, who enjoyed inflicting pain, though it seemed they were all inclined to hurt people.

"Time to go meet your fate, boy."

Jim felt his blood run cold. Were they about to execute him? His face must have betrayed the fear he felt because the man laughed.

"No, we ain't gonna kill you. General Peepo is taking you to the Mercenary Guild headquarters."

"I thought they were taking me to Betall," Jim said.

"They was. Seems your merc friends have slipped the noose she set for them. They're taking you to the guild headquarters instead. After you spill the beans, you'll stand trial."

"Slipped the noose?" Jim repeated. "Wait, Peepo lost at New Warsaw?" The man's face darkened. "They lost in New Warsaw, and the Hussars are coming for some payback." The man cocked his hand back to strike Jim, but he didn't flinch.

"Just get up, fatso," the man said. lowering his hand. He tossed Jim a clean uniform. "Get dressed. You have five minutes. If you don't, I'll drag your naked fat ass down to the shuttle. She didn't say nothing about being clothed."

"What about the other Raknar pilots?"

"They're already on the shuttle. Move it."

Jim did as he was instructed.

He'd never seen the outside of his prison. It was an unassuming series of buildings with a small spaceship landing facility. He only knew it was still Brazil from what he'd heard the Varangian Guardsmen talk about. Someplace called Ubatuba. Sounded like a musical instrument to him.

Alien mercs were lined up in formation along the open avenue leading to a trio of shuttles squatting on the landing pads. Jim could see a company of the Varangian Guards, their CASPers crisp and shiny, standing at attention next to one of the shuttles. Four platoons of Besquith in combat armor were just outside the door he was being led from. None of the slavering werewolves seemed to take any note of the Human. Neither did the squads of Oogar and Tortantula, the latter, each led by a Tortantula with Flatar on their back. It was an impressive force.

A small electric cart awaited Jim and his Varangian escort. Standing next to the cart was Major Vels Lucas. He stared at Jim with hard eyes.

"What's wrong, Major?" Jim asked as he came up to him. "You didn't deliver Peepo what she wanted?"

"General Peepo, to you, Cartwright."

"Colonel Cartwright to you, Major."

The other man's expression darkened, and he gestured to the electric cart. "I am traveling with you, so maybe we can come to an agreement prior to arrival."

"Feel free to believe whatever you want," Jim said as he climbed in. Lucas scowled even more as he got in on one side of Jim. He turned and saw the sadistic Corporal Romanov on the other. The man grinned evilly. An elSha in the driver's position glanced back at its passengers. Lucas nodded, and the elSha started up the cart, driving them to the shuttle.

Just before the cart reached the shuttle, Jim saw a blaze of light climbing into the sky. It was a huge transport, and it used three launch lasers to get off the ground. He tried to imagine how big it must be to need three of the immensely powerful launch lasers. It took two minutes for the sound to reach them, which meant the launch was at least 25 miles away.

I'm north of the starport. The cart stopped and Jim was prodded out of the cart. A Sidar/Selroth pilot team. The Sidar spoke to Lucas.

"We must hurry to make rendezvous prior to orbit on the transport."

"Why the hurry?" Lucas asked.

"Problems with the battle developing in space."

Lucas scowled and gave Jim a little push toward the ramp. "Hurry up, *Colonel.*" He managed to stuff a lot of scorn into Jim's rank.

As he was walking up the ramp, he realized two things. First, he'd understood the Sidar, which meant his pinplants were working again, as they'd translated the alien's language. Second, there was a platoon of CASPers vaulting over the building he'd just left, weapons blazing.

* * * * *

Chapter Twenty-Four

"Lead the charge!" the thirty-four members of Charlie Company screamed over their loudspeakers as they roared over the three-story building on their jumpjets. Equipped with the shiny new Mk 8 CASPers they'd found in the warehouse in São Paulo, the armored troopers unloaded on the stunned ranks of Besquith mercs with a deadly fusillade of fire. Dozens were mowed down before they knew there was even an attack ongoing.

The Tortantula were the first to respond, the ranks of riderless behemoths fairly exploding toward the CASPers as they landed from their initial jumps. The two groups collided in a crash of spider arms, armor, and blood.

"What is this shit?" Vels Lucas yelled. A pair of missiles arced over another building to land amidst his troopers. Several were blown to pieces. Their response was unorganized, and they wavered, unsure whether to go against the Cavaliers leaping into action or to pursue whoever was firing at them over the buildings.

"Yes!" Jim exulted and pumped a fist in the air. "Looks like it's time to pay the piper," Jim said, laughing.

Vels shoved him toward the shuttle and addressed Romanov. "Get him aboard!"

"Major," the corporal said and grabbed Jim's arm with frightening force. "Move it, fat kid." Jim didn't bother to correct Ramanov; it

335

wouldn't have done much good. He was half dragged, half kicked up the ramp into the shuttle. He lost sight of his beloved Cavaliers just as the weapons fire started in earnest.

* * *

CIC, EMS *Shadowfax*, Approaching Earth

Shadowfax bucked as her shields sloughed off a half dozen shipkiller missiles. "Oh, we got their attention now," she said.

"Without a doubt," Evie agreed.

"Enemy formation of seven Jeha battlecruisers is penetrating the screen," TacCom warned.

"No escorts?" Evie said, looking at her captain.

Captain Stacy had a feral grin on her face. She would have been chagrined to realize how much she looked like Alexis Crowell at the moment. "They're trying for the battleships' side. Order our screen to defend their flanks. All *Egleesius*, spinal mounts on the lead enemy battlecruisers." The five ancient ships used their oversized maneuvering thrusters to turn far faster than normal ships their size. "Match bearings and *fire!*"

The CIC lights dimmed as 90% of the power from the ship's three fusion power plants was channeled through meter-thick superconducting power relays. The *Egleesius* was built around its main armament, and the 40-terawatt particle accelerator acted as her backbone. The great ship thrummed like a bass guitar string as the charging coils discharged their deadly stream of star-hot energy.

Three of the seven Jeha battlecruisers were killed in an instant as the huge particle beams overloaded their shields, sliced through their armor like it wasn't there, and turned their interior spaces into an ever-growing shockwave of exploding matter. Two other battlecruisers were badly damaged and out of the fight.

"They're trying to disengage," TacCom said.

"Order Captain Handley in *Gallant Fox* to have his cruiser squadron exploit their flank." A few seconds later, a wave of missiles from three *Steed*-class cruisers and two *Stem*-class former Maki light cruisers tore into the rear quarter shielding of the remaining pair of battlecruisers. Their shields fell and dozens of drones, which had been holding within the cruiser squadron's defensive box, shot ahead and delivered a strike with the Hussars' devastating squash-bomb-armed shipkillers.

"Enemy battlecruiser formation is eliminated," Evie said.

Elizabeth gave some of her attention to the battlespace. Their two *Thrush*-class battleships were slugging it out with three Buma battleships. Elizabeth had never seen Buma battleships in the field. To her knowledge, it was the first time they'd ever been seen in combat. It looked like Peepo was scraping the bottom of the barrel.

<Battleship designated Tango-Beta,> Ghost said. <Its ventral three-quarters forward shield section is out. They are not covering the gap well>

"TacCom, enemy battleship Tango-Beta," Elizabeth said, and gave the shield data.

"Got it," TacCom said, shaking his head. "I didn't see it."

"No problem. *Pegasus* is in the best position. Give the data to Captain Corder; he'll know what to do with it. Remind him he's not in a *Steed*-class, and good hunting."

She watched the board as *Pegasus* disengaged and did a seven-G skew turn. She winced a little at how the crew must have suffered through the maneuver. The turn completed, he kicked her stern around and delivered 40-terawatts of energy dead on target. A section of hull the size of a battlecruiser exploded out the side of Tango-Beta, and her offensive weapons went off line. Before any Hussars could exploit the weakness, the ship's captain surrendered.

"Not much of a taste for this," Evie said.

"I wonder what race is manning the ship," Elizabeth mused. She knew it wouldn't be Buma; they weren't a merc race. They didn't even build decent ships, as was just made apparent to the crew of the ship.

"New Izlian fleet incoming," Evie said. "They were hanging out in L3."

"What were they waiting for?" Elizabeth wondered. She did a quick tactical analysis. The Hussars' allied losses had been light. While the new Izlian fleet was an unwanted surprise, it wasn't a game changer. She was about to order her battleships to maneuver for intercept when the friendly Izlians called.

"This is Admiral Epsilon on *Fresha*."

"Go ahead, Admiral, this is Commander Stacy on *Shadowfax*."

"Commander, we will handle the Izlians."

Elizabeth paused and chewed her lip a second before answering. "Admiral, with all due respect, I'm afraid that is a conflict of interest."

"It would seem that way, but I assure you, we can handle it."

Evie and Elizabeth exchanged looks. Taking the Izlians had been a gamble from the start. The Hussars were short on throw weight; otherwise, she would never have done it. She wasn't sure if Alexis would have, either. She'd rolled the dice and kept the gas bags in one sector of their advance, out front, just in case.

"Very well, Admiral. Please keep our order of battle in mind should this prove difficult."

"Understood, Commander."

Elizabeth turned to Evie. "Make the fleet aware of this situation?"

"Already on it, Captain," Evie said.

"What do you think of this Izlians?" Elizabeth asked Ghost.

<They have the situation in hand. I estimate a ninety-two percent probability there will be no additional conflict with the Izlians.>

Elizabeth shrugged and turned her attention elsewhere. If Alexis had trusted Ghost, she needed to as well. Besides, what choice did she have? She ordered the fleet to continue the approach to Earth. A short time later, the two Izlian fleets faced off.

She watched the Tri-V, expecting a battle. Just as Ghost predicted, no battle materialized. Instead the fleets merged into one. "Admiral Epsilon says his new, larger fleet is at your disposal."

Elizabeth's grin returned. Now *she* had the advantage.

<Something is not right.>

"I need a little more than that to go on," Elizabeth thought back.

<Unsure.>

"Was your advice to Alexis always this frustrating?"

<Alexis believed it was.>

Elizabeth snorted, and Evie looked at her in confusion. "I'll explain later. Scan Earth orbit. Anything unusual?"

"No, there are a lot of ships still in orbit, but they're all non-combatants. Transports and such."

<*Something with the ships in orbit.*> Suddenly, her mind was full of the scans coming from her own ship, only different. Layers upon layers peeled away like the ships were being dipped in acid. A decon-

struction like she'd never seen before. When the deconstruction reached the core of the ship, it moved to another.

"Is this how you see?"

<One way.>

"The Bakulu squadron has pushed through the defenders and is coming in range of orbit."

Elizabeth was torn between having her new allies abort an orbital approach and pushing onward. Scans continued to flash through her brain as they were shared by Ghost.

"Tell them to expect an attack," she said.

"There are no indications of anything," Evie said.

In Elizabeth's mind, the scan froze halfway through deconstructing a huge transport, one of four identical ships which had changed their orbits to face the advancing fleet a minute earlier. The scan showed the ship's superstructure was nothing more than a façade. She opened her mouth to warn about the ruse when the ships seemed to explode, and a new ship accelerated out of the debris field.

"What is that?" Evie asked. TacCom scanned the four new ships, trying to discern their shapes and specification.

<The Bakulu should flee, if they are able.>

"Contact the Bakulu commander, Glashpooka," Elizabeth said. "If they can disengage, they should."

"Captain Glashpooka says they are committed, but he isn't concerned," Comms reported.

<They will not survive.>

* * *

CIC, BMS *Trushista*, Approaching Earth Orbit

"Continue analysis," Captain Glashpooka ordered. The fact that they couldn't identify the ship types that had emerged from their disguise was a little worrisome. The tactic itself was not unheard of, just gimmicky. Useful for anti-piracy more than anything, it was wasteful in warfare. The material costs in building a superstructure to hide the smaller warship simply didn't pay off.

"They are cruisers in size, but their shields and drive emissions are completely wrong," his SitCon said.

"Weapons solutions are coming in," TacCom said.

"Admiral Galantrooka says he can have *New Era* in range within five minutes," his XO said. "Should we delay?"

"No," Glashpooka said. "Begin missile launch."

Hundreds of missiles flew from *Trushista* and her surviving escort ships. Thanks to Paka, he was somewhat low on both missiles and escorts, but he guessed it would be more than enough to deal with four cruisers.

With the relatively short range, the missiles crossed to the targets in only a few seconds. Glashpooka had been watching the Tri-V with one eye and the general battlespace with two others. When the enemy ships didn't begin firing at the missiles, all three eyes turned. *Why aren't they firing anti-missile lasers?*

"Impact in two seconds; they are not trying to stop the missiles," his XO confirmed.

Glashpooka watched with a growing sense of dread as the first of over 100 missiles reached their targets and nothing happened. As the launch reached its peak and the nuclear missiles didn't go off, his dread turned to fear. "What is happening?"

"I cannot tell," the TacCom said. The officer's eyes, pseudopods, and no doubt pinplants were working the sensor data furiously. "It is as if the missiles were disarmed. I lost telemetry just before they should have detonated." Another second later, the missile wave ended without a single explosion. Telephoto imaging showed some of the missiles physically striking the ships. Each of the four vessels had a strange, mottled hull, which reminded Glashpooka of something chipped out of rock. The four vessels were generally shaped like flattened spear points, but unique in their individual details.

"Alter rotation to bring the 10-terawatt particle accelerator bays into position," he ordered. TacCom had just acknowledged the order when all four enemy ships seemed to pulse with a crackling static discharge. *Trushista* shuddered from a series of internal explosions.

"No impact on shields!" TacCom cried.

"Reactors Five and Seven are offline," engineering warned.

"Major internal damage," the damage control coordinator warned, and he began listing a litany of destruction.

"All ships, fire," Glashpooka ordered. Laser and particle weapons lashed out. The cameras still focused on the enemy ships showed the lasers absorbed by the enemy hull, some of them reflecting away, others causing small glowing spots and puffs of material. Particle beams seemed to disperse along large areas of the hull.

"Fire is having no appreciable effect," SitCon said. The enemy ships sparked again, and damage ripped through *Trushista*'s internal spaces. "All weapons offline, helm offline!" The ship began to yaw out of control as the enemy ships opened fire on their screening vessels. Four were destroyed, one by each enemy ship.

"Send all telemetry to *New Era*," Captain Glashpooka ordered. Power failed, and the last of the emergency reserve went out. Earth was directly in their path. *I should have listened to Commander Stacy.*

* * *

CIC, EMS *Shadowfax*, Approaching Earth

"Whoa, what was that?" the TacCom asked as the new alien ships fired, and *Trushista* was torn apart by internal explosions.

<Meson weapons,> Ghost said.

Elizabeth remembered; they were in a report from an encounter in 2nd level hyperspace. The strange alien ships there used meson weapons. "*Can you alter their ship's shields, like you did with* Pegasus*?*"

<Only the Egleesius are capable of altering their shields in such a way.>

Elizabeth snarled in frustration. *Trushista* was falling past the new arrivals, uncontrolled and trailing a rapidly dissipating cloud of debris. The deadly looking spear-shaped ships accelerated at more than twenty Gs toward *New Era*, sweeping the way clear of the ships in their path. She felt her stomach tighten. Where had Peepo come up with them?

<I have identified the origin of the ships. They are Biruda, an ancient merc race. There is no evidence of their activity since the Great War. The Biruda were allies of the Kahraman.>

"How do I defeat them?"

<The Dusman defeated them. I do not know how.>

The Biruda ships didn't bother destroying all the screening ships after wrecking *Trushista*, they just continued onward toward the dreadnought.

"We are sorry, Admiral Galantrooka," Elizabeth transmitted.

"Do not be sorry, Commander Stacy," the Bakulu admiral replied. "This is a disaster entirely of Peepo's making. We seem to have underestimated her, even in the end. I was her chief admiral and knew nothing about these ships." On the Tri-V, the dreadnought was rocked by explosions as the Biruda ships targeted it.

"The enemy fleet is reforming and attacking ahead of the Biruda ships," Evie said.

"*Egleesius* to the front," Elizabeth ordered. "Screening vessels fallback."

"Enemy has launched a wave of missiles," TacCom reported.

"Charge spinal mounts and stand by," Elizabeth ordered. On the Tri-V, the missiles raced at the five *Egleesius*. "Wait for it...wait...Engage deflectors!"

TacCom brought up the deflector shields developed by Sato. In the three days before the fleet left for Earth, the Geek Squad had added them to all five *Egleesius*-class battlecruisers. The missiles exploded on target, and their energy deflected away from the ships with very little power required.

"I could get used to this," Evie said.

"Me, too," Elizabeth agreed. "Advance at best speed. Inform the rest of the fleet to prepare to withdraw if we can't damage the Biruda ships."

The mixed enemy fleet was obviously confused by the deflector shields, just as they had been when *Sphinx* employed them for the first time during the Battle of New Warsaw. They responded the same way, concentrating their fire on the deflector-equipped ships.

"Power consumption is in line with established norms," engineering reported.

"Continue on course. Prepare to target the Biruda ships." On the Tri-V, she watched the strange new ships devastating the dreadnought.

"A ship just appeared out of nowhere!" SitCon reported. "It looks like a *Steed*-class, but it's different!"

Elizabeth used her pinplants to access the view and saw the ship between the Hussars and the Birudan ships. The ship looked different, with multiple bulges around its *Egleesius*-reminiscent cigar shape. As she watched, the ship accelerated and began to spin.

* * * * *

Chapter Twenty-Five

CIC, Dusman Attack Cruiser *Hippogriff*,
Approaching Earth

"We've emerged on target."

"Good," Sly said. "Verify targets?"

"Confirmed, there are four Biruda *Maester*-class assault frigates."

"I told you," Seldia said. "I saw this. It is why we have returned to the galaxy, and why Splunk did what she did."

"Enough," Sly snapped. Seldia gave a little smile at the rear of the CIC. "We're here because you've been in communication with our scouts on the Human ships, and they alerted us the Biruda were here."

"As I foresaw there would be," Seldia said with same half-smile.

"The Biruda have taken out most of the Bakulu ships and are advancing on the dreadnought," the TacCom said, then he turned to look at Sly. "The Humans' *Egleesius* are moving up and appear to have been equipped with deflectors."

"Interesting," Sly said. "I thought that one cruiser was an experiment. It seems I was wrong." He looked at the Tri-V and verified their course. "Let's deal with the Biruda first. Spin up, prepare to launch the first *Losc!*"

The CIC quickly flooded with suspension gel as the ship spun up and began to maneuver radically. Sensors picked up a meson attack, which missed. A moment later the first *Losc* was launched.

The missile, made from one of the stolen Hussars' *Crown*-class cruisers, was mostly engine and power plant. It accelerated at hundreds of Gs toward the four Biruda ships. One of them fired on it and hit. The meson penetrated the hull and exploded inside the solid-nickel iron nose of the missile, doing no damage.

The Biruda ship tried to maneuver, but the *Losc* was mostly engine and skillfully piloted from the safety of *Hippogriff*. It hit the hull of the Biruda ship, shattering the molecularly hardened biological armor plates, as well as the magnetic bottle in the missile's nose. A kilogram of antimatter met the tons of solid metal in the missile's nose and exploded with hundreds of megatons of force. The Biruda ship was obliterated.

"Clean kill," TacCom said.

"Excellent, fire on the other three."

The remaining three *Losc* were cast free and accelerated away. A second later, the Biruda ships flashed as they activated their shunts and were gone.

"I was hoping to get at least half of them." Sly frowned. "Safe the *Losc* and clear the engagement field. Once again, we've given the Humans an opportunity; let's see if they can exploit it."

CIC, EMS *Shadowfax*, Just Outside Earth Orbit

<The Dusman are here.>

"Holy shit," Elizabeth exclaimed as the first Biruda ship was annihilated. Not exactly a ship's commander sort of thing to say, of course. She'd been pretty pissed when she realized the Dusman had stolen one of her merc company's battlecruisers, even if it had been temporarily out of operation. Then it showed up, arriving from hyperspace right in the middle of the fight like *Pegasus* was able to do. When it started launching cruiser-sized anti-matter missiles, which appeared immune to the meson weapons, her anger changed to amazement.

The former *Hippogriff* began to dodge with the agility of a missile. *How can it even be manned at those acceleration numbers?* She knew the surviving Biruda ships must be firing at it and missing. Either that, or the former *Hippogriff* was invulnerable to meson weapons?

<Not invulnerable,> Ghost corrected. <It appears this is how they defeated the Biruda. Speed and antimatter weapons.>

"So that's what those ship/missiles are?"

<Without a doubt. A kilogram or more of antimatter with a high-density metallic casing. Blast yield in excess of one hundred megatons, even with the poor conversion rate.>

"What would a high conversion rate yield?"

<Approximately two gigatons.>

Elizabeth mentally whistled. *"Why so inefficient, then?"*

<I would estimate field expediency. The ships and weapons have the feel of things quickly constructed. The Lightships employed back in New Warsaw were much more refined in design and implementation.>

"So, they were expecting the Biruda, but didn't have anything in their arsenal already prepared to deal with them?"

<A reasonable assertion.>

Elizabeth was even more impressed. *These must be the Dusman.*

"They're firing three more of those missile/ships," TacCom announced.

"Those missile/ships used to be the *Crown*-class cruiser hulls which were incomplete," sensor operators said. The Tri-V showed images of the ship/missiles with an overlay of a *Crown*-class cruiser. The lineage was obvious.

"The Dusman really helped themselves, didn't they?" Evie asked.

Elizabeth nodded. History was full of stories of the Dusman, most of which people believed were anecdotal. After all, the last time the Dusman were active was 20,000 years ago. She wondered if these really were the storied race which participated in a galactic war before man learned to write. Watching the ship, she realized they had rebuilt it in days, and they had given it the ability to tear apart ships which, only minutes before, had seemed invincible. This argued in favor of the stories' veracity. The Dusman's arrogance did as well.

The three additional missile/ships rocketed away at hundreds of Gs of acceleration. Enhancements of the weapons' launches clearly showed parts of the former cruisers' hulls shearing away from the acceleration. The builders hadn't wasted the time to cut away unnecessary components.

Before the ship/missiles were halfway to their targets, the three surviving Biruda ships flashed out of existence in an unmistakable shunt-initiated hyperspace jump.

"That was anticlimactic," Evie said. "They just ran?"

<Interesting.>

"For once we seem to agree."

"The Dusman are disengaging," TacCom said.

"You'd think they'd have more to offer," Evie said.

"Well, they got rid of the Biruda," Elizabeth said and shrugged.

"The enemy fleet is attempting to exploit the damage done by targeting the dreadnought."

"See what support we can give," Elizabeth ordered. "This isn't over yet."

* * *

Merc Guild Detention Facility, Ubatuba, Brazil, Earth

"There's your distraction," Buddha said over the radio.

"It will suffice," Splunk replied. "Shall we go?"

"One question first," Buddha said. Silence greeted him so he asked it. "Why didn't you tell anyone you were a Dusman until now?"

"I will tell you what, Buddha. If we survive this, I'll tell you whatever you want."

"Deal," Buddha said, and gestured. "You first."

The tiny powered armor suit took off with a hushed hiss of miniature jumpjets, followed immediately by four others.

"Come on," Buddha said to his squad, "let's go!" He fired his jumpjets and the seven other members of his squad followed.

They cleared the defensive perimeter in a second. The five miniature armored figures disabled the fence's weapons with deadly pinpoint fire. A few of the turrets fired on them, and the Dusmans' armor dodged with surprising speed.

"Holy shit," Corporal Solberg said. "If I hadn't watched them build those suits from parts in just an hour, I'd never have believed it."

"Dude, they're the Dusman," Private Lynch said.

"Yeah, but…"

"Cut the chatter," Buddha ordered. "Follow them. We have to stop that shuttle." With some difficulty, they followed the five racing suits of armor.

* * *

"These *Konar* suck," Ryft said as the five of them bounded into battle.

"What do you expect?" Dante asked, firing his micro-lasers at the defenses. "We made them from Human tech."

"Why didn't Sly bring any real ones with him?" Peanut asked.

"Because he knew we might not live through this," Dante said. "Besides, we don't have any fitted for Humans. They're all too damned big and have four arms."

Splunk dodged one of the slow perimeter defense lasers and took it out with her own micro-laser. The shuttle was only a hundred meters ahead. Her hushed jumpjets hissed as she set down and began to run. Jim was being rushed aboard. *Entropy, we're too late!* The shuttle's ramp was just visible on the far side as it began to retract.

"Buddha," she commed.

"I see it," he replied. The shuttle's engines began to spin up. "We can't stop it from taking off."

"Distract them for a minute?" she asked.

"Go," he said as a laser beam from the shuttle lashed out and bisected a jumping CASPer. It dropped lifeless to crash on the tarmac. Buddha cursed. "Make it count, Splunk!" Laser fire flashed around Buddha's squad, and they dodged the powerful ship-based weapons as best they could.

"We will," she said, rebounding lightly in the armor. *I'm coming Jim.* The shuttle's ascent engines roared, and it began to climb away.

"We're not going to make it!" Dante yelled.

"Yes, we are!" Splunk shouted and made a final jump. All five improvised *Konar* leaped, their miniature jumpjets screaming, as they strove to catch the shuttle.

* * *

Buddha controlled his tumbling CASPer just enough to avoid crashing face first into the tarmac as the shuttle roared into the sky. Between the wild laser fire from the escaping shuttle and the pitched battle against the alien forces a short distance away, his battlespace was a complete mess. He had no clue if the Dusman in their mini-CASPers had accomplished their objective. He was too busy trying to stay alive after one of the shuttle's lasers had clipped his CASPer and knocked out one of his jumpjets.

Private Lee Gann was gone, shot through twice with shuttle lasers, as was Private Peter Lugt. Private Chris Kadish was out of action as well. He was alive, but his suit had taken a hit in the computer/power supply and was inop.

Buddha rolled over and checked the monitor one more time. The shuttle was two kilometers up and climbing. Nothing more could be done. He checked the battlespace near the command building. Bravo and Charlie Companies were, as Hargrave used to say, knee deep in the shit. He had four men left, though, and they might be able to make a difference.

"Let's go," he said, and highlighted an approach through the squadnet. A pair of Tortantulas with Flatar riders were working around a nearby building, trying to flank Alvarado's command squad. "Time to smash some spiders!"

* * *

Merc Guild Headquarters, Ubatuba, Brazil, Earth

"Deep night!"

Although Sunshine had been traveling with Tsan for months now, it was still unnerving to hear her voice come from what appeared to be thin air. Still, she sympathized with the Depik as she watched the shuttle lift. It was the second shuttle they'd seen launch since they'd moved into position. They had no idea if Peepo had been on either—they couldn't see the back of the hacienda—but if things were still going badly, the odds continued to mount that she would be leaving soon.

It had taken the other forces longer than expected to get into position, and Sunshine had learned several new words from Tsan in that time. She had thought that she'd learned every curse possible growing up in the slums of Monrovia. She'd been wrong.

The men at the gate turned and began running for the hacienda.

"Attack!" Tsan ordered.

Sunshine charged the gate, firing her MAC at it as she raced forward. At least one round hit the locking mechanism, shattering it, and she lowered a shoulder to burst through the gate. The two scouts they'd been given from Cartwright's Cavaliers, Private Keenan Seeley and Private Teal Bridgestone, landed beside her in the courtyard, their weapons firing.

She winced involuntarily as she fired on the running Varangian Guard troopers. Jumping the gate probably would have been easier. She still had much to learn about operating a CASPer in combat, she realized—the Korps hadn't done much in the way of three-dimensional maneuvering. She hit two of the fleeing soldiers in the back, and they cartwheeled to a stop in the dirt.

She wondered momentarily where Tsan was, then saw the front door of the big house open on its own. "Let's go!" she yelled to the troopers. "She's going into the house."

Sunshine raced forward again, barely slowing for the front door, which was ajar. She smashed through it, knocking it from its hinges and launching it through the air. She also caught the door jamb, shattering it, but then she was through and standing in a huge foyer. Two more dead Varangian Guard troopers lay in puddles of their own blood, their throats cut.

"Follow me," Tsan said. "And watch where you're firing."

Sunshine looked around. "It would help if I could see you."

"Gah," the Depik said. "Here." Two invisible feet splashed into the blood puddles from one of the troopers, and created a trail to a door, which opened. "Her lair will be in the basement."

"How do you know?" asked one of the Cavaliers.

"Because she's a Veetanho." There was a pause, the "duh" strongly implied, then she added, "Well, are you coming?"

Sunshine ran forward, knowing the Depik would keep out of her way. Sunshine smiled as she looked at the fading paw prints. *Tsan was already down the stairs.* Hoping the stairs would hold the weight of the CASPer, Sunshine worked her way down them, with the other troopers closer behind her than she would have liked. The stairs groaned under the weight but held.

A passage ran down to the basement, with two doors on both sides and a single door at the end opposite the stairs. The first doors on both sides were open, and she advanced to check them out. They both held lots of computer equipment and monitors; they looked important, but no one was in either room.

356 | KENNEDY & WANDREY

She walked down the passageway as the next two doors opened. One looked like a place to have meetings—there was a big table with many chairs and a Tri-V viewer, anyway—and another room with more computers. These were also unoccupied.

The door at the end of the hall opened as large engines went to full power nearby, shaking the ground.

"Deep night!" Tsan exclaimed. "Back upstairs!"

Sunshine felt Tsan land on her CASPer and then push off again. She turned to find the Cavaliers troopers in the way.

"Go, *bass!*" she yelled. "Back upstairs!"

The troopers turned slowly—*they had obviously never operated with Depik before!*—and finally went up the stairs. She chafed as she waited for her turn to go up. While she waited, the sounds of the motors faded.

Sunshine finally made it up the stairs and ran to the back of the house where the other CASPers stood. A space-yacht was just disappearing into the sky.

"Peepo got away," Private Seeley said.

"No, she didn't," Sunshine said. "Tsan is super fast. I'll bet she caught her before that ship lifted. She's probably tearing her way into it right now."

"I *am* super-fast," Tsan said, dropping her quintessence field, "but this time I needed to be even faster." Her tail swished in irritation. "Peepo got away."

* * * * *

Chapter Twenty-Six

Hospital Samaritano, Rio de Janeiro, Brazil

Alexis Cromwell woke, though her head felt mushy, and she had trouble connecting thoughts. Everything was indistinct—her thoughts, her vision, everything. She struggled to get up, but something held her down.

"Easy…" a voice said from a blurred silhouette. There was more, but it was lost, her brain unable to follow.

"Where?" The single word was all Alexis was able to muster.

"Rio…brought here after…" The shape and the words began resolving themselves, and she was able to make sense of some of it. Everything still seemed incredibly slow.

"How…long?"

"You've been here almost three weeks," a woman said, coming into focus.

"Everything is fuzzy…and slow." She couldn't understand why, but thinking still seemed hard, even though her vision had returned to normal.

"That's the effects of the drugs they used to keep you under," the woman said. Now that Alexis' vision had sharpened, she could see the woman was young—probably late 20s—with sky-blue eyes and extremely long raven-black hair braided in an elaborate ponytail that fell over her left shoulder. "Don't worry, though," the woman added, "they shouldn't be harmful to your baby."

"My *what?*"

"When they brought you in here, you were nearly dead. You were also about a month pregnant with a son. They were able to save both you and the baby through the extensive use of nanobot therapy. Just be happy you're not going to get the bill for that; I heard Peepo picked it up. I expect she has some plans for you."

"But…I can't be pregnant. There's a war…"

"Yes, there's a war on, which is why we need to hurry. I will help get you out of here, but then you're going to be on your own." She leaned forward and did something at the back and sides of Alexis' head. A spike like a jolt of electricity went through her brain and everything seemed to speed up as her implants came back online, along with the added processing power she got from them.

"Sorry," the woman said. "I forgot they turned those off."

Alexis shook her head a little and blinked a couple of times, but then everything seemed to return to normal. "Okay, got it." She took in her surroundings. "I'm in a hospital, and I'm pregnant. The war is still going on—wait. The battle has lasted three weeks?"

"No, the Hussars lost the battle after you were shot and fled to New Warsaw. The Merc Guild forces followed your forces back there."

"I've got to go help!" Alexis said. "They'll need me for the defense!" She tried to sit up, but the woman put a hand on her chest and held her back down. Alexis found she wasn't as strong as she used to be. The woman had a surprising strength and was able to hold her down easily with one hand.

"That's not needed," the woman said. "It looks like your forces won, because they just returned and there is a battle raging in space right now."

"Can you get me to my ship?"

"Unfortunately, no. I can get you out of the hospital, but then you'll have to take it from there. There are other things I need to be doing right now. Maybe your friends in orbit can come get you."

"Where did you say we were?"

"We're in the Hospital Samaritano in Rio de Janeiro."

"Brazil?" she asked as her comm system indicated an incoming call. "Let me see what I can do."

* * *

CIC, EMS *Revenge*, Approaching Earth Orbit

Nigel watched the battle with the strange ships, wanting to charge into them, to destroy them and rush forward, but knew that if the Bakulu heavies couldn't hurt them, then his merc cruiser had absolutely *zero* chance of success. When the strange ships suddenly fled when faced with the single cruiser that had magically appeared in the system, he saw his chance. "Captain, can you exploit that gap?" he asked.

The ship's captain smiled. "I can indeed."

"All ahead full to Earth orbit."

He sat in his observation chair at the back of CIC, staring at the battlespace monitor as if his glare could keep the enemy's ships away until he had completed his mission.

"Colonel Shirazi, we are within range of Earth comms."

Nigel blinked then nodded to the comms tech as he tried to focus on something other than the battlespace monitor. "Thanks."

I hope this works, he thought, but it didn't. Nor did the second try.

Okay, Plan B, then. "Major Good, Colonel Shirazi."

After a few seconds that seemed to last an eternity, the call connected. "Um, hi, Colonel. We're kinda busy at the moment, as I'm sure you are. Is there something I can do for you?"

"Colonel Enkh told me to reach out to you. This may sound crazy, but I'm trying to find Colonel Cromwell. I have reason to believe...she's still alive. Have you any idea where they might be holding her, if she were still alive?"

"No, I...wait a minute." His voice was muted as he asked someone a question offline. "There is one thing we picked up. At one point after you were here before, there was a high value unit that was taken to a hospital in Rio, we think it was. At the time, we didn't have anyone we could send to investigate, and we never intercepted anything else about it, so we assumed the person died. The best I can tell you is Rio de Janeiro, but we can't find the name of the hospital."

"Damn. I was hoping for more. That's not enough to act on."

"I know sir, and I'm sorry. My tech wants to know if you'd like her to try calling Colonel Cromwell."

"She's not up on comms; I already tried." Nigel shrugged. "But sure, go ahead."

"Stand by, sir." There was a long pause, then Good returned. "Corporal Enkh was able to connect with Colonel Cromwell, sir!" Good exclaimed. "She's in the Hospital Samaritano in Rio de Janeiro, and she says she needs immediate extract! I'm sending the coordinates!"

* * *

MGS *Begalt*, Approaching Orbit, Earth, Sol System

J im grunted as the shuttle docked roughly with a bigger ship. He wasn't offered a window seat, but rather was shoved into a small cargo compartment and had to make do with lying on a mat to absorb the multiple Gs of liftoff and maneuvering.

From his years of living and working in space, Jim knew the shuttle was docking *during* ascent to orbit. It was a high-risk maneuver, to say the least. Despite the pain of his many bruises and poorly healed injuries, he smiled. If they were this eager to get him off the planet, Peepo's plans were turning to shit. *I hope she likes the taste.*

The door opened, and Corporal Romanov was standing there. He took one look at the semi-feral smile on Jim's face and a hand went to the pistol on his belt.

"What's wrong, tough guy?"

"Fuck you, fat boy," Romanov snarled and grabbed Jim by the arm.

Jim almost went for it. Almost. Romanov had twenty centimeters on him and wasn't more than ten kilos lighter, only his mass wasn't fat—it was iron-hard muscle and bone. Something told him a beating at this stage of the game wouldn't help his situation, so he allowed himself to be moved.

They'd waited to move him until they'd docked, which told him they were working multiple contingencies. Was Peepo running for her life at that very moment? He dearly hoped so.

He paid careful attention as he was led through the corridors of the shuttle, through the airlock, and into what had to be a transport. There were none of the signs of an armored warship—those had a different look. If the ship was lifting off the planet, it wasn't very big either. There were limits to how large you could be and still get off a planet's surface, regardless of how many launch lasers you used.

Jesus, they're really pushing it.

They came to a compartment, and Romanov entered a code Jim couldn't see. The door slid aside, and he was pushed roughly inside. The space was two meters on a side with a simple fold-out toilet designed for multiple humanoid races, and a similar hammock arrangement. It was about as simple as you could ask for.

"Like the accommodations, *Colonel?*" Romanov said, spitting out the last word. He entered behind Jim and slid the door partially closed. "I thought I'd give you something to think about on the long trip."

Jim didn't turn around. He knew what the sadistic fucker meant. The man liked the sound of his fists hitting someone else's flesh. He sighed as he looked at the far wall. Then he saw it. A symbol scratched in the paint. A triangle bisected by a vertical line, and a circle in the center.

In that second, he wasn't in a tiny prison cell where he'd wait for weeks to arrive at Capital, there to be interrogated by an alien. He was sitting in his tower apartment in the old Houston Hobby Airport, in the little sunken living room with a long circular couch covered in pillows. The Tri-V was showing an old 2D movie from the early 21st century, a fantasy about wizards and magic. Adayn had never seen it before but loved every minute of the eight movies.

"Turn around and take your medicine, fat boy."

Jim clicked the menu item in his pinplants, the one with the description 'I Open At The Close." A message appeared.

"Jim, I know you'll never understand or accept my apology. But just know this, I did what I did for a very good reason. It is true, I am not who I said I was. Neither am I who the Golden Horde said I was. I hope this gift gets you out of this situation, and maybe it will win back a small amount of your trust. If not, hopefully it will at least dim your hatred of me." It was signed "Adrianne—Section 51."

Where the empty menu selection had been, now there were three options: boost, slow, and recover. He mentally stared at the selections in amazement, wondering how Adayn, or rather how Adrianne, had accomplished this with a nanite treatment. *And what the hell is Section 51?*

"I said turn around, punk," Romanov yelled and grabbed Jim by the shoulder to spin him around. Jim concentrated on the "boost" option and felt a jolt run through his body. Romanov's fist came at his stomach. Jim brought an arm down to block, even though he knew the bigger man's punch would probably hurt his arm more than his gut. He slapped away Romanov's punch as if it were from a child.

The corporal's eyes went wide, and he took a step back. Jim grinned and followed, swinging his own fist as hard as he could. Romanov managed to get an arm up to block, and Jim felt the unmistakable feeling of bone breaking in the man's forearm from the impact. *Holy shit!* Jim got ready to punch again.

Romanov wasn't a smart man, but he appeared to know enough to realize the tables had turned. Orders be damned, he had no intention of getting his head bashed in by a prisoner. He made a quick move to draw the laser pistol at his belt.

Not so fast, Jim thought. He was no ninja of old; in fact, his martial arts' training was the least honed of his merc skills. He could handle his own in a CASPer, of course. Few aliens could brawl with a CASPer, and those that were capable of it could be dealt with by a judiciously placed MAC round to the head. However, he *had* played a lot of video games. He concentrated on "slow."

In a split second, Romanov's movements became sluggish, as if he were pushing through water. Jim found it childishly simple to reach forward, grab the hand just pulling the laser from its holster, and *squeeze*. Bones and plastic were pulverized; both the hand and the weapon were ruined. Corporal Romanov started to scream in slow motion, but Jim jabbed a fist into the man's throat, crushing his windpipe.

Romanov fell to his knees, his remaining good hand reaching for his throat as he struggled to breathe. Blood bubbled from his mouth. He looked questioningly at Jim.

"I wish I knew," Jim said with a shrug. Romanov fell to the deck, lay gurgling for a few seconds, then died.

In his mind the Slow and Boost options went gray. Jim almost fell, suddenly overcome with a desperate feeling of fatigue and dizziness. "Oh, hell," he said, and grabbed the hammock. Pain hit him. All the muscles he'd just used beyond their abilities, and the bones in his hand from the punch. "It was never like this in video games," he moaned.

Jim considered the "recover" option for a second, then decided against it. Video game training, once again. Save your resources. Gravity fell off slowly. They were approaching orbit. Time was running out. He checked to be sure Romanov was dead, then verified he was steady enough on his feet to walk. The crushed laser pistol caught his eye. *That wasn't my best decision. Still, how many can there be between me and the other Raknar drivers?*

He slid the door open and a massive, hairy, clawed hand reached out and grabbed him, lifted his bulk, and tossed him like a ragdoll.

* * *

CIC, EMS *Shadowfax*, Just Outside Earth Orbit

"N ew Era, keep pushing them!" Captain Elizabeth Stacy implored.

The remaining enemy forces were well unified now, and with Earth to their back they were able to make use of the remaining orbital platforms. There were only three in position to assist, but they were still the equivalent of three battleships. The enemy force was a match for the Hussars, even with *New Era*.

"Its shields are holding," TacCom said, referring to the dreadnought. "Though only just."

"Something will give on the other side," Elizabeth said. "*How about some magic?*" She asked Ghost.

<An opportunity is coming in 5.4 minutes.>

"We just need to hold for a few minutes," Elizabeth said. In space, lasers, particle beams, and missiles rained between the two fleets.

* * *

MGS *Supreme*, Entering Orbit, Earth Point

"W e are nearly in orbit," the ship's captain informed her principle passenger.

"Good," Peepo replied. "Are we in laser comms range of the enemy?"

"Yes, but reception will be spotty due to debris in orbit."

"Not an issue," Peepo said. She held out a computer chip. "Broadcast this on laser comms to *New Era*."

"But, General Peepo, *New Era* is in enemy hands."

Peepo glared at *Supreme*'s captain, her eyes narrowed and whiskers twitching. "Do you think I'm unaware of that?" she asked, her voice full of menace. The squad of Besquith, her personal bodyguards who hadn't left her side in hours, eyed the captain hungrily.

"Of course not, General," the captain said, bowing his head.

"Then execute my order."

The captain looked at the chip, hesitating only a second before handing it to his comms officer. "Transmit this as the general ordered."

"Yes, Captain."

A minute passed as the order was carried out. The captain watched the Tri-V representation of the battlespace with interest, wondering what would happen. Suddenly, *New Era*'s shields all deactivated. He turned to look at General Peepo, who had a small smile on her muzzle.

"I don't tolerate betrayal," she said. "Now, get me out of this stinking star system."

* * * * *

Chapter Twenty-Seven

Hospital Samaritano, Rio de Janeiro, Brazil

"Hey!" a man in a camouflage uniform yelled from the door. "What are you doing here?"

The woman turned from the window where she was working with a laser in her hand. The man tried to bring up his rifle but wasn't fast enough. The woman shot him in the chest, and he slumped back out the door. In the hallway outside the doorway, a woman screamed.

The door slammed open and Alexis dove out of the bed as a second man fired into the room.

The woman shot him in the shoulder, but then the door shut, blocking any further shots. "Take this and cover me," the woman yelled, sliding her pistol along the floor to Alexis.

Alexis scooped it up and looked at it. It had been a long time since she'd used a pistol; it wasn't what starship captains typically did. Happily, the pistol was a common model, and she was able to bring the schematics for it up in her head.

She found the safety and flipped it off as the man pushed open the door again. He was looking for the woman, though, and wasn't expecting fire from the bed. Alexis had time to aim and fire. Although her aim was off—she was low—she'd been aiming at his head and the bolt caught him in the throat. He gurgled something as he fell back out the door, and the woman in the hallway screamed again.

"What are you doing?" Alexis asked.

"Just watch the door. There will be more coming—there's a company downstairs." Alexis heard her mutter, "Fucking Varangian Guard." She stood up from her backpack with a funny looking rifle and fired it out the window. The round was attached to some rope in the backpack, and it snaked out the window after it. The woman rolled the bed to the window and tied the cord off to it, then snapped a metal piece to it that looked like the handlebars from an old-time bicycle.

"Come here," the woman said. Alexis walked over, keeping an eye on the door. "Here," the woman said, handing her the handlebars while taking the pistol. "See this button?" she asked, pointing. "Hold it down while you go out the window, then release it to go. Press it again when you want to stop."

"What?" Alexis asked, stunned by how fast things were happening.

"There is a battle going on right now. The Merc Guild may lose. If so, Peepo will probably have you killed. You have to go!"

"Wait. Who are you?"

"I'm Ad—" The woman changed her mind. "I'm a friend from Section 51. Now, you need to go so I can, too. Go!"

Alexis slid down the rope, jerking as she alternately pressed and released the button. The angle was fairly steep, going from the fifth floor of her hospital room down to almost street level. The commotion had also drawn a bit of a crowd, and a number of people had stopped to point at her. The breeze fluttering her hospital gown gave the men a great show, she realized. At any other time, she might have cared.

It didn't take long before she approached the ground, and Alexis dropped from the rope, her bare feet slapping the pavement. The rope collapsed next to her. She looked back; the woman was sliding down a different rope to a building farther down the street, above which a VTOL hovered. She dropped onto the roof as the VTOL moved in, then ran over to the craft, jumped in, and it roared up and away.

A brick on the building next to Alexis shattered. She winced away from it as she looked back to the hospital. Two men were standing in the window she had fled from. One was firing at her while the other talked into a radio.

Time to leave.

She dodged some refuse on the street and raced around the corner of the building as another laser round struck the building. She then sprinted down the street.

* * *

Dropship One, **Approaching Rio de Janeiro, Brazil**

Apparently, Earth's defenses—those of the Merc Guild, anyway—had bigger issues than a solitary dropship screaming through the atmosphere from one of the ships in orbit; no one shot at them on the way down. As the craft roared into the vicinity of the hospital, though, light laser fire reached up for them.

"I'm taking fire from the hospital," the co-pilot said. "Want me to blast them?"

"No," Nigel said. "I doubt we'll win back the hearts and minds of our people if we start blasting hospitals and orphanages. Just take us to the west a bit, and we'll jump out."

370 | KENNEDY & WANDREY

"You got it, Boss," the pilot replied, and the craft peeled away as the ramp came down. Five seconds later, the green light came on.

"All ashore who's going ashore," the pilot said.

"Thanks for the ride," Nigel said. "*Let's go save the colonel!*" Nigel yelled as he stepped off the ramp. The dropship hovered about 100 meters above the city, and Nigel used his jumpjets to land gracefully on the street below.

Cars slammed into each other as their drivers sought to avoid the giant metal figures dropping from the skies, and Nigel could see at least four accidents; one was a block away as a gawker spent more time watching them than where he was going.

"Alexis, Nigel," he commed. "Where are you right now?"

"I'm east of the hospital…and on the run," she replied immediately. She was obviously winded, and it didn't sound like she had much left. "I could…use some…help."

"Damn it!" Nigel swore. "We came down on the wrong side of town. We'll be right there." He switched to his squad net. "Follow me!" he transmitted as he blasted back off on his jumpjets. His squad—and a trail of vehicular accidents—followed in his wake.

* * *

CIC, EMS *Shadowfax*, Just Outside Earth Orbit

New Era's shields fell, and the TacCom cried out in alarm. Instantly, the enemy battleships and the functional orbital installations concentrated fire on it.

"What happened?" Elizabeth happened. "Battle damage?"

"Not a chance," her DCC said. "Their shields were still at half strength. Maybe someone on her crew had second thoughts."

"If that's the case, they committed suicide," Evie said. On screen, *New Era* was being chewed apart. A ship more than a kilometer across didn't explode so much as tear to pieces and cease to be a warship anymore. As soon as it was out of operation, the enemy fleet began to concentrate on the Hussars' battleships once more.

"Are we still going to get that magic?"

<Not the way I planned,> Ghost said. <New ships arriving.>

"New contacts!" sensor ops called out almost at exactly the same time. "Three ships, cruiser size. They're launching dozens of smaller ships that…"

"What?" Elizabeth asked.

"I don't understand, ma'am. The smaller ships just disappeared!"

"Which way were they heading?"

Sensor ops was quiet for a moment, then he turned to Elizabeth with a smile. "They're heading for the enemy fleet!"

"I have a transmission in the clear," comms said. "It's from the newly-arrived battle riders."

A feline voice came over the CIC speakers. "The Depik have come to repay the Merc Guild's treachery. Welcome to your deaths." A second later, the first of the Depik ships, wrapped in its quintessence field, slammed into an enemy battlecruiser at high speed, directly into its engine section.

* * *

MGS *Begalt*, Approaching Orbit, Earth, Sol System

The Besquith smiled at Jim, who was trying to get back to his feet while shaking off the cobwebs from getting knocked on his ass. "Yes, get up Human," the alien said, smiling with more teeth than a crocodile had any business having. "I don't know how you got out of your cage..."

"You wouldn't believe me if I told you," Jim said, searching for a weapon, any weapon. Now he *really* regretted crushing the pistol in Romanov's hand. The "boost" and "slow" icons were both shaded, and he couldn't select them. He was only a few meters from the other locked down cells. *I was so fucking close.*

"I'm not supposed to kill you Humans," the Besquith said. "But, near as I can tell, eating your arms won't kill you."

"No, but I will." The Besquith spun as a firearm roared. A burst of bullets caught the alien in its midriff, sending it sprawling to the deck. As it fell, the shooter was revealed to be a grizzled old man of at least 90 wearing light combat armor and holding a smoking rifle.

What the hell is that? Jim suddenly remembered; he'd seen the gun design a thousand times in old 20th and 21st century movies. The old guy had a no-shit AK-47!

The Besquith snarled, ignoring the horrible wounds and clawed out a laser pistol. The old man moved quicker than Jim would have thought possible, and he put a booted foot on the Besquith's hand and shoved the muzzle against its head. *Bang!* A single shot to the skull sent it to werewolf hell.

"You okay, kid?" the old man asked.

"Surprisingly, yes," Jim said. He rubbed his jaw to make sure it wasn't broken. "Who are you?"

"Name's Dodd." Dodd looked Jim up and down. "Yeah, you gotta be the Cartwright kid."

Jim wasn't wearing any logo on his uniform, so he was taken aback. "How did you know?"

"Ain't many mercs as round as you who'd be a prisoner on this here ship." Jim blushed slightly and tried to stand up straighter when a woman yelled from further down the corridor.

"Jesus Christ, Dodd, stop shooting the shit out of everything!"

"Don't get ya panties in a bunch, girl," the man said and spat on the deck.

"Can you help me get these cells open?" Jim asked Dodd.

"No, but Greenstein can."

A woman, likely the one who'd yelled, came into view. Like the man, she was far from young. He guessed she was 50 or more, with the clear demeanor of a merc. She was also dressed in light combat armor and lovingly cradling a large laser rifle, the optic tucked in under her breasts like she was protecting an infant. "That the Cartwright kid?"

"Yup," Dodd said. "Mika, call Greenstein and tell him we need a hack."

She walked up to Dodd and examined the lock. She gave a snort and removed a pistol. Jim had just retrieved the Besquith's laser pistol when Mika fired a round into the cell's controls. The door buzzed in protest, then opened.

"I'll be damned," Jim said. "I only thought that shit worked in movies like *Rambo*."

"*Rambo*?" Dodd asked, perking up. "You seen *Rambo*?"

"All five of them," Jim said.

374 | KENNEDY & WANDREY

Dodd grinned and removed a pair of laser pistol mags from the dead Besquith and handed them to Jim. "I like you already, kid."

Jim pulled the door open to see Cindy Epard against the back wall, eyes wide in fear. When she saw Jim, she sighed, ran forward, and grabbed him in a big hug.

"Thank God," she said, crying on his shoulder.

"You okay?" he asked.

"Me? Look at you? Jim, you're nothing but bruises and cuts."

Jim hadn't seen a mirror in weeks. He considered the working over he'd gotten from the Varangians and realized he probably did look a mess. "I'm fine." He turned to Mika. "These four other doors, too, but shooting them might not get the same results."

Another man came trotting up. He appeared older than Mika but younger than Dodd. He guessed this was Greenstein, because he immediately pulled out a slate and went at the other cell locks.

"Where's the boss?" Mika asked.

"Coming," Greenstein replied without looking up. "I take it that's the Cartwright kid?" Mika grunted in confirmation.

"Okay," Jim said, holding up his hands. "How the hell do you all know who I am?"

"Because I told them all about you, kid."

Jim turned at the voice; something about it was immediately familiar. Walking down the corridor was a ghost smoking a cigar. "*Murdock?*"

The huge merc grinned and held out a hand. "Great to see you, kid," he said.

Jim took it and did his best to match the grip. Murdock gave a "not bad" look and then grinned ear to ear.

"How?" Jim asked. "You're dead!"

"I get that a lot," Murdock said. Greenstein grunted, and the second door opened. "But maybe we'd better wait until later to catch up?"

As much as Jim wanted to know everything immediately, he agreed; Murdock was right. One after another, his fellow Raknar drivers were freed. Darrel Fenn next, then Mia Kleve, Seamus Curran, and Shawn Thompson last. The reunion was emotional for all of them, especially when the other five realized how horribly Jim had been treated.

"Why didn't they torture any of us?" Darrel Fenn asked.

"You couldn't give them the secrets of the Raknar," Jim explained. "Not that I have them all, either."

"They've probably taken them apart bolt-by-bolt by now anyway," Mia said.

"No," Jim said, then grinned. "They haven't made any progress at all. Just before our Fae took off, they activated a protocol which made the reactors throw tons of radiation."

"Who are these guys?" Shawn asked, indicating Murdock and his associates.

"Murdock used to be my first sergeant when I was first standing the Cavaliers back up."

"I heard about him when I signed up," Seamus said.

"We need to get you guys out of here," Greenstein said. "Our shuttle is standing by."

"Sorry about your toys," Murdock said.

"What toys?" Jim asked.

"Your robots. Ain't no way we can get them off the transport. All we got is a shuttle and a frigate."

"Couldn't move even one if we wanted to," Greenstein said.

"Where'd you get so many of them, anyway?" Murdock asked.

"Are you saying there are Raknar on this ship?" Jim asked.

"Six of them," Murdock said. "They're latched to the outside."

<Jim.>

All six Raknar drivers spun at the sound of their partners in their mind, and looked in the same direction. Murdock and his two associates were both spooked and confused by the sudden coordinated action.

"Thanks," Jim said to Murdock. "But we're heading for our Raknar."

"Kid, you're nuts," Murdock said. "There are MinSha marines on this thing, and some Human traitors, too."

"Varangian Guard," Jim said. Murdock nodded. "I wouldn't mind running into them, especially Vels Lucas." He checked the laser pistol he'd taken from the Besquith. It wasn't made for his hand, so he wouldn't be very accurate with it.

"So, you weren't shitting us about him running those giant robots?" Mika asked Murdock.

"Two things I don't lie about; giant robots and sex."

"One out of two ain't bad," Greenstein said, and Mika grinned.

"Gotta go," Jim said, and walked toward the summons.

"Jim…come on, kid; this is nuts. What can you do with those things? You aren't on the ground; this is space."

Jim stopped and turned to face Murdock. The look of determination on his face brought the old merc up short. "Murdock, I don't have time for long explanations right now. Suffice it to say, I've come a long way with the Raknar."

"Yeah, I saw what you did to São Paulo."

Jim scowled. "That was war."

"It was slaughter," Mika said.

"You going to get out of my way or…"

"Or what?" Murdock asked, a slight laugh in his voice.

The other five Raknar drivers flanked Jim and stared daggers at Murdock and his people.

"You *really* want us to answer that, old man?" Darrel Fenn asked.

"Boy," Murdock said taking a step closer. "You have no idea who you are fucking with."

"Neither do you," Cindy stepped up. "This is Jim Cartwright!"

"I know who he is," Murdock said. "Better than any of you. I was there when this all started."

"And now you're here when it ends," Jim said. "I know we're almost in space, I know there's a battle going on, and I fucking *know* we can make a difference. I'd order you to move, but you're not under my command anymore. So, I'll ask you to please just get out of our way."

Murdock stared at Jim for a long moment, his eyes searching the young man for a sign. After a time, he spoke. "Mika, Greenstein, let's get them to their Raknar."

"Are you crazy?" Mika asked.

"No, they are," Greenstein said.

"Maybe," Murdock agreed. "But this kid has the heart of a lion. Maybe he *can* help." He touched the control on his radio. "Kelso, grab some extra firepower and meet us at the corridor intersection just outside the shuttle. No, there isn't time to explain. We'll be there in ten seconds." He turned to Jim. "Come on, Colonel, let's go."

* * * * *

Chapter Twenty-Eight

Rio de Janeiro, Brazil

Alexis risked a glance over her shoulder as she turned the corner onto Muniz Barreto. She'd only run a block, but she was already spent. Like shooting pistols, running in gravity wasn't something starship captains did a lot of, and being in a hospital bed for three weeks hadn't helped.

Men were already racing toward her—men in the uniforms of the Varangian Guard. She couldn't let them catch her, but she couldn't go any further. One of the troops stopped and aimed a laser rifle at her, giving her the strength to make it a few steps farther around the corner and out of sight. A chunk of plaster blew off the building behind her.

She scanned the buildings down the street. She was too obvious in the hospital gown. She needed somewhere to hide, but most of the buildings had bars over the windows, doors, and even the access to them from the street was barred. The strains of a sad and mournful song came from the only open building she could see, and she staggered fifty feet down the street toward it.

Looking over her shoulder as she entered, she saw the men come around the corner and one of them met her gaze. *Damn it!* She wouldn't be able to hide, after all. She lurched her way into the building—some sort of music bar—and continued through the open room where two men were playing guitar.

She wobbled a bit going through the door and found herself in a kitchen area. The music ceased suddenly behind her. The men following her had obviously entered the club. There were two other exits from the kitchen—one that led to a small patch of grass behind the building and a set of stairs. With no place to hide behind the building, she mounted the steps and stumbled toward the second floor.

She had just reached the landing of the second floor when the kitchen door below her exploded open, slamming into the wall. Several doors lined the hallway—probably the private rooms for the owners of the bar downstairs—and an iron ladder led to the roof. The ladder was at least familiar—all Human ships had them—so she started climbing. "Heading to…the roof," she commed. It was all she had breath for, and she paused for a second, trying to get some oxygen to her abused body, but then she heard men yelling below her, giving orders to split up the group, and she climbed as fast as her protesting muscles would let her.

She reached a cover at the top of the ladder and struggled to lift it. The heavy metal cover hadn't been used in a while, and the hinges protested with a loud squeal. "She's upstairs!" one of the men yelled. Her adrenaline spiked, giving her the energy she needed to push the cover open as the men pounded up the stairs behind her.

"There!" one of them shouted, and a laser bolt melted the lip of the access as she flipped off it and onto the flat, rock-covered roof.

She struggled to her feet, ignoring the rocks cutting into them, as boots rang on the metal ladder, and she swayed toward the access cover. Fingers appeared on the edge of the access as she lifted the cover and jumped forward onto it to close it.

The man on the ladder screamed as the cover cut off the tips of his fingers, and she could hear a huge commotion from below as the man fell down the ladder onto the people following him. Only seconds later, though, the access cover shifted as someone tried to lift it. He obviously hadn't expected her weight, though, and was unable to move it more than an inch.

More scuffling came from below as the men organized, then, with a shout, the cover was thrown up as two men pushed up from underneath. Alexis flew to the side, landing hard on the roof's rocky surface. Her whole body hurt, and she knew she was cut in numerous places, but she struggled to her feet, looking for an avenue of escape.

There wasn't one. The building was higher than the ones around it, and she would have had to run to the edge and jump down at least one story to the next building. Running barefoot on the surface alone would have been difficult and painful. And the jump? It would have been a dangerous leap, even at full health. She was trapped.

She put her hands up and turned to meet her fate.

* * *

MGS *Begalt*, Approaching Orbit, Earth, Sol System

"Thanks, Murdock," Jim said as they reached a hatch. There were a pair of dead Besquith, both shot cleanly through the head. Mika stood next to them, admiring her own handiwork.

"You got it kid," Murdock said. "I still think you are nuts." Murdock's other associates were also there. Like him, they were all old, but they all looked dangerous.

The other Raknar drivers trotted eagerly past them to other docking points, led onward by silent callings. "You guys have a ship?"

"Yeah," Murdock said. "It's docked to this tub. We used it as cover. Long story."

"We were going to steal this thing, actually," Greenstein said, and winked.

"You can have it after we leave, if you want. But if the ship you brought is faster, I'd use it to clear the area. We're going to be making a mess."

The hatch opened toward Jim, and he saw Splunk waiting for him. The docking ring on the other side was clearly a Raknar's hatch.

"Hey, buddy!" he said. Splunk leaped into his arms.

"I missed you, <*Cooo!*>"

"I missed you, too," Jim said. Splunk looked at the older mercs and gave them a nod.

"She's a lot more than just a critter, isn't she?" Murdock asked.

"Oh, without a doubt," Jim said. "If we live through this, I'll buy you a beer."

"Not a Coke?"

"Times change," Jim said, and hurried through the hatch.

"Must hurry, <*Skaa!*>"

"Right," Jim said. The internal structure of the Raknar made it hard to hurry, but he did the best he could. In just a few seconds, he pulled the armored hatch at the heart of the mecha closed, and the system's magnetic locks engaged. "Cast us free while I get set up," he said.

Splunk started activating systems as fast as she could. He only looked up as she jumped onto her platform and reached out for his pinplants. "Kick ass time," he said.

"Akee!" They both said and were joined.

* * *

The six Raknar pushed away from the transport as gently as they could and didn't damage it *too* badly. Jim/Splunk noticed there was a Maki frigate docked, and he guessed it was the ship Murdock had mentioned.

He/She used *Zha Akee* to set up their positions and evaluate the enemy. He/She noted with some annoyance that their heavy weapons were gone, which would limit their ability to attack the heavier enemy ships. That needed to be remedied. The Maki frigate undocked from the transport and started to maneuver away. He considered using it, then changed his mind, noting it as friendly.

"Mia/Sandy, Darrel/Peanut, use the transport. Cindy/Ryft, Seamus/Dante, and Shawn/Shadow, come with us."

Jim/Splunk activated their thrusters and accelerated at 50 Gs toward the nearest enemy cruiser, with the ones they'd specified following along. Meanwhile Mia/Sandy and Darrel/Peanut rammed their arms into the transport on opposite sides and fired their engines, radically altering the transport's course.

Jim/Splunk and the other three Raknar raced toward their chosen target. The cruiser's crew saw the 30-meter-tall mecha coming toward them and fired their weapons. Missiles were swatted down with anti-missile lasers and armor sloughed off the energy beams fired at them. The Raknar spun in space and braked, though they

384 | KENNEDY & WANDREY

didn't come to a complete stop—the four 1,000-ton Raknar slammed fusion-torch-powered-feet first into the side of the cruiser, ripping its superstructure apart.

Once embedded in the cruiser, the four went to work. It only took a few seconds to get what they wanted. When the Raknar emerged, they were now armed with the lasers from the hapless cruiser. The Raknars seamlessly integrated the weapons into their own systems. The new armament wasn't ideal, but it would suffice. The cruiser's shield generators were integrated as well.

The other two Raknar, Darrel/Peanut and Mia/Sandy, finished ramming the transport into a battlecruiser and flew to rejoin the other four. More and more fire came from the now-panicking fleet as they realized what was in their midst. The two were armed as well, and Jim/Splunk handed Darrel/Peanut what had been a 5-terawatt particle accelerator barbette, the cruiser's main weapon.

"We thought you'd like this," Jim/Splunk said.

"You know it," Darrell/Peanut said. They took the weapon and merged it into their Raknar's arm. The result was a limb far too long to be functional on the ground, but since they were in space, it didn't matter. The remaining shield generators were likewise incorporated.

In *Zha Akee*, Jim/Splunk saw the new ships arrive while Darrel/Peanut and Mia/Sandy finished integrating the offensive and defensive parts from the cruiser. Jump riders dropped off the new ships and seemed to disappear, only to reappear as they rammed the enemy ships. The new ships could not immediately be quantified, nor their strange invisibility capabilities, so they were logged away for future analysis.

The enemy fleet was now trapped between advancing friendly forces and the waves of invisible suicide attacks. Jim/Splunk saw a delicious opportunity as it appeared the enemy had forgotten about them.

"Okay," Jim/Splunk said, sharing target data via *Zha Akee*. "Let's kill them all." All six ripped free from the now-gutted hulk of the former cruiser and rode plumes of fusion power toward the nearest battleship.

* * *

Rio de Janeiro, Brazil

Nigel reached the hospital but didn't see anyone there. Whoever had shot at the shuttle must have left, which had saved his or her life. While he hadn't wanted the shuttle unleashing mass destruction on the building, he had no problem ending some asshole's life with a few well-place MAC rounds.

"Movement! East along the road!" Corporal Taheri commed, blasting off down Rua Vicente de Sousa. Nigel and rest of the squad followed.

"What have you got?" Nigel asked as he covered half the block in a bound.

"Men with rifles," Taheri commed. "They turned left at the next intersection."

"Heading to…the roof," Alexis called. If she'd sounded winded before, she was now totally spent.

"She's heading to the rooftops!" Nigel exclaimed. "Bounce and look for movement."

"Got her!" Taheri, who was still in the lead, said. "On the left! I'm on it!"

Nigel spun left. Halfway up the block, he saw Alexis—the love of his life—with her hands up as men poured onto the roof with her. The first one stopped and raised a rifle at her, and Nigel was transported back in time to Planet Moorhouse, where he had been a handful of seconds too late to save his sister, and she had died in his arms.

His stomach roiled. There was no way he could get there in time; it was going to happen all over again.

"No!" he screamed, and he opened his jumpjets to full, knowing he would be too late.

* * *

Rio de Janeiro, Brazil

*S*o, *this is where it ends,* Alexis thought as the man flipped off the safety on the laser rifle. After all the space battles she'd been in, all the races and ships' crews who'd tried their level best to kill her, she was going to die at the hands of *Humans* in Rio Fucking de Janeiro. Life didn't make sense sometimes.

"Kill the bitch!" a man yelled from the access as he climbed out. His hands were wrapped in bloody rags, and blood was smeared across the nametag "Lucas" on the right side of his chest. "Do it now!"

"Sorry, *Senhorita*," the man with the rifle said as his finger tightened on the trigger.

Before he could complete the motion, a thousand pounds of man and steel slammed down onto him and continued through the roof to the floor below, leaving a massive hole, and throwing everyone on the roof off their feet.

As the Varangian Guard struggled to get up, a second CASPer landed on the roof, more gently, but with murderous intent. Its sword blade out, it cut one man in half lengthwise as it landed, then sliced horizontally to cut another man in half. The last man—the one with the bloody hands—the CASPer picked up and threw over the side of the building. The man's screams ended as he was impaled on the metal bars surrounding the establishment.

The pilot turned the mech toward Alexis as two additional CASPers landed—gently—on the roof, and she could see the stylized Huma bird logo on the CASPer, along with the number "1." The canopy opened, and Nigel jumped from the mech before it had opened all the way. He stumbled as he landed, then raced over to her and caught her up in his arms.

"I was afraid I had lost you," he said, sobbing.

"Easy," she said. "I'm hurt."

He put her back down, gently, tenderly, but she found she couldn't let go of him. It just felt too good to be in his arms again. Even if it hurt. A lot. "I'm sorry," he replied, his face going red, "It's just—"

"Don't worry about it," Alexis said, cutting him off with a smile. "It's nothing a medkit or two can't fix." She waved to the hole in the roof. "I'm just glad you made it here in time."

"Yes," Nigel said, smiling in return. "It appears Corporal Taheri was a little…overzealous in his landing, but I wouldn't have had it any other way."

* * * * *

Chapter Twenty-Nine

CIC, EMS *Shadowfax*, Sol Emergence Point

"I have new ships arriving in the emergence area!" the TacCom exclaimed.

"Whose are they?" Elizabeth asked. "They can't be ours."

"I don't know, ma'am. They aren't like anything I've ever seen before. There's one thing I can tell you, though, there are a lot of them. It's a full fleet. There are several ships that are battleship-sized, a number of battlecruisers and cruisers, and then smaller supporting cruisers and destroyers. Wait, my system has a match. They are…Goltar? I don't know that I've ever seen Goltar before."

"I know what they are," Sansar said from behind Elizabeth. "They are one of the members of the Merc Guild Council. They are an ancient race, but one I thought acted with honor at my tribunal."

"Did they vote to convict you?"

Sansar looked at the deck, unable to meet Elizabeth's eyes. "Well, yes, they did…but we did do the things we were accused of. He did seem sorry about it, though."

"If they voted against you, then they are in the Merc Guild's pocket, and they are here to help the Merc Guild. I can't think of any reason they'd be here to help us, can you?"

Sansar shook her head.

"They're moving," the TacCom noted. "They've taken a heading that will have them crossing between our fleet and the Merc Guild's. Looks like they are going to try to save them."

"Let's try to finish off the ones we have quickly," Elizabeth said, "then we can reorient on the newcomers. Message to the fleet: Move forward with all haste to engage and destroy the Merc Guild fleet. Full speed ahead."

"Ma'am," Tesk'l, her comms officer said, "we're being hailed by the new fleet…and you're never going to guess who is in charge. I have a channel open for you."

Elizabeth cleared her throat. "Station calling the Human mercenary fleet, this is Captain Elizabeth Stacy."

The Tri-V monitor lit up to show a four-armed being wearing a dark brown, hooded robe. His face was hard to see within the folds, although Elizabeth caught flashes of all three of his independently-tracking eyes. "Greetings, Captain Stacy," the figure said in a harsh whisper. "I am Peacemaker Tab'bel. By the authority of the High Council of the Peacemaker Guild and Honored Guild Master Rsach, you are hereby ordered to cease all hostilities with the Merc Guild immediately."

Elizabeth opened her mouth to say something, but the figure held up a hand. "One of my fellow Peacemakers is communicating this to the head of the Merc Guild fleet, as well. This war has gone on long enough, and we are stopping it."

* * *

Merc Guild Detention Facility, Ubatuba, Brazil, Earth

"Hold them!" Buddha cried out as half a squad of CASPers went up in a titanic ball of fire. The Tortantulas kept trying to flank, and every time the Cavaliers threw them back there were fewer Cavaliers left to fight.

"First Sergeant!" Captain Wolf called.

"Captain?"

"Sector Two, on your left. Five seconds, go!"

Buddha examined the battlespace and instantly saw what she meant. Captain Wolf had started with nearly 40 CASPers under her command. She had nine left and was just to the east of Sector Two, directly behind the Tortantula who seemed unaware. She was outnumbered five to one.

"Captain," he started to complain.

"First Sergeant," she roared. "Carry out your duty!"

"Ma'am," Buddha said, a catch in his voice.

"Lead the charge, Buddha." Her remaining command burst out of the crumbling building, screaming on their PA systems and spraying every weapon they had, then fell upon the Tortantula. Buddha had a fleeting image of Captain Wolf impaling a Flatar with her arm blade before a pair of huge Tortantula tore her suit in half.

"You heard the captain," he said over his squadnet. "Go! Go! Go!"

Buddha had gathered six CASPers of his own, all that remained of Bravo Company after Alvarado was cut down by a trio of Besquith. He'd fallen in a pile of their guts and blood, making them pay for his life with their own. This was it; they were down to the end.

His men burst through the last of the perimeter defenses of the detention facility, two more of his troopers going down to the Zuul. Every one of them had yellow indicators on their ammo supply as they neutralized the defenses nearest them.

The last five members of Cartwright's Cavaliers exploded through the wall into the detention facility. The Zuul guards opened up with small arms, and Buddha's men swept them aside with arm-mounted weapons and CASPer-sized sidearms. Buddha himself was down to his arm blade.

A laser seared into his left forearm, and he spun, impaling the gunman. The Zuul howled and bit ineffectively at the CASPer. Buddha slammed the alien against the floor and crushed his head with a boot. All around him the fighting came to a halt as the last alien died.

"Lynch, Partlow," he said to two of his survivors. "Stay here and hold the way in."

"Roger that," Partlow said. Both men were injured and running on pure guts and CASPer candy. They wouldn't stop.

"You two come with me," he ordered the other two remaining troopers.

Buddha led the mangled remains of his command through the armored gate, now unguarded, and into the largest building on the premises. Inside, a thousand eyes—their owners held in large cages with no humanitarian comforts—turned to look at the three beaten, burned, and exhausted troopers. It was completely silent.

"We're Cartwright's Cavaliers, and we're here to rescue you."

The arena exploded in a cacophony of cheers, and he had to yell over his PA to be heard.

"We don't have time for celebration. The next room over is an armory. There are dead Zuul outside. Get every weapon you can; there will be enemy reinforcements here any minute."

Faces full of elation changed to ones of seriousness. Quickly, despite the dozens of units present, the mercs organized and blazed into motion. Buddha sighed. At least their last stand wouldn't be a slaughter.

"First Sergeant," Partlow called from their entrance point.

Buddha checked the battlespace and saw dozens of Tortantula arrayed outside, ready to attack. "Go ahead, Private."

"The spiders just stopped. They were about to attack, then they just stopped."

What in the name of Ku is going on now? Buddha noticed his orbital comms was flashing for attention. He'd been too busy trying to survive to notice. He listened to the message.

"I am Peacemaker Tab'bel. By the authority of the High Council of the Peacemaker Guild and Honored Guild Master Rsach, you are hereby ordered to cease all hostilities with the Merc Guild immediately."

"The spiders must have gotten the same message," Lynch said. "What does it mean?"

"It means we stand down. Fire only if fired upon. It looks like, at least for now, the war is over."

* * *

CIC, EMS *Revenge,* Solar System

Nigel and Alexis entered the CIC to a round of applause. Nigel supported Alexis, who was looking a little pale after her multiple ordeals, although they had at least found her a uniform to wear and had treated her cuts.

Nigel smiled. "Look who I found. Apparently, she decided to sit out the war in a swanky hospital." He shook his head. "Here we are, fighting and dying, and she decides to take a vacation." He sighed. "Women."

The CIC watch crew—all men—chuckled.

Revenge had been climbing clear of orbit to rendezvous with the Hussars' fleet. Nigel had already explained some of the last three weeks' happenings to Alexis. She was of mixed feelings—proud her Hussars had managed to repel the attack on New Warsaw, but horrified at the losses they'd suffered. Nigel watched her while she stared at the Tri-V where the battle still raged. *Can she recognize her own ship? Sure, she can.*

"Any station! Any station!" a young girl's voice said over the radio, interrupting the discussion. "This is Sunshine. Peepo is getting away!"

"*What?* What was that?" Nigel asked. "Find out what that person just said!"

"Station calling, this is the Earth Mercenary Ship *Revenge,*" the communications tech said. "Say again your last."

"*Revenge,* this is Sunshine. Peepo just lifted off from the headquarters facility and is getting away!"

"Who is Sunshine?" Nigel asked.

"Must be a codename for someone," the tech said, "but I don't show it on my list."

"It doesn't matter," Nigel said. "Have her transmit the coordinates. That bitch is *not* getting away."

"Got her," the TacCom said a minute later. An icon on the battlespace monitor began flashing. "Right there."

The captain turned to Nigel. "We can be within firing range in five minutes. Will that suffice?"

"Can you make it four?" The captain nodded. "Please do so." A feral smile crossed his face. "You're mine, Peepo."

"Attention on the net! This is Commander Elizabeth Stacy of the Winged Hussars. All ships and all crews, stand down. A ceasefire has been implemented by the authority of the High Council of the Peacemaker Guild and Honored Guild Master Rsach. I repeat, a ceasefire is in place. All ships, stand down."

The captain turned to Nigel. "We've been ordered to stand down," he said. "What do you want to do?"

"Isn't it obvious? I want to kill the bitch. Continue the chase; fire as she bears."

"You can't," Alexis said.

"Can't I?" Nigel said, and winked at her. She looked unhappy, but he turned back to the Tri-V.

The captain smiled. "It would be my pleasure." He looked at the battlespace monitor. "One minute until we are in range." Alexis started to speak when another transmission came in.

"*Revenge*, this is Peacemaker Tab'bel on the emergency net," a whispering voice said, causing a small shiver to run up Nigel's back. "A ceasefire has been ordered. Be advised, if you fire upon that ship, we will fire on you, and we will continue to do so until your ship is destroyed."

The captain turned to Nigel, chewing his upper lip. "Sir, there is a battleship within range of us right now. Perhaps it would be better—"

"Unacceptable!" Nigel roared. "I swore I would kill her, and I'm going to do it. For my sister. For my family. For my friends, and everyone else who's lost their lives because of the murdering bitch. She's going to die, and she's going to die *right now!* TacCom, lock up that ship."

"Got it, sir."

"Nigel!" Alexis snapped.

Nigel stared at the battlespace Tri-V and did his best to ignore her.

"*Revenge*, this is Peacemaker Tab'bel. We show you locking your weapons on General Peepo's ship. If you fire, *you will be destroyed.*"

"Don't do it," Alexis said.

"I don't *want* to do it," Nigel said, his voice miserable. "*I have to.* For all of the people she has killed or betrayed, I *have* to kill her. I have sworn it shall be so."

"Don't," Alexis said. "There will be other times, other chances, other opportunities to settle the score—without a Peacemaker battleship waiting to kill us."

Nigel looked toward the TacCom and opened his mouth to give the order anyway, but Alexis took his hand and put it on her stomach. "If you won't do it for me, do it for him."

Nigel stood silently for a moment, then sighed and shut his mouth. His shoulders slumped and he nodded once. "Safe all weapons. Do not fire." He turned back to Alexis. "Is this how things are to be between us? Are you always going to find ways to make me do what you want?"

Alexis smiled. "Maybe." She ran a hand gently along the strong curve of his jaw. "On second thought, absolutely. You can count on it."

"Well...okay," Nigel said with a crooked smile. "I guess I can live with that."

"Good," she said. "Now, please get me back to my Hussars."

* * *

Raknar Corps, Earth Orbit

The six Raknar linked shields and rocketed toward the battleship, which fired everything it had on the war machines. They sloughed off the fire as if it were nothing. Far too big to dodge, the ship had no choice but accept its fate.

The ancient mecha spun and fired their fusion torches, and 6,000 tons of Raknar slammed into the battleship like a sledgehammer on a watermelon. Upon impact, they spread themselves out and burned their engines, wielding them like fusion scalpels to carve the great ship into pieces. One of its fusion plants exploded, turning the battleship into a growing globe of debris.

The six Raknar slowly emerged from the wreck. Drive plasma played across their shields in scintillating waves of iridescent color, bathing them in reds and oranges. The other ship captains watched the image in dawning horror. Death had come to them. Ancient, unforgiving, cold death.

Jim/Splunk reveled in the timeless chords of the dirge which was the Raknar's anthem. The galaxy was once again able to see what the Raknar would do to *any* who stood against them.

"We are Fear," Shawn/Shadow said.

"We are Pain," Cindy/Ryft said.

"We are Wrath," Darrel/Peanut said.

"We are Despair," Seamus/Dante said.

"We are Revenge," Mia/Sandy said.

"We are *Doom!*" Jim/Splunk said.

<End them all.>

"Raknar, cease hostilities."

<Ignore the mewling of the insects.> Another target was selected.

"This is Colonel Cromwell. Jim, stop it!"

A battleship died in flames. *Fear, Pain, Wrath, Despair, Revenge, and Doom!* Parts were incorporated, powers increased. There were enough of the pathetic ships to build a *Loknar*. Grow, hunt, kill, *destroy.* <*Nothing is out of our reach!*>

"Jim, this is Sansar. If you don't stop, it will all be for nothing. We've won; you can stop."

"I DO NOT WANT TO STOP!"

"You must." The voice. *Nigel?* "I know more than anyone the taste of revenge. But you have to stop at some point. You cannot kill forever."

<*Yes, you can!*> The six Raknar accelerated toward another battleship that they identified as a Goltar ship.

"No, I can't," Jim said finally, and he tried to end *Zha Akee.* Only it didn't want to let him go. The Human part of his mind felt a tinge of panic. His individuality was draining away. He was going from being Jim, to Jim/Splunk, and now to only *Doom.* The alien battleship was getting closer.

They're not the enemy.

<All who bear arms against us are the enemy!>

Beyond the Goltar were others. The Winged Hussars, friends. Jim shook his physical head, the liquid embrace of the suspension fluid surrounding him. He couldn't. This had to stop. He found the icons in his mind. Boost, Slow, and Recover. Only one still glowed. He concentrated on it and jerked as lightning seared his mind.

Zha Akee broke. Their joining shattered. The six Raknar tumbled out of control, past the Goltar battleship, and into space.

* * *

***Shuttle One*, Approaching EMS *Pegasus*, Earth Orbit**

Alexis observed silently as they approached the cluster of five *Egleesius* docked together. She recognized her beloved *Pegasus*, even among its sisters. A line of ancient welds here, a slight difference of hull shape there. The last time she had seen it was moments before her trusted second in command shot her in the back. Those wounds were largely healed, but others might never heal.

She tried to understand what she'd seen in *Revenge*'s CIC a short time before. Six 20,000-year-old mecha devastating battleships. *Fucking battleships!* After each battleship fell, they seemed to feed upon the corpse, adding weapons, shields, and other capabilities from it. When they'd called on their leader, Jim Cartwright, to stop, he'd answered with the voice of a demon. A shudder ran up her spine, and Nigel reached over to take her hand. He hadn't understood what she had—the boy had changed.

It took all three of them, the Horsemen, to bring the Raknar down. When they did, their operators had fallen into an almost-coma. Five of the six came out of it shortly afterward and rendezvoused with their ship. A ship she'd been told was Dusman. That the Fae were actually the Dusman—that would take a lot of getting used to. Entropy, she had a lot of catching up to do. Jim was missing, his Raknar lost in the debris cloud from the fight. It was hard to imagine that a mecha the size of a corvette and armed 1,000 times better could just disappear.

"We're coming aboard now," the pilot said.

"Thank you," Nigel replied.

Alexis smiled. Nigel was mellowing. Good; she didn't want the father of her child to be a testosterone-charged rage-beast. She glanced at Nigel. *Well, a certain amount of testosterone charging is a good thing.* Nigel smiled back. *Yes, for sure.*

The shuttle deck pressurized, and Alexis felt a small amount of acceleration, maybe a sixth of a G. She was sure it was on her account. When the shuttle door opened, Nigel stepped out first, offering her his hand. She hesitated a second, then took it. The hangar deck of *Pegasus* was lined with her officers and the commanders of all the ships of the Winged Hussars. She also saw Sansar Enkh, who she'd been told had led the defense of New Warsaw against all odds, and an honor guard of her Golden Horde troopers off to the side. With the losses they'd taken, calling them a horde was now a stretch.

So few, so precious few. Alexis fought back the tears which threatened to flow.

"Attention!" Everyone came to attention. She saw Elizabeth Stacy march forward. *Tricky in such light gravity.* She looked different. Older maybe. Alexis had been told that Stacy had taken command when Lech Kowalczy fell at New Warsaw and had led them back to victory.

Elizabeth stopped and said, "Colonel Cromwell, I have led to the best of my ability." Unshed tears glittered in Elizabeth's eyes.

"You did incredibly well," Alexis said. "Commander Stacy, I relieve you."

"I stand relieved." Elizabeth turned to the assembled. "Colonel Alexis Cromwell, commander of the Winged Hussars."

"Commander of the Winged Hussars!" they all roared.

Next, Captain Dan Corder came forward. "Commander, I captained your ship to the best of my ability."

"And you did it with skill and aplomb," Alexis said, smiling. "I relieve you."

"I stand relieved," he said and saluted. "Commander Alexis Cromwell, Captain of EMS *Pegasus*."

"Captain of EMS *Pegasus*!"

"What happened is in the past," she said to the assembled crewmen. "We have weathered the storm and lived to tell the tale. You held our home and defeated our enemies. I believe there are new challenges ahead. Dire challenges, that no Humans have ever faced before. We'll face those challenges together. Our fates are joined."

"Our fates are joined."

"The Four Horsemen for Earth!"

* * * * *

Epilogue

Raknar *Doom*, Entering Heliocentric Orbit, Sol

J im slowly regained consciousness. He hurt. Every part of his body hurt from his toenails to his hair. He hadn't realized hair *could* hurt. He blinked at his surroundings for a moment before he recognized the dim sphere. "Raknar cockpit," he mumbled.

"Ouch, *<Froo!>*" Splunk said a meter away.

"Yeah. I hurt, too," Jim said. He tried to remember how he ended up there. *<Doom.>*

What the fuck did I do? No details came to his mind. He took the Raknar's normal space controls and checked their situation. The mecha was fine. In fact, it was more than fine. He saw there were several starship-class shield generators attached, an extra fusion powerplant, and a 10-terawatt particle accelerator cannon mounted on his back.

"Holy shit," he said. They were tumbling through space, past the orbit of the moon and on a heliocentric orbit. "Splunk, can you dump all this stuff so we can fly?"

"You bet, *<Skee!>*" She pushed off and landed on a secondary control. A few seconds later the extra equipment began to detach with a series of loud *kachunks*.

Jim took the controls, a little fearful. He could have easily joined with Splunk, but he was reluctant. The blackout had him spooked. *I'll figure it out later.*

Together, they got the Raknar under control. Splunk seemed just as confused and reserved as Jim. Once the mecha was under control, they used a fraction of its fusion power torches to arrest its momentum. Jim had to use his slate to calculate an orbit back. He would have needed to *Akee* to use the Raknar's internal navigation. His hands shook as he worked. *Is this what coming off a drug feels like?*

The simple navigational sensors used to move the Raknars around in non-combat situations buzzed an alarm. Something was on a nearly identical trajectory and would collide with them. It wasn't part of the "extra stuff" Splunk had cast loose; that was long gone as it continued out into the solar system on their original track.

"Splunk, what is that?" he asked.

"Escape pod," she said, and used her own slate to show a Tri-V of the craft.

Jim had never seen an escape pod like it. They were usually extremely utilitarian. After all, if you were jumping into one to survive an exploding ship, who cared what it looked like? This one was more like a work of art, crafted to resemble a seed pod, or maybe a cocoon?

He used his slate to calculate velocities and orbits. Without thinking, he fired the Raknar's maneuvering thrusters and changed the collision into an intercept.

"You going to catch it, *<Cheek!>*"

"Yeah," he said. "Don't ask me why. Maybe after all the death, we can save a life or two."

Splunk nodded in agreement. Jim could tell their power situation was fine, and despite fighting the battle, they still had plenty of reaction mass, though he had no idea how. When they'd boarded the Raknar it had been down to less than 25%.

It took seven minutes to precisely match courses and come alongside the escape pod. The Raknar was hard to fly outside of *Akee*. He spent part of the time putting the mecha into a more manageable configuration, arms by its side, legs outstretched and together.

He really wished he could remember everything after they'd joined, then maybe he'd understand why he was so spooked.

"Soft dock, <*Skaa!*>"

"Good deal," Jim said, and he used his controls to latch the pod to the Raknar. Despite its unusual design, it had a Union standard collar. "Let's go see who we rescued." Splunk produced a pair of laser carbines from the small arms locker in the cockpit and tossed one to him. He nodded; it was a good idea. The two headed through the internal compartments to the small of the Raknar's back where the docking collar was located.

When they got there, he let Splunk handle the controls. She checked continuity of the connection, then the internal condition of the escape pod. It had a normal atmosphere, so they cycled the airlock.

Inside, the technology looked standard to Jim. The air smelled musty, like how a small apartment smelled if you had a pet. The inside was just as unconventional as the outside. Instead of a space for people to sit, or the military types which were just big padded open spaces, this one only had enough room for one or two humans. Or, in this case, a human and a very large cat.

Splunk leaned in and looked at the pair, and her ears went back in a sure sign of suspicion.

"It's just a cat," Jim said.

"Not cat, Depik <*Pree!*>"

Jim looked closer. It *was* different than a cat. The body was longer, and the limbs were longer as well, graceful and articulated. He guessed the alien could move on all fours if it wanted to. But it was the woman who drew his attention. She was, for lack of a better term, gorgeous. She had long black hair which was held in a ponytail, but in the course of combat, most had come loose and was now floating in zero gravity. He couldn't tell her ancestry; maybe Middle

Eastern, maybe Indian? Her features were well defined and slightly angular. She had a fighter's build but was curved in the right places. She was also obviously injured, as was the Depik. They'd been through hell.

"Let's get them aboard and find the medkit," Jim said. Splunk scowled and looked at Jim, but she helped anyway. "We'd better get them back to Earth as soon as we can." As he helped his partner maneuver the woman out of the escape pod, he was thinking how much he was looking forward to hearing the tale of how they got there, and who she was.

* * *

Mercenary Guild Headquarters, Capital Planet

"The meeting of the Mercenary Guild Council will come to order," the Veetanho at the end of the conference table said. She nodded down the table on the left to where the guild masters from the Goka, Flatar, Tortantula, and Oogar races sat, then down the right to the Selroth, Besquith, MinSha, and Goltar guild masters. She glanced out to the audience. The seats of the other twenty-seven member races were full, something she couldn't remember happening in quite some time. "For those of you who don't know me, I am Seezo, and I have been chosen to fill Leeto's position as Speaker." No one knew what caused it, but Leeto had slowly wasted away until she had died the week before, despite the best nano therapy money could buy.

Seezo had hoped Peepo would arrive to bring order to the madness, but the Goltar representative had called for a meeting of the council, as was his right as a council member, and though she'd waited as long as she could, she'd had to oblige him. That the Goltar had asked for an emergency session was strange enough on its own. They hadn't participated appreciably in guild business for centuries.

"We are here today, in emergency session, to discuss an issue the Goltar wished to bring to our attention." She nodded to the Goltar representative, an alien that looked something like a giant squid or octopus when it was in the water. On land, you could better see its snapping red beak underneath the bony crest that rose over its head. "Guild Master?"

The guild master nodded, "It is my privilege today to let you know that the Peacemakers deputized us two weeks ago to assist them in ending the war with the Humans. A fleet was dispatched to Earth, which has ended the fighting."

"You had no right to do so!" Seezo said. "This is Merc Guild business, and it should have been brought before this council before you accepted that contract! Taking it the way you did violated Merc Guild law!"

"There are many things currently occurring in the galaxy that violate Merc Guild law," the Goltar representative replied, snapping his beak. "The Humans have done many of these things, and it will reflect poorly on them when their application for full membership is reviewed shortly. However, the Merc Guild itself has also engaged in activity which violates both guild law and standard practice."

"If—if anything was done by the guild which violated guild law—I'm not saying there was anything—but if there was, then it was done under the orders of Leeto. Unfortunately, she is no longer available to answer the charges, so they are null and void."

"I dispute that the charges are null and void," the Goltar representative replied. "There are still a number of admirals and captains—and generals—actively serving, who carried out these actions, and who need to be held accountable for failing to refuse an illegal order."

Seezo shivered slightly. The interjection was obviously meant to include General Peepo. Was the Goltar representative daft enough to think they would actually try General Peepo for the crimes committed by her and her forces during the Human War? After centuries of sitting on the sidelines, he had to know that wasn't going to happen!

"Seconded," the MinSha representative said.

"Third," the Selroth representative added. "I dislike the madness I see this guild falling into."

"No one called for a vote," Seezo said, "and a proposal hasn't even been made." The Goltar indicated he wished to speak, but Seezo ignored him as a realization came over her. They'd had to put up with Goltar representation on the Council for thousands of years. But by taking an illegal contract, this was the chance to kick the Goltar off the Council. She—Seezo—would be remembered as the leader who finally brought the Council totally under Veetanho control.

"Besides," Seezo said, her lips curling into a smile, "I hardly see how it is good form to try to cover *your* illegal action by casting aspersions on members of other races in good standing. Before we do anything, I would like to deal with the illegal action the Goltar took in taking the Peacemaker contract in direct contravention of guild rules." Her smile grew. "I would like a motion to censure the Goltars and remove them from their seat on the Council."

She recognized the Goka representative. "I motion we censure the Goltars and remove them from their seat on the Council," he said.

"Second," the Besquith representative said.

"Third," the Oogar representative replied. "The sooner this is over with, the sooner we can go have dinner."

"All in favor?" Seezo asked, adding her upraised hand to the tally. She only needed one more vote, and the Goltars could be expelled for all time.

The Tortantula representative looked at the Flatar representative, who shook his head. Both hands stayed down, as did the ones of the Selroth, MinSha, and Goltar representatives.

"All in favor?" she asked again, staring at the Tortantula rep, who knew better than to block her. The Flatar rep shook his head again, and the Tortantula's hand stayed down.

"The motion fails," Seezo was forced to admit. She glared at the Flatar rep, who returned her gaze steadily.

"Sorry," the Flatar rep said, "but we don't approve of the way this war is being prosecuted, nor in the wholesale slaughter that is occurring to our forces. Tens of thousands of Tortantula lives have been lost, and there are many riders who have perished with them, as well. While we don't approve of the methods the Goltar representative took, we believe his actions were in the best interest of the guild and do not believe they should lose their seat for it. While we approve of censure, we cannot approve the motion as it stands."

"Not only are we disgusted by the flagrant disregard for the loss of MinSha lives," the MinSha representative added, "we are also…unhappy with the way this war is being spun on the GalNet. There are a number of our queens who have had positive interaction with the Humans. While they may have done some of the things which they are accused of, most of them seem to be in response to actions taken against them by this very council. It has come to our attention that the previous Speaker led us astray in some of the things she told us, and in how some of it was presented. We are no longer sure this war was needed or even justified."

"Once again, I cannot speak to the actions of my predecessor," Seezo replied. "She is dead, and any misdeeds have passed on with her."

"Have they now?" the MinSha representative asked. "I'm sure that is what you would wish us to believe, but I find her approach endemic to recent Veetanho leadership as a whole over the past century. I find myself wondering if it isn't time for a change of direction—for a change of leadership—at the top of the Council."

"Hear! Hear!" the Bakulu representative yelled from his seat. Several audience members shouted their approval.

"I will have quiet in the audience," Seezo said with a snarl. She couldn't understand how the mood had changed so quickly, but she knew she had to nip it now. "Anyone who cannot be silent will be removed." She nodded to the Selroth representative, who could always be counted on to dispute whatever the MinSha rep wanted.

"I find myself in an odd position," he said. "For the first time in my memory, I am in agreement with the MinSha representative. It appears as time has gone by, more races have become, let us call them 'client races' of the Veetanho."

"What is that supposed to mean?" the Goka rep asked.

"I mean they are happy to do whatever the Speaker tells them, no matter what it is," the Selroth rep replied. "I don't want to call them *slaves* of the Veetanho—slavery is such a harsh word, after all—but it seems the free will of some races has been suborned over the centuries."

"Perhaps it is that they've seen the things this guild has accomplished under Veetanho leadership and have chosen to embrace that leadership," Seezo replied. "Profits are way up, and deaths—before this war, anyway—were way down. Besides, I do not hold anyone's vote in sway. All members are able to vote their conscience."

"I would like to motion we have a vote to fill the previous Speaker's seat with a different race," the MinSha representative said, "rather than allow the Veetanho and their stooges to continue to run this august body."

"Stooges?" the Goka rep asked. "Was that addressed to me?"

"If the insect booties fit, wear 'em," the Flatar rep said.

Before anyone could reply, the Goka drew a wicked-looking knife from under his carapace and slashed. The Flatar's head canted and then fell to one side while his body fell to the other. The Tortantula rep launched itself onto the Goka, pinning it to the ground, and began ripping pieces off it.

The Oogar rep roared and jumped to his feet but looked unsure of whether to aid the Goka or the Tortantula. The Besquith drew a laser pistol and shot the Oogar through the head, ending his indecision. The Selroth pushed the Besquith's hand aside, making his second shot go astray, but the Besquith grabbed the Selroth's hand, stuck it in his mouth, and bit it off. Blood sprayed like a hose under pressure as the Selroth waved his hand around, until the Besquith shot him in the chest. He fell backward, but then the Besquith landed on him as the MinSha rep shot the Besquith in the back.

* * *

The Goltar rep chuckled as the meeting of the storied Mercenary Guild Council disintegrated into a pit battle, but then had to duck as a stream of the Selroth's blood arced past him. Drawing his pistols, he jumped onto the table to get an angle on the Speaker; *if nothing else, she needs to die.* While he was moving, Seezo shot the MinSha, who'd just killed the Besquith rep, saving him the trouble. He fired each of his pistols at the Speaker, putting a round into both her chest and head. She fell backward, struck also by a round that came from the direction of the audience.

He saw motion from the side, but then the Tortantula tackled him off the table, knocking aside both of his pistols as she slammed him to the floor. He tried to move, but she held him tightly as she jerked several times.

412 | KENNEDY & WANDREY

"I'm...I'm going to...let you go...now," the Tortantula said. She slowly released him, then limped backward, bleeding from a number of spots.

Realization dawned on the Goltar; she'd saved him and had been shot several times for her effort. He scanned the room quickly. The only living member of the audience was a Bakulu, who was slipping his pistol back into his shell. He turned back to the Tortantula.

"Why did you save me?" he asked.

"You would...set us free," the Tortantula replied. "Could not...let you die." She collapsed to her knees, then fell on her side and lay still.

The Goltar bowed the way his kind did to an honored enemy, then turned to the Bakulu, who was looking at him with two eye-stalks; the third appeared to have been shot off and was leaking fluid from where it lay limp. He gave the same bow to the Bakulu. "Thank you for your assistance," the Goltar said. "It appears the Council will need some new members. Are you available?"

"I am," the Bakulu replied, "although I may need some medical attention first. I would, however, like to know something."

"Yes?" the Goltar asked.

The Bakulu waved a pseudopod at the carnage. "Where do we go from here?"

* * *

Cartwright's Cavaliers Main Base, Houston, Texas, Earth

Her eyelids were so heavy. But Ziva Alcuin had lifted heavy things before. She sucked in a breath and forced her eyes to open, and then immediately squeezed them closed again as a piercing light stabbed into her retinas. A groan escaped her lips.

"Hey," a voice said. The voice was soft, male, and didn't belong to anyone she knew. She swallowed and tried again, opening her eyelids a mere slit and turning toward the sound.

"Hey," she replied. Her own voice rasped like a grinding bit on the hardest granite. She swallowed and tried again. "Who are you?"

"I was going to ask you the same question. I'm Jim. I'm the one who picked you and your Hunter friend up."

"Fssik!" Fear spiked adrenaline through Ziva's body, and she flung her eyes open and tried to push herself up to a seated position. Her entire body screamed in protest, but Ziva Alcuin had worked while hurt before, and this was important, so she kept pushing.

"Here, take it easy, let me help," Jim—whoever that was—said. He pushed a button on the side of her bed and the back began to rise, helping her to sit up.

"I have to find Fssik," Ziva said, turning her attention to the wires and tubes attached to her arms and wrists. "Get these things off me. I have to find him."

"Hey… hey, don't do that, that's your medicine drip," Jim said, his voice threaded through with distress. He put one hand on hers, apparently trying to still her fingers as they scrabbled at her various IVs. She slapped his hand away and looked up, her panic turning to a killing rage that boiled in her eyes.

And then she actually *looked* at him. His uniform was creased and rumpled, but it was unmistakably a distinctive tiger-stripe pattern. On his near shoulder, a colonel's eagle glinted in the bright lights arrayed overhead. The uniform jacket itself strained over broad shoulders that led to a large gut below.

"Oh shit," she said, her hands slowing. "You're Jim Cartwright."

"I am," he said. "And you still haven't told me who you are."

"I'm Ziva Alcuin," she said. "And my friend is Fssik. Is he okay?"

"He's alive," Jim said, but the uncertainty in his voice made fear twist in Ziva's belly.

"Where is he? I need to see him."

"In the next room," Jim said. "If you promise not to dig out your IVs, I'll take you there."

Ziva sucked in a deep breath and nodded, forcing her shaking hands to still. Jim nodded back gravely, then reached over and toggled the quick disconnects on her various lines, leaving her feeling like an idiot. This wasn't her first time waking up in a clinic or hospital; she should have known better.

"What happened?" Ziva asked as she watched Jim turn away and grab a wheelchair. He wrestled it over to the side of her bed.

"I'm going to lift you into this chair, and you're going to let me, or we're not going anywhere, got it?" he asked her in a level voice. She quirked an eyebrow at him but relented and gave him a nod. He stepped forward and slid one arm under her knees, the other under her shoulders, and then lifted her with no more effort than if she were a child. Cartwright might have been a bit portly, but he was sure as seven hells strong. He lowered her carefully into the seat, then buckled the safety belt around her.

"As I started to say before you freaked out," Jim went on as he stepped behind the chair and began pushing her toward the door. "You and your Hunter fleet showed up out of nowhere and pulled your suicide attack. It gave us an opening, but the guild frigates destroyed every ship you brought. Most of the survivors were picked up by the Hussars and others of our fleet, but your pod ended up near me and my Raknar, so I grabbed you before you went hurtling into deep space. You guys weren't in good shape, so we brought you here."

He pushed the chair around the corner into another hospital room identical to hers, but instead of a full-sized bed, it held a small glass-sided case like a baby bassinet. As the chair came closer, Ziva could see Fssik's dark shape curled inside. His chest rose and fell in time with the hissing of a nearby ventilator machine, and she could hear the quick beeping of his heart on the monitor.

"The best our vet could do was stabilize him," Jim said softly. "He's got serious internal injuries, but the Depik have always been so secretive about their physiology that we just don't know what else to do."

"Send for Esthik," she said, urgency throbbing in her voice as she forced back tears. "At my mother's outpost. I have the coordinates, you can send a ship and bring him back; he's a Hunter of Hurts, he'll know what to do…"

"We already have," Jim said, trying to soothe her as he stepped around her chair so she could see him. "But they just left yesterday, and it's a hyperspace transition both ways. Our vet is good, though; she can keep him stable until the Depik Healer arrives. Don't worry."

Ziva let out a short bark of laughter at that.

"Don't worry?" she asked. She sounded hysterical, but she didn't care. "Fssik is my companion, Jim. He's like a part of me. I owe you my life, but I'm afraid I can't make that promise."

Jim looked at her for a long moment and then nodded slowly to show he understood.

"Can…can I touch him? Hunters are very tactile, and maybe…"

"Go ahead," a new voice said, and a grey-haired woman wearing scrubs and a caduceus entered the room. As she moved closer, Ziva could see the letter "V" emblazoned on the front of the serpent and staff.

"You're the vet?" Ziva said.

"I am," the woman replied. "Joy Thompson, DVM, at your service. I don't know how much Jim told you, but we've done all we can to stabilize him and keep him comfortable. I am hopeful the Depik healer will be able to do more when he or she arrives."

"He," Ziva said, absently. "Esthik is a Deo... an honored male elder."

"Good to know," Dr. Thompson said. "But in answer to your question, if you want to touch your friend, there's a window on the side of the bassinet, there. Jim, can you help her unlatch it?"

"Sure," Jim said, stepping forward.

"But can I hold him?" Ziva asked. "Hunters are very tactile, and they are constantly touching one another when they're hurt. If I can just cradle him..." she trailed off, frustrated by her inability to express how important her gut told her this was.

The doc looked as if she wanted to say no, but then she pursed her lips and scanned her equipment.

"Maybe," she said, narrowing her eyes. "I don't want to take him off the ventilator or fluids or anything, but these lines are pretty long and flexible. Maybe if you roll right up there next to the bassinet...yes. Good. And now, Jim, you reach in and carefully lift him...what did you say his name was?"

"Fssik," Ziva said.

"Yes. Thank you. Jim, gently, gently, lift Fssik out...good. And young lady, hold your arms like he's a baby and...perfect!" The grey-haired veterinarian's eyes shone behind her wire-rimmed spectacles as she beamed down at Ziva, now holding Fssik's warmth next to her chest.

"Doc, are you sure—?" Jim started to say softly, but the doctor shushed him with a wave of her hand.

"No, the lady is right," Dr. Thompson said. "If she's Fssik's person, then close touch can only help, as long as we're gentle. His heart rate will tell us if there are any problems, but I see this with my patients all the time. Even when they're not conscious, they know when they're being held in love. Love has the power to do miracles."

"If you say so," Jim said, and even though she was focused on Fssik, Ziva could hear the bitter edge to his words.

* * *

Fssik wasn't the only one banged up after their adventure. Dr. Thompson allowed Ziva to hold him for several hours and then sent her off to meet with the physical therapist for her own injuries. It turned out she had broken both legs in the explosion. Nanites had healed the bones, but she was going to have to do therapy to get her muscles back into shape.

When Ziva woke in the middle of the night with a full bladder, her legs howled in agony when she tried to use them. She got as far as swinging her feet off the side of the hospital bed before the blackness closed in around her vision, and she nearly passed out. Sweating, she fumbled for the call button on the side of the bed and clung to it for dear life.

"Ziva!" Jim's voice preceded him into the room. He'd changed out of his uniform and was wearing a T-shirt and sweatpants. "What's wrong?"

"What are you doing here?" she asked through gritted teeth as her vision slowly cleared. "I called the nurse!"

"Our nurses are exhausted from dealing with battle casualties, so some of us are taking shifts watching over non-critical cases while they get some much-needed rest. Do you need me to wake one?"

"No…shit. No. I just…" she let out a laugh, tinged with pain and embarrassment. "I just need to pee, and I can't get there from here alone."

418 | KENNEDY & WANDREY

"Oh! Okay, let me help you." He stepped forward and looped her arm over his shoulder, and then straightened up, holding her around the waist as she leaned on him. "The bathroom is right over here."

"Look at you," Ziva joked to try and ease the mortification she felt. "Living the glamorous life of a merc commander! Piloting Raknar through the skies and helping old ladies to the toilet. I can't imagine anything better. The women must be beating down your door."

"You're not old," Jim protested. "And no one's ever been beating down my door. The last relationship I had didn't...end well."

"Oh? Well, we've all got one of those in our history. Don't feel bad. And I have a solid ten to fifteen years on you, kiddo. Don't forget that you're famous for being the youngest commander in the history of the Cavaliers."

"Don't forget that I *am* the Commander of the Cavaliers," he said tartly, but he flashed her a surprisingly sweet smile as he did so. Despite herself, Ziva felt a warmth curling low in her belly. He was really quite handsome when he smiled. "I'm no one's 'kiddo.'"

"Naturally, not in public," Ziva said as they maneuvered through the doorway. "But you're helping me pee, so I feel like that gives me some leeway."

"Um, shouldn't that be the other way around?"

"What? No, that doesn't make any sense at all. What? Were you raised in a barn?"

That got him to throw his head back in a genuine laugh, and the warmth spread through her as some of the careworn lines were erased from his face, leaving him looking as young as he truly was.

With Jim's help, Ziva got herself situated and handled her business. With hands freshly washed, she slid open the bathroom door and beckoned him over to help her back to bed. Once she was back in place, however, she reached out a hand to stop him from leaving.

"Are you going to sleep?" she asked.

"No, probably not," Jim said.

"Me, neither. Want to play cards or something?"

Jim looked at her for a long moment. "Why?"

"Why not? I'm awake and bored, and I figured you could maybe use someone to talk to. Someone not under your command, that is. Someone you won't have to later order to do something that may get them killed."

Ziva didn't miss the quickly indrawn breath that meant she'd nailed his problem. Or one of them, anyway. She gave him a soft smile.

"C'mon, kiddo. You beat me at gin, I'll find you another nick-name."

Jim let out a gusty sigh but shook his head and opened up a drawer under the counter near the bathroom door. He pulled out a new pack of cards, stripped off the old-school plastic wrapping, and tossed the pack at her.

"Shuffle them up," he said. "I'm gonna get a chair."

* * *

Laboratory, Unknown System

"I'll never tell you infidels anything," the man said, panting, as he pulled at his restraints. Sweat beaded the length of his naked body.

The reptilian creature looked down and checked the security of one of the leads running from his equipment to the Human. "I have a feeling you will," it said finally. "We have been experimenting on your kind for a hundred years. We know what makes you respond, and we know what causes you pain. You may have a great tolerance,

420 | KENNEDY & WANDREY

but I will break it at some point. I always do." Its lips twitched in what might have been a smile.

"So, let's start with New Persia," the creature said.

It pushed a button on the equipment, and the man began screaming.

* * *

São José dos Campos, Brazil, Earth

Splunk threw down the wrench. "This is stupid and a waste of time," she said. "I've been through this CASPer three times now. There is no message for the Peacemaker's Guild to be found. It isn't written anywhere on it that I can find, nor is it in the operating code. I don't think they ever got around to putting the message into your CASPer."

"They did," Sunshine said, giving every indication of a teenager about to have a temper tantrum. "The *bass* told me it was already in there."

"Well, I can't find it," Splunk said.

"That doesn't mean it's not there," Sunshine said stubbornly. "It just means *you* can't find it."

"If she can't find it, child," Dante said, coming into the workroom, "then it isn't there." He turned to the two Dusman working on Sunshine's CASPer. "Come on," he said. "We don't have time to play with this child Human's toy any longer. There's no message there."

"There *is* a message there!" Sunshine yelled as the Dusman left. "Even if you can't find it, it's still there! And I'm not a child, either!" When they didn't reply, she lowered her voice. "Fine. You can think that all you want, but I know the *bass* wouldn't have lied to me. The message *is* there, and I'm going to get this CASPer to the Peacemakers, even if I have to carry it to them piece by piece to do so."

She sighed as she looked at the disassembled mess the Dusman had made of her CASPer. If she couldn't find a good CASPer mechanic to put it all back together again, she just might have to do that.

* * *

São Paulo, Brazil, Earth

A thousand robots labored day and night, bulldozing, moving debris, cleaning radiation. A Dusman-provided manufactory turned out a new robot every few minutes. The work proceeded at an ever-increasing rate.

A third of São Paulo had been razed during the battle. Raknar and CASPer, tanks and troopers, blood and fury. Jim looked out over the devastation from the shoulder of his Raknar, inexplicably called *Doom* now. He wasn't even sure why—he'd named it Dash what seemed like a millennium ago.

A hundred meters away, another Raknar stood, this one called *Despair*. Next to it was *Fear*, then *Wrath*, *Revenge*, and finally *Pain*. Six 30-meter-tall ancient war machines standing amidst the devastation they'd caused. Each of his fellow Raknar Corps members stood in their machines bearing witness. The tens of thousands of Brazilians working with the robots looked up at the Raknar often, unsure of how to respond to their presence. Standing on the shoulder of *Doom*, he wasn't sure how he felt about it either.

"Jim!"

He turned and saw Nigel struggling up the side of *Doom*. The image made him smile.

"Help me up, you shit!"

Jim laughed and moved over, offering his hand. Nigel grabbed hold and pulled himself up. Jim was glad he'd worked out so hard over the last few years.

"I wish you'd climbed a mountain instead. What are you doing up here?" Nigel asked after he reached the top. The leader of Asbaran Solutions looked over the devastated cityscape and shook his head. "You guys did this? Amazing."

"Amazing destruction," Jim replied.

"What you were doing in space was a million times worse. Fates and hell, Jim, what happened up there?"

"I can't explain it," Jim said. *"Because I don't know either."*

Nigel stood next to him, and the hot wind from the mountains to the west blew his long hair while the two stood in companionable silence. "I've come to respect you, Jim Cartwright, and think of you as a brother."

"Thank you, Nigel. I feel the same. We've bled on the same fields, and you came back for me. I'll never forget that." Nigel bowed his head.

"What about this world?" Nigel asked, though it didn't sound like a question exactly.

"What about it? We fix the damage and go back to what we do."

"It'll never be the same."

Jim sighed and shook his head. Nigel looked at him and waited. "You're right," Jim said finally. "I don't think things will ever go back to exactly how they were."

"Then how do we change it?"

"I've been thinking about that. The Mercenary Guild has been led by the Veetanho for a long time. My father used to talk about it: how the rats ran everything, one way or another. I never really understood until this war. But I still don't understand why Peepo wanted to subjugate us."

"Maybe she just wanted another weapon to wield?"

Jim looked at Nigel then slowly nodded. After a second, he followed it with a shrug. "I don't know. Maybe we'll never know. I do know the Mercenary Guild might be back, and we can't be the way we were."

He turned to look back to the ruins of the government buildings. Peepo's first office had been in one of those piles of rubble. Maybe it was one of the ones already being removed and recycled into fresh building materials by the Dusman robots.

"How's Alexis?"

"She's fine," Nigel said. "Pretty upset about the Hussars who died and the ships she lost."

"I meant you and her."

"Oh." He was quiet for a minute as the wind whipped. "We're still trying to figure it out."

"You're going to be a father, and she's going to be a mother. Doesn't that change things?"

"It does, and it doesn't. That's why we're trying to figure it out. I'd ask her to marry me except…"

"Except you're both Horsemen," Jim finished for him. Nigel nodded solemnly, and they stood in silence, until Jim spoke again. "There is a coalition of world leaders who want to meet with us, the Horsemen."

"Oh?"

"Yeah," Jim said. "I think they want to ask for help."

"What help do the politicians need?"

"I think they want a new way of running this world," Jim said. "And I've got some ideas."

Nigel nodded. "I'm pretty sure we've shown that we're worthy of full admittance into the Union at this point. Things are going to have to change with the Merc Guild, and I'm sure the other guilds will try to take advantage while the Merc Guild is down. I've got some ideas for what to do with that, too."

Below them, the slow work of rebuilding continued.

* * *

EMS *Pegasus*, Earth Orbit

Her old office felt different. Maybe it was just the time she'd spent away? She couldn't put her finger on it.

Nigel, Sansar, Jim, and she had spent a few minutes talking, once Jim had been recovered and brought back. No words were spoken about what happened with him and the Raknar; the look on his face said a lot. The Peacemakers didn't know how to handle it either, but she understood they were putting it down as a hiccup in the cessation of hostilities. The young man looked haunted, and it worried her.

The conversation was mainly about the future. The Earth government wanted to talk to them. Jim had ideas about that, and Nigel had some about the Mercenary Guild. Sansar and she were both going to listen and provide advice, but both had privately agreed they would mostly stand aside and try to keep things from getting out of control on both sides. Even though the Omega War was over, the two women felt another was looming. Maybe a much bigger one.

Now she was back home, in her office, but without her longtime confidant and XO. Paka had betrayed her. The Veetanho probably thought she'd murdered her. The scar on her back suggested as much. Yet she'd failed, and she'd missed the life growing inside her. And what were the implications of that? *Entropy, layers upon layers.* She desperately wanted to get back to New Warsaw.

A knock on her door sounded. "Come in." Captain Stacy entered smartly and closed the door behind her. "Please, sit." It was a formality, of course, and now they were in zero G, so it was more like floating over and strapping yourself into a chair. Still, Humans were, by nature, a being of gravity.

"Did you read the report, Captain?" Elizabeth asked, addressing her by her ship's rank since they were on her ship.

"I did," Alexis said, and gestured to the slate. "I cried my tears over Katrina many years ago. Have you over Patrick?"

"He's not dead," she said. "Even riding over with it—with him—a short while ago, I think there's something of him in there."

Alexis had seen images of the new Ghost. She'd never met Patrick Leonard from the Geek Squad. She'd seen his file, of course. Kleena had given him top marks. The man would have been the obvious replacement for Kleena after he'd been killed on Prime Base. A lot of people needed replacement after the Battle of New Warsaw.

She'd become used to the look of Ghost as a prematurely-aged mirror image of herself, not a fit 40-year-old man. She hoped Ghost would take better care of this body and was more than a little disturbed about the event.

"I've lived with Ghost since the incident where it took over Katrina," Alexis explained. "Trust me, there's nothing left." Elizabeth looked down and sighed. "You did a spectacular job with the Hussars," she said, changing the subject.

"Thank you, ma'am, but I think I could have done better."

"Of course, we can all do better." She put a hand on her stomach. "It would seem the Hussars will have an heir, but we don't have a second in command. I'm formally offering you that position."

"Ma'am?" She looked surprised.

"After what you accomplished?" Alexis gave a little laugh. "Please. Normally you'd sit in my XO position, to study under me;

however, I don't think you need it, and you already have *Shadowfax*. The job is yours, if you want it."

"I accept, and thank you."

Alexis nodded. "Okay, return to *Shadowfax* and continue repairs. I'm hoping to get the majority of the fleet underway by the end of the week." Elizabeth saluted and floated out, leaving Alexis alone. The door was open to the CIC, giving her a view of her command crew. None of her original members were alive except the two Bakulu, who were now on the battleships. So much had changed. She unbuckled and floated through the CIC, out the armored door showing welds to repair battle damage, and up a deck. She arrived at her destination and hesitated.

Alexis examined the door of Drone Control for a long moment before she pressed the button. The door slid aside to reveal Ghost/Patrick. The look in his/its eyes was the same, though the body was different.

"*I wAs exPectinG yOu,*" it said in the same weirdly modulated voice.

"Yes," Alexis said. "We need to talk."

* * *

MGS *Supreme*, Approaching the Stargate

Peepo smiled as the stargate neared. All she needed was time and space, and she'd been given that by the timely intervention of the Peacemakers. Although they'd refused to bow down to her, they had served her purposes in the end. They would still have to be destroyed, of course. She couldn't risk having them show up in the future to intervene when she didn't want them to.

She would have plenty of time to think, uninterrupted by the crew and her Besquith guard. They had all gone out the airlocks, courtesy of an "anti-boarding" option she'd had installed the last time the superyacht was in the yards. By herself, with a week to plan, she would emerge stronger and with a better plan. One that would rid the galaxy of Humans…and especially the Four Horsemen.

The ship lurched as she entered the stargate, almost as if she'd hit something solid on entry. It was a feeling unlike any she'd ever had in the hundreds of transitions she'd done previously. She checked her instruments, but nothing seemed amiss. All the engine functions were nominal, and she was—thankfully—in no danger of dropping out of hyperspace.

Peepo advanced the throttles to give her one G, then unstrapped and allowed herself five minutes to rage. She swore. She threw things. She stomped around the interior of the yacht. At the end of the five minutes, she stopped and composed herself again, patting down the fur that had become mussed.

All was not lost, after all. A huge amount of resources had been wasted, which she was sure she would rue in the future. Too many lives thrown away. While it was true they were only Tortantula, MinSha, Bakulu, and so forth—and therefore ultimately meaning-less—they *were* bodies she wouldn't have in the future where she was sure she would need them.

But they could be replaced.

The plans would have to be revised, but that was part of being a leader; when plans failed, you adapted, adjusted, and overcame. The Humans had a good saying: no plan survives first contact with the enemy. She had misjudged this enemy—these Humans—somehow, but she wouldn't continue to do so. She still had no idea what had gone wrong in New Warsaw, and she would long regret not leading that assault herself. In retrospect, it was obvious she should have.

She didn't blame herself, much. She *had* given them an overwhelming amount of force to get the job done, and the plan—as modified by Paka—had been perfect, and constructed with a knowledge of the Hussars' defenses and how to beat them. It was foolproof…but apparently, it wasn't.

The only thing that could have happened to change the outcome was that either Paka had been subverted somehow, or that living too long with the Humans had done something to her mind. The fact that *Trushista* had returned with *New Era* told her everything she needed to know. Paka had betrayed her.

Paka would die slowly, in great pain. It was the least she could do for her murderous, betraying sister.

She took a step toward the planning table, but then her legs stopped working, and she collapsed to the floor. A searing pain enveloped the backs of both legs, and neither seemed to want to work correctly anymore.

"What the hell?" she asked.

"It's hard to walk when your hamstrings are cut," a voice said from behind her. Peepo rolled to her side and gasped. A Depik!

"What?" she asked with a gasp. "How did you get here?"

"One of our frigates brought me a ship that I was able to run you down with. It was a near thing; you almost got away. I don't think we had more than a second from when I latched on before you went through the stargate. Happily, though, I am here."

The Depik slow-blinked in that infuriating way that they did. "That was an impressive tantrum you threw. You almost hit me with one of the slates. And the cursing? Highly inventive, if not physically possible. Of course, with a broken limb or two, you *might* be flexible enough to do it." Tsan shrugged. "I'm willing to experiment if you are."

Tsan leveled a strange-looking gun at her and fired.

* * *

Tsan leaned over Peepo and breathed in her scent. Musk and the soil smell of a burrower predominated, with a spicy overtone that made her want to cough it back up. Veetanho. She would remember it for the rest of her life…and annihilate it wherever she found it.

"Welcome back," Tsan said with a slow-blink as Peepo woke to find herself chained to a table. "I'm sure you have *so* many questions, but I'm in a bit of a hurry. My friend Cahli swore you would bleed for every tear Sansar Enkh cried. Unfortunately, I don't know how many that was, so I had to come up with something else. I decided you should bleed for every Depik who chose death over your machinations. Unfortunately, I don't know how many *that* was, either, so I decided we would go with the number of people who died in Monrovia when you had that city destroyed.

"Now, I'm not sure you'll last more than three or four thousand cuts, much less the millions you earned for that attack; however, we *do* have seven days to find out, and I'm willing to be creative in how we go about this. I also have four medkits-worth of nanobots to help heal any major cuts and keep you from bleeding out before it's time." She slow-blinked. "We wouldn't want that now, would we?"

"You can't kill me!" Peepo said, gasping.

"Oh, but see, that's where you're wrong. Not only *can* I kill you, I absolutely *will*. Not fast…but with great certainty. The Peacemakers may have ended the war, but nothing short of your death will end this for the Hunters."

"No, you don't understand. I have information vital to the safety of the galaxy!"

"I'm sure you do," Tsan said. She slow-blinked. "And I'm sure you'll tell me all about it in time. I look forward to having you do so. I also look forward to that last cut that kills you, in spite of it."

"You stupid bitch! The Kahraman are coming, and I'm the only one who can save the galaxy!"

"Really? How interesting. I'm not sure how you're going to save the galaxy, though. Look at the state of you. You aren't even able to save yourself."

"You don't understand! I'm the only one who knows how to deal with the Kahraman!"

"Just like you knew how to deal with the Four Horsemen? How well did that turn out for you? Sansar and the rest of the Horsemen send their regards."

"You don't understand!"

"Oh, but I *do* understand. You, unfortunately, are the one who doesn't understand; however, I have plenty of time to bring you into the light. We only have 169 more hours until we reach Karma, and that time will pass *far* too quickly for me. I don't want to miss a single second."

Tsan tenderly laid her knife on the last joint of the little finger on Peepo's left hand.

"Let's begin, shall we?"

# # # # #

About the Authors

A bestselling Science Fiction/Fantasy author and speaker, Chris Kennedy is a former school principal and naval aviator with over 3,000 hours flying attack and reconnaissance aircraft.

Chris' full-length novels on Amazon include the "Occupied Seattle" military fiction duology, the "Theogony" and "Codex Regius" science fiction trilogies and the "War for Dominance" fantasy trilogy. Chris is also the author of the #1 Amazon self-help book, "Self-Publishing for Profit: How to Get Your Book Out of Your Head and Into the Stores."

Find out more about Chris Kennedy and get the free prequel, "Shattered Crucible" at: http://chriskennedypublishing.com/

Located in rural Tennessee, Mark Wandrey has been creating new worlds since he was old enough to write. After penning countless short stories, he realized novels were his real calling and hasn't looked back since. A lifetime of diverse jobs, extensive travels, and living in most areas of the country have uniquely equipped him with experiences to color his stories in ways many find engaging and thought provoking.

Find out more about Mark Wandrey and get the free prequel, "Gateway to Union," at http://www.worldmaker.us/news-flash-sign-up-page/

* * * * *

Connect with Chris Kennedy Online

Website: http://chriskennedypublishing.com/

Facebook: https://www.facebook.com/chriskennedypublishing.biz

Twitter: @ChrisKennedy110

* * * * *

Connect with Mark Wandrey Online

Website: http://www.worldmaker.us/

Facebook: https://www.facebook.com/mark.h.wandrey

* * * * *

Do you have what it takes to be a Merc?

Take your VOWs and join the Merc Guild on Facebook!

Meet us at: https://www.facebook.com/groups/536506813392912/

* * * * *

The following is an
Excerpt from Book One of the Salvage Title Trilogy:

Salvage Title

_____

Kevin Steverson

Available Now from Theogony Books

eBook, Paperback, and Audio Book

Excerpt from "Salvage Title:"

The first thing Clip did was get power to the door and the access panel. Two of his power cells did the trick once he had them wired to the container. He then pulled out his slate and connected it. It lit up, and his fingers flew across it. It took him a few minutes to establish a link, then he programmed it to search for the combination to the access panel.

"Is it from a human ship?" Harmon asked, curious.

"I don't think so, but it doesn't matter; ones and zeros are still ones and zeros when it comes to computers. It's universal. I mean, there are some things you have to know to get other races' computers to run right, but it's not that hard," Clip said.

Harmon shook his head. *Riiigghht,* he thought. He knew better. Clip's intelligence test results were completely off the charts. Clip opted to go to work at Rinto's right after secondary school because there was nothing for him to learn at the colleges and universities on either Tretra or Joth. He could have received academic scholarships for advanced degrees on a number of nearby systems. He could have even gone all the way to Earth and attended the University of Georgia if he wanted. The problem was getting there. The schools would have provided free tuition if he could just have paid to get there.

Secondary school had been rough on Clip. He was a small guy that made excellent grades without trying. It would have been worse if Harmon hadn't let everyone know that Clip was his brother. They lived in the same foster center, so it was mostly true. The first day of school, Harmon had laid down the law—if you messed with Clip, you messed up.

At the age of fourteen, he beat three seniors senseless for attempting to put Clip in a trash container. One of them was a Yalteen, a member of a race of large humanoids from two systems over. It wasn't a fair fight—they should have brought more people with them. Harmon hated bullies.

437

After the suspension ended, the school's Warball coach came to see him. He started that season as a freshman and worked on using it to earn a scholarship to the academy. By the time he graduated, he was six feet two inches with two hundred and twenty pounds of muscle. He got the scholarship and a shot at going into space. It was the longest time he'd ever spent away from his foster brother, but he couldn't turn it down.

Clip stayed on Joth and went to work for Rinto. He figured it was a job that would get him access to all kinds of technical stuff, servos, motors, and maybe even some alien computers. The first week he was there, he tweaked the equipment and increased the plant's recycled steel production by 12 percent. Rinto was eternally grateful, as it put him solidly into the profit column instead of toeing the line between profit and loss. When Harmon came back to the planet after the academy, Rinto hired him on the spot on Clip's recommendation. After he saw Harmon operate the grappler and got to know him, he was glad he did.

A steady beeping brought Harmon back to the present. Clip's program had succeeded in unlocking the container. "Right on!" Clip exclaimed. He was always using expressions hundreds or more years out of style. "Let's see what we have; I hope this one isn't empty, too." Last month they'd come across a smaller vault, but it had been empty.

Harmon stepped up and wedged his hands into the small opening the door had made when it disengaged the locks. There wasn't enough power in the small cells Clip used to open it any further. He put his weight into it, and the door opened enough for them to get inside. Before they went in, Harmon placed a piece of pipe in the doorway so it couldn't close and lock on them, baking them alive before anyone realized they were missing.

Daylight shone in through the doorway, and they both froze in place; the weapons vault was full.

* * * * *

Get "Salvage Title" now at:
https://www.amazon.com/dp/B07H8Q3HBV.

Find out more about Kevin Steverson and "Salvage Title" at:
http://chriskennedypublishing.com/.

* * * * *

The following is an
Excerpt from Book One of the Earth Song Cycle:

Overture

Mark Wandrey

Now Available from Theogony Books

eBook and Paperback

Excerpt from "Overture:"

Dawn was still an hour away as Mindy Channely opened the roof access and stared in surprise at the crowd already assembled there. "Authorized Personnel Only" was printed in bold red letters on the door through which she and her husband, Jake, slipped onto the wide roof.

A few people standing nearby took notice of their arrival. Most had no reaction, a few nodded, and a couple waved tentatively. Mindy looked over the skyline of Portland and instinctively oriented herself before glancing to the east. The sky had an unnatural glow that had been growing steadily for hours, and as they watched, scintillating streamers of blue, white, and green radiated over the mountains like a strange, concentrated aurora borealis.

"You almost missed it," one man said. She let the door close, but saw someone had left a brick to keep it from closing completely. Mindy turned and saw the man who had spoken wore a security guard uniform. The easy access to the building made more sense.

"Ain't no one missin' this!" a drunk man slurred.

"We figured most people fled to the hills over the past week," Jake replied.

"I guess we were wrong," Mindy said.

"Might as well enjoy the show," the guard said and offered them a huge, hand-rolled cigarette that didn't smell like tobacco. She waved it off, and the two men shrugged before taking a puff.

"Here it comes!" someone yelled. Mindy looked to the east. There was a bright light coming over the Cascade Mountains, so intense it was like looking at a welder's torch. Asteroid LM-245 hit the atmosphere at over 300 miles per second. It seemed to move faster and faster, from east to west, and the people lifted their hands to shield their eyes from the blinding light. It looked like a blazing comet or a science fiction laser blast.

"Maybe it will just pass over," someone said in a voice full of hope.

Mindy shook her head. She'd studied the asteroid's track many times.

In a matter of a few seconds, it shot by and fell toward the western horizon, disappearing below the mountains between Portland and the ocean. Out of view of the city, it slammed into the ocean.

The impact was unimaginable. The air around the hypersonic projectile turned to superheated plasma, creating a shockwave that generated 10 times the energy of the largest nuclear weapon ever detonated as it hit the ocean's surface.

The kinetic energy was more than 1,000 megatons; however, the object didn't slow as it flashed through a half mile of ocean and into the sea bed, then into the mantel, and beyond.

On the surface, the blast effect appeared as a thermal flash brighter than the sun. Everyone on the rooftop watched with wide-eyed terror as the Tualatin Mountains between Portland and the Pacific Ocean were outlined in blinding light. As the light began to dissipate, the outline of the mountains blurred as a dense bank of smoke climbed from the western range.

The flash had incinerated everything on the other side.

The physical blast, travelling much faster than any normal atmospheric shockwave, hit the mountains and tore them from the bedrock, adding them to the rolling wave of destruction traveling east at several thousand miles per hour. The people on the rooftops of Portland only had two seconds before the entire city was wiped away.

Ten seconds later, the asteroid reached the core of the planet, and another dozen seconds after that, the Earth's fate was sealed.

* * * * *

Get "Overture" now at:
https://www.amazon.com/dp/B077YMLRHM/

Find out more about Mark Wandrey and the Earth Song Cycle at:
https://chriskennedypublishing.com/

* * * * *

The following is an
Excerpt from Book One of the The Frontiers:

Black and White

Mark Wandrey

Now Available from Seventh Seal Press

eBook, Paperback, and (Soon) Audio Book

Excerpt from "Black and White:"

"We might as well keep looking around while we wait for Taiki," Katrina suggested.

Consulting the map on his slate, Terry could see five buildings he hadn't investigated yet. One was the biggest by far, and he headed for it. "Keep an eye out for more robots," he told the others. "I don't exactly trust them."

"They're just robots," Katrina said.

Just robots, Terry thought. That didn't comfort him at all.

They reached the big building. Terry didn't have to look far for a door; one was already open. Like the portal that hadn't responded to him, this was another first. For some reason, he had a strange feeling, and he drew his laser pistol and peered carefully around the corner.

"You see something?" Colin whispered.

"No," he admitted. *I'm getting jumpy*, he thought and holstered the gun.

This was the first building he'd found that wasn't a big open structure. The door opened into a short hallway, and he could see doors on either side, and one at the end. All of them were also open, but no lights were on inside. The lights in the hall matched the same pattern as every other building, scattered and rather dim.

They walked into the building and slowly down the hall. They still had their drysuits on, so each took one of the flashlights from their helmets to see better. Katrina pointed hers at the ground.

"Look," she said. "Dust. The robots don't come in here."

"I wonder why?" Colin asked.

"They're afraid of the vampires," Terry said. Both looked at him, agog. "I was trying to be funny."

"Stop trying," Colin said.

"Yeah," Katrina agreed.

448 | KENNEDY & WANDREY

"Sorry."

Katrina narrowed her eyes at him, and he shrugged. She sighed and put her hand on the green spot, and the door opened for her. When the light from her flashlight fell inside and she saw what was there, she screamed.

* * * * *

Get "Black and White" now at:
https://www.amazon.com/dp/B07RT821RL.

Find out more about Mark Wandrey at:
https://chriskennedypublishing.com.

* * * * *

Made in the USA
Coppell, TX
26 February 2021